PRAISE FOR DISSOLUTION

"Ranchers and university students fight to survive after an economic crisis turns American citizens against one another in this thriller. An absorbing, realistic dystopian tale with a superb cast."

—Kirkus Reviews

"Gear conjures a frighteningly realistic dystopian future in his Wyoming Chronicles series launch. Gear's impeccable detail work and timely references to MAGA and coronavirus make for a dystopian world that feels immediate and all too plausible. This harrowing future is sure to linger in readers' minds."

—Publishers Weekly

"Hold on to your hat. This thriller introduces Sam Delgado to the literary landscape in a story rooted in the archaeology and practices of the Shoshones colliding with a modern catastrophe where perhaps the only safe place to be is high in the mountains of Wyoming with some ranchers at your side."

—Candy Moulton author of Roadside History of Wyoming and Chief Joseph: Guardian of the People

"No one reads a Gear novel without being transformed in beautiful ways."

–Richard S. Wheeler

DISSOLUTION

* * * * * *

THE WYOMING CHRONICLES: BOOK ONE

W. MICHAEL GEAR

WOLFPACK
PUBLISHING
— EST 2013 —

WOLFPACK
PUBLISHING
— EST 2013 —

Text Copyright © 2021 W. Michael Gear

Wolfpack Publishing
5130 S. Fort Apache Road, 215-380
Las Vegas, NV 89148

wolfpackpublishing.com

Paperback ISBN 978-1-64734-718-5
Hardcover ISBN 978-1-64734-272-2
eBook ISBN 978-1-64734-271-5

DISSOLUTION

******

TO

HARRY AND SHIRLEY LEHMAN

FOR WHOM

DISSOLUTION HAS SPECIAL MEANING

ACKNOWLEDGMENTS

***

Special thanks to international banking consultant Brian Yarrington for his thoughtful explanation of the American banking system and its vulnerabilities.

FINANCIAL WAR

***

I would have told you that the very idea that a nation could be destroyed without a shot being fired was a fairytale. And, hey, I was an economics major at the Daniels College of Business while attending the University of Denver. I was going to be an investment banker. That was my goal, what I wanted out of my seriously messed-up life. I was doing well. Had a 4.0 grade point average. That summer I was working as an intern for Seakliff, an investment and financial firm.

COVID should have taught us that war is more than bullets, bombs, soldiers, airplanes, missiles, and warships, right?

Those things would come later. But in the beginning, even a sophomore in economics like me should have known that disabling an economy, the destruction of wealth, and the social upheaval that comes with it, would have been catastrophic.

No one would have thought that a single string of code, a silly little malware, could be much of a threat.

Excerpt from Breeze Tappan's *Journal.*

CHAPTER ONE

***

IF ANYONE, SAM DELGADO SHOULD HAVE UNDERSTOOD THE COLLAPSE OF CIVILIZATION. HE had just turned twenty-three, a graduate student working on his PhD in anthropology. The collapse of cultures—including the Harrapan, ancient Rome, Cahokia, Chaco, and the classic Khmer at Angkor Wat—fascinated him. Much of his interest stemmed from his Mexican heritage. Lots of empires rose and fell in Mesoamerica: Maya, Mixtec, Toltec, Itza, Aztec, and so many others.

Turns out that being an anthropologist didn't help. Knowing something academically was really freaking different than living it.

The day the bank accounts were hacked, Sam sat behind the wheel of a sleek black BMW 740i headed for archaeology field school in Wyoming. He was last in line in a three-vehicle caravan, driving north across a whole lot of nothing on Interstate 25 between Cheyenne and Casper.

So what if the "Breaking News" on MSNBC was that something had gone zonkers with bank accounts all across the country, and the FDIC had ordered closures? It was, like, something to do with accounting? So, figure out the numbers, make the fix, and life went on. Right?

"What's the hype? Cyberattacks happen, right?" Shyla Adams asked from the BMW's passenger seat as she stared at the passing emptiness. The ash-blonde was one of the three undergraduate students in the car. And, oh, was Sam achingly aware of every breath she took.

"The Feds will straighten it out. They always do," Kirstin announced from the back seat. She said it with authority. But that was Kirstin. The BMW was hers. A high school graduation gift from her rich parents in D.C. Bored, her earbuds in, Kirstin's head kept jerking in time to whatever played on her iPhone.

Also in the back seat, directly behind Sam, Ashley Tempest had her knees up, was streaming something on her tablet. She was the soccer- and- softball-playing jock, also called the "Dorm Queen". Looking for an easy A, she'd left her girlfriend back in Ohio. Sam wasn't sure that field school—especially this field school—was going to save her eligibility.

Sam had grown up in Hempstead on Long Island. As a kid, when he wasn't in school, he'd worked his ass off in the folks' Mexican restaurant. Called The Yucateca, it had been his private hell, prison, and salvation all rolled into one. When he wasn't in school, he was in the kitchen. Well, but for a couple of trips back to Mexico to visit relations.

That had changed when he went off to study anthropology at the university. That's when the salvation thing had come slowly and painfully clear. His years at The Yucateca had given him a work ethic most of his fellow undergrads hadn't had, and it showed in his grades. Now, for the first summer in Sam's life, he wasn't working all summer in the restaurant to make money. He was off to help run a field school.

Wyoming had him half-stunned and amazed. This was the real West. It had started to settle in while they were crossing western Nebraska. But at least I-80 had traffic. Big eighteen-wheelers, cars with plates from lots of different states. Turning north on I-25 brought the emptiness home. Miles of rolling hills, grass waving in the wind, and nothing but the vault of the sky, puffs of cloud, occasional cattle and empty interstate. Like he was driving through the middle of wide-open nothingness. He'd never driven anywhere without traffic. This was crazy. A whole interstate, and almost no one on it.

If he could conjure an image of paradise, this was it: luxury car; three female undergrads including the ethereal Shyla for company; and the open road. The destination was a back-country archaeological site in remote northwest Wyoming where he'd be crew chief for the university field school.

The news about the banks barely filtered through the rest of the crap coming out of Washington. The Republican speaker of the house was threatening to impeach the Democratic president in the endless tit for tat. Texas and California had voted for secession. Again. The country was paralyzed. COVID cases were up again.

One of the commentators said, "*Depending upon the scale of the cyberattack, we could be looking at apocalypse.*"

"Yeah, sure." Kirstin crossed her arms and leaned her head back against the leather.

Sam stared out at the distant mountains to the west. Man, there was nothing between him and infinity but grass and rolling hills.

"Apocalypse?" he wondered. "Compared to, like, the thirty million who might have died in the collapse of the Lowland Maya? Or the fourteenth century black plague?"

"'Bout time we did something different. The same ol' same ol' is a real bore." Kirstin sounded sour.

"It's just news." Shyla kept her eyes on the distance.

Sam understood why apocalyptic themes dominated his generation. He'd written an undergraduate paper on *Hunger Games, Walking Dead,* and *Divergent* and how the themes both molded and reinforced his generation's dystopian perspectives and energized antifa, BLM, and social unrest. And then there was COVID and the ever more bitter political deadlock. Most downtowns were boarded up, graphitized, and half abandoned to the armed mobs.

"Lot of nothing out here." Shyla was staring at the sagebrush flashing past the window.

"Nothing and cows," Ashley finally chipped into the conversation. "Never been anywhere with more cows than people."

That was the thing about the end of the world. Should have been more fanfare.

No one had had so much as a clue in Cheyenne that morning. Life was normal. It was Friday. The start of the Memorial Day weekend. The field crew had been driving west for three days. They had stayed that night in a Best Western, bought breakfast, fueled up, and headed out on the last leg of the journey that would take them to some ranch in Owl Creek Range in Wyoming. From there, they'd horse-pack up into the mountains, record, map, and test a remote archaeological site for two months.

Sam would find something to write his dissertation on.

Rock-shock cool.

Casper was supposed to be just another forgettable stop on the adventure of a lifetime.When the caravan exited off Interstate 25 and into the Flying J truck stop in Casper, they pulled up behind a line of cars inching through the pumps.

A hastily made sign read **CASH ONLY. SORRY!**

Even more ominous, a police car was parked off to the side, lights flashing. The cop stood with hands on his gun belt, locked in heated conversation with what looked like a really pissed-off trucker. A small crowd, many with crossed arms, watched from the side. No one looked happy.

Up in the lead, driving the college van with all the equipment and field gear, Amber Sagan waved her convoy off and led the way back onto the street. Amber was the co-Principal Investigator. That meant she was in charge along with Dr. Evan Holly, a professor from University of Wyoming. At thirty-five she was older than the rest and had a personality akin to sharp nails and jagged glass. Unkind souls in the department said that dealing with Amber Sagan was like juggling a hand grenade with a loose pin.

"What the hell?" Kirstin cried. "Hello! Gotta pee here!"

But then, Kirstin—an English major—was always irritated by something. She was a petite wiry thing with soft brown eyes and light walnut-colored hair...who'd stick a figurative knife in your belly faster than an MS13 gang banger.

Amber led the way past three stations all with signs asking for cash before she turned into a Maverick convenience store parking lot. Here, too, hastily scrawled "Cash Only" signs decorated each pump.

Sam followed, third in line, behind Dylan Collins' big Dodge Ram pickup truck. Up until then, the drill had been that they'd line up behind Amber's university van; and as soon as she'd fueled up, she'd pull forward. Dylan would then drive up to the pump where Shanteel held the nozzle, and she'd fill his rig on the same charge. When Dylan was topped off, Sam would ease Kirstin's BMW up to the pump.

He waited as Amber got out of the van and walked inside.

"'Bout time!" Kirstin cried.

"Afuckingmen," Ashley asserted.

Doors opened like butterfly wings as students headed for bathrooms, drinks, and snacks.

Sam had been behind the wheel of Kirstin's BMW since Cheyenne. The break was long overdue, or so his bladder insisted. So, like, what the hell was wrong with the pumps? He shut the BMW down.

Kirstin's folks being high-powered lawyers in Washington DC, their daughter didn't exactly want for things. Sam got to drive the BMW; it was Kirstin's attempt to prove her devotion to social justice.

As Sam waited, he savored the view as Shyla Adams crossed the parking lot in her sultry long-legged walk. Ash-blonde hair hung down past her slim waist and swung in time to her stride. She might have been the dream of every man in the department, but Sam worshipped her.

As if a Latino kid from the mean streets of Hempstead had a chance.

She was the ultimate party girl, complete with a wealthy football-player boyfriend. Word around the department was that if a guy wasn't rich—or a high-status athlete on scholarship with pro potential—don't even bother to say hello and expect her to notice. And she still kept a three-point-something GPA?

So, here he was, his academic career teetering, in search of a dissertation topic, half dying of unrequited love for Shyla Adams, stuck in Casper, Wyoming, at a gas pump, with a full bladder.

Screw it. He took the keys and stepped out, heading for the store.

As he passed, Dylan rolled down his window where he sat behind the wheel of his Dodge. "What's up with all the cash signs?"

"Hang on. I'll find out."

"That cop back at the Flying J looked pissed. Think it was a robbery?"

"Naw. Growing up in my neighborhood? I've seen robberies. That looked more like what they call an 'altercation'."

Sam stepped into the store to see the usual line outside the women's room. The field school was heavy on females.

Shyla was talking with Shanteel. As Sam walked in, she actually glanced his way and smiled. He would have liked to have believed it was his entrance that conjured such magic, but odds were Shanteel had said something amusing.

Since neither Court nor Jon were around, the men's must have been a two-holer.

At the counter, Amber was standing with a hand on her hip, the cashier saying, "...Don't know how long it will take. It's sure got everything messed up. The manager's called corporate, but it seems to be everywhere. Started a couple of hours ago. From what people tell me, it's all over town. No credit cards being accepted anywhere. Like the whole system's down. VISA, Mastercard, Amex, doesn't make any difference. Declined. Declined. Declined. Phone lines are jammed. Just an automated message when you call the bank."

"So, what do we do?" Amber's expression had the bruised-and-black look akin to an impending storm's.

"All I can tell you is that I gotta have cash. Boss says we can do a local check with ID."

Amber turned to Sam and arched a thin red eyebrow. She was five-foot-five with the light reddish hair that people called strawberry blonde. The look on her wedge-shaped face was anything but friendly, and her blue eyes had turned crystalline. Up close, a faint sprinkling of freckles could be seen on the bridge of her nose and forehead.

"It's been about a hundred and twenty for each fill up. Right, Sam?"

"Yeah."

Amber went to her purse, shelling out three fifties, saying as she did, "Keys are in the van's ignition. Could you see to gassing everyone up?"

His bladder argued vehemently against it, but he said, "Sure."

He was her crew chief—the second in command who would see to the actual running of things once they got up on the mountain. Refusing just because he had to pee? What a weenie.

"Yeah," the cashier said as she took the cash, "down the street they had to call the cops. Couple of truckers had just filled their rigs when the cards were declined. Now they can't move."

Sam made his way out to the vehicles and commenced to fill the van. One by one, Dylan drove the vehicles forward to get the tanks filled.

Pumping that much gas gave him a chance to look around. Not that Casper was much to see. First off, he noticed that a big sign was being pasted in the window of the Burger King across the avenue. **CASH ONLY!!!**

Next door, the Taco Bell had put up a **CLOSED TODAY** sign.

As Dylan drove the BMW into a parking space, Sam got his chance at the john while the rest of the crew was counting out bills and change for their purchases at the register.

Amber gestured Sam to the side as the rest trooped out to the cars. "How much cash you got, Sam?"

He pulled out his wallet and thumbed through the bills. "About a hundred and fifty."

"I've got about two hundred left."

"Hey, they'll have this fixed by the time we get to Hot Springs."

He glanced back down the road at the Flying J where a second police car had pulled into the parking lot, its lights flashing. More people were crowding around.

"Memorial day weekend? Best hope so, Sam. That or we'll have to see if we can get an advance at the bank in Hot Springs."

"Come on, Amber," he told her with a smile. "The country runs on credit cards. You can bet that they've got everybody and their dogs hopping to fix it. And God help the poor goofus who pushed the wrong button to start all this."

The tension lingered in her eyes as she looked up at the midday sun, then lowered her gaze to the mountain that rose like a wall to south. "Yeah," she said.

Across the street, an asshole honked angrily as he peeled out of the Burger King's parking lot and flipped a bird at the restaurant—a final reminder of his frustration.

Of course they'd fix it. They had to.

THE ONCE AND FUTURE WAR

***

Money is one of those things that preoccupy us. It's, like, fundamental to who we are. What we do. How we feed ourselves, clothe our bodies, make ourselves and our loved ones secure. It's how we pay for Netflix and the latest Call of Duty game. Money is everyone's major preoccupation. The need for status, sex, security, love, and approval might have been with us from the beginning of the Pleistocene, but we have only ourselves to blame for our obsession with money.

In Gone With the Wind, *Scarlet tells Rhett Butler, "Money won't buy you happiness." To which he replies, "No, but it will buy some remarkable substitutes."*

Who'd have thought something so fundamental could be so fragile?

Excerpt from Breeze Tappan's *Journal.*

CHAPTER TWO

***

TO CALL WYOMING EMPTY WAS TO OVERSTATE THE SITUATION. THE ONLY PERSON IN THE field crew from a small town was Shyla; and Rutland, Vermont, was in a completely different league compared to what they encountered upon leaving the awesome majesty of Wind River Canyon.

Hot Springs, which would be their closest town to the project area, consisted of 1300 people, a minuscule downtown, a truck stop, a couple of museums—including one that advertised dinosaurs—a tannery, and a single small grocery store.

"This place wouldn't pass for a town in Tajikistan," Kirstin muttered as Sam followed Dylan's pickup down the main street.

Sam couldn't help it: "So, Kirstin, consider it a test of character. A trial to see if you can live without Bergdorf Goodman and Amazon for a whole two months."

In the rearview mirror, she flipped him a stiff middle finger.

They had to pony-up cash again when they finally arrived at the Days Inn in Hot Springs. Nobody was happy about it; even with room sharing it pretty much wiped out Jon and Danielle's stashes.

Jon Brimmer was a first-year archaeology grad student, lab assistant, and part-time musician. The guy was always broke. This was his first field training.

Studying to be a museum curator, Danielle Cory was a junior and Sam's fellow New Yorker—though she hailed from Manhattan. Danielle lived and died by the credit card. She made no bones about being a Jew and joked about trying to keep the diet.

Sam, Dylan, Jon, and Court did a guy's supper that night, picking Pizza Hut for the economics rather than celebrating a gustatory reward worthy of having completed all but the last couple miles of the journey.

If the field crew had a misfit, it was Court Hamilton. The guy was a computer science major and a walking cliché: six feet tall, awkward, overweight, and clueless about anything in the real world. All through supper, Court sat at the end of the table looking particularly miserable. Dylan Collins—from Denver—was the only westerner and had just turned twenty-three. He was starting his senior year in anthro. The guy had brown hair, hazel eyes, and was aching to embark upon his first dig.

Sam tilted his beer, took a swig, and sighed. In the TV monitors overhead, everything was sports except for one channel set on Fox News. Figured. This was deepest darkest Wyoming after all.

"So," Jon asked, "what happens if they don't get this bank thing worked out? I'm already, like, broke. Amber was supposed to cover the travel out and back."

Dylan rocked his bottle of IPA back and forth. "It'll get fixed. It's a three-day weekend, right? Come Tuesday, everything's back to normal."

"Listen," Sam reminded, "we're up on the mountain for ten days. By the time we're back to town, it'll be like it never happened."

Sam kept thinking about the reports they'd been hearing on the radio. Kirstin's BMW had Sirius. And then people were replaying the bits of video that had come in on the phones. It wasn't just Wyoming. The whole country was paralyzed by the credit card crisis.

Even as Sam tried to picture how Mom and Dad were doing at The Yucatec, Jon said, "So, like, what's happening at home?"

Dylan used his thumbnail to peel the label off his bottle of beer. "Maybe this is kind of like COVID. Businesses either demand cash, local checks, or they simply close. Figure it will be simpler to ride it out until the banks get the problem fixed."

Jon stared thoughtfully at Fox News on the screen above where the muted monitor flashed from commentator to commentator. "The media couldn't be happier. They got their socks in a knot interviewing experts, doing stories about people caught in the middle of transactions. People pissed off where services were performed moments before the credit card machines stopped." He grinned. "Get this: airlines are actually waiving the baggage fees. People started smashing ATMs when their cards were declined."

"Yeah." Dylan leaned forward. "For whatever reason the worst has broken out in Denver. I called mom. Fight started at a grocery store in a low-income neighborhood near downtown. People were already pissed. Tempers hot over a recent police shooting. Guess it spilled into the streets. They torched an entire business district. Right in the middle of it someone with a scoped rifle started shooting at police. Twenty ended up dead, including four cops, and it's growing."

Jon stared through the amber beer in his glass. "The wages of white privilege come home to roost."

Sam kept his mouth shut. He had his own notions about "white privilege" and "social justice", but he came from a different world than the rest of his fellows.

Sam checked his phone for the latest news. The president was appealing for calm, assuring the country that it was only a matter of hours before the problem would be addressed.

"Hey, guys, listen to this: In reply to one reporter's question, the president was quoted as saying, "Martial law is a possibility when it comes to the protection of the lives and property of law-abiding Americans."

"Martial law?" Jon's voice was incredulous. "That sucks goat turds."

Sam continued to read: "The president keeps insisting it will only be a matter of hours before the problem is fixed. When asked about some Chinese incursion in Taiwan, she said that it was being dealt with."

Taiwan? Who cared about Taiwan? Sam figured the country had its own trouble. The delivery of three pizzas pretty much ended the speculation.

Back at the Days Inn, the steely look was still on Amber's face when Sam found her in the bar.

"Nothing's changed," she told him. "Tomorrow morning we're headed out to the Tappan Ranch and then up to the project. They'll have this credit thing resolved long before we're back in town for break. Then we can all hit the ATM and restock. Meanwhile, get a good night's sleep."

"Works for me."

"Oh, Sam? You were riding with Kirstin the whole way. She say anything about the Tappans?"

"No. Why?"

"Just a couple of comments over supper." Amber rubbed her face with weary hands. Sam could see the faint tracery of white scars. "We went over this in the introductory meeting back at the anthro building. No politics. The Tappans will be our hosts."

"Kirstin hitting the white privilege thing again?"

"Yeah." Amber lifted her glass of whiskey. Sipped. "The good news is that Shanteel keeps her in check."

"How's that?"

Amber shot Sam a satisfied grin. "Hard for Kirstin—given her silver-spoon background—to start preaching when Shanteel's at the table. Shanteel gives her one of those 'you don't know shit, white girl' looks, and it shuts Kirstin down like a switch."

Sam hitched his butt onto the next bar stool. "You rode out here with her, what's Shanteel's story? Why's she here? She's a social work major. Never had an archaeology class in her life."

"Looking for her Seminole and Cherokee ancestors."

"In Wyoming?" Sam raised a skeptical brow.

"Yeah, well, like you said, she never had a class in North American anthro. She didn't have what you'd call 'a fine handle on the nuances' of where Cherokee and Seminoles lived. But now that she's here, she's committed. If a little worried."

Sam waved the bartender away when he asked what he wanted to drink. "Shanteel's from one of the roughest neighborhoods in Philadelphia. She has, um, issues. Especially with red-neck cowboy types. You saw her reaction in Lincoln? Over that Confederate flag and those guys in the pickup?"

"Think she's going to have trouble with the Tappans?"

"Intense black woman, active in Black Lives Matter, face to face with Wyoming ranchers? Who are probably Republicans by the way."

"So are you." Amber shot him a sidelong look. "Oh, relax. I'll keep your secret."

"Hey, my dad and mom ran a restaurant. Running a business, dealing with the taxes, the inspections, the payoffs, the FICA, and payroll gives you a different perspective on life. But something tells me New York and Wyoming Republicans are two completely different animals. I mean, these are MAGA, God, guns, and worship the flag types, right?"

She studied her whiskey as if some remarkable truth were hidden in its amber depths. "So, why is it that anthropologists trained in intricacies of ethnic diversity—of all people—can be so righteous when it comes to the superiority of their own moral compasses?"

"Sure, there's Kirstin and Shanteel, but I don't think the rest—"

"I miss the old days when anthro struggled—if unsuccessfully—to be an objective discipline dedicated to the understanding of human diversity and complexity. The problem with being an activist, is that you've got to make baseline assumptions founded on truth. With a capital T." She hooked her fingers in quotation marks. "Which means you are nothing more than a jihadist."

Sam fought to keep his expression neutral.

She gave him a dismissive look. And to be sure he understood, said, "See you in the morning. Should be a busy day."

"Yeah. *Mañana.*"

Everyone in Sam's room fell asleep reading the insane comments on Yik Yak and Snap Chat. And there was nothing on TV but the news video of all the problems around the country.

Sam finally drifted off with scenes of angry demonstrations in Cleveland and Atlanta playing in his head. People were throwing bricks through bank windows.

THEY HAD NO IDEA

***

Most people think it was the Chinese. Doesn't matter, really. Whoever planned it, they had no clue what they were unleashing. The worry— especially after COVID—has always been that someone would use biological warfare, that lab-designed viruses would backfire, infecting the attackers as well as the target country. Spread into a world-wide plague that killed us all.

The cyberattack that corrupted the banks wasn't well thought out. Whoever infected the financial system with the malware, had no idea that it would crash the entire world.

It was brilliant. The malware corrupted less than ten percent of the nation's bank accounts. Just enough to sow distrust of all financial records. It was all about breaking the American people's faith in their financial system. After COVID and the 2020 election, maybe our faith was already broken.

Excerpt from Breeze Tappan's *Journal.*

CHAPTER THREE

***

SAM AWAKENED DIRTY-DOG-TIRED WHEN HIS IPHONE DINGED HIM SATURDAY MORNING, but part of him was relieved to be away from the nightmarish dreams.

He checked the news: The nightmares had nothing on the actual stories. Denver was no longer the only city locked down by social convulsions.

Well, shit. Didn't that just cut it?

He wondered how the folks were doing back on Long Island. All of Hempstead would be shut down. Especially at The Yucateca. No one back home paid in cash. And The Yucateca didn't take checks.

Call them?

He actually tapped out the number, hesitated, and finally cleared the phone. He knew how it would end. Dad, saying, *"Hey! What you doing in Wyoming? You're out there digging up dead Indians? Git your lazy ass back here,* cholo. *You think it's a stroll in the flowers running this place? And who got you into that school, anyway? We need the help, damn it."*

Sam left Court, Jon, and Dylan asleep, yanked on yesterday's clothes, and stepped out into the hall. True to form, he found Amber already in the restaurant, a cup of coffee cradled in her hands as if in a form of prayer. From her empty plate, she'd already eaten. This time her eyes were focused on the mounted fish and African animal heads that studded the restaurant's walls.

He pulled out the chair next to hers. "Do you ever sleep?"

She arched a red eyebrow. "Is that a serious question?"

"You were still up when I went to bed last night. Then you beat me here, coffee in hand, breakfast finished."

"Got a lot on my mind." She shifted her grip on the coffee cup, lifted her phone, and checked the time. "Evan should be on the way. Said he'd meet us at six."

"He's here?"

Dr. Evan Holly—professor emeritus from the University of Wyoming—specialized in Shoshonean archaeology and culture. Knew more about Wyoming archaeology than anyone alive.

Amber's lips twitched. "Evan has a lady friend in town that he stays with. One of his old girlfriends, I think. He has a long-standing reputation in the discipline for never sticking to one female when a multitude are available."

"What is it about archaeologists from his generation?"

"The last of the old patriarchs? They all drank like fish, and philandering was like a group sport. 'Tipi creeping' they used to call it. Maybe it was just a lustier age back before #metoo." A faint smile. "Shyla would approve."

"You heard about Denver?"

"The city's locked down according to Fox News. Denver's not the only place having trouble."

"Fox News?"

All Sam got in return was a quirking at the corners of her mouth, as if she were strangling a smile.

"Here he comes." Amber pushed back her chair and stood.

Sam did the same, turning to see Doctor Holly as he entered in a long-legged stride. The first thing that struck Sam was the man's height: well over six feet. He wore a light-canvas shooting jacket with a patch on the right shoulder, loops for shotgun shells, and lots of pockets—most of them brimming. Beneath it he'd donned a tan button-down shirt that he'd tucked into slim-fit blue jeans held up by a colorful horsehair belt. A beadwork buckle sported a beautiful red rose on a white background.

The man's battered-looking dark-gray cowboy hat was pulled down tight; gray hair poked out from beneath. Holly's long face looked weathered and tough. As a final accent to his personality, a long-stemmed pipe was clenched in his teeth.

At sight of Amber, thin lips curled around the pipe, and Holly's faded blue eyes warmed. Dropping the pipe into one of his pockets, he called, "Hey, girl!" and pulled Amber into an embrace.

To Sam's complete surprise, she didn't jack a knee into the guy's nuts and deck him with a roundhouse right. No one *touched* Amber. She actually—but awkwardly—returned the hug.

"Still a lech, aren't you, Evan?" She pushed back, grinning as if in real delight. Flinging a hand Sam's way, she added, "This is my crew chief, Sam Delgado."

"Pleasure to meet you, sir. I've admired your work," Sam said, shaking the man's big hand. It swallowed his, and Holly's grip was like being squeezed by two-by-fours.

Holly barely spared Sam a glance. "Nice to meet you."

I might have been cold lunch meat.

Holly's attention was on Amber as he seated himself and said, "You're looking good, girl. How was the trip out?"

"Long. Tense," Amber told him. "Lot of anxiety out there. COVID has most of Iowa shut down. Made it to Casper just as this credit card thing hit. You heard about Denver? The other cities? Remarkable distraction just hours before China landed troops in Taiwan, don't you think?"

"Shit's hitting the fan," he muttered, pulling off his big hat and dropping it on the floor beside his chair. "How's that old scoundrel Ricci?"

To most students, Don Ricci—the head of the anthro department—was like some sort of living god.

"Dr. Don's fine. He said to tell you to go fuck yourself."

Sam swallowed hard, a nervous quiver in his stomach as he waited for the explosion.

Holly just grinned. "Never thought much of him until he sent you my way. Good call that. Might have steered you toward those ninnies down at Colorado State. Then where would you be?"

Holly glanced Sam's way and said, "Easy, son. You'll figure it out one of these days."

Sam felt his ears begin to burn, that sense of humiliation stewing in his gut. While Amber was technically his academic equal, there was a difference between them: she had a funded dissertation topic.

Evan's eyebrow arched. "You heard that the secretary of state is on his way to Beijing to find a way to, as he says, 'defuse the situation?'"

"Yeah." Her gaze went distant. "Didn't get much coverage, did it? The news either seems fixated on cute stories about who can't buy McNuggets with their VISA or who's burning which neighborhood down."

Dr. Holly grunted.

For Sam's part, the credit card thing was a hell of a lot more important. That was *here*. Not a half a planet away.

Amber changed the subject. "Enough of the world falling apart. I've got everything on the list that you asked for. God knows how we're going to pack all of it up to the site."

"The Tappans will handle it. Their motto is, 'Ask a Tappan, they'll make it happen.' Talked to Bill last night. He said the kids had already been up to the camp, cut wood, dug a latrine, and set up wall tents. They were packing the groceries in today."

"You said you had a surprise." Amber tilted her head suggestively.

Dr. Holly leaned back in his chair; his expression smug. "There's a cave, Amber. Just down from the site in a side canyon in the limestone. Frank Tappan found it when he was a kid out elk hunting."

"Why is that important?"

"I'm going to wait until you can see for yourself." Now that he had both Amber and Sam hanging, Holly leaped to his feet, padding off for the coffee pot and cups on the buffet bar.

"Cave?" Sam asked, gaze following the old anthropologist.

Amber was tapping her fingers on the table. "He's like a kid at Christmas. Must be pretty awesome."

"I don't think he likes me."

She shot Sam a quick look. "He respects scholars who are proficient in their discipline. Beyond that, he expects you to pull your weight and then some. Go the extra distance."

Holly strode back and seated himself, coffee in hand.

"What kind of crew have you got?" he asked, forestalling any more talk about the cave.

"Typical field school. A sprinkling of graduate students and the rest undergrads. Most are anthro majors, but I've got an English major, a computer science geek, and a social work major who is going to be...interesting."

"How so?"

"Shanteel is from Philadelphia. She's twenty-two, raised in one of the tough neighborhoods. Philadelphia cops shot her mother dead in one of the early Black Lives Matter marches. Shanteel took an anthropology course because an aunt told her that some of her ancestors were Cherokee Seminoles. But instead of academic interest, I think she signed up for the field school to keep from having to take care of a younger sister in Philadelphia."

"So?"

"So, she's got an attitude about all things Western, redneck, and rural."

Holly was grinning. "I like her already."

"Did you catch that part where I said she had an attitude?"

"If she didn't, she wouldn't be worth spit." Holly took a sip of his coffee. "Cherokee Seminole, huh? She ever met an Indian?"

"I don't think so."

"Thomas Star will be up at the site in a couple of days. I thought he should see it."

"Who's Thomas Star?" Sam asked.

Holly shot him a measuring look that didn't bode well for Sam's future. "He's a *puhagan*."

Sam nodded, ever thankful for the reading Amber had made him tackle: Hultkrantz, Shimkin, Loendorf, and Stewart among others. *Puhagan.* Medicine man. A Shoshoni holy man.

Sam felt a slight lessening of Holly's disdain. Probably because he didn't ask what a *puhagan* was.

But then, Sam had never met a real Native American either.

"Why would we need a Native monitor?" Amber asked. "Don't tell me there are burials up there."

"Don't know about any burials." Holly sucked down another gulp of coffee and made a face as he stared at the cup. "That's really rude stuff."

Then he waved a hand dismissively. "You better brace yourself, Amber. You're about to blow your career wide open up on that mountain."

THE COLLAPSE

***

Looking back, I doubt the cyberattack was supposed to destroy the banking system. Just wound it. Sow suspicion and distrust among the people. I wonder what kind of "Oh shit" moment they had in Pyong Yang, Beijing, Moscow, Tehran, or wherever, when they finally realized the extent of the collapse.

See, when the US banks couldn't cope, they closed their doors. By the time they discovered the extent of the malware, could begin to implement a patch, it was too late.

Americans were looking for an excuse. The people had already turned on each other.

Excerpt from Breeze Tappan's *Journal.*

CHAPTER FOUR

***

SAM DROVE KIRSTIN'S BMW AS THEY LEFT THE LITTLE HAMLET OF HOT SPRINGS THAT SUNNY Wyoming morning. The students had settled the bill for rooms in cash. Sam and Amber had covered Jon's share. Some, like Danielle and Kirstin, were down to the change in their pockets. Their habit had been to depend on credit cards down to buying a tube of Chapstick at the truck stops.

"You'll see," Dr. Holly had promised. "They'll have it cleared up by the time we're back down from the mountain. It'll be a story you can all tell. 'Remember the time when the credit cards were all declined.'"

Worry about the banks and concern about family back home was tempered by the fact that no one who'd called home had heard anything dire.

Should have called, Sam chastised himself. But, damn it, he could imagine The Yucatec. Mama would be wound up like a spring. Her life depended upon the ritual, running the register, taking orders, and serving. The woman turned manic on the few days they had ever taken off. They'd be closed until noon anyway. Sure, they'd be insisting on cash, but he knew they'd take IOUs from long-time customers.

Again, Sam drove last in line behind Dylan's Dodge Ram. Dylan followed Amber in the college van, who in turn followed Dr. Evan Holly up in the lead who drove a battered Jeep Rubicon.

From town they wound their way up through broken sandstone anticlines and into broad sagebrush-covered valleys. Awesome geology—especially the brilliant red-sandstone uplifts. When seen against the cerulean sky, the effect was like Sam had never imagined.

This was about as far from Sam's Hempstead Long Island roots— and The Yucateca—as he could get. In that world of streets, people, traffic, and graffiti, his father ran the kitchen; Mama held dominion over the dining room and kept the books. The day he left for graduate school Sam swore he'd never bus another table, carry out the trash, or stack the dishwasher again.

His father's last words were still ringing in his ears: "Your mother and I raised you better than this. Worked our asses off so you could be the first to go to college. And you take what? Anthropology? How you gonna make a living doing that, huh? We ain't paying no more. *Comprende, niño?*"

So, here he was with thirty-five dollars in his pocket, driving Kirstin's dream car on roads it was never designed for, headed toward who-knew-what?

This was hard country. Edgy. Untamed. They barely spoke as he drove up out of the Bighorn River Valley and took the narrow blacktop country road west from the highway.

Occasional ranch houses—looking battered and dingy for the most part—stood bravely beneath spreading and ancient cottonwood trees. The antithesis of those came in the form of rudely skirted and sun-faded trailer houses, usually with a couple of junked pickups out back; rusted tractors and unidentifiable pieces of agricultural equipment looked abandoned in stands of dark-green weeds.

"Talk about Dueling Banjos country," Ashley whispered.

"What's that?" Kirstin was frowning at her phone.

"You never saw *Deliverance?*" Ashley asked.

"Vin Diesel in it?" Kirstin was lifting her phone, turning it this way and that.

"Guys from the city get raped by rednecks," Shyla supplied.

He loved it when she sat beside him. He could fantasize that they were a couple.

Yeah?

Fat chance.

In the back seat, Kirstin lowered her phone. "Um, guys, no service. Tower must be down."

"Oh, man," Ashley sounded irritated as she turned her attention from playing *Wild Rush* on her Samsung and checked her service. "Maybe that's, like, because of the riots in Denver? You think they shut down service?"

"Why would they?" Shyla murmured. "They said it was just a computer going down. I mean, banks have back-up files. What's wrong with people in Denver? Too much weed?"

Sam sneaked a glance at Shyla. Her gaze looked distant. Was she worried about her folks back in Vermont? Or missing her rich football-playing boyfriend who flew her off to places like Barbados and Martha's Vineyard over break?

A rock chipped up from one of the tires clanged off the BMW's underside.

"Hey! Careful with my car!"

"It was just a stone," Sam shot back.

"You break this car; you're going to know real trouble."

"You want to drive?" Sam asked, slowing for a rough section.

Up ahead, Dylan's big Dodge truck was chattering and bouncing over the weirdly ridged road surface. They would learn this was called "washboard", formed by the tires bouncing. It was insidious. Even the BMW's suspension was barely up to it.

"Where the *hell* is Amber taking us?" Kirstin demanded.

"End of the road," Sam told her. "You all saw the map. There's that one last ranch, then the national forest."

"People *live* out here?" Ashley asked in disbelief as she stared at the latest of the trailers we were passing. A woman in a weed-sprinkled yard was actually hanging laundry on a clothesline. It was like stepping fifty years back in time.

Ashley wondered, "It's been like an hour since we left town. They drive all that way? On this road? Just to get, you know, a carton of milk?"

"Unfuckingbelievable," Kirstin moaned as she shook her phone.

Sam was pretty weirded out himself. Talk about being alone, the only signs of humanity were the dirt road, a couple of fences, and a power line. What was that term? Dueling banjos country?

They rumbled over a cattle guard and between two tall poles. Hanging from the crosspiece a weathered sign read: **Tappan Ranch.**

The little caravan followed Dr. Holly another half mile down a lane bordered on both sides by alfalfa fields. The ranch house was built of logs with a big stone fireplace at one end. Frame additions had been added haphazardly over the years—a sort of patchwork of angles stuck on the house's back and sides.

A big tan-colored shop building—hard to even call it a concession to the Twentieth Century—stood to the left. Along the base of the slope were a cluster of small log-and-frame cabins with tarpaper roofs. A historic-looking barn, painted dark red, posed picturesquely against a series of wooden corrals. Against the slope a long, open-fronted shed stretched a hundred feet or so. Sam could see two green tractors, a couple of older work trucks, and assorted farm machinery within. Weathered horse and stock trailers had been parked in a row at the edge of one of the fields.

Sort of angled off the rear of the house stood another, cruder, log structure with a white-painted door and two stove pipes sticking up from the tin roof.

And behind it all? Sam couldn't believe his eyes. An outhouse—just like in the historical photos—could be seen to one side at the foot of the slope. From the weeds around its front—and the lack of paint—it didn't look like it was still used.

Dr. Holly's Jeep pulled up before the open-sided equipment shed; Amber parked the college van beside him, which set the pattern for the rest.

Sam shut the BMW off and stepped out. The excited bump to his heartbeat came as a surprise.Horses were all lined up at the corral beside the barn; the animals watched them with lazy interest.

"What happened to my car?" Kirstin cried in horror.

Sam turned to find her staring in absolute amazement at the powdery white dust that had covered the BMW's opalescent black paint.

"That's called dust."

She gave him a half-wild look, and Sam had to remind himself that she was a very young nineteen, and her parents were rich Washington DC lawyers.

She said, "I need a car wash. Like right now, people."

"Give it a break, why don't you?" Ashley murmured. She propped hands on her hips and looked around. "Wow, so this is home for the next two months, huh?"

If any of the students thrived, Sam thought it would be Ashley. She was captain of the women's soccer team and played shortstop on the university women's fast-pitch team. Her single goal for the summer was to get a good enough grade to get off academic probation. She stood about five-foot-five, had short-cut blonde hair, and was solid muscle.

Sam rounded the back of Dylan's truck just in time to see Shanteel climb down from the college van. Her eyes were fixed on the yellow flag hanging limp over the house front porch. Sam didn't need to see the text to know it had a snake on it and stated **Don't Tread on Me.**

Dr. Holly—his cowboy hat scrunched on his head—called, "Come on, people, let's go meet our hosts. Then there's time for a bathroom stop if you need it. After that you can unpack your gear and carry it over to the bunkhouse."

"What's a bunkhouse?" Kirstin asked.

"Like a dormitory," Dylan told her, a crooked smile on his face. "God, where'd you grow up? Washington DC?"

"Georgetown."

Sam wondered if Kirstin and Shanteel would last out the first ten-day session up on the mountain, or if they'd bail and be headed home within the week.

A man emerged from the house, thumped across the wooden porch, and into the yard. Okay. To call the packed-earth and gravel a "yard" was generous.

As Sam followed the group across the small parking lot, he kept looking up at the mountains that rose around the valley. The ranks of fir and spruce were darker green and mostly on the northern slopes. The lighter green was pine with an occasional juniper, the trees more irregular where they clung to the mountain's southern side. White patches of rocky cliff had to be the limestone Dr. Holly had mentioned. And behind it, even taller, wilder-looking mountains rose toward the sky.

What awesome country!

And he was going up there? To say it was a seven-mile pack trip on horseback while sitting in the safe confines of the Anthropology building was one thing. To stand in that valley, looking up at the mountainside, with the horses that would carry him and the crew just over yonder? That was something entirely different.

"Brought you a load of greenhorns, Bill," Dr. Holly called to the old man who limped out to meet them. The guy could have been a stereotype: With the stained gray cowboy hat on his head, he stood a little short of six feet on seriously bowed legs. A plaid snap-button shirt hung from bony shoulders on a rail-thin frame. The pointed cowboy boots that shod his feet looked so worn they should have been thrown away years back.

Word was that Bill Tappan was seventy; he looked absolutely ancient right until he fixed you with those intense eyes of his: hazel-centered and ringed by brown.

"Welcome to Tappan Ranch," his voice was firm. "I'm Bill Tappan. My people have been in this valley for over a hundred years. I'm fourth generation. Frank—who you'll meet tonight—is fifth generation, and Brandon and Celia, they're sixth, so you might say we got roots."

They went through the introductions, Tappan shaking hands all the way around, although Sam could tell that Shanteel and Kirstin didn't exactly have their hearts in it. And it wasn't because of COVID.

Sam didn't think Bill Tappan missed it, either.

An amused smile crossed Tappan's lips. "Something tells me you're in for a really interesting two months. Not one of you is going to leave here unchanged."

A vivacious woman with flaming red hair and skin-tight Levi's burst out the door. If she was fifty, it wasn't by much. She fixed them all with excited green eyes as she grabbed up Bill Tappan's hand in a familiar clutch.

"So this is the crew, huh, Bill?" she exclaimed. "Never had a bunch of archaeology students from back east before. Welcome."

Bill inclined his head toward her. "This is Meggan, and her only fault is piss-poor taste in men. Probably why she married me."

She elbowed him, grinning the whole time. It hit Sam that it didn't come off as an act.

"Until you get your legs under you," Bill continued, "don't go fooling with the horses and don't wander off. We had bear sign back of the stack yard—"

Dr. Holly interjected. "He means they had a grizzly bear just over there behind the haystack."

"—and there's been a cat lurking around on the slope yonder."

Dr. Holly interpreted: "When he says cat, he means a mountain lion. A cougar."

"Hell, Evan," Bill said sourly, "I told 'em in English, didn't I?"

Amber—a curious look on her face that Sam couldn't quite decipher—said, "In other words, people, beyond this yard and these buildings, it is wilderness. So don't go wandering. Understood?"

Sam's gaze fixed on the places where Dr. Holly had pointed. Grizzly bears? Mountain lions?

They had all known the forest service had rules about bear-safe food storage up at the field camp, and that bear spray would be provided, but *damn* they'd also been told that even seeing one would be a miracle. And the things were prowling around the ranch house?

"We'll have an orientation after you get settled in," Bill was saying. "Evan? You got anything to add?"

Sam had been watching Meggan, who'd been watching her husband. That glow stayed in her green eyes, a worshipful smile on her face.

Dr. Holly said, "Anyone who had too much coffee for breakfast and needs the facilities, they're inside through the main room. Down the hallway. Then to the right."

Meggan turned loose of her husband long enough to clasp her hands together as she faced the crew, adding, "Um, we're on a septic system. There's a sign on the toilet. 'If it's wet, let it set. If it's brown, flush it down.'" Her grin narrowed. "Should speak for itself."

"It does," Amber told her, turning. "When you're done, we'll start unpacking." With a gesture of the hand, she indicated the crew was released.

Stepping in the door, the living room was spacious with a big couch covered by some kind of tan hide. A thick wooden coffee table stood before it, and to Sam's absolute surprise an eighty-inch curved-screen TV dominated one entire wall. A stuffed elk head with huge antlers barely fit in the far corner of the room. A rack of rifles hung on the wall by the door, which caused him a double-take. A chill went down his spine. The damn things were real. He had no doubt they were loaded.

Another furry brown hide covered the plank floor. Big. And it hit him: buffalo!

The overstuffed chair by the window had an ornate floor lamp behind it. On the end table beside the chair lay a copy of Thucydides, open to about halfway.

While the rest ooed and awed in a wide-eyed procession and

crowded their way into the aforementioned hallway. Sam glanced through the arch on the far side of the room and into a dining room with a rough-hewn table and mismatched chairs that would seat ten. Dishes filled a hutch on one wall. A doorway in back led into what looked like a fully stocked and completely modern kitchen.

Going down the hall, he glanced through an open door. The room was a library, shelves from floor to ceiling. And in the middle of it, back-lit by a window, sat an antique and expensive-looking desk made of some exotic wood.

He stepped in, amazed at the titles. One entire wall was dedicated to the Civil War. On both sides and above the door, the titles were all scholarly works about the American fur trade and Wyoming history. World history and philosophy covered the wall to the right. Military history, World War II, and Vietnam were shelved in every square inch surrounding and above the window.

That's when he noticed that the top of each volume bristled with bits of paper. Pulling out Josephus, he flipped it open to a page where the note said, "Bad translation. See Whiston." The text was talking about the Jewish revolt in 70 C.E.

Sam almost jumped out of his skin when a voice behind him said, "You really have to translate Josephus from the original. Even Whiston had an agenda."

Sam spun, gulping, to find himself face-to-face with Bill Tappan. The man had a mildly curious look on his face, the piercing eyes reserved.

"Sorry," Sam almost stuttered. "I just...I mean, this is awesome. I didn't expect..."

"History is a hobby of mine. More so before Frank bought that damn TV and hooked it up to the satellite. TVs are like vampires, they suck up a person's time and intelligence...and maybe a bit of the soul as well."

Sam looked over at the desk to see another note-feathered book on the waxed surface: *The Road to Disunion: Vol. II Secessionists Triumphant, 1854-1861.*

Stepping over, he ran reverent fingers over the dust jacket.

"Not the most inspiring of reading," Tappan said wearily. "The parallels between then and today are uncannily familiar. Same jingoist quotes. Just as mindless and inflammatory...only the names are different."

"How so?"

"Look at the Congress in the late 1850's. Read their statements and speeches. Compare it to Congress today. Read their statements and speeches. The words and invective are the same, just different names. As if the intervening hundred and fifty years—let alone the Civil War—had never happened."

"What do you think will happen now?"

"Those of us who know history are doomed to watch those who don't repeat the same insane mistakes over and over." Bill Tappan gave a slight shrug of his rail-thin shoulders. "Movements create momentum and inertia until they can't be stopped. Sort of like a tidal wave, there comes a time after which you can't damp it down. I think we're past that, and we're going to have to pay for it."

Meggan leaned in the library door, asking, "Bill? Do you know if Frank dropped that check off at the bank when you and he went into town last week?"

"I know for a fact. Hannah, the gal that works the drive up? She gave me two extra dog biscuits for Mack and Talbot. Why?"

"I finally got through on the computer to order that stuff from Amazon. Some kind of problem with the credit card." She slapped a hand on the doorframe. "I'll call the bank on Tuesday. See what the problem is."

Sam said, "No one's taking credit cards. Something wrong with the system. We had to pay cash for the last part of the trip."

"Probably someone updating a system somewhere." And Meggan was gone, all energy and smiles.

"You're welcome to read anything here," Tappan gestured around after turning his attention back to Sam. "Only one rule: Nothing leaves the room."

"Yes, sir."

Back at the door, it was Amber's turn to lean in: "Hey, Sam. Let's get these people organized, huh?"

"Be right there."

Amber hesitated then, eyes alight as she took in the books.

As if Sam would ever get the time to just sit in the comfy chair behind that waxed desk and read.

The site to which the crew was headed was called "The Penthouse". A large prehistoric Native American village, it sat at an elevation of eight thousand five hundred feet and was located above a low pass where the Owl Creek Mountains met the Absaroka Range.

Amber's goal was to map and test the site. She'd found it through remote sensing using algorithms and LiDAR satellite data.

Sam's goal was to find a dissertation topic, and he needed something desperately. His father was irritated, Mama had cut off the money, and the debt was piling up.

"This anthropology stuff is crap. If you're gonna waste your life? You come home and waste it in the kitchen, huh? What kind of raising did you get, chico*? Family comes before everything else."* Those had been *Papa*'s final words just before he had slammed the receiver down.

Some of the things said by the chair of Sam's committee weren't much better. Somewhere up there on that mountain, he was praying he would find the answer.

How desperate was he?

Enough that he had signed on to the project with Amber Sagan as the project director. Sure, she was a co-principal investigator on the Forest Service research permit with Dr. Holly, but—given the rumors about her history—she was also the scariest woman Sam had ever met.

THE WAY IT WORKED

***

Here's the genius: Corrupt maybe ten percent of accounts, electronically adding money to some, emptying others. If you are VISA, Mastercard, or American Express, the careful balance between debit and credit can't be trusted. The "big-six" banks can't guarantee the accuracy of the balances in their depositors' accounts. The only way to stem the damage is to freeze all credit transactions.

Just four hours of cards not working, of more than a trillion dollars of transactions stopped, and America was in chaos.

In a nation divided, where progressives and conservatives, Democrats and Republicans, Pro-life and Pro-choice, where second amendment and gun control, urban and rural, antifa and boogaloo, BLM and Proud Boys, were all battle lines, the stage was set: Americans already hated each other.

The credit collapse struck the spark that set off the conflagration.

Excerpt from Breeze Tappan's *Journal.*

CHAPTER FIVE

* * *

"HERE'S THE BUNKS," BILL TAPPAN SAID, POINTING. THE STUDENTS STOOD IN THE "BUNK-house". Rough-cut lumber had been nailed to the log walls to create a rack of beds three-high on either side of the room's long axis. Each space had a mattress, no sheets. Sam thought it looked like something out of a prisoner-of-war movie.

"And that's a fold out," Bill continued as he indicated a cabinet beneath the far window. "Makes things a mite cramped when it's opened, but you can still sneak past."

The French windows at opposite ends of the room provided light, as did the trio of bare bulbs hanging from the ceiling ridgepole.

"You won't need to use the stoves," Bill said, pointing to the cast-iron heat stoves at either end. "But if you get chilly, there's baseboard electric heat. Just be sure to turn it off before you leave in the morning.

"The toilet's behind that door next to the table. Remember we're on a septic system. TP's okay, but paper towels, Kleenex, tampons and the like will plug it up. There's a shower stall there, too. Um...my advice is don't linger. Hot water heater's kind of small."

He touched a finger to the brim of his battered hat as if in salute. "Let me know if you need anything."

They all watched him leave the room, his cowboy boots thumping hollowly on the plank floor.

He was barely out of hearing before Shanteel asked incredulously, "This is not happening to me. Sleep here? Shiiiit!"

As if someone had thrown a switch, Amber turned hard. "Yeah, we're going to sleep here. And not a word. Not a single damn complaint from any of you, especially within hearing distance of the Tappans."

"I mean, this..." Kirstin was gesturing around at the wooden beds.

"This is primeval."

Amber stepped in-her-face close, expression grim. "Believe me, kid, there's a *whole lot* worse. When I was locked in..."

Amber closed her eyes. Fought for control. She'd been a nurse for an NGO medical clinic in northern Syria when she was captured by ISIS. They held her in a basement prison outside Raqqa for most of a year before she had been rescued. She wore long sleeves and high collars so that people couldn't see the scars.

In a strained voice, Amber stated, "In the world of living quarters, this is a paradise."

To change the subject, Sam said, "Six beds, Amber. One fold out. Are you going to make assignments?"

She seemed to catch herself on the verge of an explosion. "Call this the women's dorm. Sam, you and the guys set up your tents on the grass out front."

"Out front?" Court whispered. "Didn't he say something about bears? A mountain lion?"

Amber whirled on him, voice deadly. "Any lion or bear comes by, it'll have to deal with me."

Eyes went wide. They couldn't tell if Amber was joking. Sam thought that for the most part, they were pitying any grizzly bear that might be willing to risk pissing her off.

He had only seen Amber lose it once, in graduate seminar, when a visiting professor had been lecturing on cultural reaction to climate change. Some question about the Middle East had started him off on a defense of Islamic radicalism and the benefits of Shariah law. Amber had launched into him like a Saturn rocket, her blue eyes glittering, fists clenched, voice a half-strangled squeal. Like, she was out of her chair, headed for the speaker when Dr. Hammond and Dr. Don leaped up and escorted her out of the room.

A lot of them had wondered what would have happened if she'd got her hands on the guy.

Amber broke Sam's reverie by saying, "We've got a couple of hours before lunch. Now, *move*, people."

Like a troop of Egyptians building the pyramids they tramped back and forth from the college van and Dylan's truck, carrying sleeping bags, tents, coolers, backpacks, and suitcases.

While Sam and the guys set up tents out front, they could hear the chatter from within the bunkhouse as the females picked bunks and unrolled their sleeping bags.

Amber had insisted the crew put up their tents on the lawn behind the anthro building back on campus, had called it a trial run to be sure they knew how the tents went up and that all the pieces were there. Court, apparently, hadn't been paying attention.

The guy was twenty-two, brown eyes and hair, and just sort of loomed over things. Sam wouldn't call him obese, but he was definitely over-weight. Court hailed from Greenwood, an up-scale suburb of Indianapolis.

"You're a computer science major," Sam said as he helped him thread the poles through the loops on his tent. "What made you sign up for an archaeological field school?"

Court gave him a sheepish grin as he perched on hands and knees on the grass. Think eager and oversized dog. "I lost a bet. I mean, it was more like a dare, you know? I lost at *Pharaonic Curse*."

"What's that?"

Something lit behind Court's brown eyes. "A killer good game. Wish I'd designed it. You have to get into the pyramid, shoot all these tomb robbers trying to beat you to the treasure, and figure out the magical power that will nullify or destroy the Egyptian gods guarding the tomb. And then, if you get that far, you have to figure out how to get the gold out of the tomb. That's the tricky part."

"So, how do you do that?"

He grimaced. "That's how I lost. Matt figured it out first. You assemble the chariot that's in pieces on the tomb floor. And once you toss the mummy out, load the sarcophagus on the chariot and pack it with the treasure. Then you roll the loot out."

"After you *dump* the mummy *out*? I mean... *Tomb robbing?* You ever even taken an anthropology class?"

He looked at Sam with clueless eyes. "No."

"Just a word of advice. Anthropologists don't really get off on tomb robbing, Court. We call it looting. Think, like, big-time *bad.* Okay?"

At Sam's raised eyebrow, Court looked away. "I get your point. But dang, I thought I'd be turned down. I mean, I'd never had any of the prerequisites."

"Who needs prerequisites? Amber had to have a minimum of ten students or the university wasn't going to approve the class. Like everything else in the world, it's all about numbers and money."

"Oh," Court murmured and watched Sam slip the pole into the loop on the tent floor. "Sam, you know, actually *doing* archaeology? Might give me just the edge on my next design. This could turn my whole career around."

"You ever been west before?"

"Sure, Comicon in San Diego. Guess I'll miss this year's. And I go to the trade shows in San Francisco. You know, where they introduce the new games? If I can keep my 4.0 and win enough championships in the tournaments, there's a chance that one of the companies will take me on as an intern. So much of the business is networking."

He looked around. Everyone was checking his or her phone. "Nobody's getting cell service."

"Nope."

"A friend of mine was supposed to send me an upgrade of *Death Soldier IV.* It will be one of the games at the semi-finals. They've added a new dimension to the silicon zombies. I really have to get into the strategy and figure out how to take them down."

"It'll be waiting when we come down off the mountain."

"I've never slept in a tent before."

"There's a first time for everything," Sam told him. But then, that could be said for all of them, couldn't it?

He stepped over to see that Dylan had his house in order and was rolling out his sleeping bag inside. Jon needed help with the complex crisscrossing of tent poles that gave the thing structural integrity. It ended up being a roomy dome.

Jon had packed his guitar over, and the case was propped against the bunkhouse's log wall. The guy was good. He played gigs in the bars and coffeehouses around campus, sometimes paid, but most often picking tunes for tips.

Jon sat back on the grass, looking up at Sam with his wide brown eyes; the sun glinted in his long blond hair where it was pulled back in a ponytail. A first-year graduate student, he worked as a lab assistant in the zooarchaeology lab, got good grades, but had a reputation for a total lack of motivation.

"Holy shit, look at that." Jon's eyes had gone wide.

Sam followed Jon's point to where a mounted rider, a young man, appeared on horseback. Two big dogs followed along behind, tongues lolling. The rider trotted the dark horse across the irrigated field. All decked out as a cowboy, he rode with an elegant grace, like he was part of the horse.

At the gate to the yard, he didn't dismount, but reached down from the saddle and unlatched it. Sam and Jon watched in fascination as the rider clucked to the horse. The animal backed around and pulled the gate open. The horse then wheeled, the rider pulling the gate back closed behind them as they came through. As a final touch, the cowboy leaned down in the stirrup to latch it again before he rode off to the barn.

Sam recognized the odd protrusion on his saddle: the butt of a rifle. It stuck out just behind the rider's right leg, easy to reach.

The only people Sam knew who had guns were gangers or MS13— and the worst kind of trouble you could image. That, or they were cops, which—depending on the situation could be almost as bad. He'd been roughed up by cops for just being out on the street.

"You think he did that just to show off?" Shanteel demanded from where she stood in the bunkhouse door.

Sam shrugged. "Looked to me like he does it that way all the time."

"Sure," Shanteel murmured through a scowl. "Lazy. Make the poor horse do all the work." Then she disappeared back inside, muttering something under her breath.

Sam watched her go, fingers of unease stroking his spine like ice.

How would the tougher-than-nails Tappans react the first time one overheard Shanteel say something unkind? That hard, lean, rifle-packing young rider didn't come across as the kind who'd let an insult pass. How far could you trust a pissed-off young man with a gun? Especially when he lived out here where there was no law?

Looking around at the wilderness, at the suddenly menacing mountains, Sam came to the realization that he and his companions were a long way from anywhere. No cell service, no 911. They were completely at the Tappan's mercy.

CHAIN REACTION

***

The American banking system had safeguards. Most had the required twenty percent cash reserve, and the Federal Reserve Bank would have provided backup. But banking depends on accurate records. With no idea if the balances in the accounts were correct, how could they release funds to depositors asking for a cash withdrawal against their balances?

The FDIC acted immediately and ordered a bank holiday. Every financial institution in the country closed its doors that Friday.

It was the start of a three-day weekend. By the time the banks opened their doors the following Tuesday, the system would be reset, the malware purged, and accounts backdated to before the accounts were corrupted.

Too bad they never got the chance.

Excerpt from Breeze Tappan's *Journal.*

CHAPTER SIX

***

THE CREW WAS CALLED TO "SUPPER" THAT NIGHT AT SIX. A LONG TABLE ON THE RANCH house back porch was set with plates. Sam lingered just long enough to make sure that the students were all present and settled in.

Everyone was bitching because they had no cell service or Wi-Fi. Didn't matter that there wasn't any cell service, all of them still carried their phones around and kept checking them every ten minutes or so. Court looked half catatonic.

That feeling of being out of touch stirred a low-level panic down in Sam's gut. He'd check his phone. The little voice in his head would ask "What am I missing?" and the anxiety would build. It was like having a leg suddenly cut off. So he'd check his phone again.

Sam mentally asked himself: Remember the definition for insanity? Doing the same thing over and over and expecting a different result?

Dr. Holly watched the students and their phones with an amused pinch to his lips. Sam figured Dr. Holly probably thought of them the way psychiatric staff think of patients in a mental hospital: amused by the ones who can't leave their rooms without a special blanket or pillow.

Meggan—wearing a print-cotton shirt stuffed into tight Levi's and an apron—literally burst from the back door with a steaming, flat-bottomed pan of baked chicken and pork ribs. She held the big stainless-steel platter with hot pads as she set it in the center of the table, calling, "You all dive in. Iced tea in the pitcher. Potatoes and broccoli are coming. Hot rolls are in the wicker basket under the napkin. Butter's in the covered bowl."

As quickly, she was gone, the screen door slamming behind her.

When the crew had taken their seats, Jon asked, "Where's Amber and Dr. Holly?"

Sam told him, "Us boss types are eating inside with the Tappans. Some kind of war council."

War Council? Where had that come from? Kaliningrad, Taiwan, or Texit? All of them hot stories on the news just before the banks cratered.

"So, did you meet Frank and Pam?" Shyla asked as she used a fork to spear a thigh.

"Just a quick 'Good to meet you'," Sam told her, avoiding her turquoise eyes lest she think he was staring.

They had watched Frank and Pam from across the yard as the two rode in at the head of a line of horses that were all tied together. While Jon played folk songs from the 60s and a couple of bluegrass tunes, the crew had watched the Tappans climb off their horses and begin what looked like a laborious process of untying saddles, and odd X-shaped affairs on the pack horses.

Meggan burst out again, setting two heaping bowls of potatoes and broccoli on either side of the meat pan.

"You all okay?" Sam asked.

"Yeah, Mr. Crew Chief, sir," Shanteel said snidely, inspecting the ribs she'd speared.

He followed Meggan through the back door and into the kitchen with its steaming pots, central butcher-block island, and big Wolf stove. He hadn't seen the refrigerator before, a big two-door Sub-zero. Sam knew kitchen quality.

"This is like, commercial grade," he told Meggan as she grabbed a bottle of wine from an inset wine rack.

"We outfit," she said as if it explained everything.

"Outfit?"

She paused, studying Sam as if to determine his motive. "Outfit. People like Evan hire us to pack them into the back country. Like we're doing for you. It's extra income. Usually for tours up in the mountains and through the wilderness areas. And then there's hunting season. That's where the real money can be made. Eastern hunters will drop a couple of thousand in tips if you get them a big bull. That's cash. The damn government never knows."

Sam followed her into the dining room, thinking, *tax fraud.*

Evan and Amber were seated next to each other, Frank and Pam across the table. Bill sat at the head, an empty chair for Meggan on his right. They were talking about the Chinese landing troops on Taiwan. Bill had watched the news on the TV before supper.

The president had told China to hold position and cease any advances until the Secretary of State arrived in Beijing for talks. In the meantime, she said, the United States was sending two carrier groups into the South China Sea as a deterrent against further aggression.

The Chinese had responded that unless the carrier groups turned around, there would be what they called "irreversible consequences".

"Doesn't matter," Frank was saying. "Outside of a shooting war, there's nothing the Chinese can do. Sure, they've been building their navy, but they don't have the numbers or expertise to kick us out. They'll hold position, and we'll make concessions. In the end, they'll load up their troops, and Taiwan will have a new government friendly to Beijing." He smiled thinly. "Death of a thousand cuts."

"They can sure play us, can't they? Especially now, with the Texit vote. And California's passed a ballot, too?" Dr. Holly arched an eyebrow in Frank's direction. "You were at that last state-wide meeting to call a constitutional convention. After the Texas vote, I've heard that there's renewed interest."

"So, what's the president going to do? Take military possession of Texas? Arrest the sixty-four percent of the people who voted for secession? What's that? Twenty million people?"

Sam took his place next to Amber, directly across from Pam. He smiled at her as he seated himself. She gave him a friendly nod in return. She'd let her brown hair down, and it hung down her back. Like the rest of the Tappans, she was lean and wiry; and she shared that hard-eyed look that left Sam nervous. Even through her light, paisley-pattern shirt sleeves, he could see the muscles in her arms.

Frank, her husband, was definitely Bill Tappan's son. Square-shouldered, he had those same hazel eyes ringed in brown that seemed to see right through you.

Meggan popped the cork on the wine, poured Bill's glass full, and seated herself before passing the bottle to Evan.

Frank sipped his wine, then told Dr. Holly, "I was a precinct delegate. Voted against calling for the constitutional convention. Sure, there's a chance we might get a balanced budget amendment, some sort of restrictions and controls on these damned federal agencies. But the risks are too high. Throw it open like that, as crooked as politicians are? We could have lost a lot more than we gained. Maybe the second amendment, the tenth, and the fourth? Hell, in the internet age, and in the name of 'National Security', we might have lost a big chunk of the first amendment as well. We barely scuttled a secession vote as it was."

"What secession vote?" Amber asked.

Sam had vaguely heard of it, some passing thing in the news, but at that time, Wyoming and its weird, and supposedly backward, politics had been a universe removed from his world and the New York mayoral race.

Frank shifted his gaze to Amber. "That caught most of us by surprise. Wasn't on the agenda. But the delegations from Campbell, Carbon, and Sweetwater Counties were on the rules committee. When the motion for secession came from the floor, it had to be brought to a vote."

"What happens when it comes up again? And it will, Frank. You know it."

"I'll vote against it."

"Shit," old Bill said. "They have no idea. Secession? God, what a mess. And to think I'm hearing this in my lifetime."

"Just don't mention it in front of Brandon," Meggan said. "He's rabid at the mouth to carve the Rocky Mountain region out of the United States and form some kind of country running from the Canadian border down to the Gulf of Mexico."

"What if they do vote for it?" Amber asked, tension in her voice.

Frank stared thoughtfully at the dark red wine in his glass. "Say they changed the state constitution, the legislature approved, and we had a referendum. We'd have no national bank, no currency, no treaties with foreign countries, no trade, no passports. Hell, we couldn't even ship beef to Billings. The hotheads just think if you throw out the feds everything still works the same."

"As if that witch in the White House wouldn't drop five divisions of marines on top of us the next day," Pam said bitterly.

Witch in the White House? Sam tried not to gape.

Bill spread his hands wide. "We're off the map. Out where there be dragons. But I tell you this: If this country comes apart, you're really not going to like the consequences."

"Enough of politics," Meggan said firmly. "Want to say the Blessing, Bill?"

Oh, God, here it comes.

Nevertheless, Sam bowed his head respectfully.

Bill took a deep breath. "Good food, good meat. Good God, let's eat."

"Amen," Frank said fervently and reached for the plate brimming with chicken.

That left Sam slightly perplexed. He figured he'd be in for sin, brimstone, and calls for God to smite the heathen government in DC, and bless the NRA.

"What do you hear from Breeze?" Dr. Holly asked.

Sam wondered who Breeze was.

Frank said, "She still talks to Brandon on occasion. He says she's working for an investment firm in south Denver. Rooming with a professor. Haven't seen her in two years. Hell, for all we know, she's married with two kids."

"She's gotta make her way," old Bill said easily.

"I looked over the gear." Frank—clearly uncomfortable about the topic of conversation—changed the subject as he passed the plate to Pam. "I think we can pack it up in one trip. What about the kids? Any of them ride?"

"Not a one," Amber told him. "If any have been on horseback, it was in a riding park or at a pony ride when they were little."

"Put 'em on Shiloh's string," Pam said. "He's a good solid lead. Evan and Brandon can take the pack string, you and I will go first and handle the kids."

Kids?

Sam heard boots scuffing and, sans hat, the wiry cowboy who'd opened the gate on horseback strode in. A little younger than Sam, he had darker eyes than his father's, and his face was a mix of Frank's and Pam's. The resemblance was uncanny.

"Amber, Sam," Bill said, "this is my grandson Brandon. He's sort of the living proof that bad fruit doesn't fall anyplace but under the tree."

"Glad to meet you," Brandon leaned across the table, shaking hands with Amber first, and then Sam. As he did, he looked Sam hard in the eyes, as if taking his measure. So this was what a fiery secessionist looked like? Sam could believe it. Brandon's callused hand had a texture like sandpaper.

Brandon dropped into a chair, saying, "Got a count on the calves. Everybody's there. The grizzly didn't so much as give them a second glance as he skirted the herd. I'd guess him as a five-year-old boar."

"He hanging around?" Bill asked.

"Naw. Tracked his ass over the divide onto the reservation. I got glass on him. He'd found a dead elk, chased the ravens off, and was filling his belly. He ain't gonna be back."

This had to be bullshit. Nobody sane would track a grizzly bear into the wilderness.

But for Amber and himself, Sam could tell that no one found the statement in the slightest remarkable.

"You still seeing that Townsend girl up in Cody?" Evan asked, eyes on Brandon.

The way Brandon grinned in reply, the cute twist it gave to his lips, Sam could tell that drawing women wasn't a problem for him. "She took off for Laramie to go to school and never come back. Heard tell that she's working for a law firm in Cheyenne through some sort of college legal training program."

He took a spoonful of potatoes. "But there's a gal up in Meeteetsee I've seen a time or two. Out from Bakersfield, California. She's training to be a barrel racer up at the nightly rodeo in Cody. Hell, she might make it. She's got that pretty sorrel of hers running in the high seventeens."

"Never know how them barrel racers will turn out," Bill muttered dourly.

People laughed.

Bill made a gesture, stopped chewing long enough to say, "That's a family joke. Frank was riding saddle bronc on the rodeo circuit when he met Pam, who was barrel racing. And the seventeens are the number of seconds it takes for a rider to get her horse around barrels in the arena. The lower the number, the better the score."

Oh. Sam had imagined a girl trying to outrace a barrel. He didn't think barrels were very fast to start with.

"How's Celia?" Dr. Holly asked.

That was Frank and Pam's daughter.

"She's got a year of high school left. Working in town this summer," Pam said between bites. "Like her sister. Hates the ranch, so she's living with friends and working at the Hide Out making buffalo coats and fur hats. They get the occasional celebrity coming through since they make costumes for the movies. If she gets through high school, she wants to go off to California and learn how to be a beautician. She's got it in her head that once she moves to LA, it's all going to happen."

"Might change her mind," Dr. Holly said. "She's young."

Pam gave him a deadly look, and said dryly, "Doc, I was never that young. Even when I *was* that young."

"She's taking after Breeze. The ranch is too dull for her dreams."

Sam tried to figure out how Breeze fit into the family. Older sister?

Frank looked across at Amber, asking, "So, the site. He told you about the cave?"

"Sort of." She glanced at Dr. Holly. "Evan's being a whole lot of mysterious about it."

"Yeah, well, mysterious is a good word," Pam said, eyes hooded. "Gives me the creeps."

"Too much *taipo* in you, Mom." Brandon took a sip of his wine. "You never listen for the spirits."

"*Taipo*," old Bill translated, "that's the Shoshoni word for white person. Used to get a lot of Shoshoni up there. Last fifty years or so the Arapaho have pushed them out. Pretty much claimed the Owl Creeks for their own."

"Don't even see the Arapaho much anymore," Frank said, apparently for Amber's benefit. "Every now and then an Arapaho Ranch fence crew comes by. Other than that they pretty much stay down by Ethete. That big casino they built south of Riverton has changed everything. Hell, half the hands working for the ranch are white guys anymore."

"Thomas Star said he'd be up sometime next week. That he has a grandson, Willy, who'll pack him up from the other side." Dr. Holly reached for seconds on the broccoli.

"Better bring his medicine bag," Pam said. "That cave might send a shiver down his spine."

"What's with this cave?" Amber asked.

Dr. Holly told her, "You can't understand until you experience it."

She was giving him the most intent stare, as if trying to see into his soul.

After a pause, Meggan asked, "Frank? Bill says you dropped that check off at the bank last week. You did, didn't you?"

"Yeah." Frank lifted an eyebrow. "No doubt about it. Hannah gave us extra biscuits for the dogs."

"Gotta remember to call them after the holiday," Meggan told herself.

"Some problem, Meg?" Pam asked.

"Probably just a glitch on Amazon's part," Meggan answered.

THE CATCH

***

Banks are the most leveraged businesses in the world. The irony is that if you ran a business that say, made tires, batteries, or sold electronics that was as highly leveraged, and you wanted a loan, that selfsame bank would laugh you out of the office.

There isn't enough capital in the system, and bank assets aren't always liquid, like cash. Most of their assets are in bonds. They can't unwind them overnight. And if they all tried to sell their bonds, the price of those bonds being dumped on the market would lower their value. This is called "Mark to Market" and in a major downward spiral, is the death knell.

Excerpt from Breeze Tappan's Journal.

CHAPTER SEVEN

✻✻✻

SAM REMEMBERED IT AS A KIND OF FANTASY. HE BARELY SLEPT THAT FIRST NIGHT. SPENT most of it tossing and turning, feeling the hard ground even through the inflatable mattress he had laid out before rolling out his brand-new sleeping bag in his brand-new tent.

Everything smelled of fresh nylon.

Fortunately, Dr. Holly identified the eerie banshee-yodeling yip-pity-yipe sound that echoed down the canyon. Sam was just about to crawl into his tent when the wailing, howling chorus first sounded.

"Holy shit! What's that?"

"Coyotes," Dr. Holly said as he passed on his way to his cabin, a bottle of scotch clutched in one hand. "Bill said three packs are in the area. Don't worry about them. They won't get close to humans."

When Sam did doze off, the unfamiliar sounds of night birds—not to mention the psychotic coyote howls and the rustling of the cottonwood trees—implanted themselves in nightmares filled with Amber Sagan: The woman's eyes were burning an insane color of blue; her abused lips curled in a grimace to expose bloody teeth. She approached out of a smoky haze, step by careful step. A long, crimson-bladed knife was gripped in her right hand.

"I'm your only hope, Sam. Do as I say!"

Which was when he would jerk awake, panting and sweating, heart like a trip-hammer in his chest.

Do as she said?

Or what? She'd hack his balls off?

But then he always did vibrate with anxiety when he was around her.

Even worse, periodically, when she wasn't paying attention to maintaining her mask of flat unconcern, he had seen that scary darkness down inside her. The terrors left behind after her year of captivity in a basement outside of Raqqa. Glimpses of the tormented hell behind her eyes. A sort of madness and humiliated rage.

Sam could well imagine what she might do under the right circumstances. Could picture it even more vividly during those wee hours of the night when the doors that led to secret terrors had been flung wide.

And now his future depended on her? As if his family's disapproval of his choice of education and burgeoning student loan debt wasn't enough? Sometimes he hated graduate school and the stress it put him under.

Grinning humorlessly, he could imagine what a therapist with a copy of the *DSM-5*, the psychiatric manual, would have diagnosed.

He and the rest were rousted out of bed as dawn was turning the broken eastern horizon into a glorious pink. Overhead the sky faded into bruised purple. A few stars were still visible in the indigo west above the high country.

The girls had a bathroom line already formed in the bunkhouse by the time Sam knocked. "Wait your turn," was the sharp reprimand.

Out of habit, he checked his phone for the sixth or seventh time as he settled down for the wait. No signal, of course.

And it sank in: women and the morning bathroom?

The way he figured, it would be more than a half hour wait. Anthropologists will tell you that this is a culturally bound stereotype. Just because it is, doesn't make it untrue.

"There's always the outhouse," Dr. Holly suggested as he passed by from the small rental cabin where he'd been staying. Apparently, he read the uncomfortable postures.

Call it Sam's first gesture toward western independence, but he led the way, followed by Dylan, Jon, and a sleepless and disheveled Court. After tramping through the weeds, he unlatched the door and peered in at a somewhat dusty two-holer.

Truth to tell, Sam discovered there's not much difference between an outhouse and a campground toilet. Like at a county softball field? Same principle. One's wood, the other concrete. This one didn't smell like chemicals.

"Breakfast in fifteen minutes!" Amber announced, her voice mixing with birdsong in the clear and crisp air. "Have your gear packed and dropped off at the barn *before* you eat. No exceptions."

Breakfast consisted of eggs, pancakes, sausage, rolls from a Costco package, and hot coffee.

Court, Ashley, and Danielle were given dishwashing duty while the rest of the students paraded over to the barn.

Pam and Frank were waiting for them. Sam and the rest of the students swapped uneasy glances: Pam and Frank were wearing holstered revolvers. Big ones like in the movies. He had to wonder if it was for effect, part of a "Wild West" costume, a way to communicate authority, or if the Tappans actually thought they might *need* the things.

They certainly hadn't come across as the sort of people who had to have props to lend credence to their expertise. Just as he was considering that it was part of the act, Dr. Holly walked past on his way to the corrals, and Sam did a doubletake. Holly, too, had a pistol on his hip.

Sam cast an uneasy glance up at the looming mountains. What the hell was up there that they were afraid of? Bears and lions? Maybe people? Someone, or ones, who had fled out there, beyond the tame borders of civilized society? Every bad horror movie he'd ever seen on Sci-fi Channel began doing reruns in his imagination.

He was about to ask when Pam led the first horse up, saying, "All right, people, pay attention."

One by one they had first to observe and then to help with the process; each of the students found themselves intimidated in his or her own way. Horses, Sam discovered, were big, with a pungent but not unpleasant smell. And while bridles and saddles aren't particularly complicated, it was hard to assimilate the information the first time you did it for real.

And then came that hesitant anxiety of mounting and swinging into the saddle. Sam's legs were spread in an unfamiliar way. At the same time, he was possessed by the awesome realization that a huge living beast was between his thighs, and it was shifting. He looked over the horse's mane and head, past the swiveling ears. And then the thing moved. Autonomous. Thrilling him to the root of his spine.

As they left the ranch yard, Shyla rode immediately ahead of him on a kind of bruised-red color horse. When Sam wasn't gawking at scenery, she pretty much devoured his attention. Sitting horseback, Sam discovered, did wonderful things to a supple-woman's waist, hips, and legs; and her golden hair caught the sunlight as it swung with each stride the horse took.

A guy who'd grown up working in the back of a Mexican restaurant might not compete with her fabulously rich football-playing boyfriend. Still, a fella could fantasize, couldn't he?

He looked back where Amber rode behind him, her pinched expression adding to the severity of her wedge-shaped face. Several times she met Sam's gaze, and *Bam*, it was like an electric shock that conjured visions of his nightmare.

They headed west up the valley, following the creek past the last fence that marked the beginning of Forest Service administered lands. The trail began as something called a two-track: twin lines of tire tracks through the grass. The road ran parallel to the thick stand of willows that choked the creek bank.

It wasn't so bad on the first switchbacks as the trail climbed up through the trees. The horses were laboring, breathing harder, muscles bunching and saddles lurching as they climbed.

As the novelty wore off, the various aches in hips, knees, and ankles began. Then came the burning in the butt, thighs, and calves. But the incredible views, the animals, wildflowers, the smell of the trees were a constant reminder that he was really doing this. Fucking Awesome!

And then they filed out from the thick conifers into the sunlight on a bare shoulder of the mountain. Smack into another world.

The view was spectacular. Like a whole new perspective on the mountains. Sam could see the stratigraphic layers in the uplifted geology on the slope across the valley.

Then, after another couple of switchbacks through the timber, they emerged onto the open side of a steep slope. No more complaints. They were too terrified. Pam called back that the section of trail they were crossing was called the "slickside".

The trail clung to a nearly vertical incline, a narrow thread incised into the mountainside. On the left, a person could almost reach out from horseback and touch the grassy soil. On the other...? When Sam looked down past his stirrup the wash of terror started in his gut and leached up his spine to paralyze him. Just one slip, and he and his horse were going to tumble down that awful cliff. He'd bounce from rock to rock. Each impact breaking body, bones, and flesh. Even if he lived—if they could find his remains—he was going to be maimed for life.

"Just trust your horse," Pam and Frank kept repeating. "Stay loose," or, "They've done this hundreds of times. Haven't lost anybody yet."

The horses kicked loose rocks free to crash and clatter down the mountain. Sam heard Shyla whisper, "Fuck me," in a tone and manner she'd never have used back home.

Normally, he would have let his imagination run free with the implications; too bad he was so scared he could only buzz on the adrenaline and lipids his heart was pounding through his panicked circulatory system.

It seemed forever to cross that length of trail. Might have been bare minutes.

Then, suddenly, they popped out on a ridge top with a refreshing breeze, spectacular views of the rugged mountains on all sides, and the opportunity for the students to grin, chatter about how scared they'd been.

Every muscle, joint, and bone screamed from that point forward. Thoughts of the Inquisition lodged futilely in Sam's reeling brain. Now it was lower back and shoulders that added to the pantheon of agony. The way the skin on his butt and the inside his thighs felt, someone was grinding them down to raw meat with sandpaper.

Even so, he'd never forget the sight of those incredible mountains as the string of riders topped out on the divide. Ridges and canyons, tree-covered, with chunks of exposed rock, wound away to a wide valley running to the south. And beyond it—a most stunning mountain range, its peaks gray, glacially sculpted into fantastic crags, cirques, and rounded eminences.

"Wind River Range," Frank announced. "Look the other direction. The mountains you see to the north and west are the Absarokas."

Sam followed Holly's pointing finger to the alpine wonder of snow-capped crags that filled the western horizon. Height after height, sheer walls of rock, all gray, twisted, carved, and jagged. That looked like really tough country.

"Any way across that?" Amber asked.

"Sure. There's trails."

"And what's that peak?" Sam asked, pointing at an up-thrust pin-nacle on the divide to the east.

"Washakie Needle," Frank told him. "Named after the Shoshoni chief." He grinned. "The Shoshoni? Well, they had another name for it: Coyote's Penis. Said it dated back to the Beginning Times. That when Coyote and Wolf were haggling over the rules of how the newly created world would work, Coyote managed to lose his penis. Somehow it ended up atop that mountain."

Shyla was giving the peak a serious study, muttering, "Doesn't look like any penis I've ever seen."

"You'd know," Kirstin told her.

"And when did the Sheep Eaters move in?" Sam asked.

Amber said, "Not everyone agrees, but I side with those who think they came in as early as six thousand years ago. In my book, they were definitely here by four thousand. Look around you, people. This was their world, and they developed a culture and subsistence pattern that remained essentially unchanged for at least four thousand years. It only ended when the last of the Sheep Eaters moved onto the Wind River Reservation ninety years ago."

Didn't matter which way a person looked. The whole country was turned on its end, broken, forested, or with open meadows. Then the folded and rumpled earth gave way to the lower foothills and the sere and hazy basins before another mountain range jutted up to block the distance.

The only tangible proof of human activity was in the long lines of contrails that crisscrossed the sky and the distant roar of high-flying jets as they periodically winged their way overhead.

They were passing snowbanks now. White bands that lay in shadowed areas on the northern slopes. A marvel to see at this time of year. So, if there was snow still on the ground in June, what was this country like in January?

Hard to believe that here on the high backbone of the North American continent a group of band-level hunters and gatherers had thrived, essentially unchanged, for at least four thousand years.

Despite the pain in his body, Sam was mentally chewing on that thought when Pam reined her horse off to the side of the ridge, following a trail down into a bowl-shaped valley.

Like a cove scooped out of the mountainside, it was bounded on two sides by stands of scrubby pines, and on the north by thick spruce and fir. The bottom looked marshy, filled with willows, tall grasses, and a spring that fed a small pool of water.

Where the slope fell away beneath the cove, he could see canyons that incised the limestone like knife cuts.

As though cradled in the cove, three white-canvas tents had been erected in a line, backs to the forest. Each of them looked to be the size of a small cabin; two even had stovepipes sticking up through the roofs. Equipment was neatly laid out and tarped. A fire pit out front was smoking. Talk about a cool place to camp.

After winding down the slope, Sam was never so glad as when he swung his trembling leg over the back of the saddle. He almost collapsed onto the ground but saved that indignity for Court. The big guy was trembling, his lip quivering, tears in his eyes.

"Take a moment and catch your breath, people," Amber declared; she bent at the hips, hands braced on her knees. Then she straightened, walking forward as if powered by sheer will. From her expression, Sam couldn't help but believe she'd turned off her aches and pains. That was the thing about Amber.

They all flopped onto the cool grass, moaning, groaning, gasping and sighing.

So this was going to be home? Sam looked around the camp. The fire ring was maybe three meters out in front of what Pam called a wall tent.

Pam and Frank looked unfazed after the ride. They appeared to step off the horses as fresh as when they got on. Immediately, they turned their attention to the horses, untying ropes, unbuckling saddles, removing bridles.

Amber, moving tenderly, stepped forward to help, asking what she could do.

Damn it!

Sam struggled to his feet, feeling unused muscles twitching and wobbling as he minced his way to add his services. Frank showed him where to carry the saddles—to a series of raised poles that he had thought were hitching racks—and how to drape them over the cross piece.

Actually, working helped. Using his muscles and joints, he knew he would at least be able to walk.

Amber and Sam followed instructions as they helped with the horses, then let them loose to graze, being assured that the animals would stay close to old Shiloh, and that he'd come to a whistle.

They were halfway back to where the crew was sprawled flat when Amber stopped, her hard eyes studying Sam thoughtfully. "Thanks for offering to help."

"Well...sure."

She looked skeptically at the other males. "They don't anymore, you know? It's a change in the culture. We're de-masculinizing our men. It's really apparent when you compare Jon, Dylan, and Court to Brandon. You noticed, didn't you?"

"Not sure what you're getting at."

Her blue stare fixed on him again, as if boring down into his soul. "You didn't notice how they could never meet his eyes? How they seem to disappear when he walks into the room? If Brandon is an alpha male, what's Court? Do social rankings go down that far?"

"That's a bit callous, don't you think? The guy's a computer geek." Made Sam wonder what Amber thought of him. "What triggered this line of thought?"

She smiled thinly, as if at a shadowy memory. "It's about survival, Sam. Doing what you have to. I was thinking of the doctors I worked with in Syria. Then the SEALS, Rangers, combat vets. The people who got me out of that fucking hole. That toughness of character and soul. Of being..." she seemed to go distant "...reliable."

"And you think modern men aren't?"

She snapped back to the present. "Males used to be the expendable ones. The experimental half of the species. Now we're making them into decorations, spoiling them and turning them into pampered breeders."

"Pampered...what?"

"Got to you, didn't I? The computer age allows us to redefine masculine roles. Males still dominate business and politics. And the military. For a time."

"Okay, now I'm lost."

Her introspective gaze reminded him of an anatomist dissecting her latest specimen. "Males only make up a third of the enrolment in higher education. In the end, education and intelligence will determine who controls the power. It's a matter of time."

She pointed at where the guys lay in the grass. "I rest my case."

Ashley had been one of the first back on her feet. She'd been followed by the rest of the girls. Sam wouldn't have thought a thing of it, but Ashley was carrying cans of soda to Jon, Court, and Dylan where they reclined in apparent luxury.

"That doesn't mean—"

"Just something for you to think about," a beat, "anthropologist."

She uncharacteristically slapped him on the shoulder as she marched past and headed for the cook tent. As he followed, he heard her call, "All right! Who's willing to volunteer? Pam needs a hand getting supper set up."

Ashley, Danielle, and Shyla lifted their hands. Shanteel and Kirstin were still looking around with owl eyes, but after a moment's hesitation, both marched stiffly toward the tent.

Jon, Court, and Dylan remained in the grass. Court looked broken. Dylan was fiddling with his phone. Jon had pulled off his coat, wadded it up, and was using it for a pillow. Even as Sam approached, the guy rolled over to go to sleep.

Enough!

He stomped up, irritated to the point he'd forgotten his aches. If he'd learned anything in The Yucateca, it was that a person didn't quit until the job was finished.

"Come on, guys. Let's go ask Frank what he needs us to do."

"He's getting paid," Jon muttered, yawning, not even bothering to open his eyes.

"Yeah, and I'm—"

"This is weird," Dylan interrupted.

"You've got cell service?" Sam fought the urge to reach for his iPhone.

"Yeah. One bar. I got the news. Shock and awe. Internet's burning. Surreal, man." And then he said the words that would be burned into Sam's brain: "Banks aren't going to reopen."

Jon opened his eyes, sitting up. "What do you mean?"

"They're still closed."

"Like, yeah. It's Saturday, Dude."

"Chaos in the streets. The credit cards still aren't working. People are flipping, dude."

Sam—still stung by Amber's assessment—said, "Yeah, well, they'll figure it out. Now get your asses up. We're going to go help Frank."

"Do what?" Jon asked truculently.

"Whatever he says. Now move."

"Who made you boss?"

"Amber."

All it took was the mention of Amber's name, and the three of them struggled, moaning and whimpering, to their feet.

Pampered males?

Not on Sam's watch.

CHAIN REACTION

* * *

Whoever initiated the cyberattack probably did it to cripple the American economy. The sort of attack meant to weaken us enough that we wouldn't be able to react to some action they wanted to take in the Middle East, the South China Sea, or Eastern Europe. Maybe it was a way to strengthen their hand in a trade dispute. Maybe it was a bunch of teenage hackers in a basement in Cleveland.

The moment the Fed put a "Freeze" on the system. When credit cards were suddenly declined across the board, it began to cascade.

The "American Standard" sets the tone in global banking. Within twenty-four hours, the South American banks, which depend on American banks, failed. Banco Santander de Brazil would have gone down first, followed by Banco Santander de Chile. Globally, the bond market would have deflated. By no later than Monday, the European banks would have been frozen in an attempt to stop the inevitable collapse.

No matter how heroic the efforts, the big Asian banks would have followed. End game.

And that's assuming the malware that corrupted the accounts remained contained to North America. If it didn't? If it rode on the coattails of money transfers? Then entire world banking system would have been frozen within twenty-four hours.

Excerpt from Breeze Tappan's Journal.

CHAPTER EIGHT

***

THE PACK STRING CAME IN ABOUT AN HOUR LATER WITH BRANDON AND DR. HOLLY RIDING out in front. Sam was working on the wood crew as they "bucked up" lengths of fallen trees that Frank, and his horse Joker, snaked out of the timber with a lasso.

Call it a world of awesome. Like something come alive out of a history book. Frank would have one of the guys put the loop of his rope around the fallen timber—usually a lodgepole pine—then he would "take a dally", which meant wind his rope around the saddle horn. He'd put spurs to Joker, and sawing back and forth, horse and rider would skid the log out and drag it to be cut up.

None of them were allowed to use the chainsaw—that was Frank's baby. Said he didn't want to pack any of them out after they'd cut their legs off. Something about taking too much effort to get the blood out of the saddle blankets.

Western humor took some getting used to.

As soon as Frank bucked lengths, Sam and his crew carried them over to the firewood stack. Sam sort of figured Amber would start the fire with a fire-bow and a chokecherry-stick dowel. Instead she sloshed Coleman fuel on the wood...and tossed a lit match into the middle of it. Whoosh!

Ah, the shattered illusions.

Sam got a whole different perspective on Dr. Holly that day. Not only did the man ride like a cowboy, turned out he loved horse packing. Born in Massachusetts, Holly had come west as a hippie; he'd worked as an outfitter and guide when he was young, which is how he'd come to admire the Sheep Eaters in the first place. He'd stumbled across their camps, marveled at the country that had been their home.

When the last of the packs had been stowed, and the mules had rolled and gone off to drink below the spring, Frank showed them where to set up their tents. Again, it turned out to be a group activity—one barely finished before dinner was ready.

Chili with chunks of meat along with mashed potatoes, gravy, and something called "scratch" biscuits cooked in the fire in a Dutch oven, were served up on paper plates.

Evening was settling over the high country, casting long purple shadows down over the valleys, the temperature dropping.

The breeze began to tease, blowing smoke from the fire this way and that. Kirstin was horrified that she was getting ash in her hair.

Danielle somehow managed to figure out the balancing act required to keep her plate on her knee, eat with one hand, and scroll her thumb over her phone screen with the other.

"Jesus," she whispered. "What happened?"

"Happened where?" Jon asked, popping a can of beer as he balanced his plate and seated himself on a log.

Danielle squinted at her screen. "The headline is 'Meltdown.' It's all spelled in capital letters with lots of exclamation points."

"Stop reading the headlines," Shanteel muttered, digging her own phone from a back pocket. "Shit. Battery's dead."

By now everyone was fishing for his or her phones. Depending upon the carrier, some worked better than others on the one bar of power that faded in and out. Half the time the signal just vanished.

Dylan read from his phone: "A shaken Tony Morris, CEO of BankUltra, the nation's number-two financial institution, is appealing for calm and assuring BU's account holders that BU is leaving no stone unturned to reestablish service by the time the banks open on Tuesday.

"Meanwhile, Timothy Crabner, a leading authority on the banking industry, insists that such a universal collapse of the system should be impossible. In a statement, Mr. Crabner insisted, 'This isn't just a simple malware. While a single institution might have had problems, for credit card use to be declined across the country at precisely twelve fifty-nine EST can only be a calculated attack on the American banking system by outside interests. Ladies, and gentlemen, this is a cyberattack more insidious and damaging than Pearl Harbor.'"

"Bullshit." Dr. Holly stood outside the ring of seats. "They have to have backup systems. Banks have the best cyber security on the planet."

Everyone was tapping on their phones, then lifting them to their ears. Trying to call home, Sam guessed. From the expressions, and the way they lowered the devices, he could tell no one was getting through. Towers must have been jammed solid.

Amber muttered, "Whoever did this? They're playing with fire. People are pissed off as it is. What are they after? Blood in the streets?"

"I'm with Evan. Pretty tough to believe," Frank added where he stood back from the fire. "Everyone's credit card? The whole country? That would take a... What?"

"A really super-sophisticated malware could do it," Court said where he huddled over his plate. "Something so deeply coded it would look benign. Sort of like they did in *Hard Flash*."

"What's *Hard Flash*?" Shyla asked, waving away the smoke that drifted her way.

"One of the games on MP7," Court told her. "The Chinese crash the banking system using a malware that triggers its own replication. It implements a delete program, one that runs in nanoseconds. Before anyone can realize what's happening, everyone's financial records are gone. In the game you have to fight your way out of the city before you get killed by gangs."

"Can they do that? Crash the system?" Amber asked softly. "Seriously, Court?"

He shrugged, still not looking up. "Banks are all tied together, wiring billions of dollars back and forth millions of times a minute. It'd take a huge amount of computation. Something real fast. I mean, you could do it with a quantum qubit computer and the right program. Tricky though, you'd have to have the malware already in the system. Hidden deep. And it would have to be everywhere." Court paused. "Banks have identifying codes. To be able to hit one bank and not another? Got to be a qubit computer."

"What's a qubit computer?" Dr. Holly asked.

Court finally looked up. "To understand you've got to be familiar with quantum mechanics, but essentially a regular computer runs on I and O. Current on or off. Binary, right? A quantum computer runs at the atomic level. Charge positive or negative and spin up or down. Quaternary. Four choices, which increases computation by a power of four."

Frank was staring thoughtfully at the fire. "So, even if someone built one of these things, and the virus, or whatever, was out there, sure, we're going to be inconvenienced while they chase down the bug. But it's just a matter of fixing it, right? Writing some new security code?"

Court shrugged. "Depends on how they engineered it, I guess."

"Wow. I finally got service," Ashley said as she studied her screen. "The president has issued a state of national emergency. Says it was a cyberattack. Asks that people don't panic, and that they remain calm. That people should stay home and..."

She shook her phone as if that would fix the problem. "Lost it."

"I lost mine, too," Dylan muttered, raising his phone high and swiveling it about in an attempt to get just the right angle for reception.

Sam had fished out his own iPhone, powered it up. After tapping in his security code, he caught himself doing the same, offering it this way and that to the gods of reception. Getting nothing.

Amber had been frowning at the fire, eating slowly, her wedge of a face grim. "Good thing we got here when we did. Imagine being out on I-80, half a continent away from home."

She looked around. "No credit cards? Pooled together, we'd probably have enough cash to get part way home. But what happens when the cash runs out?"

"You'd have to get to a bank," Frank said. "Have funds wired to wherever you were stranded."

"Yeah," Pam agreed. "You and a million other people who are just as desperate. Think the banks have enough staff on hand to handle that?"

"Uh," Jon reminded, "FDIC ordered the banks closed, people."

Amber shook her head. "This is going to cost the economy trillions. And even after all this time, we've barely recovered from COVID as it is."

"Whoever did this is gonna get their asses kicked," Brandon announced darkly. He'd dropped to a crouch, plate on his knees, the spurs on his booted heels almost touching his rear. "God help 'em if it's the Chinese. Beijing will glow in the dark."

At that point, the coyotes chimed in, their warbling howls sounding lonely as they faded into the distance.

Sam could see Shanteel's expression harden. She clearly had no use for Brandon, as if the dislike were instinctual.

"Hope Dad's okay," Kirstin said after finally giving up on her phone. She'd been trying to send a text. "He's in Zurich."

"Their banks are still functioning," Amber said. "Or they were, last we heard."

"What if his credit card is no good at the hotel? What if none of the restaurants take his card?"

"Why's he there?" Dr. Holly asked.

"Business. Something for the Commerce Department."

"Government?" Frank asked. "They take care of their own."

"It's the ordinary people who get screwed," Brandon agreed, missing the flare of anger that reddened Kirstin's face.

Sam tried to tamp down the building tension. "And we thought we'd be the ones with stories to tell? People will be talking about this for years. 'Remember the time the credit cards were suddenly no good? Why, Uncle Albert and me, we had to trade a box of donuts for a package of kosher wieners.'"

"That a joke?" Danielle asked. "Just 'cause I don't keep the diet doesn't mean I don't take it personally."

"I was *referring* to the relative values of foods by invoking cynical irony," Sam growled back.

"What if I made a joke about Puerto Ricans? How they can't balance a check book, let alone a budget?" Her dark eyes were fixed on Sam's.

"Joke away. The Delgados were Mexicans a couple of generations past."

"That will be enough," Amber warned. "Just because the rest of the country is turning on itself doesn't mean we have to."

"Yeah." Sam nodded. "Sorry, Danielle."

"Shalom," she said with a faint smile. "Means peace, you know?"

He extended a fist, and she gave it a gentle bump with her own.

The Tappans had watched them with expressionless faces, but Sam knew they were taking it all in. The divisions, the way they all dealt with each other.

Everyone was thinking about what was happening back at home. About how their families and friends were doing, about the trouble this whole credit card thing was causing. Just another monkey wrench thrown into a world that was already growing more dysfunctional by the day.

People were realizing that not even their personal finances could be counted on.

"I say we consider it a day, people." Amber tossed her paper plate into the fire. Easiest way Sam had ever seen to "do the dishes". If they'd served meals on paper plates in The Yucateca, he could have had a normal childhood.

Amber stood. "Jon, Shyla, Ashley, you have breakfast detail. Wake up call for you will be at five-thirty. The rest of you can sleep until six."

"Okay, let's move, people," Sam said, sending his plate after Amber's.

He hung around, keeping an eye on things as everyone trickled away toward the tents in twos and threes, talking about the credit card thing and what it meant. In the distance, the coyote pack added to the sense of drama as they broke out in song. From off to the east, another pack answered.

Sam figured he and the crew were becoming old "mountain" hands, now. No one even remarked on the coyotes anymore.

The last to leave the fire were Shanteel and Brandon, who seemed to be in some sort of weird staring match, each with a hard expression, distaste in the sets of their mouths.

"Come on," Sam told Shanteel. "Morning comes early."

She gave him a dismissive nod and walked off.

Sam swallowed hard, glancing back at Brandon. A smoldering look lay behind the young man's eyes.

WHAT'S A DOLLAR?

***

Assuming you still have one, pull out a dollar bill. What is it, exactly? A stiff piece of paper that's probably been crumpled. Green ink on one side. Black on the other. Intricate artwork depicting a dead president, a seal, the all-seeing eye atop the Masonic pyramid. Good for all debts public and private. "In God We Trust."

In the survey course, Introduction to Economics 101, we learn that money is a store of value, a unit of account, and a medium of exchange. But, hey, it's all abstract, right?

A unit of account? Why a dollar? Or Yen? Or Pound Sterling? Or Euro?

A medium of exchange? Why give someone paper dollar for a fried chicken leg when a .22 cartridge would be much more equitable?

A store of value? Look at your dollar and tell me what value that paper and ink has.

When it comes right down to it, money is faith. Trust that your fellows will share the value you place in it.

No wonder it was so easy to destroy.

Excerpt from Breeze Tappan's Journal.

CHAPTER NINE

***

THE FOLLOWING MORNING DAWNED WITH NO IMPROVEMENT IN THE CELL SERVICE. NO CALLS possible in or out. Nothing. Not even an update to anyone's news apps. Batteries were running low or flat dead.

First thing, Amber set up one of the solar panels and plugged it into her laptop. With that power source and a USB, the phones could at least be charged. Everyone crowded around.

"I'll change the phones out," Pam promised as the last of the breakfast pots and pans had been washed and set out on a drain board to dry.

Sam wasn't sure that many of the students trusted her with their prized mobile devices. Which didn't make any sense. What was Pam going to do? Steal them? Run off and hock them to the nearest grizzly bear?

Amber and he had been working since dawn, unpacking the pin flags, the survey station and datum stakes, the notebooks and GPS equipment. Sam made sure the camera was charged, and both of the lenses worked.

Frank and Brandon had left just after sunrise, driving the herd of mules and most of the horses back down the trail. The three horses, including Pam's mare, that were tied at the picket rope made a terrible racket whinnying and stomping as they swished their tails.

"Frank's horses aren't tied together," Sam noted. "Won't some of them get lost?"

Dr. Holly lifted an amused eyebrow. "Kid, those critters know exactly where they are going. They'll be back at the ranch in a couple of hours at most, each and every one of them expecting a bait of grain for a reward. Always trust a horse to get home."

When the last of the water bottles had been passed out, Dr. Holly led the way, climbing up out of the camp hollow on a game trail that skirted the outside of the grove of raggedy-looking pine trees.

The site wasn't far, maybe a quarter mile and a couple hundred feet higher than camp. But dang! Suddenly they were wishing for the horses. It was the altitude of course. They just weren't used to eight thousand feet. Took the crew almost half an hour to climb up to the grassy shoulder of the mountain.

When they made it, everyone, even Dr. Holly, dropped to pant amidst the fresh grass.

"Wow," Shyla whispered. "What a view."

The whole of the Bighorn Basin spread before them as if they were lords of the world. The mountains stretched out on the right and left, most of the Wind River Basin visible to the southeast.

The distant Big Horn Mountains gleamed with patches of last winter's snow. The basin in between was a greenish sere, slightly hazy, and rippled here and there by ridges and hills.

"What's this stuff?" Shanteel asked, picking up a little dark-brown pebble. "There's a lot of it scattered around here."

"That's elk scat," Dr. Holly told her.

"Scat?" she asked, holding it close to peer at it.

"Elk shit," Amber told her bluntly.

Didn't take Shanteel more than a nanosecond to be rid of her little prize. And then to scoot off the scatter she'd been sitting on. "I got to go back to camp and wash my hands." She was looking ruefully back down the trail they had just climbed, her hand held out as far from her body as she could.

Dr. Holly told her, "Wipe it on your pants. It won't kill you."

To the rest he added, "This is all elk range up here. But more to the point, it used to be prime habitat for Rocky Mountain bighorn sheep. That grove of pines just below us and on the ridge to the west? Those are whitebark pine. *Pinus albicaulis.* Whitebark pine nuts are a master food. Five hundred-and-fifty calories per hundred grams, and they're a third carbohydrate, a third fat, and twenty percent protein."

Holly gestured around. "This meadow, well, we're a bit early yet, but you can see the wildflowers coming up. Most of them are edible. The reason the site is located here? We're in the middle of a wild supermarket. Elk, sheep, whitebark pine nuts, mule deer, bison, and tens of harvestable plants.

"Look to the north and south and you'll see that this saddle is a low spot, a pass in the mountains. From here people could access either the Bighorn or Wind River Basins. That, or follow the trails west into the Yellowstone caldera."

Amber added, "And that's the secret of why they built a village up here. Within a five-day walk in any direction they would have had access to every kind of environment from rivers full of fish, sage uplands and antelope, valleys with harvestable grasses, juniper and limber pine slopes on the ridges and foothills, then the Montane environment, and finally these subalpine heights."

Sam nodded as it all began to fall into place.

The rest of the day was spent establishing the datum—or reference point—for the Penthouse site. Every measurement they took would be referenced back to datum giving Amber a precise placement for every artifact and feature.

Once the datum stake with its inscribed site number was driven in, survey transects were plotted and the students began the slow job of walking along and sticking an orange pin flag into the ground at every artifact. Features which consisted of fire pits or scatters of fire-cracked-rock were marked with a blue flag; the depressions that Dr. Holly told them were house floors they flagged in pink. Stone alignments like circles and cairns got a yellow flag.

By the time Pam came riding up on her mare at noon with a pack full of sandwiches, sodas, and water, the crew had used up most of their flags and had covered a fraction of the site.

Shanteel had gotten so into flagging artifacts, she'd forgotten that she'd handled elk shit that morning. Sam considered reminding her while she was eating her sandwich. Instead, he bit his tongue and demonstrated remarkable self-control.

That afternoon they had barely begun to map when clouds rolled in from the west, blackening and filling the sky. At the first rumbling of thunder, Dr. Holly ordered, "That's it, people. Pack your gear. Off the high ridge now!"

With lightning flashing in the clouds, the occasional bolt was no more than ten seconds ahead of its cracking boom by the time they had made the camp. As they did, the first drops fell. Then came the deluge as they all packed into the community tent.

In the middle of the downpour came riders. With the thunder peeling and the rain slashing down, Frank led the way across the bowl, head down, rain running in a stream from the brim of his hat; it cascaded down his slicker in gleaming sheets.

Next in line came old Bill, and then Brandon. People might joke about cowboy hats, but when it came to a heavy rain, Sam was suddenly possessed of an understanding of why he'd want one.

The riders splashed up, each stepping down from the saddle, little waterfalls sluicing from their hats, breath fogging in the suddenly cold air.

Dr. Holly had shrugged on his coat and jammed his hat on before striding out to help with the tack.

Sam made a face—grimaced against the perversity of the gods—and forced himself out into the icy rain. Icy might be a bit of exaggeration since it wasn't freezing. He wondered if it was an understatement to just call it damn cold?

The horses flinched at a particularly loud crack of lightning and instant thunder. One of those earth-shattering bangs. Sounded to Sam like the sky had been blasted just over his head.

Brandon was blowing on his fingers after fumbling at his cinch.

"I got it," Sam told him, working the latigo loose where it was snug against the cinch ring. Latigo? Cinch ring? Who's a city kid?

"Thanks," Brandon said, and jerked his head towards Bill who was struggling to unbuckle his horse's breast collar. "Could you see to Grandad?"

"What's he doing up here?"

"Shit's hit the fan. He'll tell it his way."

Sam slogged back to where Bill was half leaned against his horse. Under his hat he looked pale and cold. Sam asked, "You all right?"

Bill gave him a thin smile. "Just need a minute to catch my puff. Whew. Ain't as spry as I used to be. Damned old leg is stove up."

Another world-ending lightning bolt flashed, and half-deafened Sam a second later with the bang. Startled him as badly as it did the horses.

"I'll get the saddle," Sam told him. "Go. Get out of this stuff and get dry."

Bill gave him a look up and down, watching Sam squint as raindrops battered on his bare head and water ran down through his hair. "Delgado, right?"

"Yes, sir."

"Buy you a drink later. Watch out for old Tobe, here. Stay close to that back leg so he can't cock his guns before he kicks you. And watch yer back when you pull the bridle off. Not knowing you for a stranger, he might take a bite out of you just to see if he can get away with it."

Horses bite? Damn!

Sam swallowed hard, shivering as cold water ran down his neck and into his shirt.

He did keep an eye on old Tobe and followed Bill's directions to the letter. He must have done well. Tobe neither bit nor kicked him, and he got Bill's tack over the tack pole and covered with a tarp called a "manty" to keep what little of it was still dry from the rain.

Brandon had led the horses over to the picket rope by the time Sam shivered his way back to the crowded communal tent. Bill stood just inside the door, hands extended to the heat stove, where a crackling fire was burning.

Sam stood by the door, arms crossed for warmth, when Bill looked his way, and said, "Hell, man. Step over here and get warm. You'll catch your death."

Dr. Holly was the next one in. Sam shoved Dylan out of the way to give Holly room. Odd that the males were the ones closest to the stove. All the girls were in the back, seated on logs, hunched over against the cold, tapping at their phones in silence.

"They getting anything?" Sam asked Court who'd gotten crowded back against the tent wall.

"No. There's no signal."

"And there ain't gonna be," Bill said before exhaling a chilled breath.

"What's happened, Bill?" Dr. Holly rubbed his hands as Amber stepped up beside them to hear.

Tappan shot them all a hard glance, his eyes oddly pained. "Television signal went preempted this morning about nine. Just text repeating that it was a national emergency and a list of rules." He paused. "Big thing is that they're admitting now that it's a full-blown cyberattack on the banks. People started to panic. Mobs of them crowding around the banks. Martial law's been declared. There's a national curfew. All travel is restricted."

"Restricted how?" Amber asked.

"Got to have a permit to go more than fifty miles. Supposedly the army's setting up checkpoints. Anyone violating the rules will be arrested. Looters, profiteers, and anyone jacking prices sky-high will be shot."

"Come on," Dr. Holly said uneasily. "Shot?"

Bill gave him an icy look, water dripping from his hat as if in emphasis. "Maybe."

Amber asked, "All this over credit cards? Martial law? Military check points? It doesn't make sense."

Bill took a deep breath. In the shadow of his soaked hat, Sam could see the lines deepening in his face. "Banks are gone."

Everyone in the tent had gone silent. They were all watching Bill as he turned, water dripping from his hat to spatter and hiss on the hot stove. "The credit cards? Apparently, that was just the beginning. That computer bug? I'm anything but a tech guy, but whatever it was, they couldn't stop it."

"NFW," Dylan protested loudly, staring uncertainly from one to another.

"Maybe," Bill said, raising his shoulders in a shrug. "I can only tell you what was reported on the news. But if what they say is true, a person can't do business unless they have cash. And there's a hint that something's wrong with the account records. Something about them being corrupted."

"They should be backed up in the cloud," Court said, his full lips purple from the cold.

"All I can tell you is what they were saying on the news before the regular programming went away. Maybe it's not as bad as they're making it sound. Hell, wouldn't be the first time the talking heads got it all wrong just to make a story and prop up their ratings."

"Which, if you think about it," Dr. Holly said, "makes the most sense of all. Hey, we made it through COVID, we can make it through this."

"Yeah, but for the president. I watched her address last night." Bill's expression thinned. "She was scared. Right down to her bones. Barely made it through that five minutes of 'stay calm' shit, and 'everything is under control'. You ask me, as soon as that camera clicked off, that woman broke down and cried."

"That's just an opinion, Bill."

The old man turned, fixing his odd hazel-and-brown eyes on Dr. Holly. "Maybe. We're cut off. No TV, no cell service. Hell, even the damn landline is silent. No dial tone. Figgered I'd better ride up here and let you folks know."

"We coulda done that, Dad," Frank added where he'd come to drip water in the tent's doorway. "No sense in you risking your neck like this."

"Slickside was a bit interesting, wasn't it?" Bill asked with a glint in his eye.

"Think we ought to go back?" Sam asked Amber.

She had a grim set to her lips. "And do what? Travel restrictions? Permits? Government checkpoints? The credit cards don't work? Fuck that. The smart thing is to stay right where we are."

She looked around, meeting everyone's eyes. "Think it through, people. We don't have the money to get home, even if we could get the permit. Go back to town? The motels would want to be paid. So would the restaurants and grocery stores."

Waving toward the cook and supply tents, she added, "Our food here is paid for. We sent the Tappans an advance, so we have a little credit with them."

Old Bill made a disgusted sound. "We *ain't* throwing nobody out at time like this. What do you think we are?"

Amber's hard gaze barely cracked. "The department is responsible for all of you. *I am responsible.* It's going to take time for the government to fix things, to reestablish order, shore up the banks, and reestablish credit. Let's be smart, people."

She smiled, actually looking amused. "What cooler place is there to ride out a crisis than up here? Mapping a site. Without having to worry about soldiers and roadblocks and whether we could afford food or find shelter."

People were sharing uneasy glances.

Amber continued, "You all know I've been there, seen what happens when things fall apart. When people are scared, they do crazy things. Looting for sure. Random violence. Setting fires. Maybe riots that will make what took place in Denver look like child's play. We stay here."

"Now there," old Bill said respectfully, "is the smartest lady on the planet."

Remembering his earlier promise, Sam said, "I'm with Amber. We stay here."

She turned a hollow and desperate look his way, as if to ask, *Do you really get how screwed we are?*

Another bolt of lightning blasted the ridge above. It just added to the fear in people's eyes.

FIAT MONEY

***

I've written about the easy definitions of money. Back in the early economies—up to the twentieth century—money was backed by physical wealth. A dollar could be traded to the Federal Reserve for a specific weight of gold.

But the economists weren't finished. They began to abstract money. Called it a unit of debt. Then it became a "contract" for goods or services. Another theory claimed that money was "chartal", that it functions as an expression of governmental power to ensure taxes can be collected. Even more abstract, some consider money to be nothing more than a tool for the creation of credit.

All of these became what is known as "fiat" money. Money that has no value except that declared by the government.

Guess what happened when the people in the streets no longer believed in the government?

Excerpt from Breeze Tappan's *Journal.*

CHAPTER TEN

***

THE NEXT MORNING DAWNED BRIGHT AND CLEAR, DEW DROPLETS SPARKLING ON THE GRASS like a billion diamonds. Birdsong filled the timber behind the field camp, and a meadowlark's musical trill carried across the bowl.

As Sam climbed out of his tent—shivering in the damp air—he could smell bacon as the breeze drifted his way from the cook tent. Waking up in the wilderness, he decided, was different than anywhere else: A person still smelled like last night's campfire. There's no sink where you splash water into your face, or hot shower to step into. He was wearing yesterday's clothes. Didn't have a mirror waiting to shock him by showing just how he really looked.

But then, neither did anyone else.

And, for the most part, no one cared.

After he had wandered down into the trees to attend to nature, he made his way to the equipment tent. There he found Amber at the portable table, a cup of steaming coffee at hand as she scanned through yesterday's field notes.

"I think I'm seeing individual domestic units reflected in the distribution of features, depressions, and lithics," she began. "If it carries through the rest of the site, and if the statistics indicate that it's non-random, and if we can get enough C14 dates to indicate long-term reoccupation of the site, wouldn't that be fantastic?"

"You mean that over generations they were using the same exact spots for houses, cooking, processing, and trash disposal. Not just randomly setting up structures every time they came back."

"If we can prove that," she mused, "it would suggest one of two hypotheses: either each family had a long-established place within the site, a sort of 'This is the traditional spot for our wickiup. The same one grandpa and grandpa's grandpa used; as will you, little squirt, when you finally grow up and become a grandpa.'"

She took a sip of coffee. "Or hypothesis two: Like us, they recognized the depressions as old dwelling locations, and for whatever cultural reason, built their shelters there, sort of like designated camping spots in a National Park campground."

Sam stared down at the point-plot map the crew had put together the day before. "Either way, it's a reflection of behavioral process. Kind of cool, actually."

She shifted, giving him a thoughtful sidelong inspection. "You don't sound enthusiastic."

"I talked to people last night. They're pretty worried about what's happening back home."

"Okay, lay it on me."

"It's like, well, they know that staying here is the smart thing, that they probably can't get home anyway, but there's this sort of guilt. Like, they're up here, without a care in the world, while their families and friends are dealing with all this shit back home."

"It's being helpless." Amber's voice took on that eerie tone. "That somehow it's your fault. You start thinking through all the moves that brought you to this place. And you start working backwards, telling yourself, 'If only I hadn't chosen medicine in the first place.' Or 'Why did I think I could make a difference?' 'What fucking possessed me to *volunteer* to help?' 'I didn't *have* to go to Syria.' 'Why didn't I *leave* when Renee asked if I wanted...'"

She looked up, blinked, as if coming back to her senses. And in an instant—like the crashing down of steel shutters—she turned angry eyes on his, snapping, "Tell them to deal, all right?"

"Hey, don't bite my ass off. You asked."

For a scary second, he could see how close to the edge she was. Brittle as thin glass. Panic, fear, some violent need to lash out, and then she swallowed hard, closed her eyes, and took a deep breath.

"Sorry," she whispered. "Just tired. Didn't sleep last night. What Bill told us...sort of set me off."

"It's okay. We're cool. I just wanted—"

"Get out. I need time to think." The anger was back, instantaneous and seething. A weird insanity gleamed behind the blue in her eyes.

Sam backed out, hands raised in surrender, and once out of sight of the door, shook his head. God, sometimes Amber was like a lit stick of dynamite. You could see the sparks, but not how short the fuse was.

Sam got his breakfast where Pam was dishing it out; then he poured a cup of coffee, watching it steam as he walked out to the fire pit. Two pieces of wood lay on the white mound of ash and were being consumed by lazy licking flames.

He seated himself next to Shanteel, who was eating slowly, her eyes fixed on the distant east beyond the mountains.

"Worried about home?"

She nodded, expression pinching. "I signed up for this class 'cause I didn't want to be home this summer. Didn't want to have to take care of my little sister, you know? Told Aunt Vee, 'I'm gonna take anthropology. Find out about those Cherokee Seminole ancestors of ours.'"

"Wrong part of the country for either Seminoles or Cherokee." He sipped his coffee. Almost burned his mouth.

"How was I supposed to know? Not that it mattered." Her eyes thinned. "I just didn't want the struggle. That little sister of mine? She's burning up on the inside with rage. Gonna get herself killed. I didn't understand at the time. But Aunt Vee did."

After she hesitated for a time, Sam asked, "Understand what?"

"She knew. Said, 'I understand what you mean about the Cherokee Seminoles.' Odd tone in her voice. Now I wonder if she wasn't saying, 'You save yourself, Shanteel. Ain't no one else you *can* save but yourself.'"

Shanteel shook her head. "If the president declared martial law, things are bad. That rage we all got? When the credit cards stopped working? When the stores said, 'We only take cash?' People who can't feed their kids? People who think they're not getting a fair deal? Not good, Sam. Not good at all."

Sad irony tainted her laughter. "Never thought I'd hear myself say this, but I hope the mayor moved in the army first thing and locked the neighborhood down tight." She paused. "Because the thing about rage is that before you destroy anyone else, you always got to destroy yourself and the people around you."

"I suppose."

"Doesn't make sense, does it?"

"Sort of Shakespearian, huh?"

A faint smile bent her lips. "Always a dead white guy to put you in your place."

He thought back to what Amber had admitted before she blew up. "We're all going to be feeling guilty, Shanteel. Second guessing if coming here was the right thing. You, me, everyone on this crew. It's the not knowing. That's what's going to make it worse. Wondering if we were back home, what difference we could be making."

"Help if we could call. Most have tried. No signal. Nothing. That's going to jack up the anxiety."

Sam couldn't help it. He had to pull his own phone from his shirt pocket. Nothing. *Mom? Dad?*

Why hadn't he tried to call?

"Sometimes things just are," Shanteel said cryptically as she forked up another mouthful of scrambled eggs. "I gotta remind myself of that. After Mama... Well, I was told that by an attorney, and then by a social worker." She nodded her head. "Sometimes things just are."

He looked off to the east, wondering about his own family. Hell, if he were there, he would have just added more fuel to an already flammable relationship.

Someday, Dad, I need to say that I'm sorry.

THE SHOCK

***

I was having lunch that Friday with a couple of people I worked with. I watched the consternation begin. The whole restaurant turned chaotic as more and more people tried to settle their bills. Everybody pays with a credit card, right?

The staff did their best as people pooled their cash. When that didn't work, the manager agreed to take checks, but how many people carry check books these days? In the end, he took business cards, personal information, and accepted what were essentially IOUs just to get people out the door.

And that was just the beginning.

You don't realize how dependent you are on money until it's gone.

Excerpt from Breeze Tappan's *Journal.*

CHAPTER ELEVEN

***

BILL TAPPAN LEFT AFTER BREAKFAST, RIDING OLD TOBE BACK DOWN THE MOUNTAIN UNDER Brandon's watchful eye. He said he'd be back when there was more news. He also said he had an old wind-up emergency radio somewhere, and if he could find it, he'd send it back up the mountain with Brandon next time the young man returned.

For the next three days, Sam and the students worked on the site. Dr. Holly said he wanted to get the crew lined out on survey, identifying artifacts and features, and up to speed on plotting and recording.

Periodically Holly would drop a teaser for Amber about this cave that was going to blow their minds. Sam was starting to think it was a joke of some kind. He wasn't sure that Amber ever began to share his suspicion; instead, she'd just arch an eyebrow, expression blank, as if a wall had been built between her mind and her face.

And no matter what the time of day, they all kept looking off to the east. Wondering what was happening back home. Talk was of family, friends, even a preoccupation about places, like Virgo's Pizza, the dive just across University Avenue from campus.

There were few smiles as they lined out for the cook tent each morning to pick up plates filled with eggs and sausage—all of which were kept in an elevated cooler about a quarter mile back in the trees. A rope and pulley raised and lowered the cache from a high branch about fifteen feet up. That was supposedly beyond the reach of mister grizzly.

No one went back to the cache unless accompanied by one of the Tappans, who carried a gun and bear spray. Given Sam's urban perspectives, the guns made him queasy. He fully understood that, yes, there were big apex predators in the area. Academically he could synthesize the concept that under the right circumstances, grizzly bears and the occasional cougar considered him a snack. Modern Americans don't grow up with the idea that something with teeth and claws might *eat* them. Outside of monster movies, it just wasn't in a Hempstead boy's operative New York cognitive framework.

And speaking of movies and TV, anyone who had watched either knew that when someone had a gun, someone was going to be shot. In Sam's anthropological universe, that was what they called culturally normative. Understood.

No one, however, sat down with the on-screen villain or tragically doomed character and ate lunch, or discussed the weather, or shared a light-hearted joke. Fact was, Pam spent all day in the cook tent with that serious-looking revolver strapped to her hip or hung within reach on a hook.

When Shyla asked her about it, Pam had barely shrugged, saying, "Grizzly country, and I'm down here alone all day frying bacon, burger, and steaks."

Sam's disquiet was further deepened every time Dr. Holly ventured farther from camp than the toilet, or accompanied them up to the site, his equally lethal-looking pistol holstered on his belt next to his Leatherman and Brunton compass.

When asked if that was standard field equipment for an archaeologist, he'd smiled. "Only in the back country. Will we need it? Naw. It's like a seatbelt. Statistically the odds are tens of thousands to one against needing it. The kicker is, on those really rare occasions when your number comes up, you *really* need it."

Like a seat belt? Call that analogy confusing at the deepest cultural level. Go back to that mythos: Unreliable people own guns. Some psychological flaw in their personality, an insufficiency of character, draws them to firearms. Or perhaps a deep-seated sense of inferiority for which they must over-compensate. Owning a gun reinforced their opinions of themselves: See me? I have a gun. I am, therefore, more masculine. Take me seriously, or you'll suffer the consequences.

At worst? Bad people carried them. MS-13 cretin types. People who wanted to rob, shoot up a school or church, unleash mass-murder, or dominate the weak. The mentally ill and unbalanced craved guns. No nightly news report was complete without a murder, or murders, by "mentally disturbed" individuals.

Watching the Tappans trot around with guns on hips and horses—not to mention Dr. Holly who most certainly didn't demonstrate any deficiencies of identity that Sam could see—didn't fit the mold.

Kirstin's words from that drive out to the ranch kept replaying in Sam's ears: *What universe are we in?*

But as the days went by, somewhere along the line, Sam stopped seeing the guns. When he realized that, it worried him to the point that he asked Shanteel. She understood guns and what they meant. She'd lost her mother to a policeman's bullet.

"Oh, yeah," she told him in soft tones. "I can *feel* them. Like the serpent in the garden, you know what I mean?" And she'd given him a squint of emphasis to make her point.

The beginning of day four dawned bright and sunny, as was usual in the mornings. The temperature was crisp, but they were all becoming accustomed to that, given the elevation.

Sam crawled out of his tent, surprised that he had slept the whole night through.

They had heard no additional news. Only Kirstin still religiously checked her phone. No signal. Speculation was that the government—as part of their state of emergency—had shut down the towers.

Everyone remained worried. Back at school, no one talked about family much. It was uncool. But since communications were down, conversation would start with "Did I ever tell you about my Dad?" Or something about a brother, or a grandparent.

After all, family, friends, colleagues, and pets were back in that world. Undoubtedly they were coping. Surely the military had established some system to ensure that people got groceries; that they could manage to get back and forth to work; and the government had to be keeping the lights on and the water running.

Dr. Holly figured they would have issued ration cards first thing.

When nature called, Sam now stumbled out into the trees just out of sight of the camp. This was another change. The guys no longer used the blue-tarp-wrapped latrine when they had to take a leak. The Tappan men and Dr. Holly sort of set the pattern, and the rest of them followed.

Sam looked up at the haze-thick sky, sniffed the morning wind, picking up a curious scent he didn't recognize. At breakfast, he indicated his nose, asking Dr. Holly, "What's that smell?"

The old professor sniffed. "Smoke. Did you notice the reddish glow at sunrise this morning? This thick haze? Something's burning. Maybe California or Nevada."

"That far away?" Danielle asked. "And you can smell it here?"

"You'd be surprised. On dry years this whole country is covered with smoke. Especially in late summer and early fall," he told her. "It's the wind patterns, where the jet stream blows. At times a smoke plume from a thousand miles away can be so dense you can't see across the valley."

He cocked his head, testing the scent. "This doesn't smell like a forest fire. It's different. More acrid. More like a burning dump if you ask me."

Amber had just stepped out of the cook tent, her plate filled with breakfast. She stopped short, sniffing. Sam saw her tense, saw the muscles in her cheeks knot tight. For a moment, she struggled to still the turmoil behind her eyes. It was hard-fought, but she forced her face into that maddening, expressionless mask.

Like an over-tensioned spring, she walked over, seated herself between Sam and Dr. Holly, and in a low voice the others couldn't hear, said, "I've smelled that before."

"Oh?" Dr. Holly asked.

"We were downwind of Aleppo during the last days." She forced herself to take a sip of her coffee, as if it steadied her. "We were under the smoke plume. It was what was left of the city burning after Assad and the Russians used high explosives to blow the roofs off an entire neighborhood and dropped incendiaries to burn the exposed rooms."

"A city?" Sam asked. "An *American* city burning?"

He sniffed again, thinking it did smell like burning garbage.

The corners of Amber's eyes had sucked down tight, the jaw muscles standing out in her wedge face. "Never mind. You're right. It's probably a dump."

Dr. Holly lowered his voice, his long face sober. "Where are you going to find a dump—even for a big city like Salt Lake or LA—that's going to burn with enough intensity to generate a plume this size?"

Sam tried to get his head around the notion of an entire city burning. He lifted his coffee under his nose to block the smell.

Dr. Holly glanced at the haze-filled sky. "We've never seen this before, not even during the Los Angeles riots in the nineties. But what happens when an entire city loses it? When everything breaks down to the point of mass hysteria and rioting? Looting the grocery stores, the liquor stores, Walmart, and Costco? When the highways are jammed and clogged?"

"If Syria is any yardstick to measure by, the electricity goes out first," Amber said. "Maybe it's a fire, or a collapsing building. Maybe someone runs a truck into a pole."

"God, I don't want to think about it," Evan said softly. "But there's something else."

He'd lowered his voice as Shyla and Ashley walked by to go sit on the other side of the fire. Now he pursed his lips and said, "Later."

"Want to give me a hint?" Amber asked.

"Airplanes. Remember the contrails when we got here?"

Amber tipped her head back to study the featureless gray sky. "They're gone."

Sam remembered Frank saying something about it that first day: *"Yeah, southern Wyoming's on the I-80 corridor. Draw a line east-west across the country and it runs through San Francisco, Sacramento, Reno, Salt Lake City, Omaha, Des Moines, Chicago, Cleveland, and Pittsburgh into that dense concentration of cities clustered from Boston, through New York, and Philly."*

Working on the site, high-flying jets had been the only human-made sound outside of the crew's.

"Things are getting worse," Amber said in a strained whisper. Sam thought her eyes looked like cracking glass. "Not a word to the crew, Sam. Not even a hint. Understand?"

He sniffed the wind again, swallowed hard and tossed his plate with its uneaten breakfast into the fire.

As he watched the flames lick up around the bacon and eggs, he asked himself: So, that's what a city smells like when it burns? Were people burning, too?

RIPE FOR THE FALL

***

I don't want to write about the things I saw, did, or survived in the days following the collapse. I relive those days with total clarity, pain, and terror every night when I sleep.

My thoughts on these pages are about the whys and wherefores. The reasons Americans turned on each other like rats in a barrel.

The roots of our discord might be traced back to the end of the Cold War. With no Soviet Union, we had only ourselves left to fight. But I think it went back to the impeachment of Bill Clinton. The proceedings polarized Republicans and Democrats. The art of political payback had always been part of politics, but I think the Clinton impeachment institutionalized it.

Excerpt from Breeze Tappan's *Journal.*

CHAPTER TWELVE

***

BOTH FRANK AND PAM RODE UP TO THE SITE WITH LUNCH. ALL MORNING, SAM HAD BEEN acutely aware of the lack of contrails. As he ate his sandwich, he stared off into the haze-filled heavens, wondering what else had gone wrong in his world.

The glass on his Brunton compass caught his attention. He lifted it, ran a finger across it. The smudge on his fingertip couldn't be mistaken: fine ash.

If cities were burning in the west, what was happening in New York? New York City had the highest urban density in the country. He'd seen the effects of COVID, how entire streets had been emptied, windows boarded up, fearful people locked in their apartments. But they'd still had money, could buy food. The lights and water had worked.

Mom. Dad. Tell me you're all right.

Now that he had no phone service, some perverse part of him *ached* to call them.

That afternoon the wind changed from the southwest to just about straight out of the north, carrying the hazy brown drift of acrid stink south where it concentrated over the Wind River Mountains. It hung there, a sickly brown miasma; Sam was thankful they were no longer breathing it. After all, it hadn't taken that long for the toxic effects of the burning World Trade Towers to show up after 9/11.

Shyla walked over and seated herself beside him, taking a finger to flick a strand of ash-blonde hair back over her ear; it had come loose from her ponytail.

"Got a lot done so far today, boss man." She stared across the remarkable vista as she took a bite from her sandwich.

"Yeah. Especially getting all the hearths and FCR scatters mapped in."

"They're pretty easy to spot now. To think, before I got here, I'd never heard the terms 'Fire Cracked Rock' or 'hackling fracture'. Now I'll never be able to look at a broken stone again without looking to see if it's been burned."

Shyla stared out at the hundred-mile view. "Why did they haul basalt in for their fires when they had so many rocks right here?"

"The site sits on limestone. Basalt is a denser and stronger stone. It didn't fracture when heated in a fire, and having more mass, it concentrated more heat. That meant it radiated for longer. If they were using it as a boiling stone, it didn't dissolve when they dropped it into cold water. Didn't leave grit in the food."

"Makes sense," she agreed. "That was a really good tip that Dr. Holly told us: 'Look for what is out of place in the environment.' Like those chipped cobble tools." Her delicate brow lined. "What did he call them?"

"*Teshoas*," Sam told her. "It's a Shoshoni word. Probably directly translates as 'big stone flake struck from a quartzite lag cobble that has hard cortex on the edge that stays sharp for longer.'"

He watched her face light up with a smile. The woman had remarkable eyes; in the direct sunlight they were a shade of blue-green, a turquoise that sparkled with vitality. He figured she could have modeled, looking a lot like the kind of woman they'd put on a magazine cover.

"Worried about your folks?" he asked when he saw her expression tighten.

"Dad works for a big company. All of his wages were direct deposit after COVID. Bet it doesn't take them long to go back to paper checks. As for Mom? When the economy goes to shit, there are worse things than running a health food store in Vermont. I mean, she knows half the farmers in a fifty-mile radius. It's not like they're going to starve to death." Her lips bent. "And if worse comes to worst, they have the church."

"Church?"

Shyla had always struck him as anything but religious.

She gave Sam a knowing look. "'God will save us, praise the Lord.' Yeah. I couldn't *wait* to get out of the house. Every Sunday, Wednesday, and Friday night we were in the pews listening to the miracles granted by our Lord to the faithful. Sure. But *Friday* night? And every summer? Bam! Off to Christian summer camp. I had no life."

"That sucks."

Finishing off her sandwich, Shyla took a swig of soda from the can. A grim smile was on her lips as she stared out at the basin. "Mom and Dad were so proud of me. Four-point-oh GPA my senior year. They'd already laid the groundwork to get me into the Christian Leadership Academy. They didn't know I'd done the paperwork for the scholarships and applied to just about everywhere else I could think of. I took the first acceptance I got and never looked back."

"Why anthropology?"

"Hey, my folks ranted about the evolution conspiracy my entire life. What's a wild, rebelling, daughter going to do? I signed up for Dr. Moore's Intro to Physical Anthro my first semester. Forbidden knowledge, you know? Loved it. Got to measure fossil skulls, study how the human body evolved. Learned something about genetics. That and intro to philosophy just opened doors."

"How'd your folks take it?"

"Scandalized." She looked uneasily off to the northeast, sort of in the direction of Vermont. "They're *good* people, Sam. I was loved, cared for, and given every security a child needs. I just had to...to..."

"Live your own life?"

"What did old Bill say the other night? 'Ride 'er while she bucks?'" A pause. "There's more to him than that aw shucks redneck cowboy image he likes so much. Soon as I was out of the house, I let her buck real good. Had years of living to make up for. Lately I've been finding out you can overdo the good times. If I never have another three-day hangover, it will be too soon."

"Amen to that."

"What about you?"

"Kind of the same story. You had church; I had The Yucateca. It was the family restaurant. From the time I could reach the sink, I was free labor. I started as dishwasher, grill-scrubber, floor-mopper, trash-taker-outer, and everything else menial. When I wasn't in school, I was expected to be at the restaurant. Hey, what's it say about quality of life when you look forward to homework, cause it was your only excuse for not being at work?"

"That explains it."

"Explains what?"

"Why you're better than the rest. More competent. Responsible."

"Me?"

She arched a slim eyebrow. "Whatever you do, you'll be a success because of what that restaurant taught you."

That was a whole different take—and one he'd have to think about.

They sat in what Sam hoped was amiable silence for a time. Partly because he was too tongue-tied to think of anything witty. He already considered it a miracle that he'd gotten a chance to work with her that morning. Kirstin—Shyla's usual partner—had asked if she could work with Dylan. Which left Shyla as Sam's recorder...then she'd come to sit next to him during lunch? Double miracle. Usually she ate with Kirstin and Ashley.

When Sam looked, Kirstin was sitting with her back propped against a limestone outcrop while Dylan was cross-legged in front of her. They were talking while he plucked up grass stems and seemed to be laughing a lot.

Ashley was down the slope, laid out on her back with Jon and Danielle, all staring up at the sky as they talked.

"Things like this bank failure," Shyla said softly, "it reminds you that nothing's ever certain. If it were to turn out bad, well, there are people I'd really like to have the chance to sit down with and have a long talk. Things I wish I'd done differently. Things I need to say. Love is a curious thing, isn't it?"

"Thinking about your boyfriend?"

"Jim?" She laughed, amused. "No. I was thinking about my family. But Jim? God, I can't imagine what this is doing to him. I mean, the biggest thing in his life? It's his Centurion card. The black one from Amex? It's got like a six-thousand-dollar fee he pays every year. I mean, that man *lives* for his credit card."

"I've got a credit card." It was lame the second he said it. Worse, she glanced his way, saw the appalled expression on his face. Next she was going to see him turn bright red.

I'm such an idiot.

"Visa?"

"Yeah."

She hooked a thumb toward her chest. "Mastercard."

Sam burst out laughing in relief, and she extended a fist his way, saying, "Here's to social justice."

He did the fist-bump and looked away, a swelling in his chest that seemed fit to burst it wide open. Sam had never had what anyone would call a winning way with women. He categorized his relationships as the Icarus kind: where no matter how high you flew in the beginning, ultimately you got too close to the sun and your wings melted. Crash and burn was inevitably a big part of the equation.

"Sam!" Amber's sharp call disrupted the perfect lunch he hoped would never end.

He looked over his shoulder. Amber had risen from where she'd been in conference with Frank and Evan. Pam was tightening the cinch on her horse, having secured to the lunch pack to her saddle cantle.

"I gotta go," he told Shyla, and extended his hand, adding, "Want me to take your can back?"

She tossed off the last of her soda, saying, "Sure" as she stood. Instead of giving him the can, she shook his hand. "Thanks for listening. You're easy to talk to."

"Some people say it's 'cause I don't have anything to say."

"Maybe they're not listening hard enough, huh?"

"Maybe." This time she handed him her can before turning to walk off for the south-side slope. It had become habit that the females trekked off to the timber patch just over the crest to relieve themselves, while the men went the other direction to the north.

"Sam!" Amber barked again.

He grinned to himself, stooped to pick up his pack, and reflected that this was one of the best lunches he'd ever had—even if he couldn't remember eating his sandwich, let alone what was in it.

PERFECTLY CONDITIONED TURTLES

* * *

Maybe we'd been trained by COVID. As a people, the vast majority of Americans reacted to the crash like turtles. They stopped dead in their tracks, pulled their heads, arms, and legs into their shells, and waited. They acted just like the government wanted them to: without initiative. The orders were: Stay calm. Do not leave your homes. Do not panic. Just wait for the state to restore the situation. Government will provide.

Americans had been psychologically conditioned to trust the government. It provided protection, medicine, driver's licenses, social security, building permits, clean food, sanitation, told us what to watch, how to think, what was correct. "Fill out the form, pay a fee, and we will take care of you."

By the millions, Americans went home, locked their doors, and waited. Even after the lights went off. And after the water stopped running.

They waited.

Because they'd been told to.

Excerpt from Breeze Tappan's *Journal.*

CHAPTER THIRTEEN

***

WHEN THE CREW HAD REASSEMBLED AFTER LUNCH, READY FOR THE AFTERNOON SESSION, Amber surprisingly placed Jon in charge and gave him instructions to continue the mapping and recording.

"If it rains," she warned, "if you see lightning, and the thunder is less than ten seconds after the flash, get the crew off the ridge and back to camp. Got that?"

"Yeah, sure," Jon told her. "Where are you going to be?"

Dr. Holly announced, "I want Amber to get a gander at the cave before Thomas Star gets here." He paused. "If he gets here at all. Not that credit cards are as big a thing on the rez, but there's no telling what's going on down there."

Frank led the way, and Sam noted that he was wearing tall, lace-up boots that he called hunting packs instead of his cowboy boots.

They angled north off the ridge and down-slope, which took them through the whitebark pine and into what Frank called "black timber". This was thick stuff, a dense cluster of fir, lodgepole, and spruce. Underfoot, a soft mat of old needles and duff covered the ground. Frank wound down through a maze-work of fallen trees, snag-like branches, and into the dim depths.

Call the sensation antediluvian. Sam felt as if he had stepped back to the Earth's beginning days. Sunlight slanted weakly through gaps in the tangle of branches overhead, when it made it to the ground at all. But for the occasional red squirrel's call, it was a subdued place, a world of dark greens, grays, and browns. Shaggy moss clung to tree trunks and bare branches. Patches of mold patterned the bark and dead wood in artistic splotches.

The silence was broken as crashing and banging sounded off to the right, along with the muffled thumps of heavy feet. A reminder that despite first appearances, this place was brimming with life...and something really big at that.

Amber and Sam stopped cold, surprised, but Frank and Dr. Holly, in unison, said, "Elk."

"Sounds more like a herd of elephants," Amber muttered.

"That or a bulldozer crashing through," Sam added.

"You'd think that an elegant animal like an elk would move with a better sense of grace," Frank agreed. "I'm not sure but that they don't make all that racket as a way of saying, 'Ha! You only thought you were sneaking up on us.'"

They hadn't descended more than another forty meters before they smelled it, first as a whiff, and then a thick cloying.

"What's that?" Amber asked the question that had been rolling around in Sam's mind.

In unison, Frank and Dr. Holly said, "Elk."

Then Frank added, "That's perfume to an elk hunter's nose. Elk are a musky-smelling animal. They have scent glands and communicate by smells in their urine. I think we miss a lot because of how poorly we can smell things."

"What are they doing in here?" Amber asked as she stared around at the tangle of trees.

"They like to bed down in black timber during the day. Flies aren't as bad, and they're safe. Nothing can sneak up on them. It's cooler in here. And when they run, they can hear if a predator is in hot pursuit."

Dr. Holly added. "I've got onto elk in the black timber. Had them bolt like we just heard. Then I spent a half day tracking their sneaky butts while they ran my ass ragged up slopes and over deadfall, only to have them drag my sorry carcass right back to the very spot where I got on them in the first place."

He paused. "Sort of like they were saying, 'Hunt us, will you? We'll show you.'"

"They do have a sense of humor, don't they?" Frank agreed.

"Yep," Dr. Holly avowed.

Frank shot a confidential look at Amber and Sam. "That's why some people just get addicted to elk hunting. People shoot deer and antelope. Sometimes you shoot elk, too. But most often, you *hunt* them."

Sam accepted that on faith, not having the slightest desire to hunt anything except the most outstanding anchovy pizza in the artsy-trendy "old town" block back home.

Still, it gave him a new perspective on the black timber. It really was a good place to hide. Not that he'd ever have to do such a thing, but even as he tried to walk quietly, the dead needles underfoot crackled, twigs snapped, their clothes swished as the cloth rubbed against itself. Branches made a scratching sound on fabric jackets. Then came the periodic metallic clink of coins in pockets, or pack strap clips.

They broke out of the trees, and Sam felt relieved to see the open sky again. They were maybe three hundred feet lower in elevation; a wild-flower-strewn grassy slope dropped away before them that indicated an old burn.

Frank followed a trail that clung to the slope's contour. Sam almost broke his arm patting himself on the back when he figured out it was an elk trail. Easy actually. Not only were the hoof-tracks the right size, but little balls of elk scat—the same stuff that Shanteel had discovered she was sitting in that first day—were liberally sprinkled along the dark soil.

They pulled up at the edge of a canyon. More of a wide crack in the limestone, actually. A place where—if Sam's geology classes hadn't failed him—the underlying bedrock had fractured as the mountains were uplifted in the distant past. Then water had weathered the rock, widening and deepening the crack enough to allow vegetation to take hold, which increased the weathering and erosion.

Looking down, the bottom was filled with currant, chokecherry, and plum bushes. Occasional fir trees rose from the narrow depths, and wild roses were in bloom. The vertical canyon sides had gone gray where the limestone supported lichens and moss. The rock was literally riddled with holes and niches, places where ground water over the eons had eaten passages through the limestone. Yeah, a good place to find a cave, all right.

"Now," Frank mused, "where's that trail?"

"Yonder," Dr. Holly pointed, leading the way farther down the slope.

Climbing down was a bit more adventure than Sam had planned on. Several times he had to brace himself on the rough stone, taking Amber's hand as she carefully lowered herself. A simple slip and fall here, not to mention a broken leg, wouldn't be good. And who knew if 911 still worked? Even if they had had the reception.

Halfway down, Frank paused. "Did you hear that?"

"What?" Dr. Holly cocked his head where he'd wedged himself in a narrow chute in the stone.

"Thought I heard a horse snuffling."

"Down here?" Holly asked.

"Probably my imagination."

Frank continued to climb down until he reached the narrow game trail in the bottom. When they all stood beside him, looking up at the narrow band of sky, it was with both relief and trepidation.

"I know there's a better way than that," Frank said. "Next time I'm marking it with flagging tape."

"You do that," Dr. Holly agreed, grinning. "Come on. It's just up here."

He led the way. Had to push through the thick growth that overhung the trail. Sam glanced up at the almost-sheer walls. Technical climbers wouldn't have any trouble. There were handholds galore, but he would hate to have to climb that.

"You found this elk hunting?" Amber asked.

Over his shoulder, Frank said, "Yeah, bailed off my horse to shoot a big bull. Didn't have a good hold on the reins. I was a sight more interested in the elk. When the gun went off, the horse went ballistic. I'd shot around him before, but that day, for whatever reason, he blew up. Knocked me on my ass, ripped the reins out of my hand, and he was gone. Kaiser Söze gone. You ever see that movie?"

"Uh, no."

"So first thing, I check the elk and start gutting and quartering, figuring Dad or Pam will realize that something's wrong back at camp when the horse comes in for oats. They'll backtrack the horse. Good tracking. About a foot of new snow on the ground. And they'll show up about the time I have the elk ready to pack.

"Only they didn't. And it's getting dark. And a storm's moving in. And it's starting to snow. I fire three quick signal shots. No answer, but the wind's blowing pretty hard by then. And I remember this canyon, figuring I can hole up until morning."

"Quite a hole you found," Dr. Holly agreed.

"What did I know?" Frank answered. "Spent the whole night in that cave and never even recognized what was right over my head."

He smiled. "Just knew I was spooked, that's all. Not that I slept much that night, but damn, I had the weirdest dreams I'd had in my entire life."

"Doesn't surprise me," Dr. Holly said as he pushed past low-hanging fir branches and led the way up a slight slope to an oval-shaped, man-sized opening in the cliff face.

Pulling some of the grass back, Dr. Holly pointed. "Notice the charcoal? Paw around in the weeds enough, and you'll find the occasional flake as well. Last time I saw a burned bone: lagomorph, probably *Silvilagus*."

That was science talk for cottontail rabbit.

"Um, Amber? Sam?" It was one of the first times Dr. Holly had used Sam's first name. "You need to understand. This is sacred space. Holy ground. Treat what you're about to see with respect."

Sacred space? To Sam that hinted at a whole bunch of burials. In his reading he had learned that various Shoshoni bands liked to put their dead in cracks and crevices in the high places under rims. This would surely fit.

"All right, let's go." Dr. Holly fished a couple of Surefire flashlights out of one of his shooting jacket pockets. Handed one to Sam and another to Amber. He flicked his own light on, adding, "Watch your heads."

One by one they climbed inside.

The first sensation was olfactory: the rich damp scent of earth and water with a not-unpleasant musk. Next came the sensation of cool air blowing across the skin. And then Dr. Holly shone his light onto the cave wall.

A being was staring back. Round-bodied, circular eyes, a rippling sort of headdress on top. Wide-spread arms turned up to five-fingered hands, as if they were startled. The legs came out from the sides, curved down, and ended in similar toes, one of which was elongated and ran down to a crack in the rock.

"Dinwoody interior-lined style," Amber said with awe.

Dr. Holly leaned close. "*Pandzoavits*. The water ghost. That's why the toe extends to the crack. That's his tie to the opening to the underworld. The hands are up and spread because water ghosts will seize and carry off people who are unworthy."

A tickle of unease ran down Sam's back.

"The Shoshoni don't believe these images were carved by men, but that they were made by the spirits themselves. I've heard elders, shamans, explain in very careful terms how they've heard pecking as they entered canyons. When they went to investigate, the sound would stop moments before they encountered the actual petroglyph. Usually unfinished."

"Let me guess," Sam said. "The pecking started again as soon as they were out of sight."

"And the next time they returned to the spot the image was complete. You've got it, Sam."

"Wow," Amber said softly. "Is this what you wanted me to see?"

"In part," Dr. Holly told her. "Let's take a look, shall we?"

Sam squeezed past Frank, who remained with his flashlight illuminating the water ghost.

"Oh, my God," Amber whispered as the cavern widened slightly. Various pictographs, images, and designs painted onto the stone versus the carved and pecked petroglyphs adorned the cave walls. Painted in red, with white-and-black accents, there were ghostly elongated beings with big eyes; almost alien linear apparitions; frog-like creatures; and stringy images that conjured notions of mutant insects.

Another of the *pandzoavits* toward the back was reaching up, but instead of straight, vertical lines, his wide torso was filled with a series of interlinked wavy lines and dots. He wore a radiant-lined headdress, but what was more amazing, he'd been painted. The body, though faded, was still red, the dots white. The headdress was in black.

"You ever seen one painted before?" Amber asked reverently.

"Nope. Nor has there been any evidence from the trace-analysis studies done on other Dinwoody-style petroglyphs to indicate that they were painted."

Sam blinked, looking around, totally and truly awed. He could feel his heart beating in his chest. It sank in. What Dr. Holly had been talking about. This *was* a sacred place. He could feel the spiritual essence that seemed to radiate from the images, what the Shoshoni called *puha*.

Sam gazed from one image to another as he shifted his flashlight. The tickle in his spine intensified. Could *feel* them looking back at him.

Had to be the place, right? The cave, deep in the mountains, and seeing cool things that just triggered his imagination. Brains did that when they were excited and got a dopamine rush.

Just past the gallery, the cave split, the larger passage leading to the left. Sam had been so blown away he had missed anything Dr. Holly and Amber were saying...was only vaguely aware of the fact that they were headed deeper into the mountain, disappearing into the left-hand passage.

Sam was about to follow when he noticed the little guy carved down by the floor next to the right-hand passage. He'd swear the thing moved to get his attention. And when he flashed his light full on the image, it was like a soul jolt: Electric. He was staring into the little guy's remarkably rendered eyes: three concentric circles with black pupils.

The image had his three-fingered hands up, and three-toed feet sprouted from the corners of his rotund body with its apparent breech-cloth and a Dinwoody-style breastplate.

"Who are you?" Sam whispered softly, struggling to remember if the image were one of the ones he had read about.

Damn! Did it just move?

Sam couldn't be sure, wondering if it was a trick of the light bouncing off the little puddle of water on the cave floor at the image's feet. Every time Sam shifted, the reflection sent soft waves of light flowing across the rock.

Drawn by the image, he took the right-hand passage, surprised to find it descended over irregular rock worn smooth by age. Ahead he could hear droplets hitting water with a hollow and musical plop that almost echoed.

The passage opened, and the first thing that caught Sam's eye was the little guy. An exact copy of the one he had left behind. The little guy was still staring at Sam through the same black pupils, his three-fingered hands held out as if in surprise.

"So, you beat me down here, huh?" he asked, figuring humor would lighten the uneasy tingle that just kept getting worse. "What was it you wanted me to see?"

As Sam shifted, the light played a trick, the little creature seeming to extend his left hand, and Sam followed...stopping short.

Even as he took in the image depicted on the cave's back wall, another drop plopped into the pool of water at the woman's feet. A sort of crescendo.

This image Sam knew: Water Ghost Woman. *Pa waip.* The mystical and dangerous siren of the Shoshoni underworld. Beautiful, seductive, with her long hair and the tears she shed. Her left arm was extended, arrowheads dangling from her sleeve like fringe and a strung bow was gripped in her hand. Broad-shouldered and narrow-waisted as she was, the artist had left no doubt about her sexuality. The breasts were well rendered with round dark nipples. The presence of her spirit helper and errand boy, Turtle, where he was carved on the wall beside her, left no doubt she was *pa waip.* Her right hand was reaching out, the fingers ready to grasp.

Sam swallowed hard, gut cold.

"You're the seductress. The stories the Shoshoni tell have you hanging out by rivers and springs. Men are drawn by the sound of your weeping. And sure enough, once they find you beside the water, they just can't resist. You flip up that little skirt you're wearing and open your legs. Then, as soon as they're inside, *Whap!* You roll them into the water just as the action really heats up."

He paused, a quivering of anxiety running through his nerves. "So, which story is true? Do you just drown them? Or do you eat them like the scary stories insist?"

She seemed to waver indecisively as his flashlight beam reflected in bars from the water.

"Making up your mind, huh?"

The attempt at witty banter didn't seem to be alleviating the unease down in his core. Something about her...

He couldn't help but think about what she would have looked like in the flesh, how her long hair would glisten in the moonlight. Imagine what animated those dark and gleaming eyes. The fantasy was good enough that he reached up with his left hand, ready to step forward and caress her full breast, feel her nipple harden against his palm. An erection began to swell in his pants.

What am I doing?

"Stop it!" he growled to himself, shaking his head and stepping back. He forced himself to remember Shyla's turquoise eyes, the delicious lines of her body, and the way the sunlight glimmered in her ash-blonde hair.

In the refracted light, Water Ghost Woman seemed to smile, as if this were just the first ploys in a most complicated game. Some faint whisper in Sam's mind said, "*You'll be back.*"

He flashed the light onto the little guy who'd brought him down there. "Am I *that* horny?"

Sam almost jumped out of his skin when a voice behind him said, "I wouldn't know, but she's remarkably alluring when you stare at her for a while."

SELF-SORTING

**

With the collapse of American manufacturing and the movement of jobs overseas to China, Taiwan, Indonesia, and Vietnam, not to mention Mexico, America began to transition into what they called the "service" economy.

A couple of generations ago, it was accepted, for the most part, that a person had one career, generally working for the same company until retirement. A couple married, bought a house, and raised their kids in a familiar neighborhood. The Ozzie and Harriet life.

For a myriad of reasons, including advances in telecommunications, the internet, cheap transportation, and evolving technology, companies rose and fell. Work became mobile. Cars were no longer being built just in Michigan, but Alabama, North Carolina, and Mississippi. It wasn't all about money. Often people began to find themselves in different communities with different politics. If they liked it, they stayed, having found kindred spirits. If they didn't they moved on to places where folks thought the same way they did. Like clustered with like.

Sociologists call it self-sorting.

In the 1850s, historians called it "sectionalism" and it gave birth to the Civil War.

Excerpt from Breeze Tappan's *Journal.*

CHAPTER FOURTEEN

* * *

SAM WHIRLED AROUND, LIGHT PROBING A DARK SIDE CHAMBER IN THE CAVERN. HE UTTERED a strangled sort of shriek as his light fell on a seated figure. A man. Black cowboy hat, red shirt, blue Levi's, beaded buckle decorated with a red rose. Old-style pointed cowboy boots and spurs on the feet. Two long gray braids draped down on either side of a beaded, star-patterned bolo at the base of his throat.

The old man lowered the brim of his hat to protect his eyes from the blinding light, and raised a weathered brown hand, as if to shield himself. "You want to lower that?"

"Who the...? Who the...?" Sam tried to stop the pounding of his heart, managed to finally both lower the light and squeak: "Who the hell are you?"

In the diffused light Sam saw the man smile and could pick out the deeply incised lines in his aged, round face. The eyes were like shining black stones as they studied him from either side of a mashed and misshapen nose.

"Oh, I know who I am," he said thoughtfully. "Ruined my life a few times, not to mention other people's, finding out. There was more than a little hell in the process, too." He paused. "What I really want to know is...who are you?"

"I...I'm Sam Delgado. I'm a...a graduate student."

"Not many *taipo* graduate students have a *nynymbi*. Why do you?" His voice sounded dry and raspy, somehow ancient.

"I have a...a *what?*"

The old man gestured with a flick of brown and gnarled fingers. "The little one. The one you were talking to before you began that fascinating interchange with *Pa Waip*."

The way he said her name, you'd think he knew her personally.

Sam flashed the light back to the little petroglyph by the entrance. "That's a *nynymbi?*"

One of the little folk—a prankster who pulled tricks on people in the back country, made them trip over their own feet, or shot invisible arrows that sent a stitch of pain through the chest or hip.

Sam finished his thoughts aloud, saying, "...And who can act as a guide to those who seek the Water World."

That was what the Shoshoni called the underworld. Sam shook his head, swiveling the flashlight back in the old man's direction. "I mean, he's not mine. I just saw one like him in the upper cavern."

"You mean you saw *him.*" Again, the brush of the fingers toward the image.

"No. I mean I saw the petroglyph that looked like this one up in the—"

"But you said, he 'Beat you down here'."

"I was just...I was...um, joking." Sam felt a red fluster warming his ears.

The old man inhaled, as if savoring the air. "Of course. Joking. Most unusual for a *taipo.* Most unusual all the way around. A *nynymbi* don't just offer his services without being asked, begged actually. It is a favor not lightly given. Yet you just walk in here, and one of the little people puts himself at your disposal."

"What makes you think he did that?"

"He wasn't here until an instant before you climbed down. He appeared just before you did."

"Wait a minute. He's *carved* into the rock. He couldn't have just appeared." What had the old dude been smoking?

"You sure?" A beat. "Be careful when you answer that, Sam Delgado, graduate student. You are in a place of passages, at the doorway to a different world. This is a place that only quantum physicists and mystics can fully comprehend. An interface between universes. The domain of the multiverse, assuming you have enough background in theoretical physics to grasp the mathematical probabilities."

The old man's head tilted skeptically. "Which, I suspect, you don't. Anthropologists generally get arrested for indecent exposure when they have to count up to twenty-one. At least the male ones do."

A voice echoed in the passage behind Sam, saying, "Down here."

The scraping of shoes and clothing preceded Dr. Holly's arrival. Sam scrunched to the side to make room as Amber crowded in.

"What the...?" She flashed her light onto Water Ghost Woman. "Holy shit," she whispered. "She's magnificent. Look at the detail. Like she was rendered yesterday."

"Who were you talking to, Sam?" Dr. Holly asked, his gaze on Water Ghost Woman.

"He was talking to *Pa waip*, Evan," the old man said from where he'd been relegated to the shadows again. "At least he was when he wasn't talking to the *nynymbi.* "

Lights flashed the old man's way again, blinding him. He took refuge under the down-tilted brim of his hat.

"Thomas? What are you doing here?" Dr. Holly stepped forward, reaching out to push Amber's flashlight beam out of the old man's face.

Thomas? Thomas Star?

"Crap," Amber whispered. "He just scared the ever-loving shit out of me."

"Yeah. Join the club," Sam muttered.

So this was the renowned Shoshoni *puhagan*? Talking theoretical physics, for God's sake?

The old man had climbed to his feet, first shaking Dr. Holly's hand, and then clasping him in a bear hug.

Pushing back, Star said, "I wanted to see this place first. Wanted to learn what the *puha* wanted done now that it's been discovered. It's *puha kahni*. A definite sacred site. The spirits and I, we've been talking about how it should be protected. What the best use of the knowledge is."

"What did they say?" Evan's voice dropped.

"They say it's their time, Evan. That they've been waiting. That they have things people are going to need. They tested this notion with Frank. They found his *navushieip* worthy, so they didn't kill him that night. Instead they watched. He and his family have always treated this place with respect and honor."

He flicked the fingers toward Sam this time. "Then, this one arrives, guided by *Nynymbi*." He tilted his head toward Amber, who had walked to the edge of the pool and was staring transfixed at Water Ghost Woman, their gazes locked together. "And that one hears. Down inside, in the *mugwa* and *suap.* You can't hear, but she does."

"I don't understand," Dr. Holly said warily. His shoulders had hunched, as though he expected some sort of a lethal blow.

"Worlds die, Evan," the old man told him. "It's the end of one world and the beginning of another. All things, all peoples have their time. Yours is over."

Sam's first reaction was to chuckle, but at the pale shock reflected in Dr. Holly's face, he scuttled it. To Sam's eyes, Evan Holly looked as if a death sentence had just been passed on him.

THE INFERNAL INVENTION

***

In Nazi-occupied Europe, having an unlicensed printing press was grounds for immediate arrest and execution. In Soviet-occupied Czechoslovakia in 1968, possession of a mimeograph machine was a one-way ticket to the "re-education camp". The state feared any uncontrolled communications among the people.

The evolution of the internet was supposed to be the death knell of despots and dictators. It promised the free movement of information, discourse, and diversity of thought. The ultimate in freedom of speech for the masses.

Who would have thought it would become a tool of self-reinforcement? Instead of broadening understanding, ideologues used it as a means of isolating themselves from those who did not share their beliefs and causes. And as a means of reinforcing their notions of "Truth". The very lack of regulation meant any vitriol could be posted without censure.

Excerpt from Breeze Tappan's *Journal*.

CHAPTER FIFTEEN

***

THE OLD SHOSHONI LED THE WAY OUT OF PUHA CANYON. THOMAS TOOK THEM TO A MUCH better trail—a place where soil had filled in a crevice to the point that deer used it. Talk about bow-legged, watching Mr. Star walk was like seeing parentheses hobbling along.

At the top of the trail two horses were tied off in the aspens, no doubt the ones Frank had heard when they had first descended into the canyon.

Seated at the base of a nearby aspen, whittling on a willow stick, a young Native man in a battered hat and Levi jacket looked up. He climbed slowly to his feet, worn boots shifting on trampled grass. His legs were long and skinny, clad in blue jeans, and he wore an old red-and-white-checked flannel shirt with snaps for buttons. A long black braid hung down his back. Wide cheekbones framed obsidian eyes and a long thin nose, and his chin dropped to a point with a dimple.

"Hey, Grampa," he called. "I see they found you."

"Huh, yeah. That's the thing about these anthropologists, Willy. Once they finally figure out you're an Indian, you can't get rid of 'em. Sort of like lice and fleas, they just cling to you. Real pests."

Willy Star grinned, exposing large white teeth, and stepped forward, offering his hand to Dr. Holly. "Hey, Evan. Good to see you again."

"You, too, Willy. It's a relief after being stuck with this old codger. Keeps hitting me up for a hundred bucks. Says it's an informant's fee for telling lies about the old times. Says he'll sell me a genuine war chief's headdress for a thousand bucks. Worn only once by some guy named Washakie when he killed some Crow Chief up on top of Crowheart Butte."

Thomas Star stroked his chin. "And if you don't want that one, for two thousand bucks, I got the war bonnet Geronimo wore at the battle of the Little Bighorn. Comes with a little card, says 'Hand made by a genuine American Indian'."

"Geronimo was never within a thousand miles of the Little Big Horn."

"That's what makes that war bonnet so valuable."

Dr. Holly leaned close to Frank, saying, "What do you want to bet it's the same headdress?"

Thomas nodded in a most sagacious Indian way. "Same headdress, but for the extra thousand you get a different card. Instead of Washakie's picture, you get Geronimo's."

Sam stared, dumbfounded, but Amber was grinning as she asked Willy, "Are they always like this?"

"Naw. Used to be worse back when whiskey was involved."

"Hadn't thought of that," Thomas Star said, looking at Dr. Holly. "You got any?"

"Back at camp."

"Good thing I don't drink no more."

Dr. Holly turned, seeing the stricken looks on both Sam's and Amber's faces. "Oh, relax! You modern 'enlightened' socially liberated crusaders in pursuit of racial justice and colonial reparations haven't a clue."

Frank laughed, a sly grin on his lips. The outfitter scuffed the grass with his pack boots, muttering, "Same old shit."

"Willy," Star told his grandson, "give Evan your horse. Him and me's gonna ride back to camp. You sort of scout the trail for these greenhorns so they don't get scalped or eaten by a bear or anything, okay?"

"Who you calling a greenhorn?" Frank asked as he laid a theatrical hand on his pistol.

Willy pushed his hat back on his head, grinned, and said, "Sure. You old guys ride. Beat's having to pack your bony asses out of here."

He untied his horse's reins, handing them to Dr. Holly, and adding, "His name is Flapjack. I don't think he'll try you, but if he does that little crow hop, keep his head up and remind him who's in charge."

"This the colt you were training a couple of years back?" Dr. Holly asked as he stepped into the stirrup and swung into the saddle. The big brown horse sidestepped and circled around as Dr. Holly called,

"Woah, now. Easy, Flapjack."

"Yeah, Evan," Willy answered. "That was like maybe ten years ago, huh."

It might have taken Thomas Star two attempts to get his old body up and onto the horse, but once he was there, it was readily apparent where he'd come by those bowed legs. The man rode like a centaur as he led the way up the slope toward the trees.

"Don't pay them two any mind," Willy said. "Grampa and Evan go way back. Maybe even to the ice age." He chuckled. "Grampa was the first Indian Evan ever met. That was back when Evan was a hippie in search of enlightenment."

"A hippie?" Frank asked as they started the hike back to camp.

"Yeah. He was doing one of them 'drive across the country in a VW bus' tours college kids did back in the seventies when he broke down in Dubois. Had to make money to fix his car, so he hired on as a logger back before they closed down the L & P sawmill. Grampa was working for them that summer, too. They kind of took a shine to each other. Talked about how the Sheep Eaters survived in the mountains. Got crazy together. Fought like wolverines when they were drunk and stood side-by-side when they were sober."

Amber walked thoughtfully for a couple of steps before she said, "I don't think of Evan Holly as a fighter and hellion."

"I came along kind of at the end of that time. But I remember one time when Mom swore Grampa was trying to either kill himself or land in prison for the rest of his life. That was just before Evan came back from graduate school with his PhD. They went up into the Wind Rivers for the summer to look for archaeology. That's when Grampa got traditional. Started hanging out with the elders, learning the stories. Did his first Sun Dance."

They stopped for a breather at the bottom of the black timber patch. Looking out over the canyons, Sam could imagine the lure. Something about those mountains, or maybe it was the lingering power of the cave, of the way the images had touched his soul, but he could understand Thomas Star's conversion.

As if it were a sign, a huge golden eagle swung into view, sailed across the sky no more than thirty feet over their heads, and drifted out over the canyon.

As they climbed over a deadfall and into the trees, Sam dared to pipe up, saying, "Your grandfather doesn't sound or act like a logger. Down in Water Ghost Woman's chamber, he was talking about theoretical physics."

"Yeah." Willy paused, studying the timber for the best path through the maze before picking a new trail. "He's got a B.A. in physics from Georgetown. Lived in D.C. for ten years as a Native American 'consultant'. Did some lobbying. I don't know which he's had more of, jobs or wives."

"How about you?" Amber asked. "You going to follow in your grandfather's footsteps?"

"I don't have the math for physics, and for the moment, the job thing is kind of illusive. I'm still working on finding the first wife."

"I meant becoming a *puhagan*."

"Oh, that? Thank God you didn't mean the whiskey and the fighting."

Amber chuckled as she panted for breath. The climb was steeper than it looked, and she and Sam were still working with sea-level lungs. Neither Frank nor Willy seemed to have any trouble at all.

Willy led the way around a tangle of deadfall. The pungent smell of elk hung thick in the air. "For now, I'm open-minded about religion. In Iraq I got to see Sunnis and Shia, Christians, Yazidis, and just about every form of extremism in the name of God you can imagine. Met some Coptics when I was detailed to Egypt. Even had a special tour of the Vatican. After the things I've seen? I think religion is more about people than God."

"You've been in the cave, though, right?"

He nodded. "Kind of awesome, huh?"

"Did you feel it?" Sam just had to ask, still bothered by his reaction to the *nynymbi* and Water Ghost Woman.

"Feel what?" Willy shot a look over his shoulder to judge Sam's reaction.

"I mean, you're Shoshoni, right. You didn't feel the *puha*?"

"What are you talking about, Sam?" Amber asked with feigned indifference. "I mean, I felt a kind of reverence, like you'd feel in a holy place. And it was fantastic to see. Especially the painted petroglyph. The site is unique and of immense academic value. Not to mention an incredibly important cultural treasure."

From the precisely structured tone in her voice, Sam could tell she was lying. That, somehow, to admit to having been touched by the place's power made her vulnerable. Put some sort of crack in that armor of invincibility she liked to paste around herself.

Time to shut up, Sam.

What was he going to do, admit that he'd been sexually aroused by a carving in the rock?

Willy was giving both of them the critical eye. "Uh, tell me you guys aren't going to be like all the rest."

"All what rest?" Sam demanded, feeling silly and defensive.

"I mean like all the crazy-sad whites who show up on the reservation looking for truth, spiritual enlightenment, and the Indian way. The wannabes. Like we've got some corner on the ultimate truth market. Go to Indian Country. Smoke dope, go through a sweat lodge ceremony, beat on a drum. Find a medicine man so you can sit at his feet, and he'll tell you how to do a vision quest. And when you do all that, you'll finally have a mystical, magical, cure for all the reasons your life is so fucked up."

"Wouldn't that be nice?" Amber said bitterly. "But no. Not interested in being something I'm not."

"I'm just here to find a dissertation topic," Sam admitted. "What happened in that cave, I mean, it was just a trick of the light." He paused for a beat. "And don't pay any attention when your grandfather says I've got my own *nynymbi.* The way I figure it, he was just teasing. Like he could get a rise out of the gullible Easterner white guy."

Willy stopped short and fixed Sam with his hard eyes. "He said you had a *nynymbi?*"

"Well...yeah."

Willy's eyes were pinning him like a bug on a board. "Grampa doesn't joke about *puha* or spirits. Especially not *Nynymbi.* I don't know the whole story, but don't fuck with him when he says you've got a spirit helper."

That left Sam even more confused. Adding to his fluster, Frank was watching him from under his lowered hat brim, those odd brown-ringed hazel eyes mindful of a gunfighter's before the OK Corral.

Amber was panting. "He also said it's the end of the world."

Willy picked a trail that led them out of the tangle at the top of the black timber. "The end of the world, huh?" He shook his head. "After some of the things I saw in Iraq, Syria, and Afghanistan, I can believe it. If I was God, I'd cleanse the entire planet."

"Can't say I disagree," Frank muttered.

They stopped for another breather. Sam could see the whitebark pine grove up ahead and knew they only needed to skirt around the bottom of the grove to find camp.

After the claustrophobic and dark confines of the black timber, Sam looked up to appreciate the sky. And stopped short.

"Guys?"

They followed his gaze up.

"Holy shit," Frank murmured.

The formations—appearing over the eastern horizon—seemed to roll across the sky. V's of aircraft, seven or eight per V, and formation after formation. Must have been a couple hundred.

Frank reached inside his shirt pocket to pull out a compact set of binoculars. Tipping his head back he studied the patterns of high-flying planes.

"Air Force," he said. "A couple of echelons of fighters. F-18s and F-22s if I'm any judge. A lot of big stuff following. A5s maybe? And some of those must be tankers for refueling. I was a Marine. Didn't get into Air Force stuff."

"That's like an entire air wing," Willy said softly. "Headed where?"

The sound was finally reaching them, a low roar that slowly built until it filled the world. They stood there, shocked, somber. Sam couldn't speak. A leaden heaviness filled his chest.

Watching that air armada pass overhead was—and would remain—one of the most horrendous sights he had ever seen.

The feeling was so intense, so devastating, Sam was slightly in shock, because he would remember biting off hysterical laughter as tears streaked his face, thinking, *You stupid fucking idiots! How could you have brought us to this?*

POLITICS BY ANY OTHER NAME

***

Can we really blame the political parties for the animosity that Americans held for each other? Clinton, Bush, Obama, Trump, Biden, Pelosi, McConnell, Schumer, and all the rest?

Ultimately the people in their districts elected them. True, the parties were partly responsible. They had, after all, finagled the districts, redrew the Gerrymandered lines to ensure that like-minded people voted together. Compromise wasn't necessary. People who didn't fit the majority moved out, if they could. Self-sorting increased. Liberals and progressives moved to the coasts, conservatives fled California for Nevada and the intermountain West.

Obviously your values and politics were correct. Everyone around you believed the same way.

Excerpt from Breeze Tappan's *Journal.*

CHAPTER SIXTEEN

***

THE EVENING MEAL WAS A SOMBER AFFAIR. THE FIELD CREW WAS SEATED AROUND THE FIRE, finishing supper as the entire western horizon glowed in an unearthly blaze-orange. The gaudy sunset streaked fire across the high cirrus and painted the Absaroka Range's irregular jutting peaks and snow patches in pink, purple, and indigo. Something about the colors hinted not of a glorious Bierstadt rendering of the wilderness, but something more mindful of the burning of Atlanta in *Gone with the Wind.*

Just enough breeze came down from the north to keep that ominous brown cloud to the south of their camp.

The evening was cool, crickets singing, nighthawks making that odd, tearing whoosh in the sky. A dancing column of swifts chased the dusk insects, and the first vesper bats appeared to flutter in jerky patterns across the wounded sky. Coyote calls could be heard, but from a considerable distance.

The fire popped and crackled, spitting sparks up toward the glowing heavens as Sam used his fork to spear the last of the green beans from his plate. Talk about a day of ups and downs. Shyla in the morning, the cave with all its spooky contradictions, and then that huge flight of bombers and transports.

When Sam mentioned the magnificent sunset, Frank pulled him aside and told him quietly, "That's more than just cities. Those are huge forest fires burning. Maybe California, Oregon, and Washington. Odd for this time of year. We'd expect to see skies like this in late summer and early autumn. Not now. Not after such a wet spring across the West."

Sam stared up at the Burning-of-Atlanta sky, awed by the irony that conflagration and devastation could contribute to such a spectacular display.

West. That's where the bombers had been headed. And everyone had seen them—had been filled with dread at the thunder of their passage.

People had spent the evening trying to call home. Didn't matter that the phones couldn't detect a signal. They still tapped out the numbers. Listened, and worried about family, friends, and loved ones. Talk was if they should try to go back, or tough it out where they were.

Dylan sat close to Kirstin, hip-to-hip. They were holding hands now. At least on their front, things were progressing. Their postures looked as if they were seeking comfort in the reassurance of touch.

Jon thoughtfully stroked a couple of chords on his guitar, and said, "Maybe the bombers were just relocating. Maybe the California banks figured out the credit card mess, and the Air Force can use their credit cards to gas up their planes in San Francisco."

No one laughed, so he strummed a discordant note.

Dr. Holly smoked his pipe where he sat on a drawn-up log. Now he removed the stem from between his teeth. "My guess? It's part of the martial law decree."

Willy grunted and took his grandfather's paper plate when Thomas handed it to him. Along with Willy's, both ended up in the fire. Thomas' expression could have been carved from granite as firelight flickered in his dark eyes.

Court—who'd been silent for the most part—jabbed at the fire with a stick. "Someone took down the banks. Remember when that bank guy said it was like a Pearl Harbor? That the records had been wiped? If the country is as damaged as we think, the president can't let this go without a response."

Shyla—sitting two down from Sam—said, "If anyone was prepared for a cyberattack, the banks were. People try to hack them a million times a day."

Court softly said, "If whoever did this used a quantum computer, they might have had the program corrupt the backups, too. All it takes in hacking is to be one step ahead of the defenses."

"How so?" Danielle asked.

Court looked around the fire. "Bear with me. I've been thinking of this as game theory. Okay, here's the scenario: For the last decade the United States has been withdrawing from the world stage, pulling back on our commitments to allies. At the same time, Russia, China, Iran, and North Korea have been advancing.

"While that's happening, the United States is dividing internally. The big story in our news is about the country splitting, and if it will happen. Texas has voted to secede, and a lot of the Rocky Mountain states want to follow. California voted to leave, Oregon, and Washington are teetering on secession. The Republican party has torn itself down the middle; two presidents, in rapid succession, have almost been impeached and forced to resign; the Democrats are distrusted by seventy percent of the American people. Everyone hates and fears the federal bureaucracies."

"Amen, brother," Pam called from where she banged pans in the cook tent.

"We haven't been this weak since the Civil War. But if Russia moves on the Baltic States and NATO, if China moves on Japan, Vietnam, and the Philippines; if North Korea invades south across the DMZ; and if Iran rolls over the Middle East, the United States could finally be pushed far enough to react, and our response would have to be nuclear."

Shanteel said, "The people wouldn't stand for it."

Amber sat hunched, posture defensive, eyes seeing something deep down in the fire's core. "What better way to shore up a failing economy than to start a war? Why do you think the U.S. is any different than, say, Assad was in Syria?"

"Because we're us," Dylan almost pleaded.

Court got back to his subject. "If you are China or Russia, Why take the chance? And for all we know they might have intel that lays out exactly what our response would be if pushed beyond a certain point. We sent those two carrier groups into the South China Sea in response to China landing troops in Taiwan, right? What if the president and joint chiefs finally said, 'Enough is enough?'"

Court looked around, taking them in one by one. "Who wants to take on the American military? There's a better way for them to win: destroy the money. A cyberattack is always deniable. It's sneaky, quick, confusing to the enemy, and most people don't really understand it. No bombs, troops, or bodies. Just corrupt the bank records."

Thomas Star asked, "How many of you get monthly bank statements in the mail anymore?"

"We do," Pam called from the cook tent. "Bank's been after us for years to put it all online. Dad refused, and well, we just followed his lead."

"Hey," Kirstin said, "Even my credit card is on my phone. All I have to do is pull up the app and press a button. Purchase made."

"Okay"—Court agreed with a shrug—"so there're a handful of people who get paper statements. Means Pam, at least, has a record of her debits and credits. But those statements were printed from the electronic record stored in a computer. And that's gone. Wiped clean. Anything you had in your bank account, maybe the account number itself, is gone. Just like pushing delete on your keyboard."

"My God," Amber whispered, dropping her head into her hands.

Sam tried to think through the ramifications. No one in his neighborhood carried cash. Not only was it dangerous—and a sure way to get mugged—but it was just inconvenient. A lot of places didn't even take cash anymore.

"A whole market economy," Dr. Holly uttered softly. "From the most sophisticated credit and debit market ever to a cash and barter economy. Overnight. And hundreds of trillions of dollars of wealth gone. Vanished. As if it had never existed."

"But the check books, the bank statements," Sam said. "They're a way that the banks can begin to reconstruct the records, right?"

Amber had a peculiar look in her eyes, a sort of tortured disbelief. "We're talking about hundreds of millions of accounts here."

"Meaning?" Frank asked as he walked up from seeing to the horses.

Shanteel rubbed her face, as if to reestablish feeling in her numb flesh. "When everything stopped, depending upon where you were, people would have reacted differently. In the more affluent part of town, they would have shrugged and said, 'Yeah, well, they'll fix it in a day or two.' In middle class neighborhoods, people would have said, 'See, things really are falling apart, this is the last straw.' And in the poorer part of town, the blue collar and minority folks who walked to the grocery and got turned away, are saying, 'I don't *have* cash. What do you mean, telling me my card's no good? My kids are hungry *tonight*.' And that's where it started."

She was firm in her use of the past tense.

The look behind Shanteel's dark eyes was nothing nice, as if she was seeing the rioting in her head. "You think tearing down the statues was bad? That's when people start throwing things through windows and taking what they can. Now it's going to a whole nuther level."

Danielle was wringing her long hair, twisting it through her fingers. "Come on, guys. Even in New York there are going to be people who say 'Let's hang together. Everyone pitch in. Throw in some cans of food. We'll work together to get through this.' I mean it happened the time the electricity went out. After 9/11 and then COVID. We *don't* just turn on each other. We're not animals."

Jon fingered his guitar. "Sure. People would have pulled together. But how long does that last?"

Sam added, "And if your business depends on customers who don't carry money, you just hit a cash-flow brick wall. The delivery trucks will demand cash. Payroll has to be met. They'll be laying off employees immediately."

Amber's expression had sharpened. "After that it all bootstraps, jacking up the pressure. I mean, who gets blamed? People show up at the local Krogers. Right there in front of them is a store full of food, but they'll only let people with cash in the door. The store is stuck, right? They have to make income on product. Outside, people finger their worthless credit cards and stare at the 'Cash Only' sign where the security guys are guarding the door. The frustration builds until someone finally just shoots down the guards."

"And cities burn," Sam whispered under his breath. Had it really come to that so quickly?

"This is nuts," Dr. Holly cried. "How can anyone destroy money. I mean, that's what they've done."

Danielle's expression had glazed, her dark eyes haunted. "We need to get home to our families."

"How?" Dr. Holly asked.

"We'll figure that out when we get there," Jon said stubbornly. "There's got to be a way. Put all of us in the van. Just the one vehicle, pool our cash, and maybe we can afford the gas."

Frank's harsh laugh grated. "Yeah, right. People, the roads are closed! There's a travel ban. Martial law. You seen any airplanes except the military flying over?" He stared from face to face. "How much cash do you all have? Will it really be enough if everything's chaos?"

Amber's voice rose. "No one's going home."

"How do you know?" Shyla asked, a tremor in her voice.

"Because that's how martial law works. Nobody travels without a permit that will allow them to get past the checkpoints."

Frank added, "And what about all the people stranded on the roads? They'll be getting pretty desperate, looking for anyone who can still travel. Anyone moving must have enough cash to buy fuel and food. You won't make it as far as Omaha."

Shanteel burst out angrily, "Shit! I've seen what happens when people start to riot." Her face contorted. "People get shot. Innocent people. Buildings and cars get burned. Won't be nothing like what's coming down now."

"You want to get home, don't you?" Kirstin asked anxiously.

Shanteel blinked, seemed to flinch. "I don't know. Not sure what I'd do...walking up that street. Seeing all the houses burned out. I tell you this, though. Any police? They're going to protect the white neighborhoods. My part of town? They're gonna let it burn."

"My *family* is back there," Danielle cried passionately.

"Barricades at the crossroads," Amber said, a far-off look in her eyes. "Probably militia. Just like Syria." She seemed to snap to, shooting Shanteel a knowing glance. "It'd be a lie to think we were any different."

"We need to go home," Ashley said firmly. "We have to try at least."

Amber stood, staring around the fire. Voice crisp, she said, "No, you do not."

"Bullshit," Jon barked. "You gonna stop us?"

"Yes."

"How?" Ashley looked sullen.

"All right," Amber said, "I'll give you all this: We'll go down at least as far as Tappan Ranch." She pointed. "Jon, Danielle, Kirstin, you'll go with me. We'll go into town and learn what we can. If anyone is able to travel, we'll hear. If there's an army detail, we'll see what the procedure for a travel permit is."

She glanced around, fire in her eyes. "Is that a deal? I mean it, do you all agree? We'll see what the situation is before any of us go charging off hell-bent to get ourselves captured, starved, beaten, and raped?"

Sam didn't think she'd realized what she said, or the tone in which it came out of her mouth: captured, starved, beaten and raped. Like had happened to her in Syria. God, she really thought that was coming down here?

"Dr. Holly," Jon cried, "you going to let her do this? I mean, you're in charge here."

Dr. Holly pulled reflectively on his pipe, shot an evaluative look at Amber, and considered his words just long enough to make his point. "I'm backing Amber."

"Why?" Ashley's voice was almost shrill. Her expression was stricken.

A bitter smile lay on Dr. Holly's lips as he said, "I've spent all of my life studying human adaptation to resources. Culture is a collection of behavioral systems that, when they're functioning, ultimately provide for the needs of the individual. I doubt any of you have read David Aberle, Ralph Linton, or Anthony F. C. Wallace about what happens when the systems collapse. It's called deprivation theory. And it's all about how human beings react when they suddenly lose their security, or hope, or can't feed their families. How they turn on each other, or toward a messiah figure offering salvation. Generally in return for total obedience."

Jon protested, "But, I mean, a total collapse of the system? What about cultural inertia? You know, how social institutions and behaviors perpetuate themselves? Americans won't just turn on each other like flipping a light switch."

"Watched the news lately?" Amber asked. "So, Evan, tell my colleagues, here, about social inertia, and just how fast it can vanish."

The old professor nodded sagaciously. "Some of you anthropology majors will have studied the Lowland Maya, Chaco Canyon, Angkor Wat, or the end of Harappan civilization. Think about how quickly those systems collapsed. Like flipping a light switch? That's a pretty good analogy, Jon."

He gestured with his pipe. "If Court's right about the extent of the attack, then Amber knows first-hand what's happening in the rest of the country. And me, I've spent my entire life studying what happens when systems break. The more complex a civilization is, the harder and faster it falls. 'Ugly' is a mild word to describe it."

He stared thoughtfully at the threads of blue smoke rising from the pipe bowl. "For the fall of ours, this is a pretty nice place to be. Clear up here on the top of a mountain. Far from any concentration of population. Safe. With resources beyond our dreams."

Dr. Holly pointed at Thomas Star and Willy. Then he indicated Frank and Pam Tappan. "We have friends here. People you can rely on who won't slit your throats just to get whatever might be in your backpack. Advisors who can help you do what hundreds of millions will dream of and then die attempting: survive."

"Best listen to him," Frank called from behind Sam.

"What if it's not that bad?" Ashley asked. "Come on, the *fall* of civilization? This is America. Have a little faith."

"*Hic Roma est! Roma aeterna! Urbs et orbis!*" Dr. Holly exclaimed, raising his hands. "'This is Rome. Eternal Rome. City and planet.' Those words were undoubtedly uttered in the Roman Forum in A.D. 410...just before Alaric and his band of barbarians broke down the gates and sacked the city."

He centered his understanding gaze on Ashley. "Faith is a fantasy. What you *want* reality to be. What we need, folks, are cold, hard, facts that portray reality as it *is*."

"I want to be with my family," Ashley insisted. "Get it? I've got a girlfriend back there. Mom, Dad, my brothers and sisters."

Amber snapped her fingers for attention. "Come on, people. You came here as part of a scientific research project. To observe, formulate hypotheses, and test them. You came to do science, so let's act like scientists. Let's do the research, find out, as best we can, what's going on in the country. Then we'll make an informed decision about the best course of action."

I'm your only hope. Images from the nightmares Sam had had at the Tappan Ranch came back to haunt him.

He stood, taking a position beside Amber. "If it's as bad back there as I suspect it is, none of us, no matter how guilty or desperate we feel, want to be there. I know. My family is on Long Island."

He looked at Shyla, who'd been listening stoically. "Maybe Vermont's dodged the bullet, but you've got to get across twenty-five hundred miles of...well, who knows what to get there. Jon, the same for you trying to get to Massachusetts; but if the cities are bad, Boston could be in flames. And Danielle, don't you think your family would *want* you to be someplace safe? To know that however bad it is in Manhattan, that you'll be out of danger until this is over? Kirstin, sure, your dad is in Switzerland and out of harm's way, but the first place the government would protect is DC, so your mom's probably okay. How would she feel if you risked yourself, and something happened to you out on the road? What would she tell you to do?"

Sam searched their faces. "Come on, guys. Think! What would your families tell you to do if you could call them right now? What would you tell your own kids if the roles were reversed?"

Awkward, clumsy, Court—of all people—stood and said, "I'm with Amber and Dr. Holly. If the rest of you aren't, it sure as hell proves that computer science geeks are a whole lot smarter than anthro majors."

Dylan said, "Hey, my family's seven hours down the road in Denver, and I've got my own truck. The rest of you do what you want. I'm going as soon as we get back to the ranch."

Kirstin crossed her arms. "I'm with him. I'm following Dylan to Denver. Anyone who wants can ride with me."

"Fool girl," Amber whispered under her breath.

Shyla took a deep breath, and Sam never thought she'd looked as beautiful as she did that night with the firelight glowing on her serious face. "I'm staying. Put me down with the smart ones."

"I've got to try and get home," Ashley said angrily, rubbing the backs of her muscular arms.

"Jon?" Sam asked.

"Stay." Then he paused. "For the time being."

"I..." Shanteel shook her head. "I don't belong here. I just..." She threw her hands up. "I gotta think! That's all."

"Danielle?" Amber asked in clipped tones.

"Stay." But she didn't look happy saying it.

"Well, can't say I didn't try." Amber reached out, touched Sam's elbow. "Thanks for the backup. We saved all but three."

He watched her walk away, legs stiff, back arched, fists knotted. That tone of resignation in her voice? Sam imagined that military commanders said that after a tough mission.

He looked around the fire, wondering, *Saved? From what? And for how long?*

AN IDENTITY OF DIVISION

***

When I grew up, my grandfather made me read Dr. Martin Luther King's "Letter from a Birmingham Jail". *And who didn't have to listen to his* "I Have a Dream" *speech when they were in school?*

What Dr. King didn't understand was that if people were to be judged solely by their personal merits—heedless of color, creed, national origin, gender, sexual orientation, or whatever—it meant they were just like everyone else. The success of a color-blind society meant a loss of individuality. To become one with the faceless mass. A negation of that "special identity" that made a person or group unique.

And who doesn't want to be unique? Distinct? But to be different, you must first set yourself and your fellows apart from everyone else.

And when the collapse came, that made it so much easier to turn on those who were not "me and mine."

Excerpt from Breeze Tappan's *Journal*.

CHAPTER SEVENTEEN

* * *

THE LAST OF THE PURPLE LIGHT WAS FADING FROM OVER THE HIGH ABSAROKAS TO THE west, and the mosquitoes were humming when Sam walked down into the trees to pee. Had he done the right thing?

His urge to head home was so desperate it was like a physical ache in his soul. Who knew what was happening back in Hempstead? Long Island really was an island. If the bridges were closed and the ferries weren't running, there was no way off, unless you were lucky enough to have a boat.

Sure, he'd thrown his weight behind Amber and maybe convinced the majority of them to stay. At least for the time being. The sad truth was, he couldn't believe his own advice. He figured that had Dad known, he would have jumped to his feet, shaking his fist, yelling, "Get your ass back here and help your mother and me keep the damn doors open! We can't even hire a blind man if we can't pay his ass. You're our son, and we *need* you to get through this."

Walking back up the slope, Sam stopped at the edge of the trees, seeing Dr. Holly talking with Frank and Thomas Star where they sat at the fire. They didn't have to fret; this was their back yard. Pam carried out a cup of something, handing it to Court where he sat next to Ashley. They were listening thoughtfully to whatever the elders were saying. Jon sat on the far side by himself, lonely cords rising from his guitar.

Sam walked to his tent, surprised when Shyla's dark form emerged from the gloom. Hesitantly she asked, "Can we talk?"

"Sure."

To his surprise, she reached out, taking his hand. Her flashlight illuminated the way. The moment they were beyond the others' hearing, she said, "I wanted someplace private."

Her destination was a stony outcrop on the slope a couple of hundred yards above the fire. Best of all, she held his hand the entire way. He was acutely aware as she turned it loose and seated herself. As he settled on the stony perch beside her, she produced a can of bug spray.

"Best use it," she said. "They'll carry us away otherwise."

"Thanks." Then he was surprised to hear myself say, "But it would be worth being eaten just for the company."

"Gallant, too, huh?"

"Actually, I don't know where that came from. I'm not known for saying witty things to beautiful women." Sam looked down at his hands, smelling bug spray. "Maybe it's a new me. Everything else is confused. I'm even seeing Shoshoni spirits on cave walls. Who knows what's going to come out of my mouth next?"

"You worried about home?"

"Scared shitless."

"Somebody said 'The times make the person'. If they're right, we sure picked one hell of a time." She shrugged, looking down at the fire below, her features barely illuminated. "I don't think you've come to recognize yourself yet. Of all the graduate students in the department, you're the smartest. In ways I don't think you realize."

"That will be news to my committee chair."

"You've got a real-world feel for things. Call it an ability to see through the academic sophistry. I was thinking of that article on Neandertals going extinct because moderns moved into Europe with better winter clothing. You stood up in class and said, 'Wait a minute. Neandertals survived in glaciated Europe for five hundred thousand years. If the weather was going to kill them, it would have done so long before the moderns moved in a mere forty thousand years ago.' And then you added, 'And if they're extinct, why does fifteen percent of their DNA still exist in the modern human gene pool?'"

Sam grinned. "That's the trouble with so much of academia. It doesn't get tested against the real world." Which was probably his disconnect with his committee chair. The guy was almost desperate to jump on any new hypothesis and make it his own, but he'd never so much as produced a research design, let alone implemented one.

Call it an epiphany.

Shyla said, "That's my point. You see through things better than the others do."

"Well...thank you."

"So, tell me, Sam. Is staying the right thing? I need to hear your take on it."

He hunched forward, staring down at the fire where its light flickered on the front of the wall tents. It looked magical and safe. "I was arguing that with myself when you showed up. Amber was right about one thing: We need to know what's happening back in the world. After that I guess we think it through and give it the best shot."

"I think Court's assessment of the situation, bad as it is, is probably more right than wrong."

"Hope not, otherwise we're in a world of shit."

"Dr. Holly seemed to buy it."

"Down in the cave this afternoon that old medicine man told him that our world is dying. A spooky kind of place, that cave." He paused. "I'd like to think Dr. Holly wasn't superstitious, but he might have been predisposed to the contemplation of disaster."

Hell, Sam would have liked to think he wasn't superstitious either. Curious, huh? Even as he sat beside the most enchanting woman he'd ever known, the image of Water Ghost Woman lurked in the back of his mind. Assuming a man actually survived an encounter with her—so the story goes—she was supposed to grant him power when it came to women. And here he was, sitting beside the one woman...

Naw. Couldn't be.

The fine features on Shyla's face pinched. "If you were China, Russia, and Iran, could you have imagined a better way to take us down? Not a shot fired? I mean, they learned a lot about us from COVID. This was genius. Just push a button and crash your adversary's entire economy. Then sit back and watch the country tear itself apart."

"Hey, lighten up. We're out here on the edge of everything. We don't have any way of knowing how serious this really is."

"I saw those jets fly over today. I may be from Vermont, but that's waaaay out of the ordinary. And big fires burning all across the west? Think of the financial system just gone. In the blink of an eye. Tell me that everything didn't grind to a halt. Sure, most people would have waited patiently—right up until it became apparent that it wasn't going to be fixed. And when the government shut down communications?

That would have been the final straw. Bet the internet's gone, too."

"Yeah."

"You ever taken Dr. Hamrah's Anthro 330 class on culture and resource utilization?"

"Yep." He glanced sidelong at her. "You're talking about his model that uses resource flow through a society? The one that gives points and different valuations to production, distribution, and consumption? I applied it to the Norse in the eight hundreds and used it to explain Viking expansion across Europe."

"I plugged the data into the modern American economy." She paused. "Granted, it was a pretty rough fit. I mean, you can only collapse so many categories of data to get an incredibly complex system to fit such a crude model, but, to put it in Dr. Holly's terms, what it suggested was pretty ugly."

"What did you get?"

"Collapse." She paused. "A really precipitous collapse. Especially if the resource was money. We've been inflating the currency ever since 9/11 without the concomitant generation of wealth. I mean, if I can read the data for a simple statistical model, why couldn't Chinese economists with a lot more sophisticated instruments, computational power, and statistical programs?"

"I'm impressed."

"Why?" Then she paused. "Oh, I see. Because I'm Shyla Adams?"

"No. Wait. It's just that..."

"Yes?" Her tone was turning hostile.

"Okay, then tell me: You're a really smart woman. Why the act?"

She studied him thoughtfully, as if deciding what to say. "Here's the thing: I know how my looks affect men. I'm the stunningly gorgeous Shyla Adams, every man's heartthrob and fantasy. More to the point, I know how I affect women. They're just plain vicious and vindictive if they perceive you as a threat. As long as I'm vivacious, half-wild Shyla, the blonde bimbo isn't threatening. But if I came off as a hard-nosed intellectual, they'd do anything in their power to cut my throat. Used to make my life a whole lot easier."

"Used to?"

"That world's dead."

"Amber'd like you."

"Watch out for her. She's brittle. If the stories are true..."

"About that year she was an ISIS hostage?"

"Nice word for the way they treated her, isn't it?"

"Yeah, well, the miracle is that she's not in an institution."

"Just be careful around her. With all the shit coming down, she could really lose it. We're talking shattered and psychotic."

"Believe me, I hear you."

After a long pause, she asked, "Do you think you could ever kill someone?"

That hit him like a blind-side punch.

"Hey, I'm supposed to say, no way. Sane, sensitive people say that, right?" He paused. "But after the last couple of days? I've had to ask myself some really hard questions. If it came down to my life...or those I loved and cared for...?"

After he let it hang, she asked, "What if a guy came in out of the dark and put a gun to Kirstin's head?"

"If he shoots her, do I get her BMW?"

"Don't joke. I'm serious. He's got a gun to Kirstin's head, demanding that we all turn over our personal property and money? You can reach Pam's pistol in the cook tent. What do you do? Your call, Sam."

He bit his lip, paused, trying to put it into words. "If we're right. If our world's dead. The old rules are gone. I once heard someone say that nations didn't live by moralities, but by laws. If we're in collapse, the laws are gone. Dr. Holly said it all when he said that ultimately it's a matter of survival."

He squeezed his eyes shut, shook his head. "God damn, did I really just say that?"

"For years we've had models for the collapse of the modern state operating right in front of us: Libya, Syria, Venezuela. That's coming here. It's already started. Amber's right, we'll be no different."

Sam gestured to the camp below. "Hard to believe, but this is my world now. Our world. It may be all that we've got left." He paused. "Dr. Holly's right. There are worse places to wait out the apocalypse. And meanwhile, maybe the president can pull some sort of a rabbit out of the hat."

"It'll mean a dictatorship." Her soft laugh was bitter. "So much for social justice." A pause. "Tomorrow, I'm going to ask Pam to teach me how to shoot." She was as serious as a heart attack when she asked, "Want to learn with me?"

If it had been anyone but Shyla... "Sure."

What the hell? These were guns they were talking about. To cover his disquiet he added, "Boy, is Jim ever going to be surprised when he sees you next."

"Jim won't make it to the end of the month. If he isn't dead already."

"That's pretty harsh."

"Jim is nothing without a football and his trust fund. Wouldn't surprise me to learn he ate every pill in the medicine cabinet. That, or jumped headlong out of Daddy's fifty-seventh story window in Manhattan."

Sam sat silently, thankful for the first time for the endless struggle he had had just to get out of The Yucateca's kitchen, let alone to college.

After a couple of seconds, she glanced at him. "What about you? Got anything to confess?"

"I meant it when I said I was scared shitless. I mean, damn, Shyla, how do you deal with the end of the world? You can fit your head around it academically: All states eventually fail. But to know that we're going to be seeing it, living it? How do you cope?"

"Yeah, why'd it have to happen to us, huh?"

They stared out at the night. The coyotes were yipping in a chorus somewhere, and the occasion calls of the nighthawks added to the empty feeling.

"Shyla, you wanted my take on whether to try and travel back East? Every fiber of my being wants to go. To get back to Mom and Dad and that crummy little restaurant. My brain, however, tells me it's a recipe for disaster."

Shyla took a deep breath, exhaling her tension. "Yeah. I'm with you. But Sam, bad times are coming, and even if I have to kill someone, I will not be a helpless victim."

THE ENEMY IS US

***

Prior to the collapse, a media personality for the Religious Right in the abortion war, stated: "We shouldn't be obsessing over if we're going to have a Civil War over abortion. Our efforts should be on how to win it." A spokesperson for Pro Choice blithely proclaimed, "They will not win this war on women, not even if it means blood in the streets!"

Fools! Fucking imbecilic fools! I saw blood in the streets. The burning buildings. Watched looters smashing store windows. Saw them destroy everything in their moment of wrath. And when they were done, all they had to look forward to was wreckage, filth, starvation, and darkness.

Excerpt from Breeze Tappan's *Journal.*

CHAPTER EIGHTEEN

***

ON THE VERGE OF SHIVERING, SAM AWAKENED THE NEXT MORNING. BREATHING THE heavy and damp air stung his nose where it poked out of the safe warmth of his sleeping bag. Shuffling over to the door, he unzipped it and stared out into a gloomy darkness. He could barely make out Court's tent next to his.

Dressing quickly in the chill, he pulled on his boots and stepped out into an opaque world. He had seen thick fog before, but nothing like this. A person couldn't see more than twenty feet.

Sound carried though; he could hear Pam Tappan in the cook tent where pans collided, and utensils clinked metallically.

He almost got lost when he ambled down into the trees to relieve himself. Talk about disorienting. For a moment Sam just stood, a sensation of panic growing as he stared around at the few dark tree trunks visible in the thick haze. But which way had he come to reach this spot?

He tipped his head back, not even seeing a lighter gloom among the shadowy branches that disappeared on their way up...

Up. Camp was up. That was the way back.

He encountered civilization when he found the back of Dylan's tent and barely avoided tripping over the tent strings. He could hear whispering inside, followed by a soft female sigh and the rustling of a sleeping bag.

Okay, so Dylan and Kirstin had hooked up. Bless them.

He tiptoed around the tent's strings and headed to the cook tent. Heard more voices. He stepped inside the door flap. A Coleman lantern cast its glaring white light across the portable spice cabinet, Coleman stoves, stacked plates, silverware, and water jugs. The big, enameled coffee pot was steaming and sending out a wondrous aroma where it sat on the flat-topped heat stove near the door. He could hear the crackle as a fire burned inside.

In the back of the tent, Pam stood pressed against Shyla, her body conforming to Shyla's back, arms wrapped around her. What Sam's confused glance first took as intimacy vanished as he recognized the deadly piece of metal held in Shyla's hands.

"That's right," Pam was saying as she pressed Shyla's elbow up slightly. "See how the sight picture stabilizes? How you don't wobble as much?"

Pam backed away a step, head cocked as she inspected Shyla's stance and the position of her head and arms.

"Now, breathe. Big breath in, half breath out. Good. Caress the trigger like you would a lover, increasing the pressure carefully."

Click!

Sam jumped.

Pam asked, "Did you see the sights wobble?"

"A little," Shyla told her.

"Try it again."

Sam swallowed hard as Shyla cocked the big gun, the hammer clicks loud over the hiss of the Coleman lantern. Shyla then carefully positioned her hands on the gun and extended it.

"Breathe like I told you," Pam said. "Sight picture. Now the trigger."

Shyla's finger slipped down from the frame to the trigger.

"Good. Now, caress."

Click!

"How was that?" Pam asked.

"Better. I didn't know it was going off."

"Perfect. We'll practice some more before..." Pam turned, stopping short as she discovered Sam in the doorway. "Oh, Sam. You ready for coffee? Breakfast is a half-an-hour out yet. Frank should have the fire stoked."

"Uh...yeah." He hoped his voice didn't squeak.

Shyla turned, smile radiant, a gleam behind her excited eyes. "It's easier than I thought, Sam. Just hold still and caress the trigger."

Pam laughed as she bustled over, grabbed a hot pad, and picked up the coffee pot from the stove. As she poured, she said, "Oh, sure.

Easy when you're dry firing. Everything changes when the gun goes off for real. Not only is the bang deafening, but the recoil jerks the barrel up and back. And you don't always have time to get in position and think it through before you shoot."

"When can I shoot for real?" Shyla was thoughtfully examining the big revolver.

"Back at the ranch. And not with that pistol. That's a Freedom Arms .454 Casull. That's my bear gun. You're going to start with a .22."

"Sam? You want to try?" Shyla asked, turquoise eyes dancing.

Pam shot him an evaluative look. "You part of this, too?"

"We decided last night," Shyla told her before Sam could find the words to back out gracefully. "Sam and I, well, we think it might be something to know given what's been happening."

Sam nodded in dumb acceptance. It had been one thing to agree up on the hill last night when it was all so academic. Another when the big silver handgun was right there, looking so lethal.

So, Sam, old pal, Shyla's looking you right in the eye.

Say no, and he'd lose her.

He stepped over, teeth gritted, and told himself: *It's not loaded. No bullets.*

Pam gave him that suspicious look, as if she could see right through to the part of him that was suddenly scared stiff.

"What do I do?"

Pam glanced at her watch. "This will have to be real quick. Shyla, show him."

"Here, step over here. We're going to point the gun up toward the tent corner, which is a safe direction. We never point the gun at anything we don't want to shoot. Now, here's how you hold it."

Maybe it was the fact that Shyla put it in his hands. He expected his skin to crawl at the touch, or that it would be icy cold and oily. The grip was warm as it slipped into his palm. Shyla molded the web of his right hand around the back, her fingers dancing on his skin. He let her shape him to the weapon as if he were a piece of clay and she the sculptor of his future.

"Feet apart a little wider," Pam coached as Shyla positioned Sam.

He wasn't ready for how heavy the gun was when she finally let loose of it. Then Shyla stepped close behind him. He caught her scent and filled his nostrils. This was pure woman after days in field camp. Not the scent of shampoo or perfume, but her, and it almost made him shiver.

She pressed close as she maneuvered his arms. His heart began to beat with an increased tension. A jet of excitement burst through him each time she touched him.

"Now, look down the barrel," Shyla said, her lips inches from his ear, her breath warm. "See the blade in the notch?"

Sam did. That was the sight picture, and it was jumping with each shuddering beat of his heart.

"Hold that sight picture. Steady," she whispered, voice almost sultry. "Deep breath. Good. Now let it half out so that your lungs are in balance. That's it. Lower your finger to the trigger. Easy. And caress it the way you would a lover."

He imagined not the hard curve of trigger, but her soft skin slipping beneath...

Click!

Sam jerked as if bitten, the image vanishing.

"I did the same thing," Shyla said happily. "Let's try again. Cock it like I showed you."

Okay, he could do this. Hell, he could do this all day. Anything to keep her so close.

Time went away, and he lost track of how many times he clicked that big heavy revolver. Somewhere in the process, he lost his old self. He wanted Shyla's approval. Wanted her to be proud of him.

And then they switched, and he got to coach her, all under Pam's watchful eyes when she could spare them a glance as she hustled about getting breakfast ready.

He might have been in dream-lust with Shyla Adams before, but that morning he fell in love with the woman. Had anyone told him "You'll find your happiness in a cook tent in Wyoming, fake-shooting a large handgun with a beautiful woman in the light of a Coleman lantern", he'd have suggested they see a psychiatrist about a prescription for Zyprexa.

Yet, there he was, cocking, breathing, finger on trigger, *click*. Sharing the growing excitement with Shyla, bonding over this crazy, taboo, instrument of death.

With it came the realization that whatever it took to keep her trust, faith, and respect, he would do.

In a complete reshuffling of his life and priorities, he *had* to be worthy of this woman. To share her company, shoulder her burdens, protect her, and keep her close.

If, by God, it took mastering a gun to do it, well, shit, Sam Delgado guessed he'd already sold his soul.

"Enough for now, you two," Pam told them with a smile. "Breakfast is ready. But first, load it up, Shyla, just like I showed you. Then stick it back in the holster so it's ready."

Sam watched in fascination as Shyla walked over to the cooler, pulled the hammer back to half-cock, and opened the loading gate. The gun clicked softly—just like in the movies—as she turned the cylinder. Her slim fingers inserted the blunt-nosed bullets one by one. Grace and elegance mastering the beast.

"Point it at the ground," Pam ordered as Shyla carefully lowered the hammer from half-cock.

"Let me see." Pam stepped over, took the gun, and turned the cylinder as she inspected the loads. She shoved it back in its holster, and added, "Always check your load yourself. Never depend on anyone else to do it. Your life might depend on it."

Then she gave them a conspiratorial wink.

In a trance-like state Sam followed Shyla out with a plate heaped with eggs, potatoes, and sausage. The sum of the events: Wyoming; the crisis; the cave; Shyla; and this morning with the gun; even then he knew it for what it was—a watershed.

The man he had been had slipped off into the past to become a shadow figure.

As he seated himself next to Shyla, he took a moment to stare into her eyes, memorizing how the blue surrounding the pupils shaded into green. "We're going to make it," he told her. "I'm going to see to that."

She gave him a special smile, reached out, laid a hand on his shoulder. "Not the sort of thing you want to face alone, is it?"

He caught himself an instant before he gushed something trite and stupid. He'd meant the overall situation; she'd taken it to a more intimate level.

Amber appeared out of the mist, got breakfast, and walked over to the fire. Taking a seat beside them, she squinted around at the dull fog, and said, "Don't think we're heading down the hill today. Not until this clears."

Sam considered the thick mist. "Can you imagine crossing slickside?"

"Might be easier," Shyla said over a mouthful of steaming eggs. "You could ride across that section like a happy idiot without seeing how far you could fall."

Amber gave a quick laugh of agreement before saying, "Sam, I want you to get the field notes packed up and ready to go. Make sure the rest of the gear is picked up and in the dig kits. We'll leave it in the supply tent for the time being."

Her weary eyes looked up at the fog. "Meanwhile, we'll pray for a miracle and hope this isn't as black as we think. That maybe we can come back and finish the project."

Shyla told him, "I'll give you a hand. With two of us, it'll be done in half the time."

"Thanks." He noticed that her hair was silvered with tiny droplets of mist. It took all of his willpower to keep from reaching out and running a fingertip along the side of her cheek.

And then there was Amber. Angular and brittle Amber, all edges, like shards of broken glass. Bestial men had done that to her, abused and broken her.

I will never let that happen to Shyla.

Memory of the revolver in his hands, substantial, controlled in his grip as the hammer fell, made him think he might actually have a chance of keeping that promise.

It wasn't until the rest of the crew had eaten that Pam stepped over to say, "Shanteel didn't show up for breakfast."

"Might have overslept," Sam said, getting up. "I'll go give her tent a shake."

But after he made his way through the thick fog, calling out, "Shanteel, rise and shine," her tent was empty.

THE INCONCEIVABLE MOMENT

* * *

We were on motorcycles. Only bikes could get through the snarled traffic. Mimi, Felix, and Jill and me were trying to get out of the city. I saw them first: three people, one sprawled woman, two men who looked like they had laid down to take a nap. Their clothing was mussed, pockets pulled out while being robbed. The thing that hit me was the half-lidded, sightless stare. The slack expressions. The realization that they were dead. That the discoloration on their chests was drying blood.

Just lying there on the corner of Wadsworth and Kipling.

Around us no one cared. Traffic lights were out. The other drivers trying to thread their way through the jammed intersection just stared. Probably couldn't believe it. And just drove on.

Pointless death was too new to them.

It wouldn't be that way for long. By the end of the week, a dead person lying at the side of the road made the same impression as a road-killed deer, raccoon, or rabbit. All you had time for was the hint of sadness, then you were past it with more important things to think about.

Excerpt from Breeze Tappan's *Journal.*

CHAPTER NINETEEN

* * *

THE FOG SLOWLY DRIFTED DOWN TO LEAVE THE CAMP IN A MAGICAL WORLD OF BRIGHT sunlight and crystal blue skies. The Absaroka Range's majestic and jagged peaks shone in the bright sunlight, gleaming, each crevice cast in dark shadow. Patchy snow fields shimmered in purest white.

Penthouse Ridge—as they had come to call it—the surrounding high country, and the distant Wind River Mountains appeared as islands of up-thrust stone floating on a silver-white sea of cottony cloud. Beyond awesome, the sight of it was enough to stop a person's breath short.

And the students hardly noticed, concerned as they were to discover what had happened to Shanteel. Shouts of "Shanteel!" carried on the morning air as groups searched high and wide.

Her tent and possessions were undisturbed, her sleeping bag top thrown back as she'd no doubt left it when she crawled out that morning. Her personal items looked as if she'd just stepped out; toothbrush and toothpaste were set beside the door, along with a water bottle, as though in preparation for her return.

"Looks to me like she headed down to the latrine and got lost in the fog," Frank declared, staring down the forested slope to where the tarp-wrapped toilet could barely be seen amidst the dark-gray maze of trunks and branches.

Sam remembered how disoriented he had been that morning. "Yeah," he agreed, "I almost got lost myself."

"Me, too," Court chimed in. "If I hadn't heard people talking up at camp, I'd have had no idea which way to go."

"Damn it!" Frank knotted a fist, expression grim. "This is my fault."

"How's that?" Amber asked.

"Forgot to give the lecture." Frank stared anxiously down into the

dark timber. "If you get lost, walk downhill. Follow the water. Every
drainage on this side of the divide will come out at the house. On the
south side of the divide, every drainage will come out at a ranch on
the Wind River."

Thomas Star took a deep breath. "Me and Willy will cut for sign
on our way back home. If she went that way, we'll find her."

"Yeah," Willy agreed. "So, if she left before breakfast, and it's
nearly eleven, how far could she have gone?"

"In a straight line?" Frank made a face. "Five or six miles, but
this country's anything but straight. Lost, she'd wind around, skirt
canyons... Hell, I don't know."

He turned, cupping hands around his mouth. "Pam! Signal shot.
Ten-minute intervals."

At the cook tent, Pam waved back and vanished inside the smaller
tent she and Frank shared. A moment later she emerged with a rifle,
stepped clear, and raised the muzzle to the sky.

The rifle's report cracked loudly, everyone in view turning in
surprise.

"She'll hear that," Amber said with relief.

"There's a catch," Willy told her. "She'll know which way it comes
from if she's in line of sight, or out in the open. If she's in timber, or
around a shoulder of the mountain, or in one of the canyons where the
echoes bounce around? That can be really confusing."

Frank kept knotting and unknotting his fist, as if he blamed himself.
"At least she'll know we're looking for her. Just knowing that someone's out there? You'd be surprised what a relief that can be when
you're lost. If she's got any smarts, she'll find a high point, listen for
the next shot, and follow it in."

At Sam's side, Shyla said, "Another good use for a gun, huh?
'Cause, if Shanteel had one, she could shoot, and we'd be able to
find her, right?"

"That's how we do it when we have elk down," Frank told her.

"Hey," Amber pointed. "There's Brandon. Maybe he's seen her."

As if out of nowhere, like a magical centaur on his mahogany-col-
ored horse, Brandon pulled up beside where Pam stood. He leaned
down from the saddle, talking to his mother. One of the ranch dogs,
Talbot, was demanding that Pam pet him as he wound around her

legs, tail whipping.

Brandon reined around, his horse sauntering their direction. "Missing the black girl, huh?"

"We think *Shanteel* got lost in the soup this morning," Frank told him, looking back toward the trail to the ranch. "Where's Grandad?"

"He's in town." Brandon gave the rest of the crew a thoughtful look. "Big meeting with some guy named Kevin Edgewater. He's from Homeland Security. Story is that Governor Agar threw Edgewater's ass out of Cheyenne. He's got his local guys with him. Including our lazy-assed excuse for a sheriff. Says he's in charge of the entire Basin. Then there's the county FEMA director backing Edgewater. That's your old friend Steve Fallow."

"Figures. He's always looking to be more than he is, isn't he?" Frank looked even more sour.

"Anyhow," Brandon continued, "Ty Rankin drove out last night special. Said that Grandad should be there along with Fred Willson, Merlin Smith, and some of the other political bigwigs."

"Why do I not like the sound of this?" Frank asked.

"Maybe because Ty told Grandad, and I quote, 'You might want to pack your nineteen eleven just in case.'"

"Shit." Frank winced, expression tightening.

"You're all ready to go?" Brandon looked around where people had piled their packs and belongings. "Meggan and I brought the mule string up. She's down watering them at the spring. You want to pack up while I go find Shanteel?"

The way he said it was no more concerned than someone at home saying, "You want me to pick up John from the office, and we'll meet for beers and burgers at four?"

"That'd be a load off my mind," Frank said.

Sam remembered the smoldering resentment between Shanteel and Brandon. How good an idea was this?

"Yeah," Brandon said easily. "I'll take something of hers for scent. Ride a circle. Have Talbot sniff while I watch for sign. If she's up high, I'll have her in a couple of hours. If she's got down in the canyons, might take a bit longer. Saddle old Theo for her to ride, and I'll take him along. Oh, and pack her bedroll in case there's complications."

Brandon reined his horse around, trotting the animal back

down toward where the mule string was drinking under Meggan's watchful eye.

"Just like that?" Amber asked. "He's going to find her?"

Willy laughed. "That kid? Brandon could track a bumble bee across a meadow. And do it two days after the fact."

Sam touched Amber on the sleeve, indicating she stay as the rest walked over to where Pam was bent over some of the packs.

"What's up?" she asked.

"Brandon and Shanteel don't exactly like each other. The other night at the fire, they were the last to leave, both of them doing this 'I could kill you' eye duel. You sure we shouldn't say something?"

Amber glanced at Shyla, who shrugged.

"Let me talk to Evan. See what he says. In the meantime, you and Shyla get everyone ready to go."

"Yes, boss lady." Sam paused. "Out of curiosity, what's a nineteen eleven?"

Amber's blue eyes had a nutty kind of intensity. "It's a gun, Sam. 1911 is the model number. Usually in .45 caliber. A SEAL once told me he thought it was the finest combat handgun ever designed."

Must have been some kind of meeting old Bill had gone to. Made Sam wonder what happened if someone denied a motion from the floor.

As Amber walked off to find Dr. Holly, he glanced at Shyla and raised his eyebrows in a "who knows" gesture. He could feel the tension in the air as he and Shyla headed over to where the crew was piling their gear. They got more incredulous looks when they explained that Brandon was going out to find Shanteel.

"Now *that* ought to be interesting," Kirstin noted with distaste. "Think he'll bring her back over the saddle, or just leave her to rot in a canyon?"

"God," Shyla said with a start, "what do you think Brandon is?"

"A redneck bigot?" Dylan suggested with fake mildness. "I overheard Shanteel call him a Cracker under her breath once."

"I think I'd rather be lost in the wildness with a chainsaw murderer," Danielle added. "Something about that guy creeps me out."

"I think we ought to go looking for her." Ashley brushed her thick blonde hair back, squinting as she looked around at the horizon as if to spot the wayward Shanteel.

Shyla asked, "What if all those clouds rise again, and we're out there? Think you could find your way back to camp when you can't see ten feet?"

"Walk downhill." Sam repeated Frank's advice. "Pay attention to this: Follow the water. It runs downhill, right? If you're on this side of the drainage, the creeks will lead you out at the Tappan Ranch. Remember that, all of you. And now, here's what's going to happen: We're all packing up. Riding down the mountain."

"And Shanteel?" Kirstin demanded.

"Brandon will find her and bring her back," Sam said firmly, hoping he wasn't lying through his teeth. "Bet she's back at the ranch before dark."

"She better be," Dylan said, "because she said she's heading to Denver with us."

"You're going to leave her up here with that cowboy racist son of a bitch?" Kirstin almost shrilled. "*Abandon* her? To *him*?"

Sam bent down to glare into her wide brown eyes. "She'll *be fine*! Willy says that Brandon's the best tracker on the mountain, and he'll keep her safe. And you believe Willy, don't you? He's an *Indian,* and they don't lie."

Sam expected her to say, "Bullshit. People are people, and they all lie." Instead, she nodded in agreement, a token to her politically correct belief in stereotypes.

"Meggan's coming with the mules. Let's get packed, people." Sam cocked his jaw, snapping, "Now!"

Pam fired off another signal shot. It sounded like the crack of doom.

SOCIAL JUSTICE?

***

When it came to social justice, I was a poser. I came from a rural Wyoming ranching background. I left home under a thundering black cloud fueled by anger and recrimination. So as soon as I landed in Denver, at the university, I shed every bit of my previous red-neck conservative life. The last thing I wanted my liberal, socialist, progressive circle of friends to know was that I had been a rodeo queen. Yeah, really. Like, horse, hat, boots, and spurs.

I was a hypocrite. Even as I adopted all those progressive Democratic ideals, I was studying to be an investment banker. The ultimate capitalist. My friends might have chattered on about the virtues of socialism, but I could never bring myself to mention its failures. I might have voted for gun control candidates, but I still kept my S&W pistol hidden in my room. Sure, I wanted free education, health care, and redistribution of wealth, but that didn't mean I was willing to bankrupt the country to get it.

Try as I might, I guess I couldn't shake that damned practical horse-sense ethic my family had pounded into my bones.

In the end, it saved my life.

Excerpt from Breeze Tappan's *Journal.*

CHAPTER TWENTY

***

SAM WOULD FOREVER REMEMBER KIRSTIN AND DYLAN'S DEPARTURE. THE CREW HAD BARELY arrived back at the ranch, maybe not as stiff and sore as when they had ridden up the mountain, but aching, burning, and hurting, nonetheless.

Nor were they the only ones. On the trail down, just after it started to rain, they had no more than made the creek-side fork when Thomas Star and Willy came riding up behind them on mud-spattered horses, calling out, "Hey, you take extra guests? The kind who can't pay?"

"What happened?" Frank had called back.

"That storm moved in thick on the south side of the divide," Thomas returned. "Me, I'd a gone for it. Willy, here, he's young yet. Filled with caution, you know? Told me, 'Grampa, we're following the Tappans down to their place.' Said he didn't want to have to pack my broken bones back home over the steep places."

"Glad Willy's got all the sense in the family," Frank called back. "Celia's room is empty."

Somehow, knowing Thomas and Willy were riding along behind had reassured Sam. He kept looking around in the shadowy places along the trail, halfway expecting to see *Nynymbi*.

Being back at the ranch came as a relief. Houses. Running water. Electricity. A shower in the bunkhouse, brief though it might have to be.

The rain had turned from big drops to fine drizzle by the time they pulled up at the barn and swung down from the horses. All of them were soaked to the bone. Most shivering.

As Sam hit the ground, he was calling out orders to the crew. And together—under Frank and Pam's supervision—they unsaddled their horses, brushed them, and turned them out into the corral.

Sam even remembered to delegate Danielle and Court, who were shivering the worst, to get the oats.

Shyla and he did the work side-by-side, helping each other. Despite their numb fingers, shivers, and puffing breath, he loved every second of it. Curious, but he thought they seemed to anticipate each other's actions, as if they'd been a team for years.

Sam, Shyla, Frank, and Pam were still pulling saddles off mules when Dylan and Kirstin walked back from a restroom break to announce, "Who all is going with us?"

Everyone stopped, staring through the drizzle to where Dylan stood, hands thrust in his pockets, one leg defiantly forward.

"Ashley? Get your stuff. We're out of here," Kirstin stated factually, her brown hair hanging in wet strands. "Anyone who wants to try for home, this is your chance. We want you all to come. Together, with our cash pooled, we'll be able to go a lot farther."

"What about the roadblocks?" Danielle asked.

"We don't believe there are any roadblocks." Kirstin flipped her wet hair back.

Amber was over at Dr. Holly's cabin, seeing to the field reports. Sam bit his lip and walked out in front of the pair. "Don't do this," he said reasonably. "Not until we have a chance to see what the smart move is."

"We may not have time for that," Dylan said firmly. "It's four-thirty now. Driving straight through, Kirstin and I are going to be in Denver a little after midnight." He looked around. "Sleeping in a real bed. After a long, hot shower. Maybe go out to a restaurant for breakfast in the morning."

"Not stuck out here shivering to death in the *fucking* wilderness." Kirstin almost spat the words. "Ashley, I said, go get your stuff."

But Ashley had stopped short, shivering, her soaked hair dripping. Her face reflected agony, tears leaking down her cheeks to mix with the rain.

"Thought you were going to wait for Shanteel." Sam crossed his arms. "Giving up on her already? What was the word? *Abandoned?* Wasn't that it?"

"No." Dylan jutted his jaw defiantly. "It's just that this is our chance. Right now. Before Amber can do anything to stop us. We wouldn't put it past her to take us prisoner or something."

"The woman's a psycho," Kirstin agreed. "And Shanteel? If you think that sociopath up there is really going to bring her back, you're crazier than Amber."

Sam was painfully aware at the way Pam and Frank stiffened, at the flaring anger on their faces.

"We're out of here," Dylan insisted. "You'll have to shoot us to stop us."

Sam said, "Last I heard, Denver was under curfew; the National Guard was patrolling the streets. The people there were shooting each other, and half the city was on fire. Or did you listen to a different radio station than we did?"

"Well, they surely got that taken care of," Dylan insisted. "That was, like, a week ago."

Dylan looked past Sam, coaxing, "Come on, people. This is your chance. Maybe your last chance. Ashley? You coming?"

Sam turned, facing the rest of the crew. "Be smart. Think. Let us figure out what's going on, okay? Dylan and Kirstin might not even make it out of the Basin before being turned back. Or worse, might make it to Casper, or maybe Cheyenne, and hit a roadblock." A beat. "Tomorrow, we'll go into town, see what the news is."

"Last call," Dylan snapped, turning around, and taking Kirstin's arm.

Sam could read the crew's growing desperation, all but Court and Shyla who stepped over to stand with him.

Shyla pleaded, "Jon, Ashley, Danielle, we already lost Shanteel when she went off on her own. At least give it another day. Damn it, people, *think*!"

"And what?" Danielle asked. "They've got the cars!"

"We've got the van," Court answered.

Shyla raised her hands in a reasonable gesture. "Hey, listen, I'm smart enough to know a good thing when I see it. I'm staying."

She raised her voice, calling, "Frank? Pam? Are we welcome here, especially if we pitch in, tackle some of the chores, earn our keep?"

"Hell, yes!" Frank and Pam had kept silent. Especially after the insult to their son. Maybe even figuring that the more who left, the fewer mouths they had to feed.

Now Frank stepped forward saying, "People, don't go out there.

Not yet. Not until we know what's going on. If you don't trust Amber, that's fine. But I've known Evan for years. He'll do right by you." He indicated Sam with a nod of his head. "So will Sam here, if I'm any judge of character."

That sort of set Sam back.

But he didn't have time to think about it as he said, "What's left of us, we'll make it. Or at least give it the best shot."

Ashley was openly sobbing now. Her voice was a miserable whisper. "I'm staying."

Dylan made for his truck, opened the door. He paused—one foot on the door frame—and called, "We're *leaving!*"

"The smart ones stay," Court said simply. "How incredibly Darwinian for a bunch of anthropologists."

Kirstin's BMW started, followed by Dylan's truck.

Sam and the crew stood in silence, rain falling, and watched as both vehicles backed out. Hesitated. Each one staring back over the seats. When no one moved, they drove off into the gray gloom.

"Okay, all," Sam said, "Let's get the mules unloaded and let them roll."

"Hope this was the right choice," Danielle muttered under her breath as she walked past Sam.

Yeah, me too, Sam thought as he watched Dylan and Kirstin's vehicles disappear off to the stormy east.

RATING OUR WAY TO APOCALYPSE

***

I've talked about social media, sectionalism, politics, religion, social justice, abortion, gun control, self-sorting, and all the manifest issues that divided Americans to the point they hated each other. But one of the real monsters was the media. The self-serving, blathering personalities who could adopt such expressions of self-righteous indignation when dissing the "other side". All they were doing was driving the wedge deeper, reinforcing the prejudices of their audience. Had they not first created the environment, the public humiliation of Americans with whom they disagreed would not have become not only acceptable, but the norm.

They did it, of course, for ratings. The larger and more radical their audience, the greater the financial reward.

Wonder who they blamed when the lights went out in their million-dollar apartments on the West Side? When their phones were cut off, and their drivers didn't bring the limo around to take them to the studio set for their next broadcast?

Excerpt from Breeze Tappan's *Journal*.

CHAPTER TWENTY-ONE

***

SUPPER THAT NIGHT WAS A SOMBER AFFAIR. THE WHOLE CREW PACKED AROUND THE DINING room table this time, every one of them brimming with worry. Shanteel and Brandon still hadn't showed up, and the rain had gotten worse; the temperature—last anyone checked—had dropped down into the high thirties. If it was that cold here, Frank said it had to be snowing up in the high country.

Thomas agreed, carefully breaking a roll in two before spreading butter on it. Of all of in attendance, he and Willy seemed the most at ease.

Most of the crew had a mixed anxiety—a fear that they'd made the wrong choice in staying, against the real concern that Kirstin and Dylan were headed off into disaster. All that was churned up with worry about what was happening to their homes, families, and loved ones back East.

That latter anxiety was fed by the absolute lack of news. Sure, the big TV in the front room worked, but all it did was post scrolling lines of rules and regulations, many of which were absolutely ludicrous: *Right of way will immediately be granted to military vehicles.*

Yeah, right. As if anyone in their right mind was going to stand in front of a tank.

Nor were those the only worries pressing down.

"Something's wrong. Bill's not back," Meggan kept repeating. Her glance kept straying to the door, no doubt praying that he might walk into the room at any second.

"Must be quite a meeting," Pam added, periodically sending her glance that way as well.

"Ah, it's Dad and his old friends," Frank answered bluffly.

"Wouldn't be the first time he and the rest stopped off for a drink and the chance to swap lies about the old days."

Sam kept thinking of that 1911 old Bill was packing.

"What about Brandon?" Sam asked. "It's long after dark. The storm doesn't seem to be letting up. Do we have *two* people lost out there now?"

Pam chuckled in a way that was supposed to ease tension. It didn't. "Sam, any time you're in the back country, it's dangerous. There's a thousand ways to get into trouble, from lightning to a tree falling on you. That son of mine? He knows that country better than the elk do."

"Don't none of you worry about Brandon," Willy said, lips oddly quirked as he sipped from his wine. "Can't think of anyone I'd rather be in the mountains with."

"What about the storm?" Sam asked.

"He and Shanteel will hole up," Thomas replied with a shrug. "There's always shelter to be had in mountain country. It's the open plains that will kill you."

Frank said softly, "He'll bring Shanteel back." He looked around the table. "I know there's some concern about how he and the girl might feel about each other, but I give you my word, if there's breath in his body, he'll get her back here safely."

"Why?" Amber asked sharply. She'd been bitter from the moment she stepped out of Dr. Holly's cabin to see Dylan and Kirstin's vehicles vanishing into the distance. Sam thought it was a feeling of having been betrayed, and it cut more deeply given Amber's history.

"Because he's a Tappan," Meggan answered somewhat stiffly. "We take care of our own. And that young woman is one of us, no matter where she comes from, or what she thinks of us."

Meggan glared around the table, eyes filled with green fire. "You think Brandon gives a damn that she's black? That she thinks we're all racist hicks? Knowing Brandon, he's all-fired amused by the notion that he'll bust his silly neck to save a woman who despises the life he lives and the ground he walks on."

"Easy, Meggan." Frank raised a hand.

"Something I gotta say." Thomas spoke softly, eyes absently fixed on the center of the table. "I know it don't work this way in the East. And it doesn't work in a lot of places in the West no more either, but here, in this place, you are judged by what you do and believe, not by where you come from, or what you look like."

"Take these *taipos*," Willy flicked his fingers at Frank and Pam. "Gave Grampa and me Brandon and Celia's beds 'till the storm blows over'. Some places they'd say, 'You Indians can sleep in the barn' but more likely they'd tell us, 'Be off our land by dark and don't come back'."

Frank smiled thinly. "Yeah, and come morning, you can help feed, then move the water on the alfalfa." He looked around the table, mildly asking, "Anyone else want more wine? I opened one of the good bottles. McNab Ridge. They make one of the best Petite Sirah wines in the world."

Dr. Holly extended his mostly empty glass. As Frank poured, he added, "One day at a time, folks. That's how we're going to get through this."

Lights flashed in the window, and everyone scrambled for the front room and out onto the porch.

Sam was hoping with all his might that it would be Dylan and Kirstin. Instead, old Bill's big dual-wheel one-ton Dodge gleamed wetly in the porch lights.

Old Bill opened the door, hitched his stiff left leg out, and stepped down. Rain pounded on the brim of his hat; beneath it Sam could see the man's steely eyes taking in just the Jeep and the van. Then those remaining on the porch.

"What's happened, Bill?" Meggan demanded, stepping down to wrap him in a bear hug despite the downpour.

"Where'd those vehicles go?" he demanded first thing.

Dr. Holly told him, "The kids that owned them struck out for Denver."

"Aw, shit." Bill tucked an arm around Meggan, using the other to wave everyone back into the house. "In case you didn't notice, it's Goddamn cold and raining. Let's get back inside. I'm only gonna tell this once, and by God I'm gonna need a stiff whiskey to get through it."

After they all filed into the big front room, Bill took off his coat—a long-tailed thing with a Western-cut yoke on the shoulders. Sam could just see the pistol grip sticking out of a brown-leather holster on Bill's right side. Then the old rancher limped over to his recliner and plopped himself down.

Meggan elbowed through the crowd, handing Bill a whiskey tumbler filled with three fingers of amber.

"Light and set," he said, taking the drink.

Dr. Holly, Amber, Pam, and Frank got the couch. The crew dropped to the buffalo rug, while Sam stood in the rear by the stuffed elk that he had once thought so garish and barbaric.

Shyla, as if sensing the gravity, stood beside him, taking his hand and giving it a squeeze. Her fine features were pinched, tension in the set of her full lips.

"All hell's broke loose," Bill began before people reached their seats. "Had a meeting today with our idiot FEMA director and some dickhead from Homeland Security. Everything's gone to shit."

"How so?" Frank demanded.

Old Bill looked at his son through eyes that seemed to peer out of Hell itself. "It's about as bad as it can get, son. Even the Homeland Security shithead didn't have all the answers. Supposedly we've been invaded by the Chinese. But no one knows if it's true. No one's heard from DC for the last week. Not in person, anyway, just spokesmen. Speaking for the president. For the joint chiefs. For the who-the-fuck-ever. No visual, mind you, just orders and proclamations."

"What kind of orders?" Meggan asked.

"Martial law orders," Bill said sourly and took a big swig of his whiskey. "Everything's frozen. No one's allowed to move. Army's got the highways shut down. That's the official version. I know for a fact though, that it's hit or miss. Fred Willson was in Cheyenne on some state business for the agriculture committee. Governor gave him a pass, and he drove back from Cheyenne yesterday. He didn't see any military, but he said it was eerie."

"How so?" Frank asked.

"'Cause of the people who are out of gas and stuck on the highway," Bill answered. "He picked up a family who'd stopped to help some guys who'd flagged them down. But when they stopped to help, it was to have the family's own car taken at gunpoint, and them left on the road."

"Jesus," Danielle whispered. "What about Dylan and Kirstin? We've got to..."

"Got to what?" Sam asked, seeing her reach for her phone. "There's no service. We can't call them. Can't warn them."

He felt a flare of anger reddening his ears. "Damn it! I told them. Begged them."

Shyla squeezed his hand, saying, "It was their choice, Sam. What were you going to do? Put a gun to their heads? Dylan said you'd have to shoot him to stop him."

"Which way were they headed?" Bill asked.

"Denver."

Bill growled, "Doubt they made it past the Highway Patrol checkpoint outside of Casper. Even if they were smart enough to figure a way around the roadblocks it's even money that those kids could make it to the state line. And, if they did, it's dollars to donuts they're not getting past the Guard. And if they do, it's a nightmare south of the state line."

Pam said, "I don't get it."

"Governor Agar called up the Wyoming National Guard first thing. Had them ready and deployed on the state line even before the martial law order. They're turning back anyone who isn't a Wyoming resident returning home. People can either head back south, or stay in a tent in a big refugee camp just south of the Terry Ranch on the Colorado line. FEMA's supposed to supply it from some warehouse. Same thing down at The Forks south of Laramie on 287."

Pam closed her eyes, seemed to sway. "But...Breeze is down there."

"God damn it." Frank's face had taken on a mask-like agony.

"Yeah," Old Bill snapped. "She's down there. In the shit-storm that's Denver. My bet? She's holed up. Locked and loaded. But that is as it is, and no changing it now."

Pam didn't look reassured.

Sam pondered the hidden meaning behind the looks the Tappans shared with each other. Call it grim.

"You said it's a shit storm in Denver?" Amber asked, her voice strained thin.

Bill studied her through hard-slitted eyes. "Electricity is out for most of the city. A lot of looting. Army was originally deployed from Fort Carson and Piñon Canyon. They just started restoring order, then they got called back. Ordered to deploy to California. Soon as they pulled out, the rioting and looting started all over again."

"You sure of this?" Thomas asked.

"That's what the DHS dickhead says." Old Bill swallowed hard, his voice a rasp of sound. "He officially informed us that the Constitution has been suspended and will remain so until the crisis is over."

The silence in the room had the weight of a tomb.

"What about...?" Jon wet his lips. Tried again. "What about back East?"

Bill took another swig of his whiskey. "Can't tell you, son. There's been no communications. No news. I did hear that you can get to western Nebraska, at least as far as the panhandle. The roads to Montana are open, but there's no news about Billings."

"What about the bombers that flew over a couple of days back?" Sam asked.

"Headed for someplace in northern California. The Homeland Security shithead got real mysterious about that. Just said that America was striking back."

"Back at the Chinese?" Frank and Pam were gripping each other's hands in a death grip.

"That's the mystery part," Bill muttered and took another swallow of whiskey.

"You keep calling him a shithead." Amber had pinned the old man with her fear-glittering eyes.

"Yeah. Something about the term fits." Bill lifted the glass to the light and studied the remaining amber fluid. "Says he's taking control of the Basin in the name of the federal government. Says he's authorized by Congress and a whole slew of Executive Orders to implement federal control and to 'conduct the administration of this district according to emergency regulations' to quote him exactly."

"What the hell does that mean?" Meggan asked.

"He called us all together to inform us that not only was he in charge, but to read us all the applicable laws, the fucking C.F.Rs, EOs, and other legal horseshit. Said he was implementing General Order No. 1."

Bill's eyes slitted gimlet thin. "Which says that within seven days every landowner in the Basin must submit an inventory of all equipment, grain, feed, and acreage under cultivation. The crops those acres are planted in. A list of all livestock, saddle stock, and poultry. And, of course, a complete list and description of all guns, including serial numbers, and a detailed accounting of any ammunition currently on the premises." He paused. "Down to the last round."

"And the purpose of this is?" Frank asked through gritted teeth.

"To make them available for confiscation and seizure for, and I quote, 'the common and beneficial use of the federal government during and throughout the current state of emergency'."

"They want to strip us of our livestock?" Meggan cried angrily. "Over my dead body."

"If that's how they have to do it," Amber said woodenly. "We can't let that happen."

All eyes turned her direction.

Amber was trembling as if every muscle in her body had gone electric. "You understand, don't you? It's...It's Daesh all over again. This is what they did in Syria and Iraq. It's happening here."

Sam had never heard her call them ISIS, only Daesh, and then rarely.

Dr. Holly sprang to his feet, hands open in a non-threatening manner. "It's all right, Amber. Ease down. That's it. Ease down."

She was still trembling when she finally nodded, swallowed hard, and exhaled. She shot a desperate glance at Meggan, voice hoarse as she asked, "You got any more of that whiskey?"

"Hell, yes. I got a whole bottle." Meggan stepped around the speechless crewmembers on the floor and hurried into the dining room. Everyone was watching Amber as she struggled to hold it together.

"Confiscation? That can't be allowed to happen," Dr. Holly said to Bill; his eyes however, stayed pinned on Amber. Like him, they were all trying to read how close she was to a psychotic break.

"Why not?" Pam asked.

"It would destroy us," Dr. Holly replied. "Destroy any chance of saving anything. Of saving ourselves."

Meggan was back with a whole bottle of the local Wyoming Whiskey. Amber took it in two shaking hands, lifted it to her lips, and took a deep drink. Closing her eyes, she swallowed, then sighed as the warmth settled into her stomach.

They all watched in horrified fascination.

Dr. Holly took the bottle next, took a swig, and passed it to Meggan. She, too, drank, passing it Court, who sat at her feet on the buffalo rug. One by one, they passed the bottle around the room. It acted as a sort of communion. That pivotal moment. A bonding, after which, they were no longer strangers.

Bill had his head leaned back; eyes closed he rubbed his temples. "You're not the only person who thinks that way, Evan. Tomorrow morning Fred Willson, Merlin Smith, Harry Farmington, Sally Hanson, Terry Thompson and I are having a meeting in town. Figure out what we can do."

Amber dropped loosely onto the couch, her eyes gone dull now, mouth almost slack in her wedge of a face. A woman would look this way if part of her soul had suddenly turned dark. "How many troops are in the Basin right now?"

"None, so far as I know. They're all down on the Colorado border, along with a whole host of volunteers calling themselves militia. If we get overrun, we lose everything. If the government takes it all? Well, that's the same thing, isn't it?"

Bill shook a finger. "This guy is another Erich Koch. If he can get his claws into us, find enough toadies to build a base of support, he'll become the iron boot that crushes us all. The officious prick almost promised it. There he sat up there at that table, dressed in his fine suit, smiling down on us like we were vermin."

"Who's Erich Koch?" Sam asked.

Dr. Holly said, "Hitler's hand-picked Party monster, selected to govern the Third Reich's eastern front from the Baltic to the Black Sea. A real piece of shit. Lived like a god, took what he wanted, and murdered anyone who even mildly annoyed him. Oh, and just in case you were starting to think he was warm and fuzzy, he also ran the concentration camps."

"That's him," Old Bill agreed. "That's what's coming here."

"So...your mister shithead just has his list of regulations and decrees to back him up?" Dr. Holly thoughtfully settled onto the couch, actually daring to tap a fist on Amber's knee, as if in reassurance.

"That, a couple of the sheriff's offices in the basin, and a bunch of slimy little shits who've latched onto his coattails as'—Bill mocked quotation marks with his fingers—"'administrators'."

"What about the Highway Patrol?" Frank asked.

"They're in the governor's pocket. No telling which way the local offices will align."

"Then we've got to move quickly." Dr. Holly tilted his head back, eyes on the ceiling. "We'll need to get messengers to the other towns in the basin: Cody, Worland, Greybull, Powell and the rest."

"What do you have in mind, Evan?" Frank asked.

"Cut the head off the snake before it can coil."

"Doing that..." Bill didn't finish but tossed off the last of his liquor. "Well, you know there won't be no way back."

"Any idea how Governor Agar is taking all this?" Frank asked. "Did Fred Willson say anything to give a hint?"

Bill arched an eyebrow. "Reckon most people know that Agar hates the Feds. He already ran the shithead out of Cheyenne. Told him he was either for the federal government, or Wyoming. When shithead told Agar the government was in charge, Agar ordered his arrest. Shithead wouldn't have made it out of town but for some of his federal cronies."

Frank laughed. "A couple of years back, a bunch of us were up at the Irma for a fundraiser in Cody. We all went up to Agar's room for a drink afterwards. My take, given some of the things he said, and the fact that he had the Guard on the border before the shit really hit the fan, is that he's about the last guy on earth who will sit back and let some federal official take over."

"We should send someone to have a meeting with him." Dr. Holly took the whiskey bottle from Pam and took a drink.

"My thoughts exactly." Bill hitched his hip up, unsnapped the holster from his belt, and laid the pistol on the reading table beside his chair. "We're talking about rebellion, people. You understand that, don't you?"

Amber asked, voice cold, "What are you going to do when they come to take your guns and vehicles and all of your cows and horses? Just stand there? Hand them over with a smile?"

Bill chuckled dryly. "Reckon we'll die right here, trying to keep what's ours."

Amber—as if in a trance—whispered, "How bloody fucking heroic. Better to kill the piece of shit before he comes knocking at your door with an armed squad of two-legged filth to back him up."

"Amen." Pam tightened her hold on her husband.

Sam's heart was pounding, an eerie nausea in the pit of his stomach. Jesus. Could this get any worse?

Shyla met his anxious gaze with one of her own. She tightened her grip on his fingers, a fragile desperation behind her pinched expression.

"Does this 'shithead' have a name," Dr. Holly asked.

"Kevin Edgewater," Bill said as if the mere utterance sullied his lips.

Dr. Holly turned his attention to the owl-eyed and stunned crew where they huddled on the floor. "As for the rest of you, none of you signed on for this. If worse comes to worst, that camp up on the hill will be your safe haven. Your retreat of last resort. No one knows it's there."

For a faint second, Sam thought he glimpsed *Nynymbi* in the shadow of Old Bill's chair. Just a faint flicker of those curious concentric eyes, the waving three-fingered hands. As Bill shifted, the image vanished as if it had been a trick of the light.

He glanced at Thomas, whose evaluative gaze was already locked on Sam. Thomas nodded, a faint and knowing smile on his lips.

Sam took a deep breath. The words, they just sort of slipped out. "I'm with the Tappans."

"Me, too," Shyla said.

"And me." Court raised his hand where he sat on the buffalo rug. The others, however, seemed too shocked to react. Nor did Sam blame them.

"Why back us?" Bill studied Sam thoughtfully.

Sam nodded his head back toward Bill's library. "Maybe because when Alaric marched on Rome, everyone expected someone else to stop him. Maybe because there's something worth saving here. Maybe because you're ready to take us in when people are being shot in the streets looking for sanctuary. The line's got to be drawn somewhere, doesn't it?"

Sam couldn't help but glance at Amber, sitting hunched on the couch, her hands clenched into rock-hard fists. She knew.

So, Sam asked himself, what lengths would he go to in order to keep Shyla from ever suffering the kinds of horrors Amber had?

Hard question to face, isn't it, Sam Delgado?

Would he damn himself?

Answer: *It's no longer hypothetical. You'll do whatever you have to. And live with the consequences for the rest of your life.*

MINI

* * *

Three friends opted to get out of Denver with me. We all rode motorcycles, or we'd never have made it as far as the suburbs. Bikes could wiggle their way through the abandoned cars and trash-clogged streets.

Mini was nineteen. A vivacious blonde with a round face and forever-effervescent personality. She was a sociology freshman. Wanted to go into teen counseling. She'd grown up in affluent Castle Rock, south of Denver. The one time I'd been to her parents' house, it was like a mansion atop a hill with an incredible view of the Rockies.

She made it a couple of miles—to the first dead bodies— before she turned back. Ultimately, she just couldn't believe that the government would fail to fix the situation. Her choice was to head back to her apartment, wait for the police, the National Guard, or the Marines come restore order. Any other outcome was beyond belief.

We watched her wheel her Suzuki around and start to thread her way back toward her fifth-floor apartment.

That was the day after the electricity went off.

It never went back on.

Excerpt from Breeze Tappan's Journal.

CHAPTER TWENTY-TWO

***

"SAM?" FRANK CALLED WHEN SAM STEPPED OFF THE PORCH. SHYLA STOPPED AS HE TURNED
back. Slushy rain was now falling, coating their hair and shoulders.

"Yes, sir?" Sam's breath rose in the air.

"You know that little cabin next to Evan's? The one with the white trim?"

"Yes, sir."

"You and Shyla. That's yours."

"Uh..."

Frank gestured back toward the house. "What you said in there. You and Shyla, you're with us now." He paused. "There's four bunks. And a divider for privacy. Just let the curtain down from the ridgepole. Best I can do for the two of you. And beyond that...well, it's just plain none of my business."

And with a final wave, he stepped back into the house.

Sam turned, another level of anxiety added to his unsettled core. "Look, I can throw out my—"

"There's a divider," she said wearily. "And four bunks. I don't think you're the type to come slithering into my sleeping bag in the middle of the night. Besides, there's only room in it for one."

"Why's it always the guy? What if you come slithering into my bag in the middle of the night?"

"Because guys think with their dicks."

She took his hand, leading the way to the bunkhouse where all the gear had been stowed. Sam and Shyla had been among the last to leave, listening to Dr. Holly, the Tappans, and Court—of all people—talking about the Bighorn Basin's resources.

"Can you believe this?" Sam asked. "It's as if there's no solid footing. Like...everything is spinning into chaos. Chinese on the west coast? And those stories about what happened at the border...?"

Shyla opened the bunkhouse door. The rest of the crew had claimed bunks, there being enough for all now that Shanteel, Kirstin, Dylan, and Shyla weren't in the mix. She recovered her backpack with its rolled sleeping bag and the sack that held her tent.

Sam picked up his own, telling the rest, "We've got other quarters. No need to hold bunks for us."

Jon, his expression a mask of disquiet, just gave them a thumbs up and went back to strumming something sad on his guitar.

Outside, in the freezing rain, Shyla said, "God! I can't *fucking* believe it! States patrolling their borders? Americans in refugee camps? Because they want to get the hell out of burning cities?"

"Part of me says, 'This is impossible. It's not really happening. You'll see.'" Sam fought back a sense of welling despair.

Side by side they walked to the little cabin with the white trim, and Sam opened the rattly doorknob. Flicking the light switch revealed a cozy log structure with a window beside the door, a second window above the table with its three ancient-looking chairs, a wardrobe cabinet, two double bunkbeds set against either wall, and a little wood heat stove in the back. The "facilities", of course, would be the outhouse at the end of the path that led off from the front door.

"Paradise on earth," Sam said, tossing his pack on the lower bunk to the left. "It's freezing in here."

"Would you rather be in one of those refugee camps?" Shyla asked soberly, dropping her gear onto the right-hand lower bunk.

Several pictures were hung on the walls, the first of a cowboy on a horse; another of autumn-yellow aspens and a bugling elk; and a third...

Sam stopped short. Behind the glass frame was *Nynymbi.* Photographed on brown sandstone, his little hands were waving, his three-toed feet protruding from the corners of his corpulent body with its breastplate. The eyes seemed to mock Sam.

Did you beat me here again?

Shyla rubbed her arms and bent to turn on the knob on the electric baseboard heater under the table.

Sam shook his head at *Nynymbi and* dismissed him as a coincidence before he pulled out a chair and sank into it.

Shyla rummaged in her pack for a bit, then turned, pulling out the second chair and seating herself. The bottle she thunked onto the old wooden table was something called Remy XO. With her slim hands, she broke the seal. Uncorking the decorative bottle, she handed it to Sam, saying, "Welcome to the end of our world."

He took a sip, marveling at the smooth taste. The label said it was cognac. He'd never had cognac.

She took the bottle, lifted it to her lips, and Sam watched her smooth throat as she sipped. He wondered what it would be like to run his lips and tongue along those sensual contours.

She set the bottle down, eyes closed, as she worked the cognac over her tongue. With a sigh she swallowed. Then fixed her turquoise gaze on the bottle.

"Parting gift from Jim." A distant tone filled her voice. Then she met Sam's eyes. "When you sided with the Tappans tonight? You surprised the hell out of me, Sam Delgado."

"One minute I was standing there. The next the words were coming out of my mouth. But you remember up on the rock, above camp last night?" He rubbed his face. "Was that really only last night? I said that this was our world now. It *has* to be. I can't think about home. Mom and Dad. The restaurant. All of my friends. I've got to block it, you know? All the people, the places, the..." He swallowed hard, fighting tears.

She said nothing, watching him intently.

"Shyla, if I go down that road, I'll die. So I'm here. Making *this* my world. Making *you* my world. This place is something to save. And to protect it and you, I will do whatever, however, and whenever. That's all that I am now. That's my promise."

He saw her pupils enlarge in pools of turquoise, noted the slight quiver of her lips. Then she blinked, as if on the verge of tears, and looked away.

To lessen the yawning sense of despair, he grabbed the bottle and took another drink, this time doing as she did, savoring before swallowing.

Setting it down, he added, "Meet the new Samuel Delgado."

When she looked back, her eyes seemed to deepen like bottomless wells. Maybe it was the effect of Meggan's whiskey mixed with Shyla's cognac, but they seemed to suck him into an eternity.

"If this doesn't get better, we're going to have to do things to survive," she said in an ironically tender voice. "Terrible things. You know that, don't you? Things we couldn't have imagined even last night. Will doing those things make us...? I mean, like those camps on the Colorado border, will we still be human afterwards?"

"I don't know." He ran his fingers down the side of the ornate bottle. "You know, after this is gone, there won't be any more."

"There won't be any more of a lot of things. Coffee, pepper, pineapples, bananas, mangos, oranges, ginger, cumin, tuna, salmon, coconuts, sugar—"

"We'll have sugar. They grow the beets here. I overheard Frank say that."

"Lot of fresh meat. Beef. Elk. Deer."

"You'll end up like Pam, you know. All whip-thin and muscles."

"God, I'd be happy to be half the woman she is." She smiled absently. "Never seen a man and a woman as perfectly matched as she and Frank."

"If you're going to be a Pam, I'd have to be at least as tough and capable as Frank." He made a face. "Tough call there. Those are pretty big boots to fill."

"Size ten if I'm to guess." Shyla pursed her lips, an intensity like an electric current between them. "It's in you. Down at the core. But I think I want you to become an old Bill."

"Why's that?"

"Because he's wise as well as tough. Like tonight. Think of the way he delivered that news, what it had to cost to tell his family that their world wasn't just at an end, but that some bureaucrat was coming to try and take it away."

"That's when I made my decision to stay and help them."

She took his hands, rubbing her thumbs down the backs, her delicate fingers tracking across the palms. Sam's physical reaction caught him by surprise. He barely stifled a gasp, the tingle was so powerful.

She laughed then, throwing her head back, exposing that elegant throat, her white teeth. Her hair went tumbling over her shoulders.

Sam had gone stiff, heart thumping like a frantic rabbit.

Her voice was filled with music: "Wow. Guess I found your switch."

He swiveled his hips to remove any visual evidence of just how electric her touch was, could feel his ears start to burn.

She clenched her jaw, tightening her grip on his hands, expression serious. "Don't. Please."

"Hey," Sam tried to laugh it off. "What do you expect when I'm sitting with—"

"A most mutually interested woman," she interrupted with a smile. Then she glanced over her shoulder at the curtain that was pinned up along the ridgepole. Let loose, it did divide the room.

To break the tension, Sam sipped the cognac again and took a deep breath.

He was falling into her stare, letting himself drift in a universe of turquoise, when she asked, "You meant that, didn't you? That I was your world. That you'd fight for it. For me."

He nodded, emotions too roiled and confused for words.

"Hard to know if this attraction is the real thing, or just that we're sitting on top of a volcano and desperate to find some kind of reassurance."

"No doubt in my mind," he told her.

She took a deep breath, swelling her breasts against the flannel shirt. Letting go of his hands, she stepped to the wardrobe, opened the cabinet, and cried, "Ah, hah!"

Tossing Sam's pack on the bunk next to hers, she dropped the folded blankets and sheets atop the mattress. When she turned to face him, a slim blonde eyebrow was arched in challenge.

Sam stood, throat feeling like it had a knot pulled tight down deep. Every nerve in his body was tingling.

"I assume you've undressed a woman before?"

Sam's chest on the verge of exploding, he admitted, "Actually, I, uh, don't have much practice in... Well..."

"Then it's a good thing we've got all night, huh? Bet we can figure it out."

They did. All the way from good to fantastic.

JILL

***

Jilliana was a sophomore in pre-law. Her goal was to be a lawyer. Wanted to work for the ACLU and campaign for Latinx and women's rights. She came from a little town in the San Luis Valley in southern Colorado.

Where US 40 splits off from I-70, she decided to head west and then cut south, take the back roads to her hometown of Del Norte.

We heard later that Summit County had set up a roadblock on I-70 just this side of the Eisenhower Tunnel. Word was that they stopped all traffic from Denver, refusing to allow their county to be overrun by refugees. No exceptions.

Grand County followed suit, but Felix and I were already across that county line.

No telling what happened to Jill. Arriving on a Honda Africa Twin? Alone? With all those frustrated people piled up against the roadblock?

Well...draw your own conclusions.

Excerpt from Breeze Tappan's *Journal*.

CHAPTER TWENTY-THREE

***

SAM DIDN'T SLEEP THAT NIGHT.

His head was a confused tangle of warring images, emotions, and nervous energy. In a moment of epiphany, it came to him that he was living a life that had been suddenly and rudely smacked out of reality. Sort of like a baseball used to being tossed from glove to glove around the infield, and suddenly, *crack!* He was over the fence and sailing out of the ballpark into an infinite unknown.

Everything about Shyla was perfect. Her spirit, her intellect, her passion, even her fear of the future. She fit like the perfect puzzle piece. Conformed to each of his indentations and protrusions as if they were made for each other. Perhaps a shitty cliché, but how true.

Against that unexpected joy, came knowledge that Wyoming National Guard soldiers and volunteer militia were herding panicked human beings into camps across the Colorado border. The military had rushed to California to fight Chinese. *California,* for God's sake?

Old Bill had reported no word from the East Coast.

What if Mom and Dad are dead? What if The Yucatec is a burned-out shell? What if, what if...

He hugged Shyla tighter to his chest, reveling in the silken feel of her warm skin against his.

Heaven in the midst of horror.

I'll never have the chance to take her home, introduce her to Mom and Dad. Never see them smile and hug her to their breasts. Never have a chance to be family again.

And the last thing he had expected was to feel this way about a woman. She was his. To have and to hold. To protect...

Dear God, can I keep her safe in this unraveling hell?

What if he couldn't? If he wasn't man enough? Wasn't strong enough, or tough enough, to stand between her and the abominations looming just over the horizon?

Pam's pistol went click in Sam's imagination. He felt it in his hand, the grip curving into his palm, that reassuring feeling as the hammer dropped.

We'll have to do things. Shyla had said those words, had understood what was coming.

And back on Long Island?

If Denver was Hell-broke-loose-on-earth with its couple of million people, what was the tri-state region like with its *tens* of millions?

If transportation had broken down to the extent Fred Willson claimed he had experienced in rural Wyoming, what was it like in New York? Were any trucks getting across the bridges?

Sam's folks barely kept a week's supply of tortillas, refritos, jalapenos, beef, and pork in the restaurant at any given time. So maybe they had been smart enough to lock the doors, barricade themselves in with enough in the larder to wait it out.

Sure. And how long would the water last if the electricity went off? What if the gas lines were ruptured? The coolers quit? The meat started to turn?

And what if roving gangs of starving people were rioting out front on Newman Street, right beneath The Yucatec's yellow-and-red sign? Sam could imagine them looking up, seeing the advertisements for food. And only that one big plate-glass window stood between their hunger and the prize that was inside.

The first of the tears leaked past his eyelids. He tried. He really did, but he couldn't stop the sobs.

Shyla had to have been awake, her thoughts paralleling his own. No doubt worried about her mother's health food store. Or maybe the children starving in the camps. Or atrocities beyond imagining than now were becoming commonplace.

She, too, broke down, shoulders wracked by sobs. As she cried, her arms tightened around him, squeezing, as if she might press herself right through Sam's skin and into his very bones.

For what seemed eternity, they lay there in the night. Two wounded souls clinging together in desperation.

FELIX

***

It was Felix and me. We made it to Granby, took the highway up to Willow Creek Pass. Three men with rifles stopped us in front of an ad hoc roadblock made with a truck and camp trailer.

They wanted our bikes. And they wanted me.

Felix chose not to have a gun. Wouldn't touch one and wanted them all banned. Had a friend killed the time he himself had survived a school shooting.

When he told the men no, one shot him through the chest. That quick. No other warning. Bang. Felix and the bike fell over.

I was staring. Disbelieving.

They told me to get off the bike. To get in the camp trailer and strip "for a little fucking".

Unreal, right? Like a bad movie.

I step off the bike, unzip my riding jacket, and start for the camp trailer. I'm shaking. Scared like I've never been. I reach inside the pocket.

That moment? It's like a haze. The pistol appears in my hand. I'm turning. I don't even hear the gun go off, but I see the surprise in the man's ruddy face.

I turn to the next...and the next...keep shooting until the Smith & Wesson clicks on empty.

Excerpt from Breeze Tappan's *Journal.*

CHAPTER TWENTY-FOUR

***

IT WAS A WHOLE DIFFERENT RIDE HEADING BACK INTO HOT SPRINGS. SAM RODE IN THE backseat of Bill's mega-cab Dodge dually. As he stared out the side window, he could have been looking at an entirely new planet.

Not that anything had changed. The same rocky ridges rose on either side of the valley, the small farmhouses looked just as lackluster, and the rusting farm machinery and stock trailers just as beat up.

The thing was that they now had the look of stubborn resistance, as if standing defiantly and ruggedly against the storm.

The periodic slap of the windshield wipers against the thinning drizzle added to the effect.

Looking through the rear window, Sam couldn't see the mountains where Brandon and Shanteel remained lost. The clouds hung too low, gray, and threatening. Thomas Star had assured everyone that there had to be a foot of snow or more on the ground up there.

Damned cold.

Exposed, without shelter, a person would die.

And up ahead Sam was going to be part of a meeting discussing an act of secession. How the hell could this be happening so quickly? It all seemed insane.

He glanced at Shyla where she sat beside him, her turquoise eyes distant as she watched the fields and bluffs pass.

"Now," Bill had his weathered hand on the steering wheel, his hat clamped tightly on his head, "it's going to be tough enough getting you in, Evan. My suspicion is that the kids are going to have to wait outside. Me and the rest, we've known each other for most of our lives. You're an outsider."

"I think I can justify my presence," Dr. Holly said easily, his arm on the pull-down armrest. "And they need to hear what I've got to say. Court and I spent half the night talking this through."

Holly made a tsking sound with his lips. "That lad's really something of a surprise. Looking at him, he's all big, overweight, stumbling thumbs. Game designer, huh? Well, he's sure got the theory down pat. Resources, transportation, logistical supply, strategy, and tactics. Says he has to employ all of it in war games. Do you know what he told me?"

"Reckon I don't," Bill said mildly, slowing for a patch of washboard.

"Said he and a team of friends played World War II against a team from Stanford. They wired a whole room full of computers and bought cloud time. He and his pals started with the same resources Hitler did, took them four weeks, but they won."

"He played Hitler?" Bill shot a sidelong look at Dr. Holly. "That's not exactly blowing my skirt up, Evan."

"It should," Dr. Holly told him. "You're a historian, you know that the Axis was doomed from the moment Hitler invaded Russia."

"So, how'd Court and his team turn it into a win?"

"They crossed the channel and took England, consolidated for a year, and kept Japan from attacking Pearl Harbor while they inspired Stalin to murder the last of his remaining generals. Launching their invasion of Russia the next March, they were in Moscow by mid-August."

"And the US?"

"Never had reason to fire a shot."

Sam glanced at Shyla. She was listening thoughtfully. He gave her hand a squeeze.

"Sounds to me like he's an asset," Frank said where he sat on Shyla's left and watched the landscape roll past. "So, you and he? What did you two figure out about the Basin?"

"It's essentially self-sufficient," Dr. Holly replied. "Or it can be. We've got everything we need. Hydroelectric power from Boysen Dam and Buffalo Bill Reservoir, assuming we can isolate the controls from Casper. Plenty of oil, including the infrastructure to get it to the three refineries in the Billings area. Other refinery choices, in order of preference, are Casper, Sinclair, and finally Cheyenne, with the latter being the most vulnerable."

"All of those refineries are outside of the Basin," Shyla noted.

"Then we might have to build our own on the Bighorn River," Dr. Holly said. "What's a refinery but essentially a distillery? No matter how it works out, one of our priorities has to be recruiting someone who knows how to build and operate one."

"What next?"

"Agriculture, of course. A reallocation of ground for staples like corn, beans, squash, melons, cabbage, peppers, and so forth. Wheat, barley, and oats are probably adequate in their current acreage, and the sugar beets are key."

"How's that, Dr. Holly?" Sam asked. "How much sugar do we need?"

"All we can get." Holly craned his head around to look back at Sam. "Trade, Sam. Sugar, like salt and spices, is going to be a hot commodity. And I doubt anyone's going to be seeing cane sugar being trucked up from Mexico or the Caribbean anytime soon."

Sam nodded.

"Oh, and, Sam?"

"Yes?"

"I'd appreciate it if you'd call me Evan."

Sam gave him a nod.

"We've got plenty of beef," Bill added. "Some sheep. Enough swine, even bison. That we can build on."

"And the wild game," Shyla added.

"What about spare parts?" Frank asked.

"That, my friend, along with pharmaceuticals, is a serious problem." Evan returned his attention to the road. The change was immediate and refreshing when the pickup hit the blacktop.

"Some things, like aspirin, we can make from willow bark."

"And there are other wild plants we can use, like coneflower," Shyla added. "I downloaded a list onto my laptop before we left home."

Evan nodded. "If I can get to Laramie, I've got a whole library. I'd love to get it away from the border before something happens to it."

"Assuming your place hasn't already been broken into and looted." Frank slapped an angry hand to his leg.

"There's that." Evan paused. "But getting back to the problem at hand, we've got five machine shops in the Basin. Most of them being run by machinists in their sixties and seventies. We need to get some apprentices into training ASAP. Some of those spare parts we can manufacture. We've got coal in the Gebo area and clay to make bricks. Won't take much to construct a primitive foundry. We can start raiding the dumps for scrap metal to recycle."

"That's down the road," Sam said. "First you've got to get through the immediate bottleneck. Especially when it comes to fuel. Without financial records, who's going to be able to buy diesel?"

"That's a subject for immediate discussion today," Bill said with a curt nod.

"We've got a thousand gallons in the tank at the ranch," Frank noted. "That should get us through until next summer if we're frugal."

"What about communications?" Shyla asked. "Who controls the phones?"

"Local company out of Worland," Frank said. "But that needs addressed."

"And more to the point," Evan said, "how can we guarantee secure communications. Something that DHS can't monitor."

"We'll figure that out." Bill slapped the wheel, slowing for the turn onto Highway 120. "Probably take a page from the OSS and the resistance forces in Europe. There's codes, ciphers, plenty of ways to keep in touch. Heard Court had some ideas based on the Enigma machine, of all things."

"And the governor?" Sam asked. "He's got command of the Wyoming National Guard, the militia, and the Highway Patrol, right?"

"That's going to be a tricky proposition," Bill said, not bothering to stop before roaring onto the empty highway.

Sam watched a herd of antelope out in the sagebrush disappear behind them as the big Dodge accelerated. They hadn't gone more than a mile before they passed the first car, a shiny Toyota, pulled off the side of the road, the hood up. As they went by Sam noticed it had Arkansas plates.

Welcome to Wyoming. He tightened his grip on Shyla's hand, eternally thankful that they had landed where they had and when they had. What if they'd been a couple of days behind? What if their little caravan had been in, oh, say, Chicago when this hit?

Between the turnoff and town they passed a total of five abandoned vehicles. One had the words, "It's yours!" scrawled in the dust on the side. Dropping down the last hill into Hot Springs, the town looked mostly asleep. No traffic. But a few people and a lot of kids were walking along the sidewalks. All watched Bill's red Dodge pass. Most waved gaily. Which was strange.

Must have known Bill's truck.

"I want you to see this," Bill said as he pulled up at the town's single traffic light, didn't wait for the signal to change since he was the only truck on the road, and made a left.

Sam and the crew had barely seen the state park with its grassy parks and hot water pools on the morning they had left for the mountains. Now, however, it was filled with an orderly array of motor homes, camp trailers, tents, and shelters made of tarps. A regular campground. The license plates were from everywhere but Wyoming.

People rose from lawn chairs as the truck drove past, looking, waving. Sam thought Bill's truck might have been the best entertainment those folks had all day.

"These are the ones who made it this far," Bill said. "Most with what was left in their gas tanks. For the time being the churches have taken up collections of food to keep them going, but we're going to have to figure out something for the long term."

"Look for Dylan and Kirstin," Sam told Shyla; but they saw no black BMW or red Dodge matching Dylan's.

"Did they have full tanks when they left?" Frank asked.

"Yeah," Sam told him. "We all filled up when we left town."

Bill took a right at the stop sign, saying, "If there was no roadblock at the canyon, they'd have made it to Shoshoni. If there wasn't one there, they could have gone all the way to Casper."

"They knew about martial law." Evan studied the hospital as they drove past. Vehicles were in the staff parking, which was promising. "They might have planned to go through Riverton, try the back way down 287."

Sam said, "The BMW could go about four hundred and fifty miles on tank of fuel. Dylan said he got about three hundred fifty."

"That would have got them to the border, all right." Bill shook his head.

"They made their choice." Shyla sounded distant as they crossed the bridge over the Bighorn River. "Me, I'd have considered turning back after passing that first Toyota, and been convinced by the time

I reached Hot Springs."

Pulling the truck into the lot behind the Bank of Hot Springs, Bill shifted into Park, and killed the engine. "Sam? You and Shyla go mosey around town. I don't think anyone will bother you, but if they do just tell them you're kin. Cousin to Frank and me. Come for a visit and got caught by this mess. Got it?"

Sam winked at Shyla. "Got it. Thank you. I'd be proud to be an honorary Tappan."

"Only 'cause you don't know what a surly bastard I can really be."

"Is that what Meggan likes about you?" Shyla asked as they all climbed out of the truck. "The surly part?"

"Girl, given what the rest is like, that's the best part I've got."

"He's mellowed over the years," Frank explained.

As the truck doors were slammed shut, the back door to the bank opened; a thick-set white-haired man cast suspicious looks their way.

"That's Fred Willson," Frank said under his breath. "We'll be inside in the conference room. Sam, Shyla? You need anything, knock twice. Hard. Then three soft. One of us will come. Meanwhile, here's a spare truck key in case it rains again."

"Got it."

Bill gave Sam and Shyla a reassuring nod and followed the rest as they filed through the bank's back door.

"Well," Sam said, "I guess we'll go see what there is to see."

"Some first date, Delgado," she told him with a smile. "You really know how show a girl a good time in the big city, huh?"

"I guess it's not quite what you're used to."

"Don't think it's what any of us are used to." Then she gave him a wry smile as she added, "But so far, so good. You keep surprising me."

"How's that?"

"You're always more than I expect you to be. As a person, as a lover, as a leader." A beat. "As a man. So, the question is: Are you really that wonderful, or is it a reflection on my dismal experience with males?"

"Every Friday night in church, right?" Sam reminded her. "Church camp every summer? Leaves a girl deprived."

They turned the corner onto the small downtown, walking slowly, looking in the shop windows. The people who passed—mostly dressed

in denim and wearing assorted sweatshirts, hats, and long sleeves—
startled Sam. Each and every one said, "How you doing today?" or
"Nice to get a break in the rain, isn't it?" or "How's it going?"

Shyla was actually quicker with a response, her Vermont roots
showing sunny as she tossed back, "Doing good. How about yourself?"
or "We needed the rain," or "Good to see you."

"It's like we're their best friends."

"Not New York, is it?" She arched an eyebrow. "People don't fear
people here. Same in upstate Vermont."

"If anyone looks you in the eyes and says hello in Hempstead, you
grab your wallet with one hand, and be ready to run. They're either out
to hit you up for money, or they've been off their meds for too long."

Shyla stopped in front of the fabric store. "Holy shit."

"What?" But she was already tugging Sam inside.

The lady behind the counter called, "Let me know if you need help."

The sign on the counter read: **Cash Only!!!**

Everything Sam knew about fabric could be put into Grandma
Alvarez's thimble, and he'd still have room for a finger.

"You think this bank thing will be over soon?" Sam asked the clerk,
breaking off as Shyla started fingering her way through bolts of cloth.

"Hope so." The woman eased back on her stool. "Can't go on
much longer. 'Course, I was one of the lucky ones. Always had my
statements mailed, so they've got something to work backwards from."

"What if they can't fix it?"

"Honey, who knows?" She tilted her head, the action almost bird-
like. "Where you from? New York, I'd bet."

"Long Island."

"You get trapped here?"

"Visiting family. The Tappans. They have a ranch west of here."

She squinted slightly, studying his darker complexion and ink-black
hair, then shot a sidelong look at Shyla. "Yeah, should have seen it.
Them blue-green eyes. She's a Tappan for sure. Gotta be Bill's side.
She belong to one of the boys?"

"The boys?"

"You know, Bill and Betty's boys. Let's see, there's Will, Tom,
and Mark. Couldn't wait to get the hell out of Hot Springs. Broke old
Bill's heart. But Frank stayed."

She gave Sam a knowing squint. "Bet if this bank thing gets worse, they're gonna be busting ass to get back to the ranch."

Bill had three other sons? That set him back. There weren't any photos, trophies, or even a sign that they'd existed, at least in the rooms he had been in. And then there was the mysterious Breeze that no one talked about.

Shyla returned with a thick bolt of heavy brown denim. "If I wanted this whole bolt, could I get a deal?"

"Gotta be cash."

"I have a little," Shyla admitted.

This was news. Sam thought she was dead broke like the rest of them. Apparently, Shyla had held back the time they were counting funds after checking out of the Days Inn.

Sam stepped back, amazed to watch the love of his life get down and dirty. He had seen haggling in Tunisia when he had booked a once-in-a-lifetime tour of Carthaginian and Roman ruins as a sophomore. Watching Shyla dicker, he could have been back in Tunis. The only thing missing was the obligatory cup of tea.

"What kind of leather is this?" Shyla had asked.

"That's bison. From the tannery down the street, but I'll tell you now, I sell that at fifty-percent mark-up to the tourists. You want bison leather, go deal straight with Ginny down at the tannery. Seeing as you're Bill's kin, she'll give you wholesale."

Most of an hour later, and with Shyla six hundred and thirty dollars poorer, they walked out with... Or, Sam would say, he *packed* out a heavy collection of fabrics while Shyla carried a sack full of various threads and sizes of needles.

"Six hundred and thirty bucks? You held out on us."

She shot him a sidelong glance. "That was before we knew how bad it really was going to be." A pause. "Jim gave me a couple of thousand. Said, 'Have a good time out west.' Call it a parting gift... and never mention his name to me again."

Sam took her advice. "Didn't Bill say not to get carried away?"

"God, Delgado, I couldn't turn it down. We got it for maybe thirty percent of retail. I mean, I understand. Small business, banking crisis, and a cash customer? She needed the cash flow."

"But why cloth and spools of thread?"

She gave him a disappointed look. "When you wear the knees out of those cargo pants you're wearing, or worse, the seat, where you gonna get another pair?"

"I...uh, hadn't thought that far ahead." Of course there would be a shortage of clothing. My God, people would eventually be in rags.

"Another week and we couldn't have touched this for a thousand dollars, Sam."

"I'd have never thought of cloth and thread."

"Okay, so I didn't have Friday nights or summers. I had quiet afternoons in my pious Christian household learning the arts of a proper young lady. I'm suddenly thankful for each boring stitch."

They rounded the corner and found Bill's truck had been joined by four other vehicles. The meeting must be in full secessionist swing.

"Tannery next," she said as Sam piled their loot in the back seat and locked the door. On an old receipt he found on the floor he penned a quick note telling Bill where they would be and stuck it under the windshield wiper.

Three blocks down, they found the tannery. A small outfit that specialized in buffalo, elk, and the kind of fur-bearing creatures that would make PETA people scream in outrage.

Thinking of the snow up high where Brandon and Shanteel were hopefully "holed up" Sam wondered if they wouldn't have desperately cherished one of the coyote coats or fox blankets.

Shyla played the Tappan angle, having overheard the lady in the fabric store. Ginny was great, an oversized and jovial woman. She had to be six-feet-four if she was an inch.

"Yeah, this bank thing's played hell." Ginny slapped her legs where she perched on a high stool behind the register. "My guess? Even if they get it fixed, it's wrecked the tourist trade for the summer. Worse than the damn COVID did, and that played hell let me tell you. You heard the stories about what's going on down in Colorado? Frickin' medieval. Tent camps full of refugees? Who'd have thought? Thank God for Governor Agar. Closing the border like that? He probably saved Wyoming."

She barely stopped for a breath. "'Course it always drives me crazy when I have to go down there. Just driving through that mess, I have to ask, 'Who *are* all these people?'"

She paused for a fraction of a second. "So, Bill's gotta line of the family in Vermont, huh? Didn't Mark end up out there someplace?"

"Bill doesn't talk about him much," Sam said.

"Yeah. Thank God for Frank. If he'd a left, too? That would have killed old Bill. As it was, drove him and Betty apart, those boys leaving. And you know about Meggan, don't you?"

Shyla shrugged. "Hadn't really met her until this trip."

"Druggie."

At their startled expressions, Ginny said, "Oh, my land, yes! Quite the story that is. She was running, strung out, trying to get away from that dealer she was living with down in Denver. I wasn't there. Heard about it, though. The night she targeted Bill in the Silver Dollar. Latched onto him like a life raft, she did. Betty'd been gone for more than a year by then."

She slapped her legs again. "Goes to show you. He took Meggan back to the ranch that night, and she never left. To see them now? Hell. You'd think they was high-schoolers in first love. Now, what can I do for you?"

"Leather. Janeen at the fabric store said that—"

"My land, you bet. You want hair on or off?"

Shyla gave her a helpless look. "It comes with hair on?"

"Let's go in the back and look at what's on the shelves."

Sam had never been in a tannery. By the time Ginny had taken them through the process, it was two hours later. Sam was starting to wonder if Bill had missed the note on the windshield and gone home without them.

Shyla was deep into the bargaining.

"That's cash," she said, running her hands over a buffalo robe.

"Being a Tappan, I'd a let you have it on credit," Ginny replied, fingering her chin as she inspected the hide Shyla had picked.

"No telling when the banks might finally get around to straightening this thing out." Shyla gave Ginny a sly look. "Power company take credit?"

"Four fifty. Final offer 'cause, Shyla, you got the charm."

"Done." Shyla leaned close and kissed Sam on the cheek.

At the register, to his amazement, Shyla counted out another seven hundred and fifty dollars from her compact purse.

Ginny had closed the register when the vehicles pulled up out front. At least seven that Sam could see through the window. Several of the pickups stopped in a semi-circle, but what really got his attention were the men with rifles perched in the beds.

"What's this all about?" he asked. "That's a lot of trucks."

Ginny had suddenly gone white. "I guess maybe I didn't turn in my inventory. In the chamber of commerce, we all decided. This is Wyoming. In the Constitution it says there's no illegal search and seizure."

Outside, a black Suburban passenger door opened, and a man in a suit stepped out. Two men in Carhart-brown coats followed on his heels.

The suit opened the front door and stepped inside. Took a couple of steps and stopped short, looking around. Light brown hair was cut long over his ears as if to emphasize his already round head with its large and oddly-fleshed jaw—the skin almost looking pulled tight. Heavy lids covered lazy blue eyes, and the man's tiny mouth below a too-small nose seemed lost in the immensity of his face.

After inventorying the room, he fixed on Shyla, a quiver of smile on his lips. Sam figured him to be five-ten, maybe forty, with the rounded shoulders of a man who'd never worked in his life.

As he studied Shyla, an almost animal intensity began to glitter behind his gaze.

"Welcome," Ginny called nervously. "Can I help you?"

"I heard about this place," the man said, walking forward. His two companions, looking like construction hands, finally broke formation. They occupied themselves by fingering the hats, gloves, coats, and vests. All the while, however, they seemed keenly aware of the man in the suit.

"Suppose I don't have to say it, but cash only," Ginny told him genially.

"Of course." His mouth bent into a smile. "You've heard of the mandatory inventory?"

The way he said it made Ginny stiffen. "Yeah. Something." A beat. "You passing through?"

"For the day. I wanted to see what Hot Springs was about. Important to know my district. Up in the headquarters we've been referring to the outlying communities as the provinces." He pointed to one of the beautiful fox blankets. "That one."

One of the burly men walked over, unhooked it from the rack and held it out over his arm for the suited man to inspect.

"Yes. Very nice. Perfect, don't you think?"

Sam had looked at it earlier, a bit shocked by the four-thousand-dollar price tag.

Time to get the hell out of there. He wrapped his arms around Shyla's folded buffalo hide. Sam had never picked one up— discovered it to be an armful. Taking his cue, Shyla filled her arms with the tanned leather she'd purchased.

"Leaving, my dear?" the man asked, eyes on Shyla. "Not so fast."

"Yeah," Sam said. "We're leaving."

One of the Carhart men—the dark-haired one—smiled humorlessly. "You don't talk like that to Director Edgewater, mister."

He stepped forward, an eyebrow raised.

Sam's heart began to do the trip-hammer dance against his breastbone. So that's who the guy in the suit was.

To the blond guy, Edgewater said, "Frederick, Take the fox hide out to the car please."

"Um." Ginny was off her stool. "Why don't you let me wrap that for you before..."

The guy was out the door.

"And I think that nice buffalo coat," Edgewater pointed at a full-length masterpiece.

"Director, you sure?" Ginny asked nervously. "That's got your total up to about seven thousand—"

"Not even close," he interrupted with a smile. "Edward, please write out a requisition receipt for the good lady, and remember that businesses always charge twice what their product is worth. They call it the margin, so deduct half. Oh, and use your discretion on anything else you think will be of value to our troops during this time of crisis."

To Ginny, he added, "To redeem the value of your requisitioned merchandise, you need only bring that receipt to the Cody headquarters where you will be given a voucher for reimbursement from the government."

"Why are you doing this?" Ginny stared helplessly at Edgewater.

"Madam, are you unaware of the current crisis? Are you not a patriot like so many of your brethren in this most conservative of states? Are you so selfish that you won't do your part and work for the common good?"

"Well, I... Of course, I will."

The man's small mouth puckered. "Without an official inventory, we have no way of validating exactly what merchandize has been requisitioned. It would be your word against the government's. It's for your protection and, of course, the government's."

"Name?" Edward asked where he penned in a small receipt book.

"Ginny. Ginny Duhaven."

Once again Edgewater turned his attention to Shyla, fixing on her long legs and breasts before raising his hands, forming a square with his fingers and thumbs, as if to frame her face.

"Such a marvelous creature."

Shyla's face burned red with humiliation.

Sam's stomach turned.

Edgewater continued to stare at Shyla as if she wasn't a sentient being. Edward stiffly said, "Miss Duhaven. You are aware that martial law has been declared? That all citizens must sacrifice during the current national crisis? We are all serving the national interest by contributing to the common good. Surely you're not one of these selfish types seeking to profit from the misery of their fellow citizens?"

"No."

Edgewater took a step closer to Shyla, asking, "And what is your name, my dear?"

"Shyla Adams." The muscles in her jaw were knotting, a tremble in her muscles.

A nervous sweat had broken out on Sam's chest, back, and neck. He had that sick-in-the-gut sensation that this wasn't going to turn out well. Like he'd had the couple of times the MS13 *cholos* had cornered him on the street.

The blond-haired guy was back, immediately picking up on the tension, the anticipatory smile bending his lips. He pulled his coat back, exposing the black semi-auto holstered on his hip.

"You live here locally, Shyla?" the blond guy asked as he stepped up and inspected her with glittering eyes. "Beautiful name, Shyla. I'll need to see your ID, please."

"Tappan Ranch," she said, voice strained as she laid her leather to one side, unsnapped her purse, and handed over her driver's license. Edward stepped forward to take it and began writing in his book.

Sam's throat had gone totally dry.

"Tappan?" Edgewater's voice turned disdainful. "Those Tappans? Not well recommended."

Edward said, "Says here that she's from Rutland, Vermont."

"Ah, not local." Edgewater remarked with a curious satisfaction.

"The Tappans are cousins," Shyla cried, and Sam could see her rising panic.

"Leave her alone," Sam said, only to be completely ignored. "We're out here for the summer. Staying at Tappan Ranch."

"ID, please." Edward asked, cold blue eyes turning to Sam. Soul squirming, Sam put the buffalo hide down; his fingers were shaking as he handed over his license. "This one's from Hempstead, New York."

Edgewater, lazy eyes narrowing thoughtfully, asked, "Ed? Is it just me, or does something about this young woman's story bother you? Sedition can come in so many forms."

"Won't know 'til you take her back to the room and interrogate her." The way Edward smiled in anticipation terrified Sam.

Sam burst out hoarsely, "She has rights. Leave her alone, or I'm calling the police."

He didn't see it coming. The black-haired guy, Frederick, hit him. Sam's head exploded like a lightning bolt inside his skull. Then pain as he hit the floor. A vicious kick landed in his belly, lofting him as it blew the air out of his lungs.

From a distance he heard Frederick saying, "Interfering with a federal officer in the conduct of his duty during a time of national emergency? That's a Class II offense."

Sam lost the world for a moment, coming to with his vision shimmering in little lights, blurry, and his head cradled in Shyla's lap, while she yelled, "Stop it! That's enough!"

"Easy, Frederick," Edgewater said. "I think the young man's learned his lesson. Now that he understands, he'll undoubtedly share his new wisdom with his friends in order that they might learn from his mistakes."

Sam tried to sit up, the world swimming around in circles.

"You've got your stuff!" Ginny was shouting. "Take the whole damn store if you want. But you leave these people alone!"

"Dear lady, we don't need your store," Edgewater said mildly, "All we ask is for your cooperation during this time of national crisis. Oh, and if you could drop your inventory off at the courthouse this afternoon, Edward will be my representative in Hot Springs."

Someone leaned in the door, calling, "Boss? There's a crowd building outside. Just thought you'd want to know."

Edgewater asked, "Are you really staying at Tappan Ranch?"

"Yes." The way Shyla bit off the words, Sam knew she was crying.

He rocked his jaw, trying to focus, reaching out for Shyla. Nor were his fingers working very well as they slipped across her sweatshirt.

"No need to make a scene," Edgewater said reasonably. "The people just need time to realize that we are all going to have to sacrifice for the common good."

As they walked toward the door, Sam heard Frederick say, "Makes you wonder, though. What's a lust-bunny like that doing with a beaner?"

Sam missed any response as he bent double and threw up.

MORALITY

***

I lived all of my life thinking I knew who I was, what I believed, and what I would and would not do. Turns out I didn't have a clue. When that moment came, I shot down three men who killed Felix, who would have raped and murdered me.

No guilt. No regrets.

Stumbled off to the side, feeling sick. Saw a pile of their previous victims dead in the ditch.

Since that day I have a very different understanding of morality. It marked a watershed, and on the other side I would be a stranger to the woman I had been.

Excerpt from Breeze Tappan's *Journal.*

CHAPTER TWENTY-FIVE

***

SIGHT PICTURE. BREATHE. FINGER TO TRIGGER. CARESS. *BANG!*

The little pistol rolled back in Sam's hand; the tin can danced on the dirt bank. Fortunately, it turned out that his right eye—the one he was supposed to aim with, was his dominant eye. His left was swollen mostly closed.

The June day was perfect, warm, the sun shining after two more days of endless rain, and three after he had been beaten in the tannery. The air smelled remarkably fresh, filled with the scent of new grass and wildflowers, periodically accented by the smell of horses.

"Frederick Zooma," Bill had told Sam as he handed Sam an ice pack. "Seriously. I couldn't make up a name like that. He's the dickhead's personal security. The other guy, the blond, he's Edward Tubb. Ex-military."

Then Bill had dropped the bombshell. "You and Shyla might have dodged the bullet. There's rumors of young women being taken in for questioning. Not local girls, but others from out of state. Women who don't have anyone to speak for them."

Sam remembered the look on Edgewater's face and cocked the little .22. Settled the grip in his palm. Sight picture. Breathe. Trigger. Caress. *Bang!*

Twenty feet away the can jumped again. A soup can is about a third the size of the human brain. And then there's the spinal cord below it. Sam hoped the day would come when Frederick Zooma and the soup can had a lot in common. That bothered him. He'd never thought he'd feel that way about another human being.

"Good work," Pam said from behind. "We're calling it for today. You're shooting superbly, so let's not muck it up by overdoing it.

Leave that memory in your head."

Sam nodded, still fighting the aftereffects of a headache.

"I hit the can more times than you did," Shyla told him as he thumbed the cylinder open and pressed the extractor to clear the brass.

Shyla had her butt propped against a tractor tire, arms crossed, her blonde hair teased by the wind.

Pam took the little .22 Smith & Wesson, checked the cylinder, and stuffed it into a holster. Then, to Sam's surprise, she pulled out a second revolver, bigger.

This one, too, she checked to ensure it was unloaded. Only then did she hand it to Shyla, cylinder still open, saying, "All right, love birds. That's my old .38. It's a Model 10. You take that home with you. Practice dry-firing it."

"Love birds?" Sam asked.

Pam just gave him a knowing squint, saying, "Yeah, right."

Shyla clicked the cylinder closed, turned, took her stance, and carefully dry-fired the Smith. "Smooth," she said.

Sam took his turn at propping his butt on the tractor tire. "We would have had to shoot them," he told her. "That's the scary thing. I mean, the only decision they leave you is to kill them."

"And then what happens to you?" Shyla asked. "Arrest, trial, execution. It's that or be carried off and gang raped. Some choice. You're damned if you do, damned if you don't."

Shyla settled against him, squeezing him over to make room, and nodded. "I've never been so scared in my life."

"Me neither. And that was before Zooma hit me. I never saw it coming, Shyla. And when it did, I was out of it. I couldn't think, couldn't see. It's not like in the movies."

"You're not going to weird out on me, are you? Filled with male guilt about not beating up the bad guy?"

"Nope."

"Good. I couldn't stand that macho shit. I've had enough of that to last a lifetime."

"We got lucky," he told her. "You saw. Edgewater's taking anything he wants. Claiming it's for the 'common good'."

Sam took the .38 from her hand, extended it, rolled the trigger back double-action as he sighted on the dirt bank. It didn't tremble as much as he thought it might in spite of the heavier trigger pull. *Click.*

"This is what happens when societies collapse." Shyla exhaled with resignation. "Who the hell appointed that piece of shit?"

"Well, we're back to rumor again, but the story is that Edgewater made it up to some kind of assistant director's position back in DC. Then there was some sort of malfeasance. Claims of sexual misconduct. Some kind of #MeToo stuff. Since no one is ever fired from the federal government, they sent him here. To Wyoming. A place that no one cares about."

"He's coming for me."

"You don't know that."

"It was in his eyes...in the way he looked at me. There was promise there, Sam."

He leaned his head back, letting the warm sun bathe his bruised face. "I think Bill would let us take two of the horses. We could hole up at the field camp. Keep both of our butts out of sight. Hell, it worked for the Dukurika Shoshoni for...let's see, four or five thousand years."

She laughed at that, but it had a nervous quality. "Yeah, I suppose. So, what happens when shithead comes here with his twenty thugs and a warrant for my arrest? What happens when Bill can't produce me? Take Danielle or Ashley instead? Take Pam? If I were a man, I'd look twice even if she is knocking on forty."

She blinked her eyes. "It's like I brought this on them."

"You did nothing." He stroked the revolver's cool steel. "He's the snake. And it could have been worse; what if Bill and Frank had walked in just as that was coming down? Bill had his .45. Tubb and Zooma had guns under those coats of theirs."

"Remember when I said I'd never let what happened to Amber happen to me? You can say that, Sam. You can mean it with all your heart, and then when you least expect it... Damn, I never saw it coming, either."

Jon burst into view from behind the barn, calling, "Riders coming! Two of them! I think it's Brandon and Shanteel!"

Sam shoved the Smith into his belt, hurrying forward, Shyla behind him.

In Sam's mind, it looked magical: Brandon, the living legend of a cowboy, riding along on his muscled blood bay. The big ranch dog,

Talbot, running ahead, tail waving. Shanteel beside Brandon on Old Tobe, the mud-spattered yellow horse. She didn't look any worse for wear. Her tent and sleeping bag were tied to the cantle, and she seemed somehow...different. More at ease.

"Hey, stranger," Pam called, striding off the porch. "'Bout time you got back and picked up on your chores. Poor Jon here has been pushing water for you."

"Obliged, Jon," Brandon dipped his head and touched the brim of his hat in salute. "Ran into a touch of bad weather up top. Shanteel worried that I might get a little snow blind, so we holed up for my comfort and to save the horses. Wouldn't want one to come up lame from slipping around too much."

To Sam's surprise, Shanteel was smiling, as if in real amusement, before adding, "Mrs. Tappan, this boy of yours doesn't have a clue about how to cook a rabbit."

Old Bill limped out onto the porch, calling, "So, you're back. What did you do? Hole up at the field camp?"

"Nope. Turns out that Shanteel, here, is something of a wilderness explorer. She'd managed to find her way clear over to Frying Pan Canyon. Since we were already there when the storm hit, we made ourselves a wickiup out of lodgepoles, packed in duff, built us a toasty fire and discussed the ills of the world until it blowed over."

Shanteel was grinning again, shaking her head, as if in amusement.

"Something's really not right about this," Shyla whispered in Sam's ear. "Think they're on drugs?"

Amber stepped out of Evan's cabin where the two of them had been working on maps. She actually let out a whoop as she hurried over, calling, "Shanteel, are you all right?"

"Better than ever, Amber. But I got to confess, think you could help me get off this horse?" She laughed from deep in the gut. "I'm so damn sore, I don't think I can move."

She had plenty of help as she swung stiffly off. Then she kept hold of Amber lest her legs fail.

Brandon reached down, taking her horse's reins. "Mom, draw Shanteel a hot bath. Let her soak it out. She just made one hell of a day's ride."

As Brandon led the horses toward the barn, Pam stared thoughtfully at the grinning Shanteel. "I don't know what you did up there, lady, but he doesn't offer praise like that lightly."

"Good man, that son of yours," Shanteel said, slightly embarrassed. "Now, was he serious about that bath? Only thing we've had to wash with was snow, and that sucks."

Sam walked over to help Brandon with the saddles, tackling Old Tobe's cinch while Shyla unbuckled the breast collar.

"What happened to you?" Brandon asked as he slung his saddle down from the blood bay. "That a bit of a domestic dispute, or did you run into a doorknob?"

"Met the new District Director for Homeland Security. One of his hired thugs hit me when Shyla declined to accompany the shithead off to his hotel room."

Brandon's lips pursed, eyes narrowing under the brim of his hat. "That's Edgewater?"

"That's him." Shyla called over her shoulder as she carried the saddle into to barn to put it on the rack.

Brandon gave a curt nod before he took a curry comb to his horse. "I see mom's old .38 sticking out of your belt, but you're going to need more than that."

"Yeah, my thoughts, too." Sam got another curry comb, and as he'd been taught, began working over Old Tobe, scraping off the mud. "Lot's changed since you went up the mountain. Seems Edgewater's got a thing for taking what doesn't belong to him. Apparently, that includes out-of-state women no one will miss."

"Someone needs to take that son of a bitch down."

"They're working on that."

"How'd Grandad's meeting in town turn out? Guess he didn't shoot the son of a bitch, or you'd not have that shiner."

"The local leaders are organizing, holding meetings. It's like...a bad movie."

"So, where do your people fit into all this?"

Shyla emerged from the barn, saying, "For better or worse, we're in it with you. At least Amber, Evan, Court, Sam, and I are. Jon's coming around. He's discovered he likes irrigating. Danielle and Ashley are still in shock."

"Where's the snippy little girl from Washington and the Colorado dude?"

"Gone. Made a run for Colorado." Sam shook the hair out of the curry comb. "My turn. You and Shanteel, how'd it work out that you're suddenly on speaking terms? Shyla thinks it's drugs."

Brandon smiled that lady-killer smile of his. "That is one tough lady. Smart, too. She just had to get her feet under her. That's all. Now, I'll admit it was a nice wickiup, but after four days of snow, two rabbits and a partridge, there's not much that two people don't know about each other."

Shyla and Sam gave each other a "who knew?" glance.

"Where's Thomas and Willy? I see their horses over yonder."

"They're up on the hillside harvesting sego lilies, blazing star blossoms, and phlox," Sam told him. "They'll probably head home tomorrow if they can get across the divide."

"Bet Grandad has Thomas in my bed, huh?"

"And Willy is in Celia's," Shyla told him.

"And the cabins? They all taken?"

Shyla arched an eyebrow. "We're in one, Evan's in another, and Amber's in the third. The rest of the crew's in the bunkhouse."

"It ain't worth pulling Breeze's bed out of storage. Guess I'll throw out in the barn. Won't be the first time. 'Cept usually it's 'cause I don't want Mom to know how drunk I was."

"Life has its little ups and downs, doesn't it?" Shyla said trying to hide a smile.

"Who's Breeze?" Sam asked.

"Twin sister. She and the folks had a parting of the ways a couple of years back." His eyes thinned. "Wish to hell I knew she was okay."

"Sorry."

"You know which one it was who hit you?" Brandon asked, touching his cheek in the spot that corresponded with Sam's bruise.

"Frederick Zooma," Sam said softly.

"There was a rumor before I left that everyone was going to have to do an inventory. That under martial law, it would all be requisitioned. Confiscated. That true?"

"They took over ten thousand worth of merchandise out of the tannery when I got this bust to the face."

Brandon nodded and worked his lips as he looked down the valley. "That means there's gonna be a war. You up to shooting people, Delgado?"

Sam glanced at Shyla. "They threatened the woman I love."

Shyla said hotly, "They were within a whisker of dragging me out and into their car. Your mother's had us shooting for two days now."

"Can you hit anything?"

"Six out of six in a soup can at twenty feet," Shyla told him proudly. "Delgado here, he misses on occasion."

"I do a lot better with the rifle," Sam told him. "Your mom says I'm a natural."

Brandon studied them thoughtfully, his curious Tappan eyes boring into them. As if coming to a decision, he said, "If you're into guns, you might want to come with me."

They put the horses into the corral with a fresh bale, scooped out oats, and followed Brandon to one of the outbuildings along the base of the slope. He fished a key out of a crack in the logs, opened the door, and let it swing open.

"Welcome to my reloading room," Brandon said. "If shithead is into confiscating things, he'll be slobbering to have this."

A big safe stood in the rear, and a bench along one wall supported curious equipment the likes of which Sam never seen.

"What do you reload?" Shyla wondered as she stepped into the room.

"Ammunition." Brandon pursed his lips, looking around. "Those kegs on the floor are filled with different kinds of powder. Primers in the cartons up above. Bullets in the boxes on the shelves, all sorted by caliber. The plastic boxes are the loading dies."

"Why show us this?" Sam asked.

Brandon stepped over, peeled a can of Copenhagen from a plastic roll, and used a thumbnail to break the seal. Taking a dip, he placed it in his lip, sighing. "Damn, I missed chew. Ran out the second day. Got so owly it's a wonder Shanteel didn't brain me with a hatchet."

He then looked them both in the eyes, saying, "If the shithead is as bad as you say, and Grandad is...well, he's the way he is. Government's gone. It's back to the will of the people. Can't fight tyranny unless you've got something to fight with."

"And we can fight with what's in here?"

"Yeah, about ten thousand rounds worth."

"Good," Shyla whispered. "Because I looked into that man's eyes. He's a monster. And he will be coming."

ULTIMATE MYTHS

***

Until the collapse I never understood how flimsy civilized morality was. We didn't know it, but the Rule of Law was already breaking down. It started in the Obama administration, corroded beyond repair in the Trump years, and disintegrated into a mockery in the last administration. From sanctuary cities, refusal of subpoenas, political activism in the Justice Department, immigration laws, COVID, economic collapse, impeachment, antifa, BLM, boogaloo, QAnon, and Americans shot in the streets to the subsequent rise of the doctrine of "Noncompliance based upon conscience". All the way from local sheriffs up to the presidency, Americans had been preconditioned to think of laws as political policy meant to infringe on their rights. As something they could pick and choose.

Was it any surprise then, that as the collapse started, people took matters into their own hands? Ignored the orders, regulations, and restrictions? If local, state, and federal government didn't follow the laws, why should the people?

Excerpt from Breeze Tappan's *Journal.*

CHAPTER TWENTY-SIX

***

A WEEK HAD PASSED. HARD TO BELIEVE. THAT LIFE HAD CHANGED SO RADICALLY, AND irrevocably, was surreal. A fantasy of tragedy and hope. Sam tried to make sense of it as he sat on the front porch stairs. He'd finished his chores—helped Frank change oil in the tractor, shoveled horse shit out of the barn—and now had a can of cold beer in his hands. The bruise had faded from purple to a horrible shade of yellow-green, and the swelling had gone down.

Shyla was in the kitchen, helping with the dishes.

As the sun sank behind the mountains, the ridges to the east glowed an unearthly orange tinged with gold. A peaceful façade that masked the terrors lurking beyond, where God alone knew what was burning.

Looking out over the valley—golden as it was with the slanted afternoon light—he saw a paradise. A fragile refuge.

It counter-balanced the worry deep in his soul; he had no clue what was happening in New York. Wondered if The Yucateca wasn't a charred hull of a building. Lived steeped in guilt over the suffering his parents must be enduring.

If they still lived.

Just because he couldn't do anything for them didn't alleviate him of the sucking sense of responsibility.

Shanteel stepped out of the door, walked stiffly across, and carefully seated herself next to him as though every muscle in her body ached. Since her return, she'd spent her days with Brandon. Riding Old Tobe. It was like she'd been avoiding the field crew. Her thoughtful dark eyes stared off across the ridge-lined horizons all dotted with juniper. She, too, had a beer.

"Word is that we're drinking the last canned beer in the county,"

Shanteel said. "From now on, it's all gonna be bottles."

"Bottles can be refilled at the brew pub in town. Cans can't."

"Bottles eventually break. What happens then? Put your beer in a ziplock?"

"Won't be any ziplocks. Shouldn't be any problem coming up with bottles though. Plenty of them in the dump."

She gave him a suspicious sidelong look. "You're telling me we're gonna dig up filthy bottles covered with rotting garbage from the dump and drink beer out of them?"

"Glass doesn't get contaminated. Washed and boiled, it'll be as sterile as the day it was manufactured."

Shanteel considered. Shook her head. "I still think I fell through the fucking rabbit hole." A pause. "You got something on your mind, Delgado?"

"None of my business." A beat. "You're different. Shyla thinks it's drugs."

"Me and Brandon? Drugs? He does booze and that Copenhagen, but that's it. I worry about the Copenhagen, but Dr. Holly told me when Brandon's roll of chew is gone, there won't be any more."

She gestured with her beer. "So, here's the thing: I got lost, and I got scared. Every way I turned in that fog was wrong. I ran, I cried, and I was in a panic like I'd never felt before."

"Didn't you hear the shots?"

"Sure. And I just knew the Tappans were killing y'all. I mean, I grew up hearing gunfire, and when I did, it was because someone was killing someone else."

Sam made a face. "We're so clueless sometimes. That thought never crossed our minds."

"I just ran harder. And then I was at this drop off on one side and trees on a really steep slope ahead, and I was getting cold and real hungry. Then it starts to rain. It's getting colder, and I'm stumbling along the edge of the trees. The rain turns to snow, and I'm wet all the way through."

She smiled at the memory. "That's when I hear this voice call, 'You might want to take that deer trail to your left. Footing's better.' And I turn around and see my worst nightmare sitting there on a horse. And beside him is this big dog. Like a scene from hell: Gun-totin' White man on a horse running down a terrified Black woman."

She took a drink of beer. "He says, 'I got Old Tobe saddled up here. We might want to make tracks back to that patch of timber and hole up. The way you're going, you're headed down into Frying Pan Canyon.'

"I mean, what am I going to do, Sam? Freeze to death, or let the man do what he will? I'm just standing there crying and shivering and miserable."

"So you got on the horse?"

"Hey, I figured this girl's already dead." She flicked her fingers in an airy gesture. "So he leads my horse off through the snow, and it's really coming down. Can't see five feet in any direction. And then we're in trees, and he says, 'Here's a good spot.' And I see a sort of tipi made of lodgepoles."

"That's the wickiup?"

"'Got to work some to make it tight,' he tells me. So we carry more poles and make the thing bigger, and by then I'm shivering so hard I'm clumsy. He almost drags me in, scoops out a hole in what he calls 'the duff', and within minutes, he's got a fire going."

She closed her eyes, a delicious expression on her face. "I never, in my whole life, felt such a wonderful thing as that fire. Meanwhile he ties a rope across the inside, and tells me, 'You need to get out of those soaked clothes. Hang them on the rope to dry. Keep the fire hot, and it shouldn't take more than an hour. Wrap up in your bedroll. If you run low on firewood, bust off squaw wood from the trees.'"

"What's squaw wood? Sounds racist."

"He tells me that's the low dead branches sticking out of the tree trunks. Then he says, 'I'm leaving Talbot. I'll be back by dark with supper.' And he disappears into the snow."

"So you did it?"

She shrugged. "Some part of my brain reminded me that I was still alive, and I clung to that. At dark he's back with a rabbit. And damn if he doesn't let me eat most of it. I ask, 'Why are you doing this?' and he looks real thoughtful and says, 'I gave my word.' Then he smiles. 'But I'da done it anyway.'"

"They consider it honor," Sam told her.

"Never had much to do with that. Honor? That's the kind of shit you read in a fairy book where I come from. But the big surprise is when he unzips my sleeping bag and spreads it open. Then he digs down into the duff and makes a hole just big enough for the two of us. He lines the hole with my tent for a covering, and explains that, given the way we feel about each other, sleeping back-to-back will be best, but I can snuggle with the dog. Snuggle with the dog? Say what? When I ask why in the same hole, he says, 'To keep from freezing to death.'"

She laughed again. "Imagine my surprise when I wake up the next morning spooned around him like shrink wrap. I may be disgusted with myself, but I'm disgustedly warm."

Her expression turned serious. "The snow was still coming down outside. We built up the fire, got soaked getting more wood, and then we started talking."

"That had to be interesting."

Shanteel gave Sam a level gaze. "Outside of my aunt, I've never had conversations like those. Never knew a man could talk honest like that. Not only does he listen, he thinks. I'm telling him about what it's like, growing up black and female in Philadelphia's squalor. About the drug houses, the burned-out buildings and the roaches and rats. About my mother being shot. He *heard* me. But no man'splaining, none of that patronizing white guilt shit."

She took a swig of beer. "We talked about everything and nothing. I told him things I've never told another human being. About what it means to be me. What I hope, what I'm afraid of."

"Did he open up?"

She nodded. "Hopes, dreams, what it means to be alive. History and philosophy. The man got out of high school with a C average, and I'm arguing intricacies of the human condition with him? Then, on the third day, we see elk. He stops short in the snow, and we're watching. I'm speechless, like having a religious vision as they stand in the timber, breath steaming. And when it's all over, he says, 'Wasn't that the most magnificent thing you've ever seen?'

"I look down at that rifle he's carrying. 'Surprised you didn't shoot one.' He gets this hurt look. 'I've lived off elk all my life,' he says. 'I'm part elk. I love them, and I cry every time I kill one. It's like I'm killing part of me.'"

Sam said, "I don't get it."

"I think you will." She tossed off the last of her beer. "I think we all will. Something about the kind of world we're living in now. What we had back east, it was an illusion, Sam. A warm cultural blanket of laws and social protection and food stamps. I'm not saying it didn't wear thin in my ugly part of Philadelphia, but we're all in the forest now. You know it. You're packing a gun these days. I ate an animal I killed with my own hands. I *felt* it die. And in the middle of all that, I found the first man I *ever* respected. The first man who ever really *respected* me."

She crumpled the can. "So, here I am, riding a horse all day to check and count the cows that will feed me. I can tell the difference between elk and deer tracks. I'm *sleeping* in a *barn*, with a *white man*, on *hay bales*, and for the first time in my life, I'm happy with myself."

"Funny, isn't it?" Thomas Star said as he walked out and settled himself next to Shanteel. He braced his arms on his knees and stared down the valley. He was wearing a smudged white cotton shirt, his graying braids hanging down in back. "Society and culture made us all separate. So here we are, having all of that ripped away and finding human beings underneath."

"You think my Seminole Cherokee ancestors understood that?" Shanteel asked.

Thomas absently shook his head. "They were all too busy being who they were supposed to be. That was Seminole, and only Seminole. Or Cherokee, and only Cherokee. In some ways I got lucky being Shoshoni. In others, not so lucky."

"How's that?" Sam asked.

"Shoshoni all came from a loosely organized ethnic band societies. Total egalitarianism. No big chiefs, no hard clan rules or stratified society like Native people had back east. No kivas, or sodalities like down south. We were 'Be who you are' Indians. Don't like the group you're with? Pack up and leave."

"Doesn't sound so bad." Shanteel leaned forward, propping her chin on her crossed arms. "What's the unlucky part?"

"Unlike, say, the Arapaho, we didn't have the tight-knit age-grade societies, the social cohesion necessary to deal with the white world and its agencies, institutions, and bureaucracies. It's a lesson I've been talking to Evan about. Something you're all going to have to deal with in the coming years."

"Where's the balance? That's what we're going to have to figure out." Sam got Thomas' point.

Thomas said, "There's going to be a lot of pressure to make an authoritarian government in the Basin. Edgewater is already setting up the foundation for it. He's the strong man, the one who is going to offer security in a time of crisis."

"I've had a taste of his security. No thanks."

"He's threatened your wife."

"Shyla's not my wife."

Thomas smiled blandly, asking, "Think outside of your Western Christian culture. You and she work side-by-side all day long. You laugh and smile and dream together. You share the burdens of the future as partners, and at night you make love and sleep in the same bed. In Shoshoni terms, what else would you call your relationship?"

"But, I mean..."

"Oh?" Thomas asked. "This is just a quick dalliance? A brief affair for the sex?"

"No!"

"You want to build a life with her?"

"Yes, damn it."

"Because you love each other."

"I... Okay, yes."

"But for the Judeo-Christian religious baggage and legitimacy requirements for the rearing of children in a patrilineal system, isn't that usually the way marriage is defined in the anthropological literature?"

Sam wasn't the only one staring wide-eyed at Thomas.

"Shit," Shanteel whispered, a stunned look on her face. "According to your terms, I'm married to a *white* man?"

Thomas slapped hands to his Levi's. "I'm always amazed by anthropologists and how blinded they are by their own cultural biases. A white man? Is that how you really see him? Answer honestly, Shanteel, and think about the inherent hypocrisy practiced by those who shouted the loudest about racial equality in the past."

She bowed her head onto her crossed arms and nodded. "Lot of comeuppances out here aren't there?"

"You're in love with Brandon." Thomas made a tsking sound with his lips. "The rebellious part of you is reveling in the new wonder.

You're breaking the taboo, blaming it on the place, the times, on the precariousness of your situation. Another part of you is insisting that it can't work because of who you really are. Because of what he is."

"How you know?" Shanteel only slipped into street slang when she was really upset.

"My first wife, Angie, was white. Met in college. She was from Amherst, Massachusetts. In the end, we called it quits because once the exotic and daring part wore off, we both thought we had to be different people than our souls wanted us to be. She went back to Massachusetts and married a lawyer who was a partner in a Boston firm that specialized in corporate law. I went back to the reservation and married a Crow pow-wow grass dancer. It wasn't what society thought of us that made us do that, it was what we thought of ourselves. We were such fools. Angie was the one real love of my life."

"*Yeah, makes you wonder. What's a lust-bunny like that doing with a beaner?*" The words from the tannery came back to haunt Sam.

Made Sam wonder how much deep-seated and festering ethnic baggage he might have in some dark recess of his mind.

"Why are you still here, Thomas?" Sam asked. "The pass has been open for days."

The Shoshoni thoughtfully watched an eagle come soaring over the valley. "The spirits haven't told me it's time to leave. They want me here for a while. Speaking of which, you seen *Nynymbi?*"

"Just the picture of him hanging on the cabin wall."

"*Nynymbi?*" Shanteel asked.

"I have a spirit helper."

"Trouble is coming," Thomas said. "He'll warn you before it breaks, you'll see."

"Thomas," Shanteel asked, "what you were saying about not being who we think we are? Who do you think Brandon thinks he is?"

"What you're really asking is whether deep in his soul he ultimately sees himself with a white girl? I think he finds some amusement that he'd fall for a black, big-city woman from back East. A sort of divine joke because he's been looking in the wrong place. But Brandon doesn't care what his wife looks like, or where she comes from, or if she's black. The woman he craves in his heart is a partner: strong, capable, and fearless like his mother. He will stand with whichever woman stands with him."

"How'd you get so damn wise? The spirits tell you all this?"

"Spirits? I wish. I got this wise from sixty years of making stupid mistakes." He squinted at the distance, and said under his breath, "Ah, yes. I see."

A black suburban came roaring down the ranch road.

Sam leaned in the door, calling, "Vehicle coming! Just one."

Evan and Bill rose from where they were sitting at the dining room table; dishes stopped clinking in the kitchen.

Everyone came trooping to the front porch, and Sam recognized the Wyoming State Patrol emblem on the door panels as the Tahoe pulled to a stop in the yard. A uniformed officer stepped out and fixed his hat to his head. He looked around at the mountains, before slamming the door behind him.

"Bill. Frank. Evan," he greeted, and then added, "Pam, Meggan, good to see you."

"Sully," old Bill cried in delight as he hobbled out and took the officer's hand. "What brings you out this way?"

"Got a message. Governor wants to see you." He glanced warily at the rest of them. "Wants to see you and Evan in Cheyenne tomorrow afternoon."

From a pocket he produced an envelope. "Here are passes and travel permits for you, Dr. Holly, and Frank. You'll have an escort. Lot of trouble on the roads these days. Car jackings, gangs stopping and looting vehicles. Gets worse the closer you are to the border."

"What's Pete want to see us about?" Bill asked as he took the envelope.

"The governor wants a briefing on the committee and what you're planning. Wants Dr. Holly to interface with some of his people. And there are..."—the patrolman shot a wary look at the rest of us—"some other matters."

"Oh, it's all right, Sully," Bill said. "These are my people, and sure as hell not Edgewater's." To the field crew he said, "This is Captain Sully Richardson. He's the honcho for the Highway Patrol in the Basin. Go ahead, Sully."

"Doug showed up today. The Cody committee says they're about a week out from ready to roll. The Powell group is with us, and so are the eastern Basin towns."

"By God, that's good to hear," Frank said. Then he winked in a conspiratorial way at Pam. She clasped his hand and gave it a squeeze.

"Got time for a cup of coffee? Something to eat?" Bill asked.

"Can't. I've got to be back in Cody. People are watching. Keeping track. Bad as it is with Edward Tubb in Hot Springs, it's a hell of a lot tenser in Cody now that that son of a bitch Edgewater has set himself up in the South Fork. He's got a lot of people crawling to him. Folks I never would have thought would suck up to a piece of shit like him."

"How about a sandwich to go?" Meggan asked hopefully. "It'll only take a second. And give me your travel cup. I've got hot coffee. The real thing. Won't be any more when this is gone. The grocery store is sold out. Last there is."

"Sure, Meggan." He opened his door, reached in, and handed her an old Maverick travel cup.

As Meggan hurried inside, Evan asked, "Any more news from the east?"

"It's like a friggin' black hole. Just rumors. Our guys on the Nebraska border heard that Washington's gone. Some sort of dead zone. Nothing alive within a hundred-mile radius. No one's said anything about a nuke. But—and brace yourself for this—we're at war with someone. Warren Air Base launched four missiles up over the pole in some kind of retaliation. People coming in from the west say there's real warfare around San Francisco, Seattle, and Portland. A guy from South Dakota on a motorcycle said that the whole northeast is like something out of a bad horror movie. Roving gangs, cannibalism, bodies piled and rotting. Gutted and burning buildings. Eerie."

Evan asked, "Well, if DC's gone, where's Edgewater getting his orders?"

"That's just it," Richardson said. "As best we can figure, there's no one calling the shots. We think he's making it up on his own. The governor will fill you in. He's been in touch with the governors of Nebraska, Utah, Idaho, Montana, and South Dakota. As far as I know, it's anarchy, Bill. Even the military command structure is in complete disarray above the divisional level. Or so we hear from General Kyzer at Warren Air Base."

"Somebody *has* to be in charge," Bill declared.

"Do they? I mean, I'm on the radio all day long. We've got one of the few functioning communications systems left in the state. If even a fraction of the stories I hear are true?" Richardson ground his teeth. "I'm not even sure that God can save us."

Sam reached out, took Shyla's hand, pulled her close. He shared a worried glance with her. With his wife. It felt oddly reassuring to think of her that way. Somehow full of promise when nothing else was.

"What about on the other side of the Colorado border?" Amber asked as she stepped out. She was wiping her hands with a dish towel.

Richardson's eyes narrowed to a squint. "Heard that the FEMA warehouses outside of Denver were looted by one of the gangs. Shot down the few soldiers left guarding the place after the army pulled out. Gangs carted the last of it away. Not that there was much left." He made a face. "I suppose that eventually these gangs are going to set their sights on Wyoming. We're bracing for the worst."

Amber sagged against the porch support, a look of despair on her face. "They going to let those people through the barricades?"

"No, ma'am. At least, those are the standing orders."

Old Bill pulled on his ear as he said, "We had never before seen so clearly the law of war: 'You or me.'" His lips twitched. "That's a quote from a survivor of the Eastern Front during the last days of the Second World War. Guess that's what we're finally left with."

ULTIMATE TRUTH

***

Civilization. The theory of law. Morality. The Ten Commandments. The Constitution. Ethics. All are geared toward functioning societies—rules by which numbers of people can moderate their behavior and act for the common good. A means of providing for social order, security, confidence, peace of mind and the protection of self and property. All highly advantageous in a functioning and stable state.

In the chaos of complete collapse, they become anathema.

Here's the moral dilemma Governor Agar faced: He had resources, industry, and energy to sustain a little over a half million people. Just over his border, nearly ten million traumatized human beings were going to starve to death. If they flooded north, they would consume everything, destroy the infrastructure, and ten-and-a-half million people would eventually perish in the ruins. Do you stop them? Hold that border?

What would you do?

Choose. Right now.

I don't hear your answer.

Choose.

Excerpt from Breeze Tappan's Journal.

CHAPTER TWENTY-SEVEN

***

THE SEX FELT DIFFERENT THAT NIGHT. SAM WASN'T EVEN SURE HE COULD PUT IT INTO words. He and Shyla shared a deeper intensity and richness, and he realized they had crossed some threshold into a realm that went beyond just being lovers.

In the aftermath, Sam lay with his legs tangled in hers, her head on his breast. He tried to put it all into perspective. What were the long-term prospects for their relationship? He assumed they could still get a license at the Hot Springs courthouse, could wrangle a marriage through one of the local churches. But if they did, somehow, he thought it would kill what was special between them.

Because that's who we expect ourselves to be.

"Thomas Star, you're the smartest man on the planet," Sam whispered softly.

As a cloud passed, a shaft of moonlight shone through the window and splashed on the floor. As it did, it filled the room with a soft white glow.

He thought he caught movement, blinked, and glanced at the opposite bunk. *Nynymbi* sat there, half hidden in shadow.

The spirit messenger's three-fingered hands wavered in a ghostly fashion; the concentric round eyes peered at Sam as though from another world. Outside, the mild wind blowing down the canyon whispered through the cottonwoods and hissed along the cabin eaves.

Nynymbi seemed to wave more frantically. Did Sam imagine it, or did the being slip away through the door?

Shyla murmured, "What's wrong?" as Sam disentangled himself.

"Outhouse, call," he fibbed, and kissed her pearlescent cheek. She sighed and rolled over, crushing the pillow into a wad.

Sam pulled on his pants, kicked into his boots, and stepped out into the night.

The breeze caressed his naked chest, flipped his hair around. Overhead the three-quarter moon was bright in the sky. Somewhere up the canyon, the great horned owls hooted to each other.

Nynymbi danced in the shadows beneath the long grass where the wind caught and played with it. No sooner did Sam notice him, than the little spirit helper led his eye to the solitary figure standing in the middle of the yard. Thomas had his head back, long braids swaying with each gust of wind.

Sam walked out into the yard as quietly as he could, not wishing to disturb the old man's solitude.

"I suspected that he'd bring you out." Thomas Star said it as if it were a casual remark over coffee.

"I'm still having trouble with this spirit helper thing."

"I have a B.A. in physics," Thomas told him. "While I was amazed by the principles and laws by which the physical world is governed, I was awed by theoretical and quantum physics. It's the multidimensional element that fouls most people up."

"I speak anthropology, not physics."

"I'm saying, in my clumsy way, that there's more to reality than we can perceive. Call it perturbations, ripples of energy, the jostling of particles from dimensions we can't imagine."

"You're saying *Nynymbi* is real."

"I'm saying trouble's coming."

Sam took a deep breath and stepped up beside Thomas to look up at the moon. "What kind?"

"The spirits don't say. All I know is that we have to be ready. Don't know how it will come. Or from where. Just be glad we were warned."

"Then maybe I'd better not go to Cheyenne."

"No. You need to go. The spirits didn't tell me why. Or did *Nynymbi* tell you?"

"I wasn't aware he could talk. But why would the spirits bother? Why go out of their way to warn us in the first place? What makes us so special?"

"We're not special. They warn us because we're willing to listen. And don't bother to deny it."

"But Thomas—"

"Otherwise you wouldn't have left a nice warm bed filled with a beautiful woman and followed a *nynymbi* out here."

"Okay. I'm warned. Now what?"

"Go to Cheyenne and find out."

THE LINE

***

I talked my way past the militia blockade on the state line at Woods Landing. Wyoming people share an identity. Once you get out of Casper, Cheyenne, and Sheridan, it's a tough state. Develops a sense of independence and self-reliance given the weather and distances.

Agar had decided to save his state—and to damn his soul in the process. Right or wrong, he had determined to preserve a sliver of civilization. Probably because unlike the governors of Colorado, California, New Jersey, and Maryland, he could.

It came down to population, resource production, and most of all, distribution. Wyoming had farming and ranching, oil and coal, railroads, and most of all, electricity. And none of it had been destroyed by rioting.

Agar established "The Line", a string of armed outposts, called OPs, along the Colorado border to turn back refugees. He manned it with Wyoming National Guard, the local militia.

I'd seen the alternative. I'd survived the insanity and mayhem. For my part, I joined a group of young women who used their motorcycles to run critical supplies to outlying OPs.

I'd given up part of my soul on Willow Creek Pass when Felix was shot.

I lost the rest of it on The Line.

Excerpt from Breeze Tappan's Journal.

CHAPTER TWENTY-EIGHT

***

IN THE RANCH YARD SAM HUGGED AND KISSED SHYLA GOODBYE. THE EARLY MORNING CHILL made hugging her close even more enjoyable. She gave him a saucy wink and promised, "Don't worry about me. I've got the pistol. Thomas and Willy and Brandon are here. And you know that no one would mess with Amber or Pam."

"We'll be back tomorrow night," old Bill called. "God, I'd think you two love birds were held together with superglue."

Sam grinned, reluctantly let loose of Shyla, and climbed into the truck.

"Hey, Delgado!" she shouted in the moments before the door was closed. "I'm making you a coat! I love you!"

The words hummed in Sam's memory like the endless chime of an old church bell. He sat in the Dodge's back seat with Evan and Court while Frank drove, and old Bill offered commentary from the passenger seat.

True to promise, a Highway Patrol Dodge Charger awaited them at the Highway 120 junction and took them all the way to Shoshoni where another patrol car escorted them to Casper and I-25. Sam was retracing his path into Wyoming. And how different it was from that day when the banks had failed. He saw the empty rangeland and distant mountains through entirely different eyes.

Along the way they passed occasional cars and trucks that had been abandoned and pushed off the side of the road.

"You know," old Bill said, "as long as the fools left the keys and didn't leave the ignition on and kill the battery, there's a living to be made hauling gas out and driving these abandoned vehicles back to town."

"Don't you think there's already enough abandoned vehicles in town?" Frank asked.

"Oh, stop being such a damned pessimist and think it through. Each of these abandoned vehicles is a collection of spare parts, tires, wires, and things we can't replace with a simple trip to the auto parts store."

"Hadn't thought of it that way."

And that was the thing. They all had to start thinking differently.

"I don't really know Governor Agar," Evan said. "You're the expert, Bill. What's he like?"

"A no-bullshit pragmatist. A lot of people, especially the state employees, didn't like him. The delicate art of diplomacy isn't one of his finer attributes. Government people like to chrome-plate and polish the barbed wire so it's all sparkling and gleaming before they shove it up your ass. Tell you it's just a gentle rain while they're pissing on your head. Pete Agar tells it like it is."

Frank added, "Which is why the people of Wyoming reelected him. Up until the shit hit the fan, I think a lot of the kiss-my-ass career people in state government, and probably the feds, too, were counting down the days until the next election. Agar would have been term-limited-out. Now? Well, do term limits even matter anymore?"

"Why did he call us down to Cheyenne for this meeting?" Sam asked. "Couldn't he move against Edgewater himself?"

Old Bill stared out the window at the passing grasslands. "Agar thinks on a state-wide basis. He might have started out as a lawyer in Casper, but his uncle ran a trucking company with offices in Rock Springs, Gillette, and Cheyenne. Cousins still have ranches in Lincoln County, Uinta County, and Crook County. A brother runs the biggest hotshot company in Casper."

"What's a hotshot company?" Court asked.

"Oil field service," Evan told him. "If You Betcha Oil Company is drilling a well sixty miles from town and discovers they've got three sections of drill stem that won't thread. The company calls the hotshot service, and, day or night, they run a truck and trailer over, pick up the stem, and deliver it right to the well."

"That's just it," old Bill said as they began passing the occasional house north of Cheyenne. "Agar knows the state from the grassroots up. I sure don't envy the decisions he's been having to make."

Evan reflected, "Do you save your own citizens, at the expense of thousands of lives, or do you let the refugees in to overwhelm your resources? The ultimate us or them. Either way, you're damned."

They had passed a surprising number of pedestrians headed north with bundles on their backs, and more than a few headed south. The farther south they went the numbers were up. Including knots of people sitting on the roadside across the way on the northbound lane. Mostly families, or small groups of adults, all had signs describing their plight. Most waved, even though Sam's party was headed the other direction.

"Doesn't look nearly as rough as Sully Richardson said it would," Bill muttered.

"Yeah," Frank added, "especially when we've got a Highway Patrol escort. You think anyone would have the balls to try and flag us down?"

Old Bill growled, "If the number of refugees grows, and they steal enough guns, a couple of patrol cars won't make much of a difference."

A checkpoint had been set up in the north-bound lane at the Highway 85 exit ramp. Orange construction barrels funneled traffic into a bottleneck, and a Highway Patrol car was backed up by four pickups filled with armed men and women.

"Must be the vaunted Wyoming Militia," old Bill grumbled.

Sam kept his nose to the window as their escort took the ramp at exit 12 and led the way into Cheyenne. He watched the tent city in Frontier Park pass: the signs people along the street displayed read: **Need Help! Starving Children! WFFF! Will Work For Food. Jewelry For Sale. God Loves Us So Help Please.** and so on. One stated: **Trade: 22s for food.**

This can't be America. Not my America. Sam knotted his fists as he took in the refugees.

Their Highway Patrol escort led them to a spot in the Capitol parking lot. After Frank pulled into the space the officer indicated, Sam was delighted to get out and stretch.

"Straight through the front door, gentlemen," the trooper told them. "Have a good day."

Sam looked up at the Capitol. The building was imposing, with the requisite soaring golden dome. A fortress mix of grayish-tan stone, classical columns, and high, arch-topped, windows.

Court shot him a "who knows?" look as they walked to the main entrance. Armed guards, dressed in Tee-shirts and light denim jackets, stood posts at the doorways.

Climbing the main steps, a soldier in fatigues asked their names.

"We're the Tappan bunch," old Bill told him. "We're supposed to confab with the governor."

Sam stifled a whistle as they were led into the rotunda, and he looked up. Okay, so it was a pretty cool building.

A second soldier led them down a hall and to a conference room.

Here, a young man was placing notepads before chairs around a central table. As he finished, he asked, "Anyone need coffee?"

"All around," Bill said. "Thanks."

After the young man left, Court meekly said, "Um, I don't drink coffee."

Bill gave him a sour look.

At that juncture, Merlin Smith and Sally Hanson entered. They shook hands all around, Sam and Court getting their first formal introduction to the Hot Springs movers and shakers.

The next two men to arrive were older. The first, a tall, elegant-looking sixty-year-old with silver hair, was introduced to Sam and Court as Terry Tanksley, or just plain "Tank". He wore a Western-cut suit, gleaming-black pointed Western boots, and bolo tie. His companion was Barry Lehman, the mayor of Cody, Wyoming, and an ex-state senator.

No more had introductions been made than the young man was back with a tray of cups, followed by a capable-looking woman with a large coffee pot that she plugged into the wall. One by one, she poured, handing cups around.

"Cheers." Sam clicked his cup against Court's. The computer geek just stared glumly into the black liquid.

"Looks like the cabal is here," Sally said as she glanced around the room.

"When did you get here?" Frank asked.

"Two days ago. We gave Agar a rundown on Edgewater's doings. How it almost ended in a riot in Hot Springs."

Lehman took a drink of his coffee before saying, "Same here. Agar said he wanted to consider his options, and that when he was ready, he'd make his decision about the Basin."

"Think he'll stick to it?" Evan asked.

Sally stated in her hard-as-nails voice: "I watched the governor execute four death sentences the night we got here. He pulled the trigger himself. Shot them in the back of the head. Agar is as serious as a heart attack when it comes to holding this state together."

At that moment, the governor himself stepped into the room.

Sam thought that Pete Agar should have been ten feet tall, built like a line-backer, wearing a ten-gallon hat, with twin six-guns on his hips. The man who walked in might have topped five-foot-six, with close-cropped black hair, thoughtful dark eyes, and was wearing a regular suit and tie. Even his loafers looked average.

Again, the introductions, though a curiosity lay behind his gaze as he was introduced to Court and finally Sam. From the order of things, Sam had no illusions but that he was low man on the totem pole. He and Court took the chairs at the far end of the table.

"Thanks for coming down," Agar began. "We don't have much time, so let's cut to the red meat: What's the latest situation with Edgewater, and what are we going to do about it?"

Tank spread his hands wide. "Essentially the guy's dug in up the South Fork. Took over the Clark Ranch. He has forty-some hard cases on his payroll who act as his enforcers. About half of the more influential of our citizens have offered their services. Most of them, I think, because they're seeking to avoid having their property seized or possessions taken. Some of his more vocal supporters think that by licking his ass, he's going to be their ticket to prestige and status. In short, he's got guys, and guns, and the willingness to use them."

"How is he paying them?"

Evan interjected. "With luxury items. Guns, booze, new vehicles, fancy clothes. Nice places to live. And he's making appointments. Lick his boots, and he'll set you up as high minister of fuel supplies, with your own armed guard to back it up."

Lehman added, "He's taking whatever he wants. Food, new trucks, merchandise off show room floors. Hell, he even raided the Buffalo Bill Center of the West. Took some of the most famous Western art, then he went through the Winchester museum and confiscated weapons. Not just the machine guns and combat stuff, but some of the really expensive guns for his personal collection. The guy's a whole new Herman Goering."

"And we think he's taking women," Lehman said distastefully. "Out-of-state girls if the stories are true. The piece of shit calls them his 'livestock' and is keeping them in that big horse barn back of the property."

"If we just had proof of that, every man, woman, and child in Wyoming would rise up and cut his throat," Old Bill growled.

Agar took this in, fingers tapping on the tabletop. "What are you planning to do about it?"

"Depends," Bill said. "How much leeway do we have?"

"As far as I'm concerned, as much as you need. I want the guy gone, but I don't want to start a small war. Where are the county sheriffs in this?"

"Big Horn and Washakie Counties are with us," Lehman said. "Sheriff Madden from Park and Hank Kapital from Hot Springs have taken the fawning sycophant route. They back Edgewater."

Agar looked back, making a tent of his fingers. "I'll leave it to you people to clean up your own messes in the counties. As for any action you take, if you want official sanction, we can do it in one of two ways: The first is through the Highway Patrol. Sully Richardson can swear you in as special agents, or whatever. The other option is that we can do it through the militia. I'll have my staff write you commissions. That way you report directly to me."

Sam glanced at Court, awed by what he was hearing.

"So we have free rein in this?" Bill lifted a questioning brow.

Agar gave him a dead-blank stare. "Within reason, Bill. I want the guy taken out. I don't care how you do it as long as we don't end up with a home-grown *Game of Thrones* in the Basin."

"What about Federal repercussions?" Tank asked. "The guy's the designated state director for the Department of Homeland Security, for God's sake."

Agar chuckled dryly. "Tank, operate under the assumption that there is no DHS. We've heard nothing from back east. It's as if Washington has ceased to exist. If some kind of ad hoc government shows up somewhere down the road, I want Wyoming to be in a strong enough position to brush them off."

"So, we take him out," Evan said. "What's next?"

"I want the Basin operationally functional. Self-reliant, and *part* of Wyoming."

"What else would it be?" Lehman asked.

"Part of Montana," Evan answered thoughtfully. "Geographically, the Bighorn Basin is an extension of the Yellowstone Valley, and economically it has closer ties with Billings."

"You had any feelers from either Billings or Helena?" Agar asked.

"Nothing we're aware of." Tank sounded slightly bewildered, as if this were all brand new.

"They've been too busy in Helena with their own problems and seizing the Bighorn Basin isn't in their political paradigm," Evan replied.

"Yet," Agar told him. "They'll get around to it."

Old Bill, a subtle smile on his lips, said, "Odd you'd think of it, Pete. What's brought this on?"

"Rawhide," Agar answered.

"What's Rawhide?" Frank asked.

"Rawhide Energy Station." Agar pointed south. "Big coal-fired power plant about twenty miles south of the border in Colorado."

"You've seized it?" Sally asked in her whiskey voice.

"Wyoming needed it. Most of Rawhide's electricity went to the Greenies, but Cheyenne, Laramie, and most of all, F.E. Warren Air Base, are on their grid. That's big enough that General Kyzer and I have guaranteed Rawhide's managers that we'd keep them safe, keep them fed, and supplied with coal. And, by God, I will do it even if it means formally annexing that part of Colorado. Electricity is my first priority."

"And you think you've got that covered?" old Bill asked.

"I can't save the state without it. I've got Wyoming's power-generating stations under Guard protection from Gillette, to Douglas, to Wheatland, south to Rawhide on the east, with Bridger and Flaming Gorge on the west. I have your hydro plants in the Basin, Alcova, Seminoe, and Pathfinder; that covers the rest of the state."

"And after that?" Evan asked.

"Fuel. I've got three refineries: Casper, Cheyenne, and Sinclair. Your crude in the basin is going out to either Laurel or Billings. But with the mountains in the way, I don't know how I can help that."

"We do," Evan told him. "We want to build our own refinery."

Agar smiled warily. "I think I'm going to like you, Dr. Holly."

"You're going to like Court, here, even more. He's got a head for logistics and problem solving."

Court flushed red, staring self-consciously at his coffee cup.

Agar said curiously. "What have the two of you been working on?"

"Self-sufficiency for the Bighorn Basin." Holly leaned back in his chair and smiled. "A two-year plan."

Sam thought that Agar was almost vibrating with interest as he said, "What are you doing tonight after seven?"

Holly chuckled. "Well, we all had tickets to *La Boheme* at the Met, but somewhere along the line I heard the performance was cancelled."

Agar laughed.

Sam glanced unsurely at Court, who shrugged and whispered, "What's La Boam?"

"*La Boheme,*" Sam whispered back. "It's an opera."

"I don't get it."

"It's a... Oh, never mind."

"Getting back to the problem," old Bill said. "None of this happens if we can't take Director Dickhead out of the equation. So, just to be sure we're all on the same wavelength, Governor, you don't care how we do, as long as we do it neatly?"

Agar smiled. "I like that word. Neatly."

"Do you want a trial?" Tank asked, knuckles thoughtfully against his lips.

"I'll leave that to your discretion. Mostly I just want results. And the sooner, the better."

Sam fought to keep from gaping like an idiot.

ATROCITY

***

There is no moral ambiguity when it comes to survival. Human values disintegrate in the struggle to still be breathing at the end of each day. German and Russian soldiers learned this in the horrendous caldron of the Russian front during the Second World War.

I learned it on The Line. Did things that would have been incomprehensible—beyond even my blackest of fantasy before the collapse. We all did.

I think we all asked ourselves: Are we heroes standing between barbarian hordes and the last vestiges of civilization? Or are we monsters committing a modern version of the holocaust?

The closer I came to believing the latter, the crazier I got. See enough death. Deal enough death. Witness enough despair. And what's left to live for?

Excerpt from Breeze Tappan's *Journal.*

CHAPTER TWENTY-NINE

***

SILVERWARE CLINKED, CONVERSATION WAS DESULTORY AS SAM SAT AT A TABLE IN THE rear of the Hilton Hotel's restaurant in downtown Cheyenne. After everything he'd been through since the collapse, his current situation hit him as totally unbelievable. The whole world had been kicked upside down and was rocking like a capsized turtle whose clawing legs couldn't find enough purchase to right itself. Yet here he sat, surrounded by normal-looking people who chatted, drank coffee, and ate sandwiches as a waitress bustled around them.

Frank had driven old Bill, Evan, and Court back to the Capitol for the seven o'clock meeting, which left Sam on his own for the evening. So here he sat, trying to make sense of the tumbling events in his life.

I just heard the governor of Wyoming order the murder of an appointed official of the United States government.

The notion floored him as he stared into the foamy head atop his glass of stout.

Not that he had any love for dickhead Edgewater, his thugs, or his arrogant despotism. Like Stalin's chief of secret police, Lavrentii Beria, or Hitler's Reinhard Heydrich, Edgewater—a minor functionary—suddenly found himself unleashed to practice his most sordid fantasies without fear of reprisal.

Sam fingered his cheek where the deep bruise remained tender. No love lost there—let alone for the fact that Edgewater had been on the verge of abducting Shyla.

And I couldn't do anything about it.

He'd been powerless, hit without warning, and worse, so scared he could hardly stand it. Which left a deep-seated sense of shame in his Latino-macho soul.

So, good riddance to Edgewater.

A part of him wanted to be there, to see the monster taken down. Another part understood that getting to the man would be dangerous. Edgewater's armed goons—at least the ones Sam had stared eyeball-to-eyeball with—would shoot without hesitation at the first hint that their patron was threatened. Work was that before Edgewater's retreat to the Bighorn Basin, he'd seized weapons from the Wyoming National Guard Armory in Guernsey. Any frontal move would be met with serious resistance.

"So, Bill, how are you and your merry band of conspirators going to take the bastard out?" he asked himself.

As he pondered various scenarios of ambushes and midnight raids, the young woman walked in. Maybe a couple of years younger than he, she immediately drew his eye.

Something in her walk reminded him of a soul-wounded warrior. Thick brunette hair hung down over her back in a ponytail. She wore a heavy yellow-and-tan motorcycle jacket, open to expose a light shirt tucked in at a thin waist. A belted pistol was on her hip, an ugly black rifle hung from one hand, and worn Levi's conformed to slim legs.

The way she carried herself, Sam immediately placed her as a Wyoming woman, possessed of that same quality he saw in Pam. Mindful of her, in fact. While not movie-star beautiful, her looks and presence made her damned attractive.

A heavy canvas military bag hung over her shoulder.

Sam did a double take. Thought at first glance that he knew her. Then dismissed it. Something about the eyes, the planes of her perfectly proportioned face.

He gave her a smile when she glanced his way—and let it fade at the haunted look she gave him in return.

The young woman slung the heavy bag against the wall and propped the rifle beside it. Her coat rustled when she peeled it from her shoulders and draped it over the back of her chair. She seated herself in the corner booth, her back to the wall.

The waitress called, "The usual?"

"Yeah, Bess." Something in her voice communicated a sense of futility.

From the corner of Sam's eye, he watched her prop elbows on the table and drop her head into her hands. The slump of her shoulders hinted at exhaustion and defeat.

Sam pursed his lips and stared into his beer. Lot of that going around. Hell, how did anyone really see a glimmering for the future?

Well, except for me.

He had the woman of his dreams waiting for him back at the ranch. Idly he asked himself: *If I had to make the choice between keeping the world as it was, saving Mother and Father, the whole economy, and all those people's lives, or giving up a future with Shyla, what would I choose?*

"Damn, Sam," he whispered. And with a flutter in his gut, he answered, "I'd choose Shyla."

Which made him decidedly uncomfortable.

Who the hell have I become?

As he mulled a way to bargain with the universe in an attempt to both save the world *and* keep Shyla, a soldier came striding in: fifties, silver hair, hard gray eyes, and hat tucked under his left arm. The man's uniform had seen better days.

The soldier didn't hesitate, but walked to the woman's booth and seated himself across from her as he placed his hat on the corner of the table. "Saw your bike out front. I hoped you'd made it back."

The young woman tilted her face up, leaving her chin supported on her palms. "Glad I could make someone's day."

"Got a call from the guys out at Able X-Ray. They were worried. Said you seemed really upset, on the verge of tears. Asked me to check and make sure you didn't do something dumb like pile the bike into a bridge abutment on the way back."

From the corner of his eye, Sam caught the woman's grim smile, the hardening of her brown-and-hazel eyes. "Hey, Captain, if I'm going out, I'm not trashing the bike in the process. I *love* that beast too much to hurt it."

"Glad to hear it."

"Heard that the guys over at Charley Echo had a tough day."

"Somebody down south got the bright idea that if they welded plate to a dump truck, they could smash their way through the line. Figured the plate would stop 5.56 rounds, and the truck was heavy enough to bash the Humvees out of the road. I guess their intelligence was flawed."

"Charlie Echo has Ma Deuce don't they?"

"Good memory. That big fifty tore the dump truck into scrap. Turned into a merry little firefight for about an hour or so."

"Any of our guys hurt?"

"Two. Nothing that stitches won't take care of."

Sam sat rapt, trying to picture what these people lived with every day. Charlie Echo? Had to be the code names for the line of defensive posts established along the Colorado line to keep refuges south of the border.

The brunette asked, "When are you going to let me back into Charlie sector?"

"What set you off today?"

"Who says I was 'set off?'"

"The guys at Able X-Ray." The Captain arched a knowing brow. "Come on, you know how the whole line feels about you. What happened out there today?"

Sam endured the long pause as the young woman and Captain engaged in a steely-eyed staring match.

Finally, the woman said, "A little girl, Cap. In a tent in a gully. Her family had somehow managed to get north of the line, found all the ranches burned. Ran out of water. She must have died first. Dad capped her big brother, then the mom, then did himself. And here's this little girl. In the damn tent, propped up by her favorite toy. A filthy stuffed sheep if you can imagine."

"You pass dead people on the side of the road all the time. What was different about these?"

"They had nothing." She paused. "No food. Empty water bottles. Nothing in their pack." She knotted a fist as she fought for control. "But they carried her stuffed sheep. And when she died, they left her, propped up with her beloved..."

The woman looked away, before adding, "Captain, how many of them have I just driven past? I mean, all it would have taken was a water bottle. Just a single..."

The silence stretched; Sam's stomach gone hollow.

Finally, the captain said, "There's no law that says you have to be a hero twenty-four seven. God, girl, take a break. Even my people on the line get a rotation. You're out there every morning. Taking chances my people wouldn't take on a dare."

"I'm not doing anything the other girls aren't. Lauren Davis, Audra Barkley, we're all— "

"Last time you came back with two bullet holes in your coat. Even you admitted that you just got lucky."

The captain pointed a hard finger. "You and I both know that from here on out, it's just going to get harder. Like that armored dump truck. It's not families anymore. We're looking at raiders. They've killed all the livestock, horses, and pets south of the line. Burned and looted everything lootable. These are desperate people willing to punch a hole in the line, hoping to hit outlying ranches and homes, load up what they can, and hightail it back south."

"All the more reason you need us to keep the OPs stocked in ammo and food."

"I'm calling it," the captain told her. "You've got a choice: enlist in the Guard, or take a break, but your days of traipsing around the border on the bike are over."

"You can't do that," she said hoarsely.

"Bet me. You gonna enlist?"

"Not a chance. You'd order me into some office somewhere."

"That's the nice thing about being an officer."

"Why are you doing this?" Her voice sounded empty.

"Because you've lit the slow-burning fuse, and it's just a matter of time before you detonate. You're dancing ever closer to disaster out there. Every man and woman in the Guard would die for you, but I'm not going to let you get yourself killed just because you don't see any way out."

She sat there, muscles tense, on the verge of shattering.

The captain pushed his chair back and stood. "I've got to go. Meeting. Something's cooking up north. But I mean it. You're relieved, and I've given orders at the quartermaster's. You are officially 'stood down'."

Her voice might have been an overstretched wire. "Want me to beg?"

"Nope." He paused. "But I'd ask you to do me a personal favor."

"What?"

"Go home. Take a break. Give it a month or so. After that if you want, yeah, come on back." He paused. "But not until then. You got me?"

"Yes, sir." It was said in total defeat.

The captain turned and strode rapidly for the door.

The waitress placed a sizzling steak and potatoes in front of the woman, along with a glass of beer.

Sam lingered for maybe another half hour, nursing his stout, trying to cast surreptitious glances at her. In that entire time, the young brunette never so much as reached for her fork. While her food went stone cold, she just sat there, as if paralyzed, and stared. Without expression. At nothing.

THE BALANCING ACT

***

As far as havens go, Cheyenne wasn't much in those days. But the lights were on, the water worked, there was food and places to shelter from the rain and sun. For most people, it might not have been high living, but compared to the palls of smoke rising over the Front Range cities down in Colorado, it beat the hell out of alternatives.

Getting off the line, back to Cheyenne, made the difference. If we killed people trying to smash their way across the border, seeing the folks in Cheyenne, alive, struggling to go on with their lives gave us a justification. Others died that these might live.

And the madness and total despair were held at bay.

Barely.

When the only thing left is a hopeless battle, the will to live vanishes. When I, or the other girls, asked what made me any different from the desperate starving wretches trying to sneak across the line, we had no answer.

I'd committed ugly acts. Lost my balance. I had nowhere to go. The hole was too deep, too dark to find my way out of. I was just falling, with no bottom in sight.

Excerpt from Breeze Tappan's *Journal*.

CHAPTER THIRTY

* * *

SAM AWAKENED WHEN COURT ENTERED THE ROOM. THE BEDSIDE CLOCK READ 11:38. SAM sat up in bed, squinting in the harsh light. Court closed the door and flipped the lock closed before walking over to his bed. There, he dropped onto the edge, head hanging.

"You look like it's the end of the world," Sam told him.

"It is." Court rubbed his tired eyes.

"How bad?" Sam propped himself on the pillows.

"The east is gone, Sam. All of our people. The cities, Washington DC, New York, Boston. They think it was two nuclear strikes. And the EMP took out all the rest. As far west as Iowa."

"What the fuck? When? How? I mean..."

"I'm just telling you what General Kyzer told the governor. So this is hearsay. Best guess is that everyone was caught off guard trying to deal with the economic crisis. It was bohungus brilliant. See, they destroyed the money. Who would have ever thought money was vulnerable? It's just there, right? Money is faith. People believe in it. But a dollar bill's just a piece of paper. And the electronic accounts? They were corrupted. So the president declared Martial law to keep order."

"I thought money was backed by gold or something."

"Nope. Not since Nixon. A dollar is worth something because you, Sam Delgado, and everyone else, believes it is. It's an abstract. A measure of account for perceived value." He paused. "They didn't have to corrupt all the accounts. Just enough to shake confidence in the system. Then it all cascaded after that."

"But the records?"

"Couldn't be trusted not to have the malware. By the time it could be fixed, the country had already come apart. Whoever did this played upon American distrust of other Americans. Democrats and Republicans, liberals against conservatives, East against West, Antifa against Proud Boys, Q-Anon against BLM, urban against rural, racial resentment, distrust of government, you name it. We were ripe to turn on each other."

Sam pressed a hand to his gut, thinking about what he'd heard about the line. Americans. Down in Colorado. Starving. Being shot by Americans. From Wyoming. Trying to protect their homes.

"Meanwhile"—Court interrupted—"some humongous container ship unloads an entire Chinese army in San Francisco."

"A what? A whole army?"

"Yeah. Right there. At the port. Container after container, all holding troops, guns, tanks, fuel, food. A whole fricking army. In a container ship! And the longshoremen do the heavy lifting."

"Chinese? So...it was the Chinese who did this to us?" Sam tried to concentrate, to kill the images of Hempstead. Of what his parents' last moments might have been like. About the immensity of everything he'd known. Just gone.

"Nobody knows." Court stared at his pudgy hands. "Iran, North Korea, China, Russia, Pakistan? Maybe all of them working in unison for all anyone in Wyoming can tell. Those four missiles that were launched by the missile command at Warren Air Base? Rumor is they went to China. That the order to launch came from the Joint Chiefs."

"Holy shit." Sam suffered through the image of what Manhattan would look like after a nuclear blast. The glass blown out of the towering buildings. The fires. People burning alive by the millions. Washington DC. The Capitol collapsed into rubble, the Smithsonian buildings and all they contained, incinerated. The Washington monument blown away. An entire history and heritage vanished in an instant.

"We're it," Court told him. "Wyoming, Montana, the Dakotas, Nebraska, Idaho, Utah, and Nevada down through New Mexico and Arizona. Most of Texas. That's who still has electrical grids, working infrastructure. Any kind of social cohesion."

"What about California? Oregon and Washington?"

"All Agar knows is that there's supposed to be fighting around San Francisco, Seattle, and Los Angeles. Agar wasn't sure. Might have been additional Chinese landed at other ports. It's all pretty confused with the chaos, rioting, and looting."

"So...what do we do?"

Court met Sam's gaze, a vision of Hell lingering in those wounded brown eyes. "We save what we can. Who would have thought it would be out in the wasteland of the West, but if there's any chance for who we are as a people, it's out here."

"I don't understand."

"No one does," Court told him. "I tried to explain it to Agar, but I don't think he quite got it. Any place with a large urban population is doomed. So what if the army is fighting Chinese outside San Francisco? There's no infrastructure to send them ammo, food, spare parts—and the civilians around them are starving and turning on each other. If China was nuked, the EMPs would have blacked out the entire country. Just like the US, China's economy stopped in its tracks. They can't resupply their army, either."

"Why not?"

"Because nothing works, Sam!" Court gave him a half-panicked look. "Don't you get it? Everything with a computer chip, phones, banks, cars, trucks, clocks, airplanes, trains, industrial robots, power plants, cargo ships, tablets, the cloud, security systems, traffic lights, pump controllers, washing machines, TVs, anything electric." He swallowed hard. "It all stopped."

"All of it?"

"Everything that ran on transistors or a chip. Which is everything. Talk about the Achilles heel of the world economy."

"Then why would anyone have started the cyberattack in the first place? I mean, they had to know we'd retaliate."

Court's shoulders slumped even further. "Name a war, any war, that anyone's started in the last century that worked out the way it was supposed to. Hitler didn't figure he'd be living in ruins within four years. Japan didn't anticipate we'd blast their cities to radiated ruin. Korea was supposed to become a paradise. Vietnam? Did the Russians stop Islamic radicals by invading Afghanistan? Did Bin Laden initiate world-wide jihad on 9/11? Is Iraq a shining example of democracy that reshaped the Middle East? Did Iran neuter Saudi Arabia by turning Yemen into a conflagration?"

"Guess not."

Court sighed. "So, I can guess a thousand reasons why another country would want to knock the US off the top of the heap. As far as plans go, the bank cyberattack was pretty good. Destroy the money. Then step in with a way to stop the chaos."

"But?"

"But it worked too well." Court pulled off his shoes and flopped onto the bed. "If American banks went down completely? They'd take the international banking system down with them. Maybe the malware doesn't stop in the US, maybe it spreads across the globe? We're talking a world disaster. Like a fire that burns out of control. Chaos everywhere."

"And someone panics?" Sam suggested.

"Could be. They know the damage to the US is so great it will require retaliation, so they hit first. Try to disable our ability to strike back by taking out the East coast, the White House and Pentagon."

"But it doesn't work. We launch missiles."

"And there's the submarines, the strategic bombers."

"Or it could have been someone besides the Chinese who nuked the East Coast. Maybe North Korea or Iran who wanted to capitalize on our weakness?"

Court made a snuffing sound. "You'd be a pretty good gamer yourself."

"Yeah. Lucky me."

Which didn't ameliorate the fact that everything he'd ever known, home, Mom, Dad, Sammy, Tico, Paco, and all the kids he'd grown up with, his high school, the New York skyline. All those people and places. Dead.

As it sunk in, the keening began in his soul. He closed his eyes as Court got up, flicked the room lights off, and left him in miserable darkness.

To cry.

And mourn.

ROCK BOTTOM

***

*It is going completely numb and senseless. Can't think. Can't compre-
hend sight, hearing, smells, sensations. A total blank out.*

*I'd seen it on the line. That point when a human being finally
lost the last glimmer of hope. The empty despair beyond which they
couldn't feel. Like flicking a switch. The brain just turns off. Goes
dark. Doesn't process.*

I was that way.

The night I was pulled off the line.

Excerpt from Breeze Tappan's *Journal.*

CHAPTER THIRTY-ONE

***

THE RAUCOUS SNORE—LIKE SOMEONE STRANGLING ON JELLY—JERKED SAM FROM A TOR-
tured sleep. He blinked awake, could see gray morning light filtering in past the curtains.

The wracking snore repeated, almost shaking the walls. Sam winced, sat up in bed. Across from him, Court lay with his arm across his eyes, mouth agape. As Sam watched, Court sucked in another snore that might have been chainsaw teeth clattering on metal.

"Jesus," Sam whispered, dressing in the half-light. Sure as hell, there was no sleeping with that kind of caterwauling. Besides, his dreams had been tormented enough. Mostly consisting of dark visions, imaginations of death, billowing smoke, and misery.

The worst part was knowing. And not knowing. His brain worked overtime with memories of his childhood. Times that Mom smiled, or Dad had been beaming with joy. About their upstairs home on the second floor of the restaurant. It had been a warm place to grow up.

The time they'd gone into the city, to Cipriani. The three of them. "Tonight," Papa had declared, "we celebrate. As of today, The Yucatec is ours! The bank has sent the title. We owe no one for anything! *Ninguno para nada.*"

Sam ground his teeth, fought down the grief. Busied himself with brushing his teeth. Tried not to dwell on the painful knowledge that he was alive. Safe. And they... They...

No. Don't think it.

Stepping out into the hall, he took the stairs down to the ground floor. Looked out onto Lincoln Way. No traffic this morning. A soldier—Guard from his uniform—stood by a silver and yellow motorcycle. Obviously, a sentry of some sort.

"Can I help you, sir?" the doorman appeared at Sam's side. He looked barely old enough to be out of school.

"Must be a pretty important bike to merit a guard like that."

"Yes, sir."

"Sam?" Frank called from the elevator. "You're up early."

"Court snores, and I couldn't sleep."

"Coffee? According to the story, two semi loads made it as far as the Pilot truck stop when the crash hit. For the time being, Cheyenne has it in spades."

"Until it runs out," the doorman said. "Makes us the premier hotel in Wyoming."

Sam took one last glance out at the street. Across the way a woman sat on the curb, her head down, blonde locks falling over her knees. Beside her was another of the hastily scrawled signs proclaiming **WFFF**.

"What does that mean?" Sam pointed.

Frank had come to stand beside him.

"Will fuck for food," the doorman said uneasily. "Cheyenne police will be along soon. They try to keep them away from the hotel. It's just...well, the way things are."

Sam put a hand on the door, started to push it open.

"What are you thinking, Sam?" Frank asked.

"I've got twenty dollars. It's not much. It'd keep her fed for a couple of days."

"We're supposed to discourage that sort of thing," the doorman told him. "The hotel doesn't want to get a reputation for handouts."

"Yeah. Right." Sam stepped out, glanced up at the heavy sky. Smoke haze hung low, somber and threatening. The silence was equally oppressive. This time of morning, before the crash, Cheyenne would have been alive with traffic. People on their way to work in any of the state and federal offices, or the support services that made the city function. Now the streets were empty.

"Hey," Sam called as he walked up to the woman. "Excuse me."

She started, looked up with bleary hazel eyes. "'Scuse me. Guess I nodded off. You got somewhere we can go?"

"Go?"

"Don't want to do it here on the sidewalk, do you?"

She might have been in her early thirties, would have been attractive if she'd been washed and dressed in something besides a filthy tee-shirt and stained jeans.

"Here's a twenty," he told her. "Go buy yourself a meal."

"But?" she frowned at him. "You mean, like, just take it?"

"Yeah. No strings."

She snapped the money away, muttered, "Thanks." Before he might change his mind, she was trotting away as fast as she could. Didn't even look back.

Sam chewed his lips as he watched her go. How many like her were there? Where was the food going to come from?

He found Frank in the restaurant and asked exactly that as he seated himself at the table and signaled for coffee.

"Agar's trying to figure that out," Frank told him, rubbing his temples. The rancher looked as haggard as Sam felt. "We've got the beef out there. More than enough. But the cows are still nursing calves. And how does the state compensate the producers for the beef? And if they do, the animals have to be hauled to a slaughter plant, who has to be paid, and the boxed beef has to be trucked from there to the consumer. So, in a state with very little cash floating around, how do people—most of whom have lost their means of income—earn enough to pay for a steak?"

"It's kickstarting an economy from nothing," Sam agreed, thankfully accepting the cup of coffee from the waitress. "And here we are, room and meals paid by the governor, drinking coffee, and living large."

Frank tilted his head in the direction of the street. "She taken care of?"

"Yeah. I guess." Sam fought down the turmoil in his chest. "Just got too much to get my head around. Been thinking about my folks. Home. I mean, I know they've got to be dead. But there's that part of me that can't believe it. And worse, I'll never really know. That's maddening."

"Yeah." Frank was staring at something way far away in the distance of his mind. "It's the not knowing."

The words were no more than out of his mouth before old Bill came rushing in, hitching along on his bad leg. He had his wide-brimmed hat clamped down on his silver locks, a passion burning in his Tappan eyes. He pulled up, saying, "Come on, Frank. Move your ass."

"What's got your tit in a wringer?"

"Got word. About Breeze. I think she's here. In Cheyenne."

Frank leaped to his feet, crying, "No shit? I was just thinking about her. Where? How? I mean, where is she?"

"That Guard captain, Ragnovich. Heard the name Tappan, asked if we were related to Breeze. Come on. I've got the truck running out front."

"See you, Sam. Be back as soon as we can."

Breeze? The missing daughter? The center of the great Tappan mystery?

Sam watched them go, then stared down into his coffee. When this was gone, there would be no more. Along with things like toilet paper, oranges and bananas, pepper, canned soda, tires, running shoes, movies, and how many other things? The dying of his world. So much was going away, he had to wonder what would remain. Well, outside of pain, loneliness, and suffering.

He'd seen it in the woman's eyes as she took his twenty.

Desperately, he hoped that if Bill and Frank found Breeze, she wouldn't be standing by a WFFF sign.

ESSENCE

***

Prior to the collapse, very few people ever asked themselves: When it comes down to it, what would I do to stay alive?

And, even if they did, any answer they came up with—with the exception of 'I don't know'—would have been meaningless.

You really don't know. Not until you're there. Face-to-face with the ugly reality. From my direct experience, some do draw the line. Accept to die rather than debase themselves. Too appalled by the prospects of their situation. Unwilling to live with the consequences.

Others surrender to whatever is necessary, groveling, accepting any humiliation to keep breathing.

Once upon a time, I would have scorned those poor wretches. Told myself, "I'll never allow myself to stoop that low."

It's like being shot at. You might insist to yourself, "I'll do this," or "I'll do that." But until the instant that bullet snaps past your ear and you get that runny feeling in your gut, you don't have the foggiest clue.

Anything you tell yourself until that moment is a lie.

Excerpt from Breeze Tappan's *Journal.*

CHAPTER THIRTY-TWO

***

IT WAS MAYBE AN HOUR AND THREE CUPS OF COFFEE LATER THAT COURT SHOWED UP.
Looking rumpled, he pulled out Frank's chair and dropped his bulk
into the seat. Around them, the restaurant had picked up. Most of
the tables occupied. But for the creeping reality that lay just beneath
Sam's thoughts, it might have been a normal morning. Plates clinking,
silverware on ceramic, the low conversation of the patrons. Even the
waitress hustling about in her uniform, with the pot of coffee.

"You snore," Sam greeted. "I thought I was sharing the room with
a buzz saw."

Court gave him a sheepish look, his brown gaze slipping away. "I
can't help it. I'm, like, asleep when it happens."

"At least you slept last night."

"You didn't?"

Sam shook his head. "I guess, given what we talked about last
night, we picked the lock open for too many nightmares. Couldn't help
thinking about my folks." A beat. "How about you? Indianapolis is
farther to the west. Would have been out of the blast zones."

Court stared sadly down at the coffee cup the waitress put before
him but waved the pot away when she was about to pour. "Just
water," he told her.

To Sam, he said, "Greenwood's a bedroom community. Sure, it's
suburbia, but the EMP would still have shut everything off. Anyone
driving would have been stranded when the pulse took out the car's
ECU. Stopped. Right there in the road. No lights, stores dark, no
gas pumps, and the credit cards were already worthless. Think of the
freezers at the grocery stores. All that ice cream. God pity the people
who were in elevators, or flying, or...well I guess everything."

"But it was the suburbs," Sam reminded. "They might have had...I don't know. Something."

Court sucked on his lips as he nodded. "Yeah, something." Then he added, "Dad's diabetic. Doesn't matter that he was personnel supervisor for Indiana Parks and Rec. There won't be any more insulin. Mom is a home-care nurse. EMP would have taken her pacemaker out." He snapped his fingers. "Just like that."

"Sorry."

Court watched the waitress shoo a customer away from the booth across from them, saying, "Sorry, that one's reserved."

"Who for?" the man demanded. "I'm the state oil and gas commissioner."

"Well, commission yourself up front to that table by the door. This one's reserved for a woman who's earned it by keeping your oil-and-gas ass safe."

After the waitress had chased the commissioner back to the front, Court asked, "Wonder who the celebrity is? Buffalo Bill?"

"Woman was seated there last night. Maybe our age. Some kind of hotshot-like runner for the posts on the line. She looked pretty tough. Had that soldier's stare like Hell had opened up and she'd stared into it for too long. Had some officer come chew her out for taking risks. The guy told her to go home. Didn't look like she took it any too well."

Court had fixed on something over Sam's shoulder. "She wear a motorcycle jacket? Brown hair?"

"Yeah? So?"

"So, here she comes. And, uh, if you ask me, she looks a little rocky. Like she tied one on last night."

Sam kept his eyes down as the woman stepped around their table and slung the heavy military bag onto the seat opposite her. She unslung a black military rifle and laid it atop the pack. Then she slid into the booth, back to the wall. For a moment she sat there, eyes closed, hands on the table as if to keep the room from spinning.

Court and Sam fixed on the rifle where it sat so close at hand. Damn thing set his teeth on edge. Some kind of hero huh?

The waitress was back, bearing coffee and a cup. "Good to see you're up and about. Bess said you'd need coffee. The special for breakfast?"

"You're a Godsend, Jen. You see the sentry? Cap's put a guard on my bike."

The waitress stared down, concern in her eyes. "You ask me, it's about time they 86'd your ass off the line. Why Ragnovich lets you girls ride out there is beyond me. You've done enough. Kept people going through the tough—"

"'Scuse me. Be right back." She almost ran for the women's room.

At Sam and Court's stare, the waitress told them. "Not one damned word out of either of you, you hear me?."

"What'd she do?" Court asked.

"She's one of the Line riders. She single-handedly saved the I-25 check point. One of the posts was being hard pressed, she'd run ammo, water, food, whatever. Them frayed spots on her coat? They're bullet holes, mister. They came that close to killing her."

"Sounds pretty tough." Sam indicated the women's room. "She all right?"

"Bottle flu. It'll pass." Then Jenn hurried to the back, calling, "I need a special."

"Combat hazards of being a hero, I guess." Court raised his eyebrows. "Any of that make any sense to you?"

"A little. Agar's taken some pretty extreme measures to keep the chaos south of the state line from rolling over the top of the people here. That captain last night, he was talking about armed dump trucks, fire fights. Sounded like the kind of talk you hear in a war zone."

"Here she comes." Court averted his eyes as she reseated herself.

Sam thought the brunette looked a little better; her face was freshly washed.

Court swallowed hard, said, "Excuse me, but I've got aspirin if you'd like some."

Her eyes were dark around the edges of the iris and faded into a tan. Striking, actually. And hard when they pinned Court. Then a quiver of a smile bent her lips. "Yeah, thanks. My head feels like someone split it with an ax."

Aspirin. Was that another thing that they'd never see again?

Court fished a bottle out of his pocket, uncapped it, and fiddled through a collection of pills until he had two aspirin. These he handed over.

To Sam he said, "Mom's a nurse. You think she'd send me off to Wyoming without a pharmacy?"

Sam asked, "That's your bike out front?"

"Yeah." She swallowed the aspirin, proving herself to be one of those tough kinds of people who didn't need water to wash it down. This was followed by a resumption of the hard stare. "Do I know you?"

"I was here last night. Left before you did."

"Before I ordered the whiskey. Yeah, must have been. That part of the evening's a little fuzzy." A beat. "Whiskey always gets me into trouble."

Again, that penetrating stare. "You're not from around here. Got marooned passing through? If so, you're doing better than most."

"Court and I were working on a project up in Hot Springs when the collapse happened. It's sort of our new home."

Her eyes softened. "How are things there? People doing all right?"

"Like everywhere," Sam told her with a shrug. "Trying to hold it together. The basin has a chance. We're down here with a delegation trying to put together a plan."

She blew on her coffee, took a sip, and let her eyes close. "God help us when this finally runs out. Mornings are going to be hideous after that."

Even as she said it, the ghosts were back; her gaze took on that thousand-yard stare. She might have been peering into Hell again.

What was it she'd said last night? A little girl and a stuffed sheep? The brother, mother, and father dead of murder suicide? That she passed dead bodies every day? Shots fired? That she'd almost been killed how many times?

"Sam asked softly, "Anything we can do?"

She vaguely shook her head, eyes still unfocused.

The waitress was back, setting two plates on the table. Sam and Court dove in. The meal consisted of steak, eggs, and potatoes. The former, so the Hilton claimed, were locally raised. The potatoes, they asserted, were freshly imported from Idaho.

Wow. The new beginnings of interstate trade.

It was maybe five minutes later. In an instant, the woman cried out, jerked half out of the booth, her hand clawing at a pistol that had been obscured by her coat. Even as Sam and Court started, she pulled up short, breathing hard. Her frantic eyes came into focus. She fixed on the room, on the people staring, and almost wilted into the bench.

For a moment she sat there, hand to her heart, eyes wide. Sam heard her say, "It's all right. I'm at the Hilton. It's breakfast. It's all right."

She glanced Sam's way, actually blushing. "Sorry. I was just...I mean..." She swallowed hard. Forced herself to ease back on the bench.

Yeah, sure. Sam figured he'd just seen a flashback. Like the kind that came with PTSD.

Giving the woman a sidelong glance, it was to wonder: What the hell had she endured? And the frayed spots on her heavy fabric motorcycle jacket? Bullet holes?

"Bill and Frank are coming through the door." Court used his napkin to wipe his lips. "Got some kind of soldier with them, and Dr. Holly's tagging along behind."

Sam craned his neck. Tried to make sense of the expressions on both Frank and Bill's faces as they entered the restaurant. Something anxious, almost afraid, but incredibly desperate. Not at all like the Tappans he was used to.

And yes, the soldier, he was that same captain from last night. Probably coming to check on the woman. Maybe ensure his orders were being followed?

Glancing at the brunette, it was to see her frozen. Stunned, and wide-eyed. Her lips parted, her color draining.

As Frank stopped short at the table, she asked, "*Daddy?*"

"Hey, baby girl."

In a shot she was on her feet, locked in a desperate embrace, repeating, "I'm sorry. So, so sorry, Daddy."

RANDOM CHANCE

***

Survivor's guilt? Divine intervention? Plain dumb luck? Chosen for a higher purpose? Who the hell knows? I was given another chance.

Sometimes it takes the end of the world before what would have been an impossible chasm can be bridged. For me, it happened in a second. One moment I was contemplating inevitable surrender, the next I was forgiven.

But for what?

How did a family squabble—no matter how serious—compare to the atrocities I had committed? Callous and numb, I had turned myself into a self-destructive machine. As mindless as a drone, fixed on a mission without thought or care that it would ultimately destroy me. Don't feel. Ignore any hint of humanity. Just do the job.

Given my sins, why did I deserve a second chance?

And how did I live with it?

Excerpt from Breeze Tappan's *Journal.*

CHAPTER THIRTY-THREE

***

SAM TRIED TO KEEP FROM GAPING AS FRANK AND THE YOUNG WOMAN CLUTCHED EACH other with the passion of drowning victims.

Frank's daughter?

This was the mysterious Breeze?

The restaurant had come to a stop; people gazed upon the reunion with knowing smiles. A brief flicker of shared enjoyment in their expressions before they turned back to their meals and ever-so-precious coffee.

Old Bill eased his way forward, laying a hand on the young woman's shoulder, unwilling to separate her from Frank's hug, but patting her fondly. "By God, girl, I can't tell you how happy I am to see you again."

"Grandpa?" She tore herself loose from Frank and threw her arms around Bill's shoulders. For long moments they swayed back and forth, the woman's eyes closed, her face awash with tears.

Both Tappan men were sniffing, their own cheeks wet and shining.

"Don't break an old man's ribs, Breeze," Bill told her, finally pushing her back far enough to take a couple of swipes at his leathery cheeks.

"Tappans can cry?" Court asked under his breath, awed. He and Sam had stood and retreated to give them room.

"This is the mysterious Breeze?" Sam asked Evan, who was a couple of steps back, a curious twist to his lips.

"Daughter. Brandon's twin."

"And why have we never heard of her?" Court asked in his barely audible whisper.

"Had a falling out about three years back." Evan shrugged. "May

Sarton once wrote: 'Families murder each other.' She was more right than wrong. A reason I've always steered clear of having one."

"Falling out? Over what?"

Evan shrugged. "Guess whatever it was doesn't matter anymore."

Ragnovich stepped close. Fixed on Breeze. "For everything, Miz Tappan." He stiffened, knocked off a perfect salute. "It's been both an honor and a privilege."

Breeze looked stunned, cheeks wet. Then the silence in the room was broken with applause. The captain pivoted on his heel, striding purposefully from the restaurant.

"How'd you get out of Colorado?" Frank demanded. "You were in Colorado, right?"

She shifted her hug from Bill back to Frank, saying, "Denver, Daddy. Yeah, I got out. Barely."

Frank, voice breaking, on the verge of tears again, said, "I was so scared. And your mother. We've spent the nights since this began... We prayed, Breeze. We hoped against hope. We'd have come. You have to know that. If we'd had a clue about where you were, we'd have moved heaven and earth to get to you."

"I know. I just couldn't..." She fought tears again, gesturing helplessness. "How is mom?"

"Leather and whipcord. Just a little older and tougher than she used to be. But hearing that you're safe? She'll feel ten years younger."

"And Brandon?"

"Still half wildcat and complete hell on a horse," Bill told her. "You know Brandon. Does it all his way. You'll be proud, Breeze."

"And Celia?"

"In town. Finishing high school. She's living with Merlin and Patricia Smith. Wanted to be a beautician. She'll be overjoyed to hear that you're safe."

Breeze's eyes, so similar to her father's, narrowed. "She as much trouble as I was?"

"Not by half!" Bill added with a snort, then he grinned wickedly. "Compared to you, she's almost cussed boring."

Evan indicated Court and me. "Maybe we should get our own table. Let them have some time..."

"Naw," Bill grumbled, overhearing. "We'll miss you and Court for the next week or so as it is. Let's pull these tables together. In this case, the water under the bridge is so long gone it's halfway to the Gulf."

As Sam helped pull the table against Breeze's, Bill was saying, "Girl, I reckon you know Evan Holly, here. Family was working for him when everything went south. And these fellas, well, the skinny one is Sam Delgado. He's an anthropology graduate student from New York. This big dude is Court Hamilton from Indiana. He's a... Well, let's say a logistical planner and Governor Agar's new best friend. He and Evan are going to spend the next week in high-stakes-planning with the governor's team."

Court was blushing bright red as he shook Breeze's hand.

When she turned to Sam, her gaze slipped away self-consciously. "Guess I made a hell of a first impression."

Sam grinned. "Made a few of my own."

"Jenn?" she called. "Coffee all around."

"Coming, Breeze!" the waitress chimed back with an obvious and new enthusiasm.

Frank seated himself, a look of rapture on his face as he studied his daughter. "Captain Ragnovich just said, 'There's someone I want you to meet. I think it's important.'"

"Could have skinned me with a chainsaw when I saw who it was," old Bill added in delight. "I served in the legislature with Doug Ragnovich. That man doesn't have a frivolous or over-dramatic bone in his body. What the hell did you do? And that man don't salute nobody but a superior."

Sam watched Breeze Tappan's gaze harden. "I'm no hero. Everything I did, I was either scared to death, or being stupid."

For an instant, her expression failed, eyes revealing a flicker of desperation, then she pulled it together in an instant. If Sam hadn't been watching so close, he might have missed it.

The waitress delivered the coffee. As she did, old Bill looked at Court and said, "Just drink it. It'll put hair on your chest."

Court frowned. "But I've got..."

"Shhh!" Sam cut him off as Court pulled his shirt out and stared down the front.

Breeze took a deep breath. "When I left, I went to Denver. Got accepted at University of Denver. It's called the Daniels College of

Business. One of the top-ranked business educations in the country." She smiled sadly. "Hey, I'd made up my mind. I was headed for Wall Street. Get as far from the ranch, from Wyoming, and Hot Springs as I could."

Frank's expression looked strained.

"For the summer," Breeze continued, "I took a job as an intern with Silver Pinnacle. In a branch office working for the broker. That's where I was when everything fell apart. Danny, the guy I was dating, was in Florida on a consultation. Told me to get out of Denver. By the time I tried, I-25 was hopeless. Took the car back and got the bike. Three of us on motorcycles took the back roads through the mountains. Hit trouble. Jill... She turned tried to go south. Felix...he was a broker. Thought he could..." She winced. "They shot him for his bike."

The table was quiet. Breeze stared sightlessly. "Three guys with rifles. Felix never had a chance. They'd have shot me if I wasn't a woman. You know what men do with women."

Sam ground his teeth, saw the anger stewing in Frank and Bill's eyes. Court just stared into his untouched coffee.

"I couldn't stop the bleeding," she said, voice distant. "Felix was scared. Like, he never thought..."

"And these three guys?" Bill asked, voice gentle.

"They didn't know I had a pistol." Her jaw muscles clenched, her gaze thinning.

"Kill 'em?" Bill asked.

"Yes, okay? And that's the last I'm going to talk about it!" she snapped back.

Could I have done that? Sam wondered.

Breeze seemed to shake it off, said, "At the border, it took a while. Had to talk my way through. Heard Ragnovich was allowing women with bikes to supply the line. Tried to do my share. I'd seen the shit coming down south of the line. Things you wouldn't..." She gave a dismissive toss of the head, as if to rid herself of the memories.

"And then there was the I-25 checkpoint. I did things. Men, women, and children. I held the line. Bought time for the Guard to plug the hole. But the time will come when God will judge me for that."

The tone and manner in which Breeze narrated it, she might have been in a trance, almost like a third party. Eyes vacant, the expression on her smooth face hiding a quiver in her deep muscles. The pain and loss, the horror, the distance she tried to keep and the way she understated it, became even more palpable.

Men, women, and children? The way she's talking, it's like she killed them.

"It was the little girl in the tent," Breeze finished. "Maybe Ragnovich is right. Maybe I've lost my edge. It's like I don't know myself anymore. Not unless I'm on the bike. Running supplies to the posts. That's the only time I'm alive."

She glanced up at her father, the desperation back in her Tappan-family eyes. "So, am I crazy?"

Frank chewed his lips for a couple of heartbeats, nodded, and said, "Yeah. But then I figured that out just after you turned three."

A flicker of smile died on Breeze's lips. "Could be, Daddy. Could well be."

"So, what's next?" Bill asked almost hesitantly. "You said Ragnovich told you to take a break."

The hollow look was back in her eyes. "I...don't know."

"Home might not be any safer than here," Frank told his father softly. "Not with us going up against Edgewater."

"Kevin Edgewater?" Breeze asked. "DHS director? Governor Agar came within a whisker of arresting him. He and a bunch of his cronies tried to declare themselves in charge. The guy barely got out of Cheyenne ahead of Agar's people. As it is, he skipped with a truckload of M2s from the Guard armory. Guns we could have used on the line. Heard he landed in Cody."

Old Bill told his granddaughter all about "dickhead" and his inventories and confiscations.

Sam squinted uncomfortably when Bill got around to Sam's encounter with the director in the tannery, and how he'd almost lost Shyla. Something about the way Breeze fixed on Sam during that part of the story made him uneasy. As if she were judging, finding him unworthy.

Or was that just his imagination?

"Just so you know, Edgewater's a real piece of work," Breeze told them. "Story is that he was sent here because DHS couldn't fire him. Some sort of sexual impropriety with a minor. Word is that he had some kind of dirt on the Attorney General or one of the Supreme

Court justices. Anywhere but Wyoming, and with any governor but Agar, he'd be running this state."

She leveled a hard finger at Bill and Frank. "So, you two watch your asses. He's got federal law and a slew of regulations to back him. And he's known to be a real shit."

"And where will you be?" Frank asked. "I know we're a little obtuse about these things, and not too bright, but we're trying to make a point here."

For the first time, Breeze actually laughed. "Any reason you won't just come out and say it?"

"Please," old Bill said kindly, "come home."

"Damn, I'm a screwed-up wreck. I've dreamed it. And now, I just... Well, I've really done a job on my life haven't I?"

"Runs in the family." Frank grinned to hide his desperation. "Besides, you can have Brandon's room. He's sleeping in the barn."

"Mom throw him out for drinking again?" Breeze asked, a flicker of amusement showing for the first time.

"He has a girl." Old Bill gave her a saucy wink. "Black gal. From Philadelphia. Shanteel's different. Showed up tough as nails. Totally out of her element. Big-city eastern girl that didn't have clue. Then she and Brandon had to hole up in the mountains for a spell. Just the two of them. And when the weather breaks, they come riding down the trail acting like two kernels out of the same cob."

Bill shrugged. "Got no clue how it'll work out, but they seem to make each other happy. She's got a place with us for as long as she wants to stay."

Frank grinned. "She stumbled in the other night looking like she came in last place in a fight with a wildcat. She and Brandon spent the day fixing fence. Said she'd be damned if any barbed wire would get the better of her. Brandon said she could stretch wire like an old hand by the time they were done."

Sam watched old Bill struggling to keep the hope out of his voice as he asked her, "So, what's keeping you here?"

"Free room and board," she waved around. "The Guard started picking up the tab for the Line riders' rooms and meals. Drinks I pay for."

"Huh, well, I guess we can at least meet their offer." Bill scratched under his chin. "As full as we are, we can put you on the couch until Thomas and Willy head up over the mountain."

"What about the guest cabins?" Breeze asked.

"Evan's in one. Amber, one of the archaeologists, is in another, and Sam and Shyla are in the third. My call is that we kick Willy out of your old bedroom and move Amber into the bunkhouse with John, Court, and the girls. Then Willy can have the third cabin."

"Call it done," Frank agreed easily.

"What?" Bill read Breeze's reluctance.

She glanced uncertainly at Sam, Court, and Evan. "What's this thing with Edgewater? You really going to move against him?"

Frank glanced uneasily around, leaned close, and said, "I won't lie to you, sweetheart. He's building a power base up in Park County. Governor Agar, along with the rest of us, we want him gone. We're working on a plan with some of the other Basin leaders. Like Sam found out, he's a mean son of a bitch, and he's probably not going peacefully."

She nodded, expression thoughtful. "I watched Agar shoot four looters, rapists, and murderers in the back of the head. Public execution. We talking that kind of justice?"

Sam tensed in anticipation.

"That a problem?" Old Bill narrowed one of his bullet-like eyes. "He's taking women. Looting stores. Bastard's making himself the only law. I won't have it. Lot of us won't."

"You said he's got a small army?"

"Forty guys. Some ex-military. Others who just act like all-around tough guys." Frank took a deep breath. "I suspect we won't be able to keep our intent completely quiet. The Park and Hot Springs County sheriffs have sided with Edgewater. Call him the 'duly constituted authority' and think he's going to be calling the shots. If either of them catches wind, they'll rat us out."

"When are you heading home?" she asked, brow lined as she studied her father and grandfather with worried eyes.

"We were supposed to be leaving this morning. Then we heard you were here." Frank was chewing his lips when he wasn't talking. "But now? Hell, girl of mine, I can't just have a cup of coffee and run."

"Son," old Bill told him, "it's not like we're calling the shots.

That Highway Patrol escort is waiting on us. And I sure as hell can't leave you behind."

"I just *found* my daughter," Frank barked. "Your *granddaughter.*"

"Yeah, you knot-head, and we're supposed to be planning a war." Bill looked adamant.

"We'll go when we're ready. We don't need to tie up the Patrol."

"Bad idea," Breeze snapped. "You damned well *don't* want to be on the roads at night. Not anywhere around Cheyenne. And definitely not in a truck with a full tank of fuel."

"How'd they stop us?" old Bill asked.

"About fifteen or twenty different ways that I've seen. Women and children lying in the road is a real good one. Angle vehicles across both lanes. Stretch a length of chain at windshield height. You'll stop to see what's wrong. And they'll have you. Some guy leaps up and into the truck bed. After he shoots out the back window, there's nothing between you and his shotgun." The stare Breeze was giving her father and grandfather looked harder than granite.

Sam's stomach did an inside-out.

"No shit?" old Bill muttered uncertainly.

"No shit."

Evan looked up as a Highway Patrol officer entered. "Looks like our escort just ran out of patience. Head's up, folks."

Evan and Court were staying in Cheyenne at the governor's insistence as they worked on a plan to stabilize the Big Horn Basin's economy. Word was they'd be back in Hot Springs in another week.

All heads turned as Sam watched the patrolwoman cross to their table. Her expression was anything but happy.

"I know," Frank told her. "We're discussing—"

"Mr. Tappan," she cut him off. "I've just had a call from Captain Richardson. Sully wanted me to get you a message soonest. He says you need to know that Edgewater's people made a call at your ranch last night. Shots were fired. While Edgewater's people fled from the scene, they left a vehicle and several casualties behind."

"What about Pam?" Frank cried. "Meggan? Is everyone all right?"

The patrolwoman's expression went even more steely. "Pam Tappan was shot in the exchange. She's at Hot Springs Memorial Hospital. All I know is that she went into surgery last night."

Frank sank back in his chair, facial muscles strained.

"Anyone else hurt?" old Bill demanded, stumbling to his feet.

"I'm told a woman was killed."

"*Who?*" Sam and Bill cried in unison.

"I'm sorry, gentlemen, I don't have that information."

Sam felt the world tilt. He grabbed the table edge to steady himself.

THE WEAPON

***

I wasn't a soldier. I'd never joined either the Guard or Militia. I'd just shown up at an opportune and desperate moment when Captain Ragnovich needed to get water to a distant OP. I was there, waiting a chance to enlist, and was told, "You have a fast motorcycle. Here's a map. If you can get that case of water to them, you're a Line rider."

The job just evolved from there. Along with the other riders, I'd run whatever the OPs radioed that they needed: bandages, water, ammo, food, spare parts, whatever. As the days passed, the role of the OPs changed from refugee interdiction to repulsing raiders. Fewer and fewer families were trying to sneak across the line as gangs of looters down south figured out how to organize. Most of the cattle, sheep, pigs, chickens, horses, and pets had been eaten. The looters had figured out how to overwhelm outlying Colorado farms and ranches. They started probing the line soon after.

Wasn't long before I was riding out to OPs in the thick of the fight.

On that long ride back to Hot Springs—worried about Mom—I considered that. My father thought he had his daughter back.

I knew he carried a lethal weapon, and it was me.

Excerpt from Breeze Tappan's *Journal.*

CHAPTER THIRTY-FOUR

***

ALL THINGS CONSIDERED, HAVING THE HIGHWAY PATROL ESCORT MIGHT HAVE KEPT THEM alive. Not because of ambush or the threat of robbery or the people walking the roads, but Frank's driving. He kept growling, "Come on. Come on" at the rear of the Highway Patrol Charger that led the way up the Interstate at eighty-five. From Casper to Shoshoni, their second escort had run at seventy-five. Now they were careening through the Wind River Canyon at a breakneck seventy, centrifugal force slinging them back and forth around the curves.

Sam sat in the back seat; beside him, Breeze fidgeted. In the pickup bed, the yellow-and-silver BMW 650 rocked against the tie-down straps every time the big Dodge thumped over bridge approaches. Breeze's boogie bag—as she called the military duffle—was stuffed down next to the bike's front wheel.

Despite assurances that she wouldn't need it, the M4 rested on the seat beside her. Her pistol hung on her hip. When he wasn't overwhelmed by his concern for Shyla, he was shooting surreptitious glances at Breeze Tappan. Wondering what it was about her that left him on edge. The feeling was like riding next to an angry tiger, the kind that might turn and rip him apart at any second.

He had tried talking. She'd reciprocated. Each attempt at small talk had died as it gave way to worry and introspection.

Sam kept squirming. In a voice thick with desperation, he'd insist, "She's got to be all right. It's okay, Sam. She's fine." Then he'd squirm some more, knot and unknot his fists.

But then, all four of them were fuming, fretting, and terrified at what they'd find as they hurtled their way north.

Sam heard Breeze absently whisper, "God, it's like my soul's hanging from a meat hook." She was looking out the side window at the passing river. Probably had no idea she'd spoken out loud.

He heard her softly pray: "Make it, Mom. Please. Just let me say I'm sorry."

Sam stared up at the towering rock walls as they flashed past. *Yeah, I know what you mean.* But he'd never say any of those things to his parents. Offer his eternal thanks for those endless days in the kitchen and the work ethic Mom and Dad had beaten into him.

The Highway Patrol car slowed to forty as they hit town and led the way to the hospital, pulled up at the front door. Lights still flashing, the trooper gave them a nod and salute, watching as they all piled out of the Dodge and headed for the entrance. Sam followed along behind, feeling like an appendage. A voyeur to a drama where he was an uncomfortable interloper.

"Where's Pam Tappan?" Frank demanded at the reception window.

"Intensive care, Frank," the woman told him. "Down the hall and right. But you check with Doc before you go barging in."

Frank practically ran, Grandpa hitching along behind on his bad leg. Breeze lagged, her face a mixture of hope and anguish.

A deputy stood before the Intensive Care ward—an older man, maybe late forties, with a sagging belly that grotesquely stretched his uniform shirt and hid his belt buckle.

"Whoa!" the deputy called. "Who are you people, and where are you going?"

"I'm Frank Tappan, and my wife's in there."

The deputy fixed on Old Bill. "You William Tappan?"

"I am."

"All right, and who are..." His eyes stopped on Breeze, and then the muzzle of the M4 sticking up over her shoulder. "There's no weapons in here."

Frank barked, "She's with the Guard. Take it up with Governor Agar if you've got a problem with that."

The deputy seemed confused.

"And you?" he asked when he looked at Sam.

"Friend of the family." God, get it over with! He had to know about Shyla.

"Five minutes," the deputy told them. "Then I've got to have a word with you two." He pointed at Frank and Bill.

Sam followed the Tappans into the room, remembering what hospitals were all about: cabinets, glowing monitors, IV stands, wires, and tubes.

Pam lay on her back, the hospital bed tilted up. Old Doc Willson stood beside the bed where he tapped at his laptop, and stopped short at their entry.

"Shhh!" He put a finger to his lips and motioned them to stop.

Frank, never one to take orders, stepped over and took Pam's hand, whispering, "I'm here, babe. Right here."

Breeze ground her teeth, fists clenching. "Mom? It's Breeze. I came as soon as I heard."

"How is she?" Bill asked. "What the hell happened?"

"She was shot through the lower right lung," Willson replied. "Now, Bill Mason's a pretty good general surgeon, but I called in Tommy Tharp."

"He's a vet," Bill growled.

"You know anyone else with more experience sewing up gunshot wounds in the Basin? Normally, we'd fly Pam out to Salt Lake or Billings. Well, those days are past," Doc Willson growled back. "Tharp and Mason worked together with a combat-trained nurse. I stood back and assisted. The wound's debrided, the major bleeders are tied off, and her lung's re-inflated. But don't jump for joy. She's still critical."

"Hey," Pam whispered softly, and tightened her grip on Frank's hand. "I'll be all right."

Frank bent down and gently kissed her lips. "You gotta make it, babe. I can't do this without you."

"Feel like I was bucked off a horse onto rocks."

"Got a present for you." Frank stepped back, gesturing Breeze forward.

Pam's eyes were opened to slits, looking dazed and unfocused. "Hey, baby, that you?"

"Hi, Mom." Breeze took her mother's hand. "I'm back. I want you to know I'm so sorry."

Sam saw tears trickle past the tiger-woman's eyes.

Her mother squeezed her hand. "I know, sweetie. Me, too."

"Get well, please. I want to go riding with you again."

"I think," Doc Willson said, "that that will be about all."

"Sweetie?" Pam whispered. "Come close."

Breeze wiped at her tears, bent her head down. Sam heard her whisper, "Overheard the deputy. They're forming a posse to go get Brandon. Get to the ranch. Warn him. They're gonna kill him. Understand?"

Sam gaped. *Kill Brandon?*

Breeze blinked, met her mother's now flint-like eyes, and nodded. "I'm on it."

Doc Willson motioned them out of the room as he said, "Nothing could have been better for her. She's got the will now."

In the hallway, Sam faced the deputy. "Heard a woman was killed out there."

"Yeah, tried to resist arrest. Heard that when she pulled a pistol, Ed Tubb took her out." He nodded toward the hospital room. "Like Mrs. Tappan, here. You people better understand. There's a whole host of charges, from federal all the way down. You get it? Director Edgewater is the duly appointed federal authority, and we're in a state of emergency and martial law. So, yeah, there's a shit storm brewing."

"What about the woman? Who was she?" Sam insisted, his heart like trip hammer.

"I didn't catch the name. Just that she was some transient from Vermont."

The world seemed to fade. Hollowness, emptying his gut. "Where is she?"

"Probably still out at that ranch." The deputy had his right hand on his weapon now, pointing with his left index finger at Dad and Grandpa. "You two, I'm supposed to detain. Heard you were out of town. Sheriff Kapital and Steve Fallow want to have a word with you. Something about sedition."

"You got any paper on me?" Breeze asked, stepping forward. "I'm Breeze Tappan. Been in Cheyenne on the border. You can check with Captain Ragnovich. Give him a call."

"I've got nothing on you."

"Then I'm out of here." She asked her father, "You coming?"

Frank tipped his head back at the room. "I'm not leaving her."

"And they're going to face the sheriff before the day's out," the deputy insisted. "So my advice to you, young lady, is keep your nose clean, or you'll be in shit as deep as the rest of your family."

"Go on," Old Bill told her, a grim sort of fighting smile on his lips.

Sam's thoughts kept dissolving, the word *No* repeating in his brain as images of Shyla smiling, her eyes agleam replayed in his memory. *Had to be a mistake. Had to.*

"Let's go," Breeze told him. "I need your help getting the bike out of the truck."

As they turned to leave, Sam heard the deputy: "Sure. Give a silly girl a big gun. My bet? If she ever gets close to action she'll be so busy pissing herself, that if she gets a round off, it'll be through her own foot."

For a half second Breeze hesitated, probably considered going back and blowing chunks of his heart out through a hole in the middle of his back.

"Vermont," Sam said as if in a trance. "That fat fucker said she was from Vermont."

"Who?"

He didn't answer as he dumbly followed her out the doors, just worked his mouth. Choking on something impossible.

Outside she lowered the tailgate, vaulted into the back of the Dodge, and released the turnbuckles. As she backed the bike, she called, "Sam, help me keep it upright."

He pitched in with all the enthusiasm of old wood. Somehow, they managed to roll the BMW back and down without dropping the bike onto the unforgiving parking lot. She flicked out the kickstand and pulled the boogie bag from the back. As she strapped it on the back of the seat, Sam stood there, back arched, staring off to the west past Round Top hill.

Shyla's still out there. Got to be a mistake.

Breeze fetched her helmet and worn jacket, squinting up at the slanting light. Maybe an hour or two left before sunset.

Sam said, "That guy said her body's still there." He tried to swallow. Couldn't. "Please, Breeze. She's... She's... I've got to get to the ranch."

She swung a leg over the seat, reached for the key. Got a good look at the desperation in his eyes.

"Oh, fuck." She leaned the bike back on the stand, saying, "Yeah, help me repack this load."

On the way out of town, Sam clinging behind her, they passed the fairgrounds where deputies were loading horses into stock trailers. The slanting sunlight glinted on rifle barrels.

"Mom wasn't delusional," she called over her shoulder. "They're really coming."

DEATH'S HEAD

* * *

Before the collapse, lots of people were into stylized skulls. They cast them into rings, painted them on motorcycles or sewed them onto jackets. Used them on art to promote music. Molded them into candles or cast them as hood ornaments or shifter knobs. Hung them on keyrings. Spray painted them onto walls or railroad cars. Death's head skulls hung on bar and nightclub signs, and millions were tattooed on the arms, backs, and chests of guys and women who'd never seen a dead body, let alone an abandoned corpse, or real skull.

After the collapse, I never saw a death's head used that way again. Those of us who survived? The death's head didn't need to be painted or tattooed. It peered out from behind our eyes.

Excerpt from Breeze Tappan's *Journal*

CHAPTER THIRTY-FIVE

***

SAM KEPT HIS FINGERS KNOTTED IN THE TOUGH FABRIC OF BREEZE'S COAT AS WIND TORE at his hair and pooled tears in his eyes. The heavy boogie bag pulled his shoulder down where it hung from the strap.

Through a slitted and watery gaze, he watched the familiar terrain pass. He'd never ridden on the back of a motorcycle, watched in curious unease as the ground flashed past just below his hiking boots. Breeze's short black rifle jabbed uncomfortably into his thigh. All that, and somehow, he couldn't make himself care.

Brain-numb, the time seemed to compress. Lost in moments with Shyla, he barely recognized when the bike chattered across the cattle guard and down the lane.

"Got a sheriff's car, Sam," he heard Breeze's muffled voice from behind the curtain of her helmet. "If this goes bad, you drop like a rock, all right?"

"What?" he asked softly.

She obviously didn't hear as she pulled into the yard, circled around, and stopped the bike before the barn door.

A single deputy stood from the chair where he'd been sitting on the porch.

As Sam climbed fragilely from the bike and swung the boogie bag down, the deputy racked a shell into the chamber in his shotgun. He came forward in a wary walk, as if feeling his way. His eyes focused, laser-like, on Breeze as she stepped off, unstrapped her helmet, and placed it on the bike's mirror.

Unslinging the black rifle, Breeze called, "We going to war, Eddie?"

"Breeze? That you?" The deputy lowered the shotgun, a pleading on his face. "Please, Breeze. I don't want to have to bury you."

Breeze stepped up to the guy, her black rifle resting at half-mast. "You still married to Kelly Ann?"

"Yeah. Jennie's just two. Little Cody's four this year."

"Eddie, we go back, you and me. Hell, you're the guy gave me my first drink of whiskey. Remember that?"

"Wyoming State Fair. What? Six years ago? You finished fourth in the barrel racing finals. Thought the world had come to an end." The deputy smiled. "I should have stopped at the first drink. The only reason I'm still alive is you didn't tell your dad who got you drunk that night."

"You in love with Kelly Ann and your kids?"

"What the hell kind of question's that?"

Breeze cocked her hip, bracing the rifle on it. "You're a good man, Eddie Lawson. You don't want to be part of this. And I sure as hell don't want to watch Kelly Ann crying at your grave."

"Breeze, you don't underst—"

"Go *home*, Eddie! That bastard Kapital is bringing a posse."

"I know."

"You swing that Mossberg around and shoot me. Right here." She unzipped her coat and jabbed a thumb into her chest. "Come on. Do it. And look me in the eyes as you do."

"Breeze, this is just crazy. You don't—"

"You heard what kind of man Edgewater is? About why he came here? About the looting? Word is he's taking girls. Arresting people who don't lick his ass."

Eddie made a face. "Breeze, those are just rumors."

"Take the Anchor Dam road south so you don't run into Kapital's people. Go home to Kelly Ann, and if you have a lick of sense in you, hold her and love her, and wait until we can bring some sense to this."

"Breeze, I swore an oath."

"You torture yourself over getting an underage girl drunk? How are you going to live with yourself knowing you were part of what's coming down now?"

Sam watched the deputy swallow hard, nod his head. Then Breeze gave the man a fierce hug, one made awkward by the weapons.

"Where's Shyla Adams?" Sam heard himself call, the voice coming from another universe.

"Buried her," the deputy answered over his shoulder as he walked hurriedly to his car. "Ask the old Indian."

Buried her.

The words hammered around the inside of his head.

Sam stumbled aimlessly backwards into the barn wall. Propped himself against it. He stared dully at the ranch yard. Tried to piece it together: A black Chevy Yukon—its windows shot out—had been pulled to the side; the University van in front of the tractor shed; bullet holes that pock-marked the front of the house. The empty ranch yard where tires had spun and torn the gravel. Gleaming brass cartridge cases lay scattered across the ground.

And there, just before the door, the blackened blood stain in the beaten ground. Shyla's?

He vaguely heard the deputy's cruiser start, spin around, and roar off down the lane.

"Sam?" Breeze was there, like magic, staring into his eyes. Images of Shyla, like an old movie pastiche, flickering inside him. "Why did this...?"

"Because the world's dying," a familiar voice said, and Thomas Star appeared in the barn door; the .44 caliber Marlin that once sat on the rack inside the ranch door hung in his right hand.

"You'd have been proud of her," Thomas told him. "Tubb sent two guys to get her. Amber stepped out with a shotgun. Gave Shyla time. She pulled that .38 and shot one before the other one could grab her and twist the gun away. Then she fought like a wounded panther."

Sam hadn't felt himself sink to the ground, held up only by the barn. "Who killed her?"

"Tubb did when he saw there was no way. Shot her, then ran for his truck. He was the first one to run."

"Saw him in town," Sam whispered, "loading horses."

"How you doing, Thomas?" Breeze asked. "Long time, no see."

"Good to have you back. I thought I was going to have to shoot that deputy. Got Joker saddled for you. I put a pack saddle on Molly, and Old Tobe is saddled for Sam."

"Joker? My saddle? How'd you know I was coming."

"Spirits told me." Thomas bent down, staring into Sam's eyes. "Shyla's body is buried on the hillside. The rest of her, her soul, has gone up the mountain with the others. That's where she's waiting for you."

Sam blinked, trying to make sense, teeth gritted against the urge to sob. "She's...waiting?"

"You need to be a warrior now." Thomas stood. "Not much time. They'll be here soon."

"Thomas. Pack that army bag on Molly, if you would," Breeze called over her shoulder as she ran for the house, clunking across the porch in her motorcycle boots.

"Come on. I need some help." Thomas extended a hand and pulled Sam to his feet. "We don't have much time. They'll be here just about dark. You and Breeze need to be up the mountain by then."

Tubb shot her? "Where is everybody? Meggan, Brandon, Amber, and the rest?"

"Up at the field camp with Willy."

"Why are you here?"

"Because this is where I have to be. I'm in no danger." Thomas grinned showing his stained yellow teeth. "I'm just the Indian who does old Bill's chores for whiskey money."

"But you don't drink."

"Those stupid *taipo* don't know that." He grinned. "Come on. Help me with that bag."

Moving, working, just the mechanical motions allowed Sam to block off the grief. *She shot one of the men who tried to take her.*

And they were coming here. Bringing horses. Ready to track Brandon and the rest into the back country.

"What about the ranch? Will they burn it?"

"Nope," Thomas said as he flipped the lash cinch around Breeze's boogie bag. "It's too nice a ranch. Tubb wants it for himself. No sense in busting up something you think is going to be yours."

"What about the animals?"

"I'll be sure they're fed and watered." Thomas tightened the diamond hitch, then fixed his dark eyes on Sam's. "You and Breeze. When this is all over. Go to the cave. Do you understand?"

"What?"

"You will both need to heal. To have the death and corruption cleansed."

At that moment, Breeze came hurrying out of the house transformed. She now wore western boots, slim jeans, and a thick flannel shirt. A black, scuffed cowboy hat with a stampede strap topped her head. A bundle of clothing was wadded in her arms.

"You about ready?" she called as she entered the barn and stuffed the clothing into one of Molly's panniards. Then asked, "Whose sleeping bag?"

"Sam's," Thomas told her. "I figured he wouldn't be thinking when he got here. His tent's in there, too."

Meanwhile her attention was fixed on Joker. She wrapped her arms around the horse's neck, hugging him fiercely. "Hello, old friend. Do you forgive me?"

The horse nuzzled her shoulder, lips pulling at her coat, as she whispered, "I'm so sorry. It was all my fault."

Breeze stopped, pulled back, and wiped at a tear. She studied the old man thoughtfully, then gave him a big hug, too. "You watch your ass with these guys. They're itching to kill."

"You, too, almost-a-daughter."

She shot him a fleeting grin, slung her rifle, and swung into the saddle. "*Use kaan kwaisi*, almost-a-father."

Thomas grinned as Sam clambered into the saddle. Then the old man thrust the Marlin into the empty saddle scabbard beneath Sam's right leg, adding, "Bullets are packed in the right side of those saddlebags tied on behind your butt. Watch for *Nynymbi*, he'll guide you."

Like a passive observer from another universe, Sam watched the ranch pass as they rode out. From the higher vantage of horseback, he could see more blood spots now. In places he could see where bullet strikes had furrowed the dirt.

"Must have been a hell of a fight," he heard himself say.

"You were face-to-face with Edgewater, what possessed him to attack us?"

"My wife," Sam answered bitterly. "And I wasn't here to keep her safe like I promised."

"Yeah, well, the world's a really fucked up place, isn't it?"

He could see Breeze's jaws knot as she stared bitterly ahead from beneath the brim of her hat.

"That last thing you said to Thomas. What was that?"

"Shoshoni. Translates to 'in a packrat's tail'. Sort of like 'the end' in English. A final goodbye." Breeze kept studying the long shadows. "We'd better make tracks. It's going to be dark before we're up top as it is."

"Why'd Thomas give you Frank's horse?"

"Dad's horse? Joker's mine. My barrel horse. I trained him up from a foal."

"I've never seen him ride any other."

Her lips pursed. "Oh, Daddy. You're such a soft touch." She patted Joker on the neck.

Sam suffered a spear of grief. He had no homecoming. Nothing to look forward to.

Sure, there is. There's standing over Edward Tubb's lifeless body.

THE POSER

***

I dismissed Sam right off the bat. I'd seen too much of the Line—that hard "I'm already damned" expression in the eyes of the men and women who'd been called upon to commit acts they thought were unconscionable. And seen them through.

Sam's demeanor spoke of worry, a bit of insecurity, and discomfort with the world he now found himself in. Untested. Unsure. A sort of kite who'd be batted this way and that until an inevitable gust blew him into the power lines to incinerate.

Didn't matter that he wore Mom's old Model 10 Smith & Wesson stuffed into his pants. The guy was a poser. Soft. Like a sort of marshmallow.

And there I was. Enraged. The Death's Head staring out from behind my eyes. Mom was shot. Might die. They were after my brother. Didn't matter what was behind us. This was family.

And I was stuck with a sobbing city kid who'd just lost his girl?

But that was before slickside.

Excerpt from Breeze Tappan's Journal.

CHAPTER THIRTY-SIX

***

THE FIRST HINT OF DAWN CAST A SHINE ON THE DISTANT SILHOUETTE OF THE BIG HORN Mountains. Between them and where Sam and Breeze had camped stretched a deep indigo shadow that filled the Basin.

Sam yawned, crawled out of his sleeping bag, and tossed sticks on the fire. Somehow, he'd managed to sleep. Had chewed his lips, knotted his fists, and raged until he was sure Breeze was asleep. Then he'd buried his head in the depths of the bag and wept. Punished himself for leaving Shyla alone.

If only I'd been there.

He shivered in the cold morning. Stared across the purple basin. Like he'd seen Brandon do, he leaned down. Blew on the coals until the sticks caught fire.

Breeze winced and stretched in her bedroll. "God," she whispered. "Every muscle in my hips, thighs, calves, and lower back is sore. Haven't forked a horse for three years."

"Pam said it takes about a week." He stared at the distant Bighorns. Thought that this was how God must see the world. The endless vistas. No wonder He let people like Tubb murder beautiful young women whose only crime was being beautiful.

When they had crossed slickside the night before, Sam had stepped off Old Tobe. He had pulled the Marlin from its scabbard, saying, "This is it."

"What's it?"

"The place I'm going to be standing when they come." His face a mask of determination, he'd declared, "This is the place I pay them back for what they did to her."

She'd looked around. Considered. "Not a good place for a last stand. One of them will shoot you from those trees across the way."

"They already took everything I lived for. What do I care?"

"Got a point there, Sam. But I'll do you one better." She'd pointed up the slope's steep face. "I think we ought to set up there. Behind those rocks."

He'd followed her eyes to the rocky outcrop sticking out from the mountain. "We?"

"What makes you think you're the only dog in this fight?"

She'd led him to the second switchback above slickside and showed him an elk trail that ran back to a timbered cleft in the mountainside. Here they'd made camp on a tiny patch of level ground. Ate the sandwiches she'd found in the saddlebags and checked their equipment before rolling out their sleeping bags.

As Sam watched the flames lick around the firewood, it really settled in. This was his last morning. Shyla was dead. Mom, Dad, all of Hempstead, the whole East Coast, everyone he'd known. Gone. Like a nightmare gone wrong, he was going to wage war on a posse. After he killed Edward Tubb. They'd kill him.

And I don't care.

He wondered if his laughter at the thought sounded insane.

Stepping to the edge of the timber, Breeze cocked her head and listened. Said, "Knowing townies, they won't be saddled up and out of the ranch yard until full sunup."

Breaking off a straight branch, she used her knife to sharpen the tip into a wedge and, Sam following, proceeded to wage war on the field of biscuit root and sego lily growing on the slope. With a pocket full of bulbs and roots, she stopped short, listening.

Sam heard the crunching sound. "What's that?"

"Breakfast."

Following the sound to its source, they found the porcupine about ten feet up, back feet braced on branches as it chewed pine bark. The big rodent hunched down at their approach watching with glistening small eyes.

"Simple pistol shot," she told him, "but the last thing we want is the echo traveling all the way down to the house where that damn posse is forming up."

"We're going to eat a porcupine?"

She arched an eyebrow. "You don't like the taste?"

"How would I know? It's not on anyone's menu."

He watched as she took out her knife, lopped off a squawberry twig, split it into four supple strips, and used them to bind the knife handle to her digging stick. Then she climbed up to within a couple of feet beneath the grumbling porcupine and thrust.

Maybe it was because he was already numb, emotionally exhausted. He'd never seen anything killed before. It should have traumatized him. Watching the creature kicking, bleeding, and finally going still.

He'd shut himself off. Awed at the warm blood and meat as he helped her gut it and carefully skin the thing. How funny. He was ready to murder human beings, and he still had to turn his brain off over the killing of an animal.

The meat was sizzling, and the roots roasted on the coals as Sam checked his rifle. The sun was maybe a hand's breadth above the distant Big Horns. "How much time do we have?"

"A couple of hours I'd guess. We'll hear them coming a good hour before they get here."

He seated himself, and she handed him one of the front legs. With her stick, she fished the baked roots from the ashes. "Don't worry about eating the ash. Believe me, it's sterile."

He smiled. "Used to get people who'd never eaten Mexican food in the restaurant. Always amazed me when they'd try to eat the tamale cornhusk wrappings."

"You think your folks are all right?"

He shook his head. "Word is the East Coast was nuked. My folks lived right next door to the highest population density in the country. Surrounded by solid city. I just..." He struggled, got control. "I just hope they went fast. Even if they were outside the blast, Long Island would have been a nightmare as soon as the trucks stopped running and the electricity went off."

"Yeah. Lot of that going around."

He nibbled cautiously at the ends where the meat had cooled: a sweet pale meat with a unique tang. He hadn't thought himself hungry. But once he started, he couldn't stop.

A half an hour later, only bones remained.

Sam was staring thoughtfully at the distance, eyes fixed on the dark rise of the Pryor Mountains a hundred miles off to the north. "Shyla would have loved this. For a girl from Vermont, she was really game for everything."

"She must have been something."

"She was a magical goddess, you know? Way out of reach for some Mexican kid from Long Island." His lips twitched. "And then we came here...and for those precious moments..." Unable to finish he just shook his head.

"How'd Edgewater get involved?"

"Just that one time in the tannery." Sam looked at her through misting eyes. "She was beautiful, Breeze. I mean, like, Victoria's Secret beautiful. And smart. And that fucking monster saw it in her." He knotted a fist. "If she hadn't been gorgeous, and precious, and perfect..."

He swallowed hard, looked away. Then added, "And I'm going to kill that mother fucker. Didn't matter that Tubbs pulled the trigger. Edgewater ordered it."

Was that really him talking?

"Getting out of Colorado. Same thing came within a whisker of happening to me. They stopped us. Like your Shyla, I was going to die rather than let them touch me."

"That was when your friend got killed, right?"

"Yeah. Never gave him a chance. I blew the brains out the back of the first guy's head. Shot the second through the heart."

A faint clink carried up from the canyon below. Breeze tensed.

Sam took a deep breath, fighting for control. His heart had begun to pound again. "Guess they're coming."

Breeze stood, slinging the M4 before checking the horses one last time and apologizing. "Sorry, kids. We'll have to finish some business here, but we'll get you a drink up at the camp."

She led the way on foot as they traversed the steep slope above slickside. From below, a faint shout could be heard. Then nervous laughter.

The outcrop wasn't quite perfect, the top of it sloping like it did. She and Sam took enough time to hack out hollows that at least accommodated their butts.

She got herself situated as comfortably as she could. "You ever shot anyone before?"

"No."

"But you have shot a gun before."

"This very one. I could hit a soup can at fifty feet."

"Pick something in the middle of his body to aim at. A button. The base of his throat. I'll remind you when the time comes."

"Thanks."

"Don't shoot the horse if you can help it." She made a face.

Sam ground his teeth. Didn't matter that he was a city kid. He was smart enough to know they were going to kill a whole lot of horses when the animals went over the side.

Shut it off, Sam. It's just how it is.

The sounds were louder now: metal clinked, the strike of a shod hoof on rock. Then he heard the snuffling of horses.

"Sam, I want you to wait for my order, all right? I've done this before. You've got to trust me to let as many of them as possible get out in the open."

"Okay."

"Here they come. Wait now. Relax."

He nodded, cheek welded to his rifle. He wanted to scream. To do anything to stop the building terror.

"Is your heart racing?"

"Yeah."

"Breathe deeply and clear your mind. Relax, Sam. Breathe. Slow your heartbeat. Will yourself to relax."

"Okay," he whispered. Closed his eyes. Breath by breath, he filled his lungs. Blew it out. God, why was he so hot? He could feel the sweat on his neck, chest, and upper arms.

Relax. Trust Breeze.

Somehow, he did. Saw the first of the horsemen appear from the trees. The man in the lead rode on a dapple gray. Behind him came rider after rider.

"Shit," Breeze whispered. "It's Bradley Cole. Of course, they'd have gone to the outfitter. Who better to lead the posse?"

"Know him?"

"We used to go camping and hunting together. And now he's *leading* the posse sent to hunt down my brother?"

"Second one in line is Tubb," Sam whispered.

"Wait for my word. Like I said, we want them all in the trap."

How the hell can she sound so damned calm?

The adrenaline high had started to buzz Sam's muscles and nerves; and then a peculiar sense of calm inevitability settled over him like a soothing blanket.

"Holy shit!" one of the men called. "We're riding *across* this?"

"Trust your horses, guys. Just relax, and don't do anything stupid," Bradley called back over his shoulder.

"Too late," Breeze whispered as she settled the M4 into her shoulder.

Sam sighted the Marlin, the gleaming sight bead on Tubb. He was a muscular man, awkward in the saddle, with a black submachine gun hung around his shoulders.

Breeze said, "See how Tubbs' shirt pattern makes a cross on the sleeve halfway down the upper arm?"

"Yeah."

"That's your target."

She almost sounded maternal as she said it.

More horses had emerged, but Bradley was almost across the steep section. Fifteen riders and mounts now filled the trail from end to end.

"Get your aim, breathe. Tell me when you've got your sight picture," Breeze coached.

Sam glanced back, seeing a gap between the last horse and the trees. Bradley was almost across to the firmer footing at the end of slickside.

He heard Breeze's strained whisper. "He's riding with the enemy. That's picking sides."

Sam focused on his rifle sight, the bead on the cross pattern on Tubb's shirt. "Got it."

"Caress the trigger, and let the gun go off."

Sam's Marlin banged. Beside him, Breeze fired a short burst into Bradley Cole's shoulders.

Sam had a frozen image as both men jerked at the impact of the bullets and went limp in the saddles, sliding off to the side as their animals went with them.

That's all it took.

Sam was swinging around to shoot at the last man in line when the whole party erupted in slipping, bucking horses. Sam watched a man on a buckskin, obviously a good rider, try and wheel away from the horse in front of him as it lost footing and fell, only to go over backward himself.

Men screamed, horses shrilled; then they were tumbling, bouncing down the slope accompanied by a clattering of dislodged rocks and cascading dirt. The farther they fell, the faster they went, hitting, bouncing insanely, flying out only to bounce again. Dust rose, blanketing the nightmare below.

As quickly the trail was empty. The cracking and banging down in the trees coming loud as rocks, men, and horses crashed into them.

"Holy shit," Sam whispered.

Breeze closed her eyes, sagging forward over her M4. Her shoulders were convulsing as the woman wept.

SLICKSIDE

* * *

I can tell you the difference between the I-25 checkpoint and Slick-side. At I-25, I shot people down as they swarmed to overwhelm the checkpoint. They'd been warned. Told to turn back. And among those women and children there were men with guns popping off rounds in our direction.

Our guys fired over their heads, and they just kept coming. If they'd overwhelmed the checkpoint, they'd have killed a lot of our people.

What mattered was that they had warning. Knew the consequences. Made a choice to rush us.

Slickside was an out-and-out ambush. Bradley and his posse had no warning. We murdered them. I shot my father's good friend. Saw the rounds hit him. Mea culpa.

By then, so much of my soul was dead, I thought there was nothing more to lose as I triggered the M4.

Turned out there was. But what really broke me down was the horses. I couldn't miss the terror in their eyes, the fear that sent them crow-hopping, bolting, and tumbling to their deaths.

No matter what damnation I had condemned myself to up to that point, no pit of Hell will be deep enough after what I did to those horses.

Excerpt from Breeze Tappan's *Journal*.

CHAPTER THIRTY-SEVEN

***

THE FIRE POPPED AND CRACKED, SPARKS SHOOTING INTO THE AIR. HIGH ABOVE, THE MOON was barely visible in the haze. Sunset had been like burning blood tinged with glowing orange. Even now, when the wind was right, Sam smelled the slightly acrid tang mixing with the scent of conifers.

The entire day had been a struggle. Disbelief and grief, that welling sense of loss, then rage, all to be followed by abject horror. The stunning realization that he'd shot Edward Tubb. Just like that. Bang. Not only had he coldly murdered a human being, he'd contributed to the mass death of all those men and horses.

The memory of them falling, the horses screaming, the men bellowing their terror... Sam winced, held his stomach, and wanted to be sick.

How much more can you take?

He drew a quick breath, blinked, aware of Breeze and Amber staring at him from across the fire.

"Think they'll try it again?" Shanteel asked where she sat on an up-ended log, holding Brandon's hand.

Breeze—tough as titanium again—told her, "We didn't get them all by any means. Must have been a second group. Maybe ten of them from the sounds they made high-tailing back down the trail. We waited until they'd hit the canyon bottom to be sure."

"Bradley Cole?" Brandon shared a disbelieving look with his sister. "That'll break Dad's heart when he hears."

"Outside of Mom and Dad, he was the best outfitter in the southern basin. My guess is that pus-gut Kapital is going to have a hard time recruiting anybody else to guide a posse up here to get us."

"What happened?" Sam swallowed hard, trying to organize his reeling thoughts. "Back at the ranch, I mean. With Shyla?"

"They showed up at about three in the afternoon," Amber told him where she sat cross-legged with a .30-30 across her lap. She glanced at Meggan. "We were just finishing up with butchering a pig. One of the neighbors brought it to trade for a quarter of a beef next time we kill one. Danielle called, 'Somebody coming.'"

Where she sat to one side, back bent, elbows on her knees, Danielle said, "I mean, a whole line of cars like that? Ashley and me, we were hoping it was Kirstin and Dylan coming back from Colorado. Or maybe Bill and Frank coming back early from Cheyenne. Never thought it would be trouble."

Ashley shook her head, blonde locks gleaming in the firelight. "This shit doesn't happen, right?"

Brandon told him, "Shanteel and me, we were up fixing fence on the south slope when they drove in. Thomas and Willy were on the ridge to the north looking for sacred sage since Sun Dance is coming up. Tubb's people just drove in, formed a half circle with their cars. We made fast tracks for the trees and came down the back way to the barn."

Meggan said, "I stepped out on the porch, drying my hands with a washcloth. Pam, smart as always, stopped long enough to strap her revolver on. Then we all sort of crowded out onto the porch to hear what was what."

Danielle stared sadly Sam's way. "They asked if everyone was there, and Pam said yes. That's when Tubb read out this proclamation that under some CFR and Executive Orders, that during time of emergency, arrests for sedition... Dah, dah, dah. He ended saying they had an arrest warrant for Shyla Adams for inciting sedition."

"Shyla said, 'No way,'" Amber told him through gritted teeth. "Pam stepped out, one hand on her pistol, and said that no one was being arrested. Not that day, not on her property. That if they wanted, they could set a court date in town, and that Shyla would be there to answer any charges."

Amber's eyes glittered. "That fucking beast just laughed and said, 'And who, do you suppose, these other girls are? More transients working to undermine the security of the United States?' And he tells his goons, 'Arrest them all. All of these women. Even if some are local, we need to sort out who is loyal and who isn't.'"

"And Sheriff Kapital is there," Meggan said. "So Pam addresses him. 'You know who is local and who isn't. And you know me, Frank, and Bill. You damned well know these girls aren't seditious.'"

"And Tubb says, 'You Tappans are already on our list. This whole ranch is suspect. Under section seven of Order Number One, the government can seize any property for the good of the people.'"

Amber then said, "I was still inside, behind the door. That's when Tubb says, 'By my order, each and every one of you is under arrest. You are surrounded, and any action to hinder my men in the conduct of their lawful duty will be considered an act against the government and punishable by the most severe consequences.' And he orders two of his guys to start with Shyla."

Sam could see it all in his imagination. The growing disbelief that this could happen in America. The sudden fear each of the women must have been feeling. The impossibility of it all.

Amber stared thoughtfully down at the sleek rifle in her lap. "It was happening again. Syria all over. I couldn't let it." Her facial muscles jumped, eyes blinking. "Not again."

Amber's gaze went eerily distant, reliving it. "So I step out on the porch with the rifle, screaming, 'Leave her alone.' And I lift the rifle..."

Amber broke out in an insane giggle, blinked, coming back to reality. "Shyla pulled that pistol she always carried and shot the guy closest to her. Then the other guy had her and twisted the pistol out of her hand. So I blew the mother fucker away where he stood."

Danielle said, "Ashley and me, we just turned and ran. There's bullets everywhere. I mean, freaking unreal."

"Pam pulled her pistol." Meggan glanced around. "And she just stands there like it's the old West, banging away as these guys scatter. Amber was shooting as fast as she could work the lever. Bullets are smacking into the wall behind us. I pulled Amber back inside and crouched down by the door, waiting for them to rush the house. I didn't see Pam go down, but when I looked, she's on the ground. Then these guys just start dropping. I mean you can hear the bullets slapping into their bodies. And there's gunfire everywhere."

"That's when Shanteel and I started in on them," Brandon said. "Call it a hunch, but I'd left the 6.5 284 up in the loft. These guys immediately hid behind the cars, you know? Like, right there in front of me. Sitting ducks. So I just started taking them out as quickly as I could fix one in the scope and work the bolt."

Shanteel added, "I'm handing Brandon bullets, and I look across, and Thomas and Willy are shooting from the other side behind the stock trailers. Got 'em in a crossfire. That's when Tubb and that fat sheriff scramble for their car and run. The others try to break, and there's nowhere to go. Finally, they make it to a car that still runs, and what's left are rocketing away on the road to town."

Amber said, "I got to Shyla first thing, Sam. There's no kind way to say this; Tubb had shot her through the heart. That's when I hurried to Pam. I dealt with enough hemothorax in Syria to get her stabilized. Meggan pulled the college van around, and we rushed Pam to the hospital. Worked with Doc Willson and his people to get her into surgery, and as soon as Pam was stable, we were told to make ourselves scarce." A pause. "So, we drove back to the ranch."

Brandon added, "By the time they were back, we'd collected the bodies, picked up a lot of cool guns and ammo, and were packed to go. Left Willy and Thomas behind to take care of the..."

"Bodies," Sam finished what Brandon couldn't say.

Willy had been sitting in the rear, quietly listening. "We put Shyla up on the rise, overlooking the valley. Grampa sang over her," he said. "I think she would have liked that. Said he sent her spirit up here. That he knew you'd be coming. That when it was all over, you'd send her soul in the direction she needed to go."

Brandon kept his grip on Shanteel's hand as he said, "The others? Willy used the backhoe and piled all nine of them in a hole and covered them up."

"So, how long do you think you can stay up here?" Breeze asked.

Amber spread her hands wide. "We've got everything we need. Just like the Dukurika, we can live here for the next six thousand years. Plants, animals, water, and shelter. That's pretty much it considering the rest of the world is gone."

"They're going to be back," Sam said. "As long as Edgewater's out there. You didn't see him like I did that day at the tannery. He was bloodied at the ranch, and then again at slickside. That's intolerable for a man like him."

He looked around the fire. "Governor Agar wants him gone. Four days from now, if everything works right, there's going to be a move to take him down and return control of the Basin to local folks."

"Agar sending troops?" Brandon asked.

Breeze shook her head. "I doubt it. The Guard's pinned down on the border. He might dispatch Militia, but honestly, they're not the sort to go toe-to-toe in a stand-up fight."

"Oh my God!" Danielle cried. "Are you people *listening* to yourselves? Hearing what you're *saying*? Stand up fight? We're just trying to stay alive. Get it?"

"Danielle," Shanteel said before anyone else spoke, "I'm *tired* of you and your shit. You and Ashley, both. Maybe it's about time you start pulling your weight. Tappans are good people. Let you wash the dishes and do house chores, while they kept food in your mouths and got shot keeping you from being hauled off to be gang-ass-raped by them white savages."

"Hey!" Danielle snapped, eyes glittering. "We're living a nightmare here! We didn't sign on for any of this shit, you get it?"

Shanteel thrust a hard finger her way. "We're *all* living a nightmare, bitch. My family, hell, all of Philadelphia's *gone*. And you think Manhattan's survived? It be *gone*. No Fifth Avenue. No Madison Square Garden. No Grand Central." She gestured around. "This is *it*. And you are *alive* where millions are not. Now, get your white-assed Karen shit together and *deal* with it!"

Danielle's expression broke. Glancing at Ashley—who stared slack-faced at her hands hanging in her lap—Danielle stumbled to her feet and vanished into the dark in the direction of the tents.

"Sorry," Shanteel murmured. "Guess I lost it."

"No," Amber answered wearily. "I should have taken care of that days ago."

"Been too worried about other things?" Sam asked kindly. "Like the fact that American is now Syria?"

"I am such a coward," Amber whispered, a curiously fragile smile on her face. "Should have been me they shot."

"No coward steps forward with a rifle while surrounded by a half dozen armed men, my dear," Meggan told her and reached over to pat her on the shoulder. "First you, and then Shyla. You bought us the time."

"And Pam, standing where I should have been, paid the price,"

Amber added.

Breeze's hard-eyed glance shifted from face to face. "Look, I don't know you people. But I've been out there where the shit's coming down. Shanteel's right. It's gone. All of it. Ask yourselves, who comes out on top? People like Agar and Old Bill, or guys like Edgewater?"

Sam thought he felt Shyla's hand on his shoulder as he said, "We do."

He glanced around, wondering if he were insane. "Look around at who we are: Shanteel, black Philadelphia. Me, Long Island Latino. Brandon, back-woods Wyoming. Amber, freed captive. Willy, Native Shoshoni. Danielle, and, no, I don't count her out yet—Manhattan Jew. Breeze," and he chuckled "whiskey-drinking rodeo queen."

She grinned and flipped him the finger.

He slapped hands to the Marlin in his lap. "And we can't forget Court the computer geek. He's in Cheyenne, planning how to build us a sustainable future."

"Or Jon," Amber added, "misguided musician graduate student and tonight's lookout guy up on the ridge."

"What about me?" Ashley asked softly.

Shanteel said, "So far? You're shit."

Breeze, not unkindly, said, "Ashley, one way or another, you'd better figure it out."

"Meanwhile," Brandon said, "What are we going to do about Edgewater? Sis tells me that if Mom lives, she's going to be tried and executed. My granddad and dad may be under arrest even while we sit here. And Sam's right, they'll be coming for us eventually."

"Can we hit them first?" Sam asked, glancing around the fire. What the hell, without Shyla, what did he have to live for?

Brandon glanced at Willy, who nodded and said, "Might be a way. If you don't mind taking a chance on getting killed."

"How's that?" Sam asked.

Brandon had narrowed his eyes as he stared into the fire. "Clark Ranch, where Edgewater's holed up over the on the South Fork? It's got a back door. My guess is that they won't be expecting anyone to be opening it."

WORD COUNT

***

There are just shy of 200,000 words in the English language. But there is no word for being thrown from one insane mess of a situation to another. There should be. Like, from the Greeks who were really into tragedy.

So, I'm home. Forgiven.

Mom's shot and in the hospital. Dad might be arrested. I've killed men, including a dear friend. I'm in elk camp with Brandon and a bunch of Eastern city college kids who don't have a clue.

Well, but for Amber Sagan. She's haunted half-crazy by her own bad shit. Spooky woman. Reminds me of cracked glass.

On the Line I was helping our people keep it together. Giving the state a chance.

Protecting.

Now I'm going off to kill people in order to give my family a chance. Still a warrior.

Protecting.

When does this shit end?

Turns out the answer is never.

Excerpt from Breeze Tappan's Journal.

CHAPTER THIRTY-EIGHT

***

BREAKFAST THE NEXT MORNING TURNED OUT TO BE A CHILLY AFFAIR WITH THE TEMPERA-
ture in the high thirties. The camp woke up in a hazy gray world of
fog and falling mist.

Sam crawled out of his tent, wandered down into the trees to pee.
One of the chickarees, the little red squirrels, was chattering down in
the branches.

Shyla, Shyla, God, he missed her. Felt like someone had twisted
his soul out of his body with a bent stick. One instant he wanted to
rage, to kill and murder, and the next to weep.

He made his way up to the cook tent.

Breeze had slept in the equipment tent, her sleeping bag wrapped
in a survival blanket from her Guard boogie bag.

Sam met her as she stepped out into the morning. Asked, "How'd
you sleep?"

"Like shit. One fucking horrible nightmare, after another. Each
more disturbing than the last. Couple of flashbacks that had me
scrambling for the M4. Good news is I caught myself before I shot
up the camp. You?"

"'Bout the same." Sam yawned and blinked.

While Breeze folded up her bag, Sam went about helping Meggan
with the cooking as the crew drifted in for breakfast. What was the
point of living so much of his life in a restaurant if he couldn't help
make a breakfast?

"God, I hope Bill's all right," Meggan confided, her face lined. "I
just lay there all night worrying about him."

"Yeah, me, too." Sam stirred the potatoes sizzling in the big
frying pan atop the Coleman stove. "He's got his fight, we've got

ours. Different battlefields, same war."

Meggan's green eyes took on a pained look. "Hope to God we make it out of this. I owe that man my life."

Breeze heard as she stepped in for coffee. "After Grandma left, Grandpa was headed to 'Hell in a hand basket' as he used to say. You saved him, too. Gave him a direction."

Sam bit his lip, miserable enough to begrudge the Tappans their family. Suddenly he couldn't take it. The urge to scream built in his chest. Fit to burst him wide open.

He dropped the spatula, picked up the .44 Marlin, and stalked out into the morning. Anywhere. Just to get away.

Maybe it was Shyla, her hand like a mirage in his. But his wandering feet took him to the outcrop. The one where he'd sat with her that first night. Where they'd touched, shared their souls.

He could hear the crew. They all ate in the big tent, people shivering and taking turns crowding around the small heat stove.

They were his people now. Turned to outlaws in the eyes of some. Freedom fighters by the values of others.

"How the hell did we end up here?" he asked Shyla, as if she were there, beside him. That all he had to do was hold his gaze just so, and she'd be there. That her death had all been a delusion. A nightmare gone wrong.

Doesn't matter how, Sam. It just is.

Was that her? Had Shyla said that? Or had it been his tortured imagination?

He thought if he really concentrated, he could see her. If he saw her, she'd be real. Not dead. Not buried. Not stolen from his life.

He blinked to clear his sight. Squinted. Willed himself to see her. "Shyla," he ordered. "Shyla. You're coming to me."

Staring as hard as he could, he thought he saw shapes wavering in the gray mist. Waving, weaving slightly, like she was walking toward him. And yes! She moved! He could see her forming from...

"Sam? You out here?"

He jumped. Almost cried out. And the wavering form emerged from the mist: Breeze Tappan.

"Go away."

Cutting across the slope, she settled herself on the rock beside him, saying, "Thanks for leaving me a space."

"I didn't," he told her. "I wanted to be with Shyla so I took her spot."

"Breakfast's ready."

"Not hungry," he told her bitterly.

"Um, you got a reason for sitting out here in the cold and wet?"

"Leave me alone."

"Yeah, I get it. I spent all night jerking awake. God, I hate the nightmares." She paused. "You dream about slickside? Keep seeing it in your head?"

"Yeah." He suffered through the shivers, his hands clenched in his lap. "I killed him. Saw the bullet hit. That flap as the clothing jumps, and the guy's body jerks under the impact. And all that screaming, and the horses, and it's...it's almost too much to..."

"That's the price you and I have to pay for saving those people down there eating breakfast." She hunched against the cold.

"They weren't all Tubb's men, were they?"

"Nope. Some of them were just deputies. The guy in the lead, he was an old family friend. Just hired to guide. Another fucked-up thing I'll have to answer for."

"All night long," Sam whispered. "Shyla kept coming to me. And when she did, I just couldn't stand it. If I could, I'd crawl down under the dirt in that grave just to be with her. Touch her. Feel her."

Breeze reached out, put her arm around him. "I'd bring her back for you if I could."

When he'd sniffed himself back into control and wiped the tears away, he added, "Then, last night, lying there alone, it all hit me. My *home* is gone. My family is gone, my neighborhood, all those people that I knew, grew up with. My friends back there. Zinny, Thomaso, Torpedo, and Shank. All the guys from the block."

"Some of them may have gotten out."

To end the long silence that ensued, she asked, "So, last night, you were the strong one. Now you're up here drowning in grief. What happened?"

"I pull that macho shit up because that's what they need to hear. It's just an act, Breeze. A fucking lie. I'm not the strong one. That's Amber. Me? I'm just a scared dude from Long Island who's lost it all."

"Damn, don't I know."

He glanced skeptically at her. "Thought you were the Guard's superhero."

"All those brave and daring deeds?" She grunted at the absurdity of the notion. "Either I was scared shitless, or I was just trying to get myself killed. First 'cause of Felix. Then over all the people I shot down at the I-25 checkpoint."

Her voice went distant. "You get it? They were men, women, and children. Families. They were scared. Desperate. All they wanted was a chance. But they were coming in a flood. Someone started shooting at our guys. I didn't think. Just stepped into the gap and picked up Bill's M4."

She glanced down at her hand, frowned as if seeing for the first time. "I emptied three magazines into those people. Was reaching for a fourth when they finally broke and ran." A pause. "I'm a monster. A mass murderer that people call a hero. And every time I tried to atone, I just got more famous."

"That night at the Hilton, the captain said you were trying to kill yourself."

"Sometimes there's nothing left inside." She snorted under her breath. "Slickside just added to the ledger. Now I've got Bradley Cole and those horses to add to tally. I figure I'm not getting out of this alive. But for the moment, I've got to keep it together."

"So, what changed?"

"Mom getting shot. Edgewater. In the end, Sam, I'm damned. For now? Someone's got to stand between the bad guys and my family."

"Yeah, Edgewater," he said softly. "There's still Edgewater."

He paused, the hollow inside expanding. "After yesterday, I guess I'm damned, too. I just wanted revenge. But watching those horses and men tumble down that slope?" He shook his head. "They didn't all die immediately, did they?"

"Nope. But that's just the way it is."

"Shyla told me that. Just before you arrived." Sam closed his eyes, shivering in the wet cold.

She asked matter-of-factly: "You're sure Edgewater is at Clark Ranch?"

"That's what Tank and Lehman said. You been there?"

"Oh, yeah. I'll say this for Edgewater, when he declares himself

God, he goes whole hog. Nothing else like it in this part of the state. Old man Clark was a multi-billionaire. The house is like ten thousand square feet, huge garage, and that fancy horse barn with its varnished wooden stalls. Even got a building with a classic car collection. Tennis courts. There was talk for a while he was going to put in a nine-hole golf course."

"So, where's the South Fork from here?"

She tipped her head to the west. "Just over there. About thirty miles as the crow flies. About three days' hard travel by trail on horseback. Willy, Amber, Brandon and Shanteel are in. So am I. What do you say we go kill the son of a bitch, or get killed trying?"

"I guess I could do that."

"But here's the deal: No suicide shit. No just walking into the guns to get it over with. See, the thing is, like down on the border, you've got to make it count. Gotta have that high in the blood, be totally jacked for the action."

"Like yesterday at slickside as they were riding out in that perfect line," he said with an understanding nod.

"Kind of a strange feeling, wasn't it? The pounding of the blood, the excitement?"

"Never felt anything like it before."

"Hey, if you're going to die anyway, might as well go in a rush, right?" Breeze gave his shoulders one last squeeze and stood. "So, remember Shyla. Love her for all that she was, and all the hope that Edgewater took from you and her. Like me, you'll pile up more ghosts, just make it pay at the end."

He nodded.

"Let's go get breakfast," she told him.

CHANGED

***

When I started this journal, it wasn't about me. I wrote this in an attempt to understand, to put everything that happened in perspective. The end of the world as you knew it doesn't just happen every day.
I should have died in Colorado, or on the Line.

I'm home now, in the high country; I'm going to be leading a bunch of college kids on horseback over slippery trails across the backbone of the Absaroka Mountains. When we get to Clark Ranch, we're going to attack it. This is how much reality has changed. Before the collapse, this would have been insane fantasy, the improbable stuff of fiction. Today it seems a matter of course.

Somehow, I've become the leader, the "hero of the Line".

They all turn to me. Even Willy who was deep in the shit in Afghanistan.

How did I get here?

When it comes to understanding, I'm as much in the dark as when I started.

Excerpt from Breeze Tappan's *Journal.*

CHAPTER THIRTY-NINE

***

THE CLOUDS AND DRIZZLE LIFTED A LITTLE BEFORE TEN, AND BY THAT TIME THEY HAD saddled and packed the horses they'd need. Meggan, Jon, and Ashley, each for their own reasons, had chosen to stay and keep the field camp occupied and supplied.

"I'll shoot a deer or elk," Meggan told them. "With Jon and Ashley to help, we can cut wood, have everything ready with fresh horses when you come back."

If we come back.

Sam found a macabre amusement in that thought. Hell, they were only heading across thirty miles of mountainous wilderness to try and kill a bipedal piece of shit protected by his own army.

The day's ride, however, left him speechless. If it wasn't heart-stopping vistas of angular basalt peaks, dramatic valleys that dropped away into stunning depths, remnants of glaciers nestled in their high cirques, it was the incredible thrill of riding on horseback along some of the most perilous trails in the Rockies.

While Willy, Brandon, and Breeze stayed on horseback, in the dangerous sections they ordered the greenhorns—as Sam and the rest of them readily admitted themselves to be—to lead their horses across the rougher sections on foot.

The route consisted of a series of game trails that led west along the base of the high peaks and skirted the head of alpine valleys. But for the occasional saw-cut trees that betrayed a previous human hand, Sam could well have believed that he was the first human to pass this way.

And there were delays from recent deadfall blocking the trail. There they would dismount; Brandon would pull the chainsaw from one of the panniards on a pack mule and cut away the fallen tree.

"God, I *love* this!" Brandon chortled as he shut the saw off. "I mean, this is all wilderness area. We'd have had to cut this out with a handsaw. If the end of the world was good for anything, it's that now I can use a motor."

"A handsaw?" Shanteel wondered. "To cut trees?"

Breeze stood with hands on hips after wrestling a section of fir tree off the trail. She watched it tumble down to catch against the trunks just below. "They don't call them idiot whips for nothing."

It helped Sam cope, all of it. Keeping busy—paying attention to his horse, gaping in wonder at the mountain splendor, and the hard labor of walking his horse up and down steep slopes—kept his mind from the grief and pain.

Mostly.

So many times, he longed to point at some new marvel and say, "Shyla, would you look at that?"

But he kept it together. Somehow. Throwing himself into the moment, making himself live on the trail, concentrate on the horse, or the next task.

"We're not making very good time," Amber noted when they took a break to rest and water the horses in a pool below a snowfield.

"We're doing fine," Brandon told her. "Right here we're at more than ten thousand feet. Nobody with sense pushes themselves, or their horses, in the high country. Not unless they're idiots. Hurrying up here is a fast way to get yourself killed."

Sandwiches gulped down, water bottles full, the trek continued, and Sam was finally able to look back and recognize Penthouse ridge behind them in the distance.

They were crossing an open patch of tundra when Danielle rode up and matched her pace to his. She kept looking in every direction except at him. Wind had tangled her long black hair in a mess that hung down the back of her jacket.

"I figured you'd have stayed back at camp with Meggan, Jon, and Ashley," Sam said.

"I was going to. Then, I got to thinking about what if those men tried the trail again?"

"Jon and Ashley are going to take turns keeping watch. You'd have been another set of eyes."

"I know."

"So, why'd you come?"

She scowled, fidgeted. "So, like, you're a New Yorker. I mean, we come from the same place. But you, like, get it, you know? I just feel..." She paused, searching for words. "Is it a guy thing?"

"What?"

She made a sweeping gesture from the saddle. "All this. The horses, the guns, the whole Western *thing*."

"God, no. Most of the time I feel like I'm a five-year-old dealing with a world that doesn't make sense. It's all alien. This is the hardest learning I've ever done. More so since, anymore, someone else's life depends on it."

She waved at where Breeze, Brandon, and Shanteel rode three-abreast, talking and laughing on their horses. "I'll never be like them. Even if I dedicated my life to trying to be a cowboy, that's not who I am."

"So?"

She shot him a brown-eyed look of disbelief. "Isn't that the only thing that counts these days?"

"No one expects you to be a cowboy or a soldier. No one expects that of Court or Jon. But Court's making a difference in Cheyenne. Jon and Ashley are doing the physical labor that Meggan can't. You just do what you can, and then do a little bit more."

"What about when we get to Clark Ranch?" She looked away. "I don't think I could shoot a gun. Not at a person."

"Someone has to stay back and take care of the horses. You can do that, can't you?"

In a small voice, she said, "Horses scare me."

"Yeah? So you going to live like a mouse for the rest of your life?"

"That's just it. I *can't* do these things." Her face contorted. "This isn't my world. I don't belong here."

"You're Jewish."

At that she flared, eyes going hot. "Where you going with that? Some anti-Semitic, racist, shit that—"

"You got any Israeli friends?"

"What's that got to do with anything?"

"It's got everything to do with it." Sam narrowed an eye her way.

"How do you think all those urban European Jews felt after the Second World War? There they were, survivors of the Holocaust, half-starved, haunted, and plopped down in the middle of Palestine surrounded by people who hated them. Cobblers, bankers, musicians, all trucked out to a kibbutz and handed a hoe before being told, 'You're going to work, or you're going to starve.' And a couple of years later, they whipped combined Arab armies to make a nation."

As she digested that, he said: "Jews. Relatives of yours. You wanted to know where I'm coming from as a New Yorker? My family's dead. So's yours. The collapse is our holocaust. You going to be an Israeli, or a statistic?"

"Shyla was a fighter, and she's dead."

"She's not being gang-raped and humiliated by a bunch of thugs." He jerked a head toward where Amber brought up the rear. "Go ask Amber if Shyla made the right choice."

Danielle shot a furtive glance back, then bit her lips, face flushing red. "What if I'm scared?"

"The Jews in the Warsaw ghetto were scared. That's in your blood, too, Danielle."

She took a deep breath, held it, gaze locked on the distant peaks. "I guess I never thought of it that way."

"Back in that world, we didn't have to. You're an anthropologist, figure it out."

"I wanted to be a museum curator like my uncle in the American Museum of Natural History."

"So you end up as a band-level hunter gatherer. Life's full of little surprises."

To his relief, she laughed at that. "Nothing to fear but fear itself, huh?"

"Yeah." And loss, and defeat, and hunger, and endless grief.

But he didn't tell her that.

CONTEMPLATION

*** * ***

The fire crackles and spits. The temperature is in the forties. The archaeologists sit in a circle around the fire, faces lit by the flickering yellow light. They don't talk much, huddled, hands in pockets or clasped before their knees.

I am reminded of that old movie Red Dawn. *The original with Patrick Swayze. Grandpa loves it. Has it on DVD. The archaeologists have that same expression on their faces, like they can't believe what's happening to them.*

Amber Sagan seems the most unfazed. She's older, harder, and should be more of a leader for the rest, but she's withdrawn. Locked inside herself, a distant reflection of hell in her eyes. I don't know her story, but by instinct, I'm wary of her.

Brandon and Shanteel amaze me. Talk about coming from two incompatible worlds? My red-neck Copenhagen-chewing brother and an intense social-activist black woman from the Philadelphia slums? Should be oil and water, yet there they sit, holding hands, leaning shoulder-to-shoulder, a halo of desperate intimacy around them. I've seen Brandon in lust. This is different. The two of them seem to mesh like gears.

Willy sits back, apart. Not because he's not one of us, but because, like me, he knows how this raid is likely to end. It's a guess, but I think he's preparing himself to be killed.

Danielle comes across as a wide-eyed mouse, ready to freeze and cower at the first shot. I don't know why she volunteered for this, being the most out-of-place of all of them. I suspect that when her moment comes, she'll either crater into a weeping mess, or find herself. Call it fifty-fifty.

And finally, there's Sam. He's the most complex of them all. City kid for sure, but the toughest of the newcomers. His problem is that half of him wants to break down and bawl, wallow in the grief that's bubbling in his soul. The other half wants to rage as he stands over Edgewater's body and rips the director's guts out. But with Amber's retreat into herself, he's assumed responsibility for the archaeologists, so he can do neither.

Excerpt from Breeze Tappan's *Journal.*

CHAPTER FORTY

***

BRANDON SAID THE TRAILS WERE IN WORSE SHAPE THAN HE REMEMBERED. NOT ONLY DID deadfall have to be cut where it blocked the path, sections of trail had to be built in places where it had washed away. They were running a day behind when they finally made camp in a hanging valley high on Boulder Ridge above the South Fork of the Shoshone River.

More of a mountain than a "ridge", the north-south trending mass of Boulder Ridge would be their last refuge. From where they had situated camp—hidden from sight by the shoulder of the mountain slope—Clark Ranch lay some five hundred feet below and a mile and a half down a steep slit-like canyon.

Having grazed and watered the horses, Breeze and Danielle brushed them down. The animals rested, heads down and exhausted where they were tethered to a picket rope strung between two lodgepole pines.

A low fire crackled as a pot filled with creek water, packages of freeze-dried macaroni-and-cheese mixed with a packet of Mediter-ranean-style fettuccini alfredo, and two rabbits, boiled. Willy had potted the bunnies with a .22. Whatever the meal lacked in culinary sophistication was rendered mute by the growling-and-empty stomachs around the fire.

"Here's what we've got," Brandon said where he'd scuffed the duff and grass back to expose dark earth. "These two ridges"—he drew them on the damp dirt—"are the two you see leading off to the west." He pointed into the sunset, indicating the high ground to either side of the intervening drainage.

Brandon said, "Shanteel and I will take the ridge on the north, Willy the one to the south." He fixed on Willy. "Our job is to find a position overlooking the ranch. You and me, we're the best long-range shots.

I'm good for a guaranteed cold-barrel first hit on a man-sized target out to about six hundred yards with the 6.5 284. I've seen you pot an antelope out to four hundred fifty with your .270."

"Yeah." Willy was nodding. "I've got a box of twenty cartridges and another four in the gun. So let's don't make this a long, drawn-out affair."

Brandon looked at Shanteel. "We've got a box of fifty, so I can lay down a covering fire for longer, but, love of my life, I want you to spot with the binoculars and generally keep track of what's going on. Breeze's bunch will be moving, and I want you to monitor their location, so I know who's on our side and who is an enemy."

"Got it," Shanteel gave him a nod. "And I'll hand you bullets as you run low. Just like last time."

Breeze took her stick, drawing a line between the ridges. "My party starts out a couple of hours before dawn, following the trail down the cut and into the valley. If some of these guys are ex-military, they might have laid traps along the trail. Maybe trip wires, or who knows what? So, we'll take our time, sticking to the slopes as much as we can."

She fixed on Sam and Amber. "That's us. Sam's got a box of fifty rounds of .44 mag for the Marlin. Amber, you've got forty cartridges for the .30-30. I've got three mags for the M4, which is sixty rounds and another forty in loose rounds that I can use to top-up the magazines if I get the time."

She turned back to the contents of the boogie bag where they were spread out behind the fire. Among the bag's myriad contents were two walkie talkies, one of which she gave to Brandon. "That's our only communication. I'm turning it on low, but if we find ourselves in a situation where it could give us away, I'll turn it off. That doesn't mean you should panic if you don't hear from me."

Brandon spared her a mischievous grin. "So, that's about like normal, huh, Sis?"

She flipped him the finger. "If I've got the radio off, it's because bad guys are close and could hear it. If you can't raise me, and it's an emergency, fire two pistol shots. Just like when you have an elk down: Pop. Pop. I'll turn the radio on if I can. Three shots. Pop. Pop. Pop. We'll know that something's going really wrong, and we have to get the hell back up the canyon."

"You got that, Willy?" Brandon asked his friend. "You're the guy who doesn't have a radio."

"I'll be fine." Willy lifted a shoulder in a lazy shrug. "Something tells me I'll know when the shooting's done. That'll be my clue to ghost my way back up to camp."

Breeze finished laying out the contents of the boogie-bag gear and kit she'd acquired during her days on the Line. The rest were looking on with definite interest.

Brandon gave her the old familiar nod. "I gotta tell you, I'm really starting to like your friends down in Cheyenne." He pointed. "Those real?"

Sam picked up one of the three hand grenades and hefted it. "Yeah, they're real. Never realized they're so heavy."

"What's the thing with the umbrella?" Amber asked, pointing.

"Satellite phone with a directional antenna." Breeze shrugged. "I've fiddled with it before, no one ever answered when I tried to make calls. So either I don't know how to work it, or no one's left on the other end."

"And the can things?" Willy asked, pointing.

"Smoke grenades. If we get into a mess, I'll pop one and toss it over my shoulder. Use it to screen a rapid retreat."

The four-goggled night vision set wouldn't be necessary since they were hitting the place at dawn. The roll of cord she stuffed in her pack along with the flashlight. The tarp, slicker, and other gear would stay behind.

"We need to set priorities," Amber stated in clipped tones. "The captives have to come first."

"Agreed," Sam rejoined.

"No." Breeze shot back. "The priority has to be Edgewater."

Amber leaned forward, face possessed of a new-found intensity. "Fine. You do your thing. I'll do mine. There's three of us, and two shooters. You go after Edgewater. I'm breaking the hostages out. And when I do, I'm getting them the hell out of there. If you don't like it, you can shoot me now."

Breeze bit her lip, studied the woman. "All right."

Sam committed it to memory as Breeze drew the ranch layout in the dirt as she remembered it. "The stables are here, just to the left of the canyon mouth as we come out. We should encounter it first thing.

If the rumors are true, that's where the hostages are supposed to be."

She glanced around, drawing another square. "This is a big garage full of fancy cars just to the right as we leave the canyon. Storage for maybe twenty vehicles. It sits up against the hillside. Below it is a large lawn that slopes down to the main house. It's a big place. Took ten to fifteen million to build, with a stone patio and plate-glass windows, so anyone inside is going to see us crossing the lawn."

Brandon pointed. "That's the hard part. That yard. It's wide open. Or it was. No cover. No way to cross it without being exposed."

Breeze flexed her fingers. "That'll be something we have to solve when we get there." She paused. "What about this attack that the governor wanted? If it came off yesterday like it was supposed to, maybe this is all a moot point?"

"We can hope," Sam said where he'd been crouched, hand to mouth, studying the drawing. "But I really want to kill that piece of shit."

"Stand in line," Amber whispered, clutching her .30-30 as if it were a life preserver.

"What about the hostages?" Willy asked as he stirred the pot-pourri stew.

"I'll lead them up the canyon," Amber said, voice distant. "Don't want them milling around where there is shooting. Getting in the way. Most will be willing to run. Some may just want to huddle into a ball and cry. I'll get them back here, to camp."

Amber glanced at Danielle. "You'll be here, keeping the fire going. Maybe have soup or something ready. Something hot, simple. It can make a huge difference. Like the first reassurance they have that it's really over."

Sam watched Danielle bite back a shudder.

But it was Amber that he worried about. That glassy-eyed fanaticism. The almost desperate and unbending dedication, as if there would be no failure. Rigid insistence that everything be done just so.

Yeah, I just hope she doesn't break down at the first sign of trouble.

Because surely, Amber Sagan had to know that if this went wrong, she was headed right back into hell.

Sam tightened his grip on the unforgiving hand grenade he held. *That's the great thing about being male. They'll just shoot me dead on the spot.*

THE DIE IS CAST

***

In Colorado, down on the Line, things happened so fast. Most of what I did was react. The call would come in, OP Bravo Whiskey was taking fire and needed belt of ammo for Ma Duece. I'd slap a couple of belts of .50 caliber ammo into the saddle bags and maybe a case of bottled water and roar out along I-80 as fast as the BMW would run. Take the exit and fog it down the dirt roads to the OP.

I never had time to think. Just do the job. Fast. Because our people's lives depended upon it.

Bullets tear through air, like a crack or snap. I'd be aware as I killed the bike, kicked the side-stand down, and started stripping supplies from the saddle bags and luggage rack. Same thing at the I-25 checkpoint that day. No time to think. Just act.

Being thrown into action is really different than what I experienced descending that trail down the canyon. I had plenty of time to fill my head with what-ifs. And this time it wasn't just me. There were other people at risk, like my brother, whom I loved. Nor could I trust Amber or Sam when the bullets started whacking past. Either might fold up on me.

Here's the thing: After everything that I'd survived, if Edgewater's people hadn't shot mom. If he hadn't ordered the arrest of my family, I'd have turned around and walked right back out of that pre-dawn canyon.

Excerpt from Breeze Tappan's *Journal.*

CHAPTER FORTY-ONE

* * *

HARD TO THINK HE WAS MAKING HIS WAY DOWN THIS NARROW MOUNTAIN DEFILE WITH THE express purpose of shooting people. Had it only been a month since he'd left his rented room just off campus? That Sam Delgado? What had ever happened to him?

This man was a stranger. Some elemental, hurting, and pissed-off remnant of a human being. Something confused, having been batted so quickly and violently from reality that he half thought of himself a human handball. Smacked so hard that he didn't have a clue which way he was going.

He had come to Wyoming in an attempt to find academic salvation. Instead he'd found love and a refuge—and lost it all. As he followed Breeze and Amber down that dim trace, all he had left was hatred for the men he would find at the end of this winding game trail.

The scent of the forest filled his lungs. He listened to the early morning sounds of the birds, the last hooting of the great horned owls, a distant chorus of coyotes, and the faint rustle of night creatures in the brush to either side.

He tightened his grip on the Marlin hanging in his right hand, feeling its reassuring heft. Images of Shyla, laughing, that teasing look in her turquoise eyes, lingered just behind the veil of his memory.

He remembered other eyes: the intent look Edgewater had fixed on Shyla that day in the tannery. How the man took what he wanted, heedless of what it cost.

Just get me close, Sam promised himself, *and I'll blow a hole through Edgewater like I did Ed Tubb.*

After that, nothing much mattered.

Those few days with Shyla had been worth a lifetime. Looking back, he'd been loved, raised by decent, hard-working people. Instilled with values that had won him the woman of his dreams.

A man could do worse.

Fragments of unsettling visions clung to his memory: images of death. Shyla's body, staggering along, bleeding from a ragged hole torn between her breasts. Her face twisted in a grimace of agony. She'd kept calling out, "Why weren't you here?"

Once, he'd been awakened when Breeze poked him with a stick, calling, "Hey, Sam. It's all right. It's just a dream."

He had blinked, looked up at the haze-blurry stars. Glanced around the camp with its smoldering campfire. Breeze had been propped on an elbow, little more than a shadow in the night.

"Nightmare."

"Yeah, well, I've got enough of my own that I don't need to listen to yours. Either dream happy or move your bedroll somewhere else."

He didn't "dream happy" but Breeze hadn't jabbed him with a stick again.

Breakfast had been a hurried affair, the last of the stew from the pot.

And then they started down the trail, the way lit by Breeze's red-lensed flashlight that cast a dim cone of light that barely illuminated the roots, rocks, and holes in the winding game trail.

One either side, the canyon walls closed in as they descended, dark against a glowing sky whitened by the sliver-thin and waning moon that hung low in the east.

They took their time, Breeze explaining that the last thing they wanted was to hurry, for someone to trip, to send the sound of breaking wood, or the clink of metal to warn any sentry that they were coming.

They proceeded step by step, no one rushing in the darkness.

"If there are deer in here," Breeze also explained, "going slow lets them drift out of the way instead of sending them off in a crashing panic that will alert any guard."

"Never would have thought of the deer," Amber admitted in a hoarse whisper.

"You okay?" Breeze asked the woman.

"Better now than I've ever been."

Breeze let them stop at the bottom of a particularly steep section. Gray twilight had filled the canyon, exposing stands of silent fir and spruce that darkened the slope. Outcrops of cracked rock jutted from the canyon walls above cluttered scatters of talus. A creek gurgled musically in the bottom as it tumbled over boulders and splashed down stone. Willows and currents choked the flats.

Sam took a seat on a canted slab of sandstone, Amber dropping next to him and shedding her pack. She looked distant.

"Tired?" Sam asked.

"Not in the way you think."

"How then?"

"I thought that killing that bastard trying to take Shyla would have brought a little relief. I mean, I'm glad I shot him. Piece of shit deserved to die."

She shook her head, as if baffled at something inside. "I'll kill more of them today, God willing."

"You sound sad."

"Just exhausted. Tired of hurting. There's no getting away from what happened. It lives inside you, down in your bones. I see him, over and over..."

"Who?" he asked, staring up at the violet-and-orange tinged sky. It was the smoke, always a constant, blowing in from the west.

"Abu al Palmyri. I can't get away from his eyes, dark and gleaming as they...as they..." She waved it away. "And his laughter is there. It echoes, you know. Endlessly. Pulsing with my blood. The louder I screamed, the harder he laughed. His crooked yellow teeth flashing behind that thick black beard of his."

"The guy's dead, isn't he?"

"They missed him that day they got me out. Shot down most of them, but that miserable maggot-fucker was trying to get to Raqqa on some sort of Daesh business. So...he skated. And that haunts me. Knowing that he's out there, somewhere."

"Like how I feel about Edgewater, I suppose." Sam squinted up at the brightening sky.

"Edgewater didn't rape you day after day. Didn't burn you with cigarettes and attach jumper cables to your nipples," Amber said hotly. "Or have let his fawning creatures crawl on you and..."

She blinked, lowered her head. "Over and over. It never stops. Never has an end. Just lives inside me. Down in the bones."

"Well," Breeze said from where she'd been listening a couple of paces away, "let's go kill as many of these rat bastards as we can."

Amber smiled in a wistful way. "Two men, our guys, died taking me out of that hole. Given what little was left of me, I've always thought they shouldn't have taken the risk."

"That's what those guys do," Breeze told her. "They knew going in—"

"They died *for me*!" Amber snapped. "I've *tried*." She squeezed tears out from the corners of her eyes. "I tried so fucking hard to be worth their sacrifice. Pushed myself. Fought to shut the demons out of my head."

Her voice dropped, "But they showed up again at the ranch, Going after more women. They are *here*, don't you understand? In America. In *our* country. Abu al Palmyri. Same demon, just masquerading as an American. You've got to understand the kind of men we're dealing with"—she knotted her hands around her rifle—"and why we've got to kill them all."

THE VALUE OF LIFE

***

I would like to think there were absolutes when it came to ethics, philosophical truths, and morality. The Ten Commandments tell us: Thou Shalt Not Kill. And, of course, the Bible goes on to expound upon the battles and conflicts waged by the Hebrews. So, we're left with the implicit understanding that Thou Shalt Not Kill is limited only to not killing Jews who keep the laws of God. Anyone else is fair game.

In American jurisprudence life was sacred; murder had no statute of limitations. No other crime had the same status. I prove my point by noting that an entire genre of film and literature—the murder mystery—existed on its own. Didn't matter how hideous your neighbor might have been, how evil, twisted, and malicious. Killing him was forbidden, even if he poisoned your dog. People were known to go to jail for killing burglars and rapists who broke into their houses. Self-defense wasn't an excuse.

And in a single day, that changed. I knew it the moment we saw those three bodies on the sidewalk at Alameda and Kipling.

I lived it when I shot the bastards that murdered Felix. The fear and horror disturbed me, but I never regretted or mourned snuffing those guys.

Then came the Line, the I-25 checkpoint. People whose bodies I blew apart with bullets. Or passing corpses along the side of the road like they were roadkill.

The little girl in the tent, her family dead at their own hands.

Now I was purposefully headed to take people's lives.

Without a functioning society the only right and wrong is what's needed to keep your loved ones alive. The final reality is that all morality and ethics are situational. They change with the wind.

Excerpt from Breeze Tappan's Journal.

CHAPTER FORTY-TWO

***

TO SAM'S RELIEF, BREEZE SAW IT FIRST. SHE HISSED, MOTIONED THEM INTO THE LEE OF A slash-pile of branches. The clear-cut slopes on either side of the V-shaped valley gave it away. The pile of slash—or cut branches—lay at the base of a slope at the upper end of the clear cut. Crews with chainsaws had logged out all the timber, dragged it down to the trail in the canyon bottom, built a barricade and skidded the rest out.

The chest-high barricade was no more than a hundred yards down the canyon. The breastwork was made of limbed and stacked logs and piled earth.

"Son of a bloody bitch," Breeze growled as she pulled one of the dead limbs out of the way. She had her small set of binoculars to her eyes.

"What's wrong?" Sam asked.

"Behind the log breastwork, see the Polaris side-by-side with racy paint and the big tires? That thing in the weather cover? That's a pintle-mounted Browning M2 machine gun atop its roll bar. And the thing's sitting butt-ugly in the middle of the trail. I've got four men just visible from the shoulders up behind the barrier."

"So?" Amber asked.

"So, we're screwed," Breeze told her. "See why they cut the slopes bare all the way up to the limestone cliffs? It's to provide a full field of fire. Anyone trying to bypass the position would stand out like a Santa Monica street walker at an Atlanta cotillion."

"Can we shoot them from here?" Amber asked as she peered through the screen of branches.

"Not and live," Breeze told her, looking around. "Even the boulders have been chained up and pulled out of the ground around the slash pile."

"Shit," Breeze muttered, "You know why they left this slash pile out here? Why even the boulders had been dragged away? We're in the jaws of a God-damned trap."

"How?" Sam whispered.

"If they'd been alert. If they hadn't been telling lies and drinking coffee down there, we'd already be dead. It's just luck we got to the slash before they noticed."

"I don't understand," Amber said warily. "Don't these branches give us protection?"

"That's Ma Deuce down there."

"What's Ma Deuce?" Sam asked.

"That machine gun mounted on that ATV. It's a fifty caliber. Get it? With enough power to blow our little stack of kindling apart like tissue and turn us into hamburger."

"But this is the only place to hide," Amber hissed back.

"Exactly. We're hunkered down in a death trap. The instant they figure out we're here, they're going to cut us into doll rags."

"Why the fuck can't they be somewhere else?" Sam asked angrily.

Breeze smiled bitterly. "The narrow walls here, that's what they call a choke point. A bottleneck. Any descending force will be packed together, in the open, and set up for shooting. Think three hundred Spartans and Thermopylae. And they're the Spartans."

"What do we do?" Sam almost cried. "How do we get past?"

"We don't," Breeze said with a weary exhale. "This is it, kids. End of the line. Our biggest problem right now is how do we get back up the trail and around the bend before they shoot us in the back?"

"Why can't we shoot them from here? Each of us pick one and kill them?" Sam asked.

"It's a hundred yards. Doable if we were all excellent shots, with scoped rifles. But all it takes is one guy jumping onto the back of that Polaris, getting a sight on this position, and thumbing the spade." She made an exploding gesture with her fingers. "Poof. We're gone."

"What if we could get past these guys?" Amber had her eyes fixed to a gap in the branches. "Think there's another barricade down yonder?"

"I doubt it." Breeze scratched under her chin where a mosquito had found a free lunch. "My memory is that the canyon opens up after this. And you can see the trees, narrow-leafed cottonwood, growing thick along the creek. Lots of cover that they didn't take down. No, my bet is that they think this has their butts covered. The pisser of it is, it pretty much does."

"Damn it, damn it, *damn it*!" Sam gritted through clenched teeth, his hand knotted so tightly around the Marlin his knuckles were white.

Breeze carefully crawled back, studying the trail back up the canyon. It wasn't much, maybe fifty yards to a house-sized boulder next to the trail. Once behind that, they'd be out of sight all the way back to camp.

"Got a plan?" Sam whispered.

"We can crawl about twenty yards before they'll see us. At that point, it's get up and run like a striped-assed ape for that rock. Duck behind it, and you live."

"If we can get that far," Amber noted. "It's, like, turned into daylight since we've been hiding here, folks."

"Any chance we can do a distraction?" Sam asked. "Buy us some time?"

Breeze chewed her lips, trying to think.

"I know a way we can get past that barricade," Amber said, eyes fixed on that eerie distance she so often stared at. "Something I saw used in Syria in situations like this. They won't be expecting it here, that's for sure. And I know these men, the kind of animals they are. That's a weakness, you know. A vulnerability that can always be exploited."

"What plan?" Breeze asked skeptically. "Lay it out, Amber, and it better be good."

"I'll need a hand grenade. Can't take the rifle. That'll tip them off for sure."

Sam was looking skeptical. "You're just going to walk down there and lob a hand grenade over that barrier? What makes you think they'll let you? And why won't they shoot you down the second they see you pull the pin?"

"Because they're not going to see the grenade until it's too late."

Breeze stared across at her in the shadows cast by the branches. "You ever even laid fingers on a hand grenade before?"

"Actually, yes." Amber snorted in amusement. "Took one out of a guy's gut in Syria. A bomb blast in Aleppo blew it, unexploded, like a piece of shrapnel right through his navel. Still had the pin in it when they brought him into the hospital."

"That's just the point—"

"I've been around a lot more grenades than you have, Breeze. Now, do we want to get past these guys and be in position by the time Brandon and Willy get set up on the hill? Or do we want to give up the whole thing and take a chance on getting shot in the back getting out of here?" She narrowed one blue eye. "It's a risk either way, but I think I can take those guys out."

"What if it doesn't work?" Sam asked in a whisper.

"Then you and Breeze hightail it while they're taking me down." She reached out, took Sam's hand. "Do you trust me?"

"Well...sure."

"Then you're a fool, 'cause you know I'm an emotional basket case." Amber's grin got wider, a kind of crazy behind her eyes. "But just this once, trust me."

Sam nodded, unconvinced.

Breeze still hesitated, her fingers wrapping around the grenade she pulled from her pack. "So, what's the plan?"

Amber nodded as she spoke, seeing it in her head. "I walk down all alone, a lost woman from the forest. My hands are out and open, no weapon. They let me close. You and Sam have to be ready. The second I toss the grenade over the breastwork you've got to run like you've never run before. Get to that barricade and shoot down any of the dazed men behind it. When it's all finished, I'll go back for the .30-30 and my pack."

"You think *that* will work?" Breeze hissed in disbelief. "You'll be standing there, in the open. All it takes is one shot, and you're down."

"Would you be expecting a hand grenade from a backwoods camper?" Amber lifted an eyebrow.

Sam had a creepy feeling along his spine. Something that screamed of wrongness. But, what the hell, light as it was, they'd be shot down like fools if they made a run for the boulder.

From her expression, Breeze, too, could sense the wrongness, but handed over the grenade. "You just pull the pin and throw it. You've got—"

"Three seconds. I know." Amber took the grenade, held it close, and shrugged out of her pack. Over her shoulder, she whispered, "The only thing that matters to me is freeing those women down there.

Promise me."

"Promise," Breeze and Sam answered in unison.

Amber, like a snake, wiggled her way to the edge of the slash and slipped out of her jacket and pistol belt. Then she froze, intent gaze fixed on the men below. She waited until all eyes turned away and stood.

Amber made it ten good paces down the trail, calling, "Hello! God! Am I glad to see you! I've been lost for three days! Where the hell am I?"

"Who're you?" one of the men called, the others lining up on the breastwork, leveling rifles.

"Amber Sagan! I was hiking outside Cody. Got turned around. Haven't seen a soul for days."

"Keep your hands where we can see them. Come on in."

"What's she doing?" Sam asked as Amber, apparently unfazed began unbuttoning her shirt.

"I haven't a clue?" Breeze muttered in amazement as Amber discarded her shirt to flutter down onto the trail.

The men were watching with rapt attention as Amber strode toward them; reaching behind to unhook her bra, she let it fall. Then she shook her red hair loose from the clip restraining it, letting it tumble down over her shoulders in a wave.

"Duck. Freeze," Breeze hissed as one of the men pulled up binoculars and searched the slash pile. It seemed forever before he lowered the glasses, apparently satisfied that Amber was alone.

"Where's your friends?" one of the men called.

"Just me. I wanted to get, like, elemental with nature. Like you guys, camping up here in the wilds." She ran her fingers through her hair. "You know, *El le men tal*! Whoo!" she shrieked and whooped, then skipped a step. "Got the *wild* in me."

Breeze pulled up her binoculars, scanning the men's expressions. Even from where he watched, Sam could see them grin, nudge each other behind the wooden wall of their fortress.

"So, where's the hand grenade?" Sam asked, eyes to the gap in the branches. What did Amber do? Stuff it down the front of her pants?

"Got me. But you get ready, Sam. She's almost there. Ease your way over to the side but stay down. Just like Amber said, when she tosses that grenade, we run faster than we've ever run before."

And my priority target will be the first guy to climb up on that Polaris and reach for the big fifty. He checked to be sure the safety was off on the Marlin. All he had to do was thumb the hammer back and shoot.

Sam belly-crawled after Breeze, his heart beginning to hammer with that unnerving sense of dread.

It looked like Amber was really going to pull this off.

What the hell? When Amber reached the breastwork, she didn't stop, but climbed up and jumped lightly over. She was laughing, almost maniacal as the men pressed around her.

Across the distance, Sam barely heard one of them say, "Sweet Jesus, where'd you get all those scars?"

Amber almost squealed as she announced, "Wait till you see what I've got in my pants, you big stud."

Sam couldn't see, but from the look of Amber's shoulders, she was undoing her fly. As she reached out with her right hand, offering something to the men, she threw her head back, shouting, "Abu al Palmyri, this is for you, you piece of shit!"

Breeze hissed, "Sam! Now!"

Sam stumbled to his feet, vaulted the last of the branches, and pounded for the breastworks; the grenade exploded with a muffled bang.

He saw Amber's red hair blow out straight, head punched back. The men standing in front of her were blasted back like rag dolls, guns flying, heads jerking forward and back.

Beside him, Breeze was running for all she was worth. The Polaris rocked on its suspension as men and shrapnel thudded into it.

And then everything went oddly still. The only sound came from Breeze and Sam's boots slapping into the trail, the air rasping in and out of their lungs.

Side by side, they reached the breastworks, literally ran up the logs and vaulted, coming down to one side of where Amber Sagan's body lay against the rough logs, her face tilted back, eyes wide like blue glass. Her mouth gaped wide, her hair in a spray.

Her gut...

Sam glanced away, turning his attention to the men.

Breeze dropped beside him, stunned as she stared at the woman's torn remains.

The guy to Breeze's right, wearing a shredded Tee-shirt, his arms a maze of tattoos, jerked, sucking for air where he lay propped against the Polaris. Blood ran red from punctures up and down his torso.

The two men who'd been tossed to the side lay in a tangle of limbs and torn flesh. Neither moved.

The fourth—a Levi jacket partially blown from his body—lay on his back. His lungs were spasming, one eye wide, the other a bloody mass of tissue where shrapnel had torn its way into his brain. Another piece of shrapnel had broken his arm, which lay askance and crooked.

"Amber?" Sam wheezed, dropping next to the eviscerated corpse with its bits and ropes of bloody intestines. His breath caught, mouth working, as he took in the carnage. The blood. The ruined meat.

Peppered with jagged holes torn by metal fragments, the Polaris leaned, both the tires on the left now flat.

Breeze bent down, checking the tattooed dude. He kept blinking, trying to suck a full breath. Blood had begun to bubble on his lips.

At the tangle of corpses, she did the eye test, tapping her finger to a fixed eyeball on each one. Neither so much as flinched.

Even as she turned to number four, his limbs twitched and jerked, and what was left of the air rattled from his lungs.

The soft crackle of the radio on her belt brought her back. She lifted it, saying, "Yes?"

"We're in position," Brandon's almost whispered voice told her. *"We can see Willy across the way. All set. Status?"*

"The way's clear all the way in. They hear the grenade go off down there at the ranch?"

"Is that what that was? No. Just a muffled bang. The guys down here just looked up the canyon, then went back to what they were doing. Only counted four guys so far. Two at the stable. Two down by the house. No telling how many might be inside at breakfast."

"Got it. We're clear all the way in."

She holstered the radio, getting to her feet. "Let's go, Sam."

But Sam just crouched there, appalled gaze fixed on what remained of Amber Sagan's ripped and scarred body. The world seemed to fade, as though he was seeing it from an ever greater distance...

THE HERO

***

The ultimate hero is the one who sacrifices himself or herself to save others. That's what made the Jesus myth so powerful. Think Congressional Medal of Honor recipients. From Katniss Everdeen to Harry Potter, those heroes are the most powerful. Even Spiderman gave up what he wanted most: the girl of his dreams. They all served a higher calling than themselves.

Did Amber Sagan?

Excerpt from Breeze Tappan's *Journal.*

CHAPTER FORTY-THREE

***

"SAM? *SAM!*" HE HEARD THE WORDS, FAINT. COMING FROM ACROSS ETERNITY.

A keening seemed to grow, to encompass him, enfolding him in a blanket that wrapped tighter and tighter, crushing the breath from his lungs.

He tried to comprehend what he was seeing: Amber's pale arms, lined and blotched with patterns of white scar tissue, hands missing, lower arms ending in bloody and shattered bone. Her face, untouched by the blast. The eyes stared vacantly at the sky, her gaping mouth, dentures hanging loose to expose pink gums.

Dear God, they broke out her teeth!

Only smooth scar tissue remained on her breasts where the nipples should have been. He couldn't breathe. Felt his heart straining in his chest.

In that instant, *Nynymbi* appeared, seemed to hang in the air. Sam stared into the creature's eyes, the dark rings like an infinity of midnight time and space.

"Sam!" Breeze barked. "Snap out of it!"

He realized he was panting, throat catching at the sickening smell clogging his nostrils.

"Sam, we've got to go." Breeze continued to glare. "Get it together."

"Yeah." He swallowed, fought the urge to throw up.

She pulled him to his feet, where he wavered unsteadily. Somehow, he clung to the Marlin rifle, but every nerve in his body had gone rubbery.

"Sam?" Breeze was back, her face thrust into his. "You with me? You gonna make it?"

He jerked a nod. Ground his teeth. "Yeah. I... I'm just... Got the shakes."

"If you're going to fold on me at the last minute, I'm better off going without you. You can cover my rear, here."

An image of Shyla—of what they would have done to her—made him close his eyes. The thought of what men had done to Amber, lent him the rage and energy. "No. Let's go."

He followed on unsteady feet as she led the way past the listing ATV with its canted machine gun.

Only as he walked did he grow aware of the valley again, of the now-gouged-out trail where logs had been dragged. His brain continued to stumble; his soul might have come loose from the rest of his body.

Sam tried to comprehend, failed. "What kind of shit are we living?"

Breeze turned, leveling a finger. "We're stopping Edgewater. That's what Amber bought us...a free shot to kill that motherfucker and get those hostages out."

Shyla's face hung in his memory. He kept catching flickering glimpses of *Nynymbi* as the spirit helper darted ahead. "I want the bastard dead."

"When we get down there, Sam, there's no time for second guessing. No mercy. We're there to kill and do whatever it takes to get those prisoners out. And then we'll do anything it takes to buy them enough time to get away."

Filling his lungs with the fresh morning air, it came home that—horror aside—he really hadn't planned to get out of this alive. "Just get me close enough that I can put a bullet through that piece of shit's heart."

"With an attitude like that, you'll do, Sam Delgado."

Breeze kept them to the trees as they emerged from the canyon. She led the way, hopping over the creek and crouching down in the willows that overlooked the barn. She lifted her radio. "We're in position, bro. Maybe fifty yards from the northeast corner of the stables. I don't see anyone."

"*The two guards went inside maybe three minutes ago. Yard's clear. You want to chance it?*"

"No. Leaving two guys behind us is a death sentence. We're going for the barn. Cover us." Breeze slipped the radio back in its holster, saying, "Safety off on your rifle, Sam. Anyone gets in your way, shoot him."

She watched him click the Marlin's safety button into the receiver, adding, "Just walk. Like we're out for a morning stroll. Anyone sees us running, it'll be a dead giveaway."

Sam's heart began to pound as he followed her out of the willows and got a good look at Clark Ranch. "What the hell?"

The camp filled the lawn area behind the big house: a tall, fenced enclosure maybe ten feet high, topped with a roll of concertina wire. The center of the square was filled with wall tents. Through the wire, Sam could see five, six, no an even dozen men and women. They stood at the far end, some with hands extended to a smoking fire.

"Looks like a prison," Breeze muttered. "Shit. It's like a fucking little mini concentration camp."

It hit him like a dash of cold water. "Split up. You get the guys in the stable. I'm taking out the fence."

"How?"

"I'll think of something."

On the left, the stable building was a beautiful thing made of cedar with a red-tin roof. Off at an angle sat a sizeable barn-like arena. The creek ran down out of the canyon, under an ornate bridge, and skirted a wide lawn that sloped down to a multimillion-dollar mansion.

A huge, sprawling thing built of logs, with soaring river-rock fireplaces, and low-hung eaves, the great house was a masterpiece of design. From this angle an artistic, stone-paved patio with a fire ring, barbecue, and glass patio tables abutted huge floor-to-ceiling glass windows. Behind them, Sam could make out what looked like a sunken bar and lounge. The distance coupled with the angle of sunlight on the windows was such that he couldn't really discern the room's contents, but it looked like plush sofas, a pool table, and designer woodwork.

"Holy shit," he murmured before glancing north to take in the long garage with no less than eight large doors. A yellow D8 caterpillar was parked at the side, and a raised fuel tank could be seen above the far end.

Beyond the house, lush, green alfalfa pastures sloped gently down to the South Fork of the Shoshone River. A paved driveway led down, crossed a bridge, and met the county road that ran along the west side of the valley. The whole place looked remarkably peaceful, hardly threatening at all.

A shot rang out, carrying down from the slope above the garage. Sam heard the meaty *pock* of the bullet and just caught sight of the man on the patio as he collapsed. The only sound beyond the echo of the shot was the man's gun clattering on the stone paving.

The people inside the wire, started, looking around. Others began to emerge from the lines of wall tents.

"Hey!" an armed man called out, stepping into view on the far side of the wire compound. "Don't none of you fuckers get any ideas! First person to get close to the wire gets shot!"

The prisoners were now milling, the knot of them growing larger where they gathered around the fire.

"Okay, Sam. Armed guard on the concentration camp." How was he going to get the wire down? He looked around. Breeze had reached the barn door; she didn't even hesitate, but threw it open, M4 leveled, and charged in.

A second later, two shots could be heard from inside the barn.

Don't think. Just act.

Sam beat feet to the garage, slipped behind the Cat and opened the side door.

The line of automobiles glistened in the diffused morning light coming through translucent panels in the roof. Closest to him, a 57 Chevy two-door, turquoise with a white roof, gleamed. Next to it, something Italian, like a flying wedge, maybe a Ferrari or Lamborghini? A couple of 60s muscle cars. No help there.

And on the back wall, sitting atop a steel stand, rested a barrel-shaped fuel tank, complete with filler hose, marked **LEADED GASOLINE ONLY.**

The popping of gunfire could be heard outside.

Sam hustled to the fuel tank, unhooked the hose, and used a WD-40 can to prop the filler handle wide. Gasoline spewed as Sam dropped it to the floor, stepped back, and found the lighter in his pocket. Flipping the flame on, he tossed it.

The spreading pool of gas went up with a whoosh. Liquid fire ran under the bright red Italian job. As it did, a bullet whacked into the garage with metallic clang.

Sam ducked back out the door. Shot a glance at the stable. The door gaped, but he couldn't see Breeze. Bullets, however, were cracking into the walls.

Sam ducked behind the Cat. Shot a glance around the side. Across the cleated tracks he could see the prisoners behind the wire; most were ducked down. Some were screaming, calling for help. Others shrieked. There were maybe forty of them visible now, some scuttling this way and that. One woman ran for the wire, only to be shot down by some unseen gunman.

How the hell was he going to get that wire down? There was no gate in the back. No lock he could shoot. He'd have to somehow make his way around the front, open the gate in full view of the big house.

With a runny feeling in his guts, he tightened his grip on the Marlin, charged out. Made two steps before something tore the air just to his side.

Fuck me! That was a bullet!

Skidding to a stop, he almost fell in his rush to get back behind the safety of the Cat. From there, he peered past the wire camp, could see the shooters now. A line of men who'd advanced to the end of the stone patio. Shots were banging out, echoing off the mountain behind, followed by a periodic rifle report from up on the slope.

Inside the garage, something let loose with *whump* that shook the building. The roar inside was getting louder. Across the way, Breeze leaped out of the stable, her M4 rattling as a line of young women raced out.

Sam watched the last of them fleeing pell-mell for the canyon, flinched as a bullet tore past his ear with a crack.

He dropped to his knee, taking a sight on the house. Even as he picked out the shooter, a shot rang out from Willy's ridge, and the guy dropped.

"Bless you, buddy."

The line of women was running for all they were worth, Breeze still shouting orders.

Another rifle shot came from Brandon's location.

"Sam," Breeze shouted. "Get back. We've done all we can."

He stared at the panicked people in the fenced yard. How could he get that damn fence...?

Breeze slid to a stop behind him.

With a ping, a jacketed high-velocity round whined off the Cat's side.

"Think there's a key in this?" Breeze asked, her eyes on where the last of the women were vanishing into the canyon. One, not so fortunate, a blonde, lay face-down in the grass beside the willows.

"You can drive a Cat?"

"Never had the chance, you?"

"In Hempstead? Get real."

At the sound of feet, Sam raised his rifle, leaned out, and saw the guy in a red tee-shirt and Dockers who rounded the garage. One instant, the man was lifting his rifle. Sam triggered the Marlin. And then the gunman was flat on the ground. Lost in the recoil Sam didn't even see him fall.

He glanced past the track, down to where the house now swarmed with men, he could see them behind the huge picture windows.

"Breeze?" he called to where she was crouched behind the cat. "Think we could drive this down through those windows?"

"Are you out of your..." Her brow lined. "Cover me."

Breeze made a leap to the track, made four steps, and Sam saw her wrench the cab door open. As she dove inside, a bullet blasted a star-patterned hole in the window where her head had been but an instant before.

"Breeze? Talk to me."

"Give me a second, will you?"

He could hear banging inside the cab.

The .44 Marlin at the ready, Sam tried to control his breathing and watched the corner of the garage lest another guy appear from there. The man he'd shot through the chest had ceased gasping for breath; frothy blood continued leaking from his mouth and the hole in his blood-soaked shirt.

To Sam's surprise, the starter ground, and with a clattering of diesel, the Cat rumbled to life. White smoke puffed from the stack.

"Breeze, what are you doing?" Sam shouted over the rumble of the exhaust.

He heard the *pock* of glass breaking as a bullet found the windshield.

"I don't know the gears!" She called over the engine's rumbling.

"Whatever you're doing, do it fast!" Men were starting forward.

The engine raced. The Cat lurched forward, transmission howling. Even as it gathered speed, Breeze leaped out, fell, and scrambled to her feet. Staggered sideways as the supersonic crack of bullets filled the air. She was running full out, hair flying behind her.

Sam barely heard the popping of shots from Willy's and Brandon's positions as he slid behind the garage's bulk. Breeze threw herself behind the garage's protection as something inside exploded, blowing a hole in the back wall no more than thirty feet from them.

"I gotta see this," Sam said, pressing against Breeze so he could look past the corner.

The cat was howling, full throttle toward the high fence, doing all of ten miles an hour. Caterpillars, it turned out. Weren't very fast.

"It's all downhill from here," she told him. "Throttle's wide open. They can only stop it if they get inside."

The shooting from the house had turned serious, men spilling out the doors to fire at the screaming D8.

Sam stepped out, knelt, and took aim. Call it two hundred yards. He figured the bullet would drop, put the front sight on a man's head, and triggered the gun. The Marlin went off with a bang. In the distance, the man dropped, screaming, and grabbed his crotch.

"That a payback for the women?" Breeze asked dryly.

"I was aiming for his head."

"Which one?"

The Cat thundered onto the high wire. Ripping the posts out of the ground, it clawed its way forward, snagged enough wire to pull at an angle, and tore through the chain-link like it was tinfoil.

The huddled captives were staring in horror as the yellow beast—pulling shredded wire behind it—bore into the first wall tent. Fabric wrapped around the blade, having all the resistance of tissue paper.

The sight of the diesel beast collapsing wall tents around and on top of it, must have been mesmerizing. The shooting had stopped, everyone staring.

"Come on," Sam gritted. "Get the hell out of that compound!"

But the hostages had been just as ensorcelled by the spectacle. Some barely managed to gather enough wits to scramble out of the way as the Cat, shrouded in wire and canvass, clattered its way past.

"Damn it!" Sam charged out, running for the compound. As he passed the front of the garage, smoke and flames burst out of one of the middle garage doors.

"Hey!" he bellowed. "Run! Get out of there. This is your chance!"

The hostages turned, torn between his screams and the impossibility of the caterpillar crashing into the downhill fencing, tearing down the entire wall.

"Come on, damn you!" Sam was waving, wishing them to move by will alone.

The Cat continued to thunder its way toward the house. It was almost to the stone patio now, grinding along, the tracks ripping and shredding bits of fencing shroud that were pulled beneath the high blade.

"Someone stop that damn Cat!" came the bellowed order from below.

Edgewater's shooters, were leaping to their feet, charging the bulldozer. Some tried to find a way, but the thing was wrapped in wire and torn canvas. A whipping snake of the razor wire that had once topped the camp caught one man by the thigh. Like a chainsaw, it cut through his leg.

The rest of the men jumped back, some lifting their weapons, shooting entire magazines into the Cat, the staccato reports mixing with the spatters of bullets on steel.

Sam had reached the torn ground where the compound wall had stood. "Everyone run!" he bellowed. "Get out now! Head for the mountain!"

"Go!" one of the older women ordered, pointing. "Let's get the hell out of here!"

And like sheep finding sudden comprehension, they ran. Only a few headed for Sam, the rest, for whatever reason, were headed north. Apparently making for the valley where it headed for Cody.

"Sam!" Breeze bellowed. "Let's go! Now!"

He turned, followed by the older woman, a couple of men in their fifties and sixties, and a few middle-aged men and women.

Throwing a glance over his shoulder, he saw it happen. Slowed. Couldn't help but watch. The Cat didn't hesitate as it plowed through the patio furniture and smashed into the high, plate-glass windows.

It bounced over the sill in a shower of falling glass, went snarling into the recessed den, the mantle of wire and canvas trailing around and behind. Crashing and breakage, like chaos could be heard as it crossed the sunken lounge, veered right, and tore into the great river-stone fireplace. For a moment, the Cat stopped, tracks clawing on the floor. Then the fireplace toppled. Tons of round rocks smashing down.

A giant cracking sound came from the house. Like a series of tree trunks being snapped in two. Then Cat's roaring exhaust could be heard as it caught traction. The thing disappeared into the depths accompanied by more banging, cracking, and snapping sounds.

Armed men came boiling out through the smashed windows, firing blindly.

Sam tried to estimate the drop, worked the lever, and shot. Beside him, Breeze's M4 let loose with a staccato of fully automatic fire. As quickly, the men below broke, running for the sides, leaving their dead and dying behind.

In the sudden silence, Breeze's radio crackled.

She pulled it from her hip. "Yeah?"

"I think it's time to get the Dodge out of Hell. Shanteel says that a whole bunch of trucks are fogging down the road in our direction. We'll cover you."

"Got it."

"Now, run, Sis!"

After Breeze stuffed the radio into its holster, she fished one of the smoke grenades out of her pack. Their small party of freed hostages was running full-out for the canyon. Shooting Sam a glance, she asked, "You ready?"

"Yep." He waited long enough for her to pull the pin and toss the smoke grenade. Then he lurched to his feet, pounding for the canyon mouth. Shots echoed down from Brandon and Willy's position, and a couple of bullets snapped angrily past. Sam got the surprise of his life when just the sound of their passage energized him like a cattle prod. He never knew he could run that fast.

Then they were in the trees.

He looked back just in time to see the mansion's roof fall. It sagged, then let loose with a sound like distant thunder. A moment later, it was followed by an explosion. A huge ball of fire rose from what was left of the lounge roof. Sprays of glass from every window shot out like bursts of diamonds in the morning light. The force of the blast had flattened the milling men, some batted like rag dolls to crumple as they hit the ground.

Bits of debris, fire, and twirling pieces of house rose high to arc and cartwheel back to earth. Splintered wood, sections of buckled plywood, and shreds of Tyvek danced in the sky.

"Son of a bloody bitch," Breeze wheezed.

"Wooo Hooo!" Sam chortled.

Breeze's radio crackled. "*Sis? Couple of vehicles headed your way with some serious guns on them. Worst is a Jeep Rubicon with what looks like two big guns on the roof.*"

Even as Brandon said it, the cackle of gunfire could be heard. Different. Louder and deeper than the rifles they'd been hearing. "What the hell?"

"Big stuff," Breeze told him, whipping her radio out. "Brandon! Get the hell off that ridge! They spot you and Shanteel, those guns will tear you apart!"

And then she wheeled, running flat-out for the canyon. Over her shoulder, she cried, "Run like hell, Sam, or we're going to die here."

CHAPTER FORTY-FOUR

***

BREEZE LED THE WAY, FEET HAMMERING ON THE TORN TRAIL LEFT BY THE LOGS THAT HAD been skidded out of the valley. Behind, Sam ran for all he was worth. He could hear the growling of vehicles, occasional gunshots, and then the deep-throated staccato of the heavy machine guns.

A trail of blood spots led to the body of a brown-haired young woman who sprawled face-first in the trail, her clothes matted in coagulating crimson. The freed hostages barely spared the dead girl a second look, they just ran harder.

That was two who hadn't made it.

Sam felt oddly better as the valley closed around them, the high walls rising to either side. Once they were past the breastwork, across that open area and behind the boulder, they were safe. They'd have made it.

If the hostages could make it that far. They were all wheezing, half staggering, those in street shoes slipping and sliding on the grass. The older man in his sixties was red-faced, huffing, and bug-eyed as he kept running slower and slower.

A secondary explosion sounded from behind and echoed its way up the canyon.

Sam followed the skid path past the last of the narrow-leafed cottonwoods and stared in disbelief. Five of the freed young women were milling hesitantly, glancing unsurely toward the wounded Polaris and the torn bodies, and then back down the canyon where occasional shots could still be heard.

"What the hell are you doing?" Breeze shouted, her breath already coming short from the hard run.

The women, dressed irregularly as they were, started back down the trail toward Breeze in a shambling trot.

"Run! Damn it! *They're coming!*" She lifted her M4. Sam could see it as she fought the urge to fire a burst over their heads to provide an incentive that words couldn't.

Sam cast a desperate glance over his shoulder, half expecting to see the Jeep Brandon had warned about appear on the trail. It remained empty, but a pall of black smoke was rising beyond the canyon gap.

"Where do we go?" a panicked black-haired young woman asked. "Up there? Into the wilderness? And to what?"

"Someone *murdered* those people?" an ash blonde almost whimpered, tears streaking down her red face.

"You want to be...back in that mess?" the slim gray-haired woman demanded. "The only way out is up this canyon."

"What...about...the rest?" the red-face man puffed. A hand to his heart.

"They'll be hunted down!" Breeze declared. "Now, all of you. Get your asses over that barricade!"

Sam cursed, charging forward as he shouted, "Get your *fucking* asses moving. Amber died to get you silly bitches out of there. Now move, 'cause if they catch any of you, it'll be worse than a bullet to the brain."

"So, run, God damn it!" the gray-haired woman thundered.

Breeze lifted her M4. Fired a round to motivate them.

Three of the women turned and scrambled over the piled logs, two, to Sam's absolute disbelief, fell on their knees, weeping, arms up, pleading. The hostages had no such confusion. They were slipping and sliding over the piled logs.

"Breeze," Sam said as he stopped, heart hammering, before the kneeling women. "Go! I'll get these two. You get the rest up to that boulder. We might need the cover."

And then he bent down, shifted his rifle, and bodily picked the smaller woman off the ground. Threw her over his shoulder, shouting to the other, "You, red shirt. Get up and come along, or I'm leaving you."

"I *can't*," she sobbed. "I'm scared."

Sam bent down, used the rifle barrel to lift her chin, and calmly said, "You can. You have to. Safety's just there, up ahead."

Breeze didn't take time to listen.Over her shoulder she called,

"Damn you, Sam, *leave* them. Call it Darwinian selection."

The three who'd followed instructions were tip-toeing past Amber's body and the corpses of the men, trying not to step on blood or body pieces.

"Go, damn you," Breeze bellowed as she pounded her way up behind them. "Climb."

From the mouth of the valley, Sam could hear the Jeep now, coming slowly, the driver no doubt worried about ambush in the trees.

To Sam's relief, the black-haired, bawling woman he had so calmly talked to, was right behind Breeze. Bringing up the rear, Sam pounded along, breath blowing as he labored under the smaller woman's weight.

Puffing like a steam engine, he made the breastwork as Breeze was pulling the black-haired woman over.

"Come on," Sam urged as he swung the woman down and onto her feet. "Over you go."

She wasn't more than a girl, Sam realized. Redheaded, fifteen if she was a day, and wearing slightly too big jeans with one shoe on, her other foot bare.

"Here, take my hand." Breeze practically hauled the girl over.

"Shit," Sam said, his eyes fixed down the trail. "They're here."

He turned, lips working. "Breeze, give me one of the grenades."

"Sam, we can make it."

"Now, damn it!" He measured the distance. "Grenade. I can take them out, and I'll be right behind you."

"Sam, you can't single—"

"It's the only way." He reached out, snapping his fingers. "I've got a plan."

Light on painted metal now. It would only be a moment more and they'd be visible. Reaching into her pack pocket, she slapped the grenade into his hand and turned, running behind the redheaded girl, shouting, "Go! Run! They're right behind us."

"My foot—"

"Turn your *fucking* mind off and *run*."

Ahead of her, scattered along the trail, the others were running with various amounts of speed.

Sam watched as Breeze unslung her M4, fired a burst over their heads, and saw a singular and most sudden display of enthusiasm.

The lithe young redhead in front stumbled, almost fell, and then ran like a gazelle.

How far yet?

The first of the fleeing women passed the slash pile, feet flying. Making distance on the rest.

Sam turned as the Jeep broke cover. The only thing between him and the muzzles of the two mounted machine guns was empty air.

Only thing left is to buy time for Breeze and the rest.

He smiled as he dove for the bloody dirt.

See you soon, Shyla.

CHAPTER FORTY-FIVE

***

AS BREEZE THREW A GLANCE OVER HER SHOULDER, SHE COULD SEE LIGHT ON PAINTED metal as the vehicle ground its way up the skidway in the valley bottom. It would only be a moment more and they'd all be visible.

As she charged forward, it was to find the redheaded girl limping, shoulders jerking as she sobbed. The older man was puffing and stumbling, at the end of his endurance. The other hostages, the freed women, were calling reassurance to each other. All of them winded, pushing themselves as hard as they could.

From somewhere down in the valley, gunfire crackled on the morning air. Breeze guessed that some of the errant hostages had been run down.

Catching up with the redheaded girl, Breeze shouted, "Go! Run! They're right behind us."

"My foot—"

"Will heal. That big boulder is safety."

Ahead of her, scattered along the trail, the others staggered along. Breeze slowed as she reached the flagging man. He wore a dirty white shirt, suit pants, brown loafers. Looked like a businessman. His mouth gaped, face red, sweat shining. He shot her a sidelong glance. "Can't...go...farther."

"You've got to. There's a truck coming with guns."

He stopped short, then, bent to wheeze. "Go on. Get them...out of here. I'm...dead."

She saw the vehicle emerge from the trees.

The fleeing hostages were moving too slowly to make the boulder. Without a second thought, Breeze raised her M4, fired a burst over their heads. The lithe young redhead in front of her stumbled, almost fell, and then ran like greased lightning.

Breeze dared not look back. "Run. Run," she prayed between breaths. *Damn it, Sam. What possessed you?*

Her lungs burned. She had run, uphill, all the way from the garage, most of it at full speed. She hadn't slept well the night before, had awakened long before dawn. The days on the trail had been hard work, constantly pushing, and little quality sleep. Just dozing at night...and fitful dreams.

How much did she have left? Her legs had that rubbery feel, muscles aching from fatigue. She couldn't suck enough air. Her heart thundered painfully in her chest.

She passed the slash pile, wishing she had a lunge whip to slash the black-haired woman across her buttocks. The little redhead had passed her and was now hot on the heels of the rest. Only the black-haired woman lagged, and she was trying. She just didn't have the wind.

"Fucking run, bitch," Breeze panted, hating to take the breath necessary to make words. "Don't...give...up."

The first of the hostages staggered their way past the boulder.

Almost there!

Ten yards. The redhead had almost reached the rock.

Thudding, rasping hisses tore the air overhead; the valley above them exploded in flying dirt, burst rock, fragmenting bullets, and splintered wood. Even as it did, the hammering of the guns came from behind.

Then she heard a shout: "Halt! Freeze, or we shoot to kill!"

"Go! Run!" Breeze bellowed in the sudden silence as the hostages staggered to a horrified halt. "Behind the rock!"

She whacked the black-haired woman on the butt with the muzzle of her M4.

I'm going to die here.

It would come now. Any second.

She wouldn't feel it—just have that quick image of her body being blown apart. A sensation of impact as large caliber bullets ripped her flesh, bone, and muscle into pieces.

The world seemed to slow into a weird and oddly tranquil reality.

As the hostages staggered for the great boulder, a detonation behind her made her throw a quick glance over her shoulder.

The Jeep—a copper-colored Rubicon—pitched rear up. A yellow ball of fire caught in the instant. Men, like black silhouettes, were catapulted forward and out. The twin machine guns were frozen in that moment as they were ripped from the Jeep's roll cage.

Down the valley, she could see men with rifles who stood rooted just this side of the narrow-leafed cottonwoods. Five of them, they were staring at the burning Jeep. The Polaris lay on its side.

Below the slash pile, the businessman lay sprawled, blood on his white shirt.

The men started forward.

Breeze raised the M4, figured the range at three hundred yards. Bracing against the boulder to steady the sight picture, she fought to steady the rifle, couldn't with her pounding heart and puffing breath.

She triggered a burst. The distant men ducked; a couple threw themselves flat. They shouted back and forth, turned. Then they were running back the way they'd come, disappearing down the trail.

Slipping behind the safety of the boulder, she stopped, braced herself as she sucked her lungs full and blew it out. Sweat was beading, slipping down her sides under her shirt, tickling and drawing flies on her face.

"Can we rest now?" the older, gray-haired woman asked from behind the boulder's safety. She was bent over, sucking air like a bellows.

"For a minute," Breeze whispered hoarsely.

Come on, Sam.

She kept expecting him to clamber up onto the breastwork. Pictured how he'd shoot a look back, just to make sure, and leap to the ground before trotting across the open area, that old Marlin hanging from his right hand.

But he didn't.

Her radio crackled. "*Sis? You okay?*"

"Yeah. You and Shanteel?"

"*We're out of their range now. Keep catching sight of Willy across the way. He's okay.*"

"I've got the hostages. What we could get anyway."

Should she go back? Look for Sam's body?

Torn, Breeze shook her head. The Polaris now erupted in a ball of smoke and fire. Rounds were detonating in the heat, cooking off with hollow popping.

"God bless you, Sam." She wiped the sweat from her forehead. "When you get there, tell your Shyla she's got herself one hell of a man."

She turned, meeting eyes with the hostages—singled out the women who'd stopped at the barricades. Crap on a shingle, they looked like field mice come face-to-face with a bobcat.

"Why the hell did you stop?"

The ash-blonde cried, "Just run off into the wilderness? Just because we're told to by people with guns?"

Breeze raised her M4 their direction. "People died to save your worthless skinny asses. Two *good* people. If you don't follow my every direction from here on out, I'll shoot you myself. Now, get your asses up that trail. They can still send a party after us, so we're not even close to out of this yet."

The panting hostages from the wire enclosure just nodded, turned their clumsy and stumbling steps to the trail.

Breeze watched them line out.

Think any of them are worth Sam and Amber's lives?

With one last look, she touched the M4's barrel to her forehead in salute to Sam and Amber and turned her weary feet to the trail and the long climb ahead.

CHAPTER FORTY-SIX

***

COMING OUT OF DISORGANIZED AND FRAGMENTED DREAMS, SAM BLINKED HIS EYES OPEN to a blurry white light.

Heterodyne.

The whole world...vibrating out of tune.

Worse than any hangover, his tongue had no feeling and just rattled around between his teeth.

As his mouth finally began to water, he had the first glimmering of understanding: The heterodyne. The dissonant ringing, it was his body. Like that stunned feeling after landing hard from a long fall. His head was filled with a dull, deep-inside-at-the-core ache.

Thoughts wouldn't come, just the endless ringing tingle in his body, and as his vision cleared, a sense of vertigo, nausea, and being really, really sick.

He had no clue where he was. Had no sense of time or place. Just floating misery.

A door opened, and he realized that his vision had cleared enough that he could recognize a room. Even knew the kind of room if he could just put his thoughts...

He frowned, having lost track as the man walked across to his bed. Older man. Black short hair. Blue-green smock. Stethoscope.

The man did something with a little wheel on an IV tube. Bent over Sam, flashed a light into Sam's right eye, and then left. Took his wrist and lifted his right arm. Poked Sam's finger, and nodded when he flinched.

Even as this happened, the room came into clearer focus. Scattered thoughts beginning to fuse.

"How are you feeling?" the doctor asked. Doctor. That's right. The room...In a hospital.

"Who's paying for this? I only have student insurance."

The doctor laughed. "It'll take a couple of minutes for your brain to clear. You're lucky to be alive. They found you under a wrecked Polaris."

"What happened?"

"Well, that seems to be the subject of a great deal of debate." The doctor leaned close. "Do you have a name?"

"Samuel Michael Delgado. My mother was an Alvarez."

"Where are you from, Sam?"

"New York."

"How long have you been working for the Director?"

Sam blinked. *Director?* His scattered thoughts were running around in circles. "What director?"

"Director Edgewater. Up at Clark Ranch." The doctor watched him carefully.

"Piece of shit." He swallowed. "Edgewater. Killed Shyla. Wanted her for his..."

Image by image, it began to coalesce in his brain. "They had hostages. In a fucking wire enclosure. Like Nazis did. And women. Out-of-state girls. Locked in the stable. Sex slaves. Had to save them."

"You sure?" the doctor asked. "Word around here is that the stables were a barracks for the director's men."

"We used a Cat. Tore down the fence. Hostages...they all ran." Sam smiled to himself. "The girls. The hostages. Old guy, red face. We got them out. Breeze and I."

"Tell me about the soldiers who raided the director's ranch. Where did they come from?"

"Soldiers?"

"Some kind of paramilitary force. Commandos. Twenty or thirty men. Whose unit? National Guard?"

"Just five of us. Students, can you believe?"

The doctor's eyes narrowed, voice even lower. But then, he'd been speaking softly the whole time. "This is important, Sam Delgado. Whose side are you on?"

Sam blinked. "Wyoming's. With Governor Agar. Us...or Edgewater."

"Who ordered the attack on the ranch, Sam?"

"No one. We did it to get the prisoners out."

"Sam, this is a really important question: Where are those hostages and girls now?"

"Some ran the wrong way. Got the others up the canyon. Breeze would have taken them up. High. Back to field camp."

The doctor's lips pursed; the man was obviously thinking. "Can anyone prove that?"

"Tank. Lehman. They were at the meeting. Down in Cheyenne. With Governor Agar."

The doctor took a deep breath. "Wow. Okay. Outside of them, do you have a contact here in Cody? Someone you'd turn to in the event of an emergency?"

"Cody? Sully Richardson?" Sam frowned, something inside yelling for him to shut up.

"Sully would vouch for you?"

Sam was finding it hard to breathe, his chest was really beginning to hurt. "At Tappan's. Meggan gave him a sandwich and thermos of the last coffee."

The pain began to intensify. "What hurts so bad?"

"Broken ribs, cracked pelvis, fractured cheek bone, internal bruising." The doctor stood, fiddling with the little wheel on the IV.

Sam felt a slight rush of relief flow through him like a cool breeze as the doctor said, "You go back to sleep now, Sam. I think things are going to get a little grim around here."

Sam watched the doctor step out the door where a guard with an AR15 stood; dressed in black, hair close-shaved to his scalp, the guard didn't look happy.

"How's he doing, Doc?" the guard asked. "The director really wants to talk to him."

"He's in critical condition," the doctor said. "Be a couple of days. If I can keep him alive that long."

The floating sensation was coming back, the pain receding. Sam almost sighed in relief.

Down the hall, he heard a man shouting, "My son's been shot in the genitals, damn you. He's going to spend the rest of his life without manhood, dribbling into a bag, and that son of a bitch in there might know who's responsible!"

"Now, now," a reasonable voice replied. "One thing at a time, Commissioner. We'll get to the bottom of this, and when we do, the punishment will be excruciating. *Ex crux*. Meaning from the cross. Crucifixion. Yes. That's how we'll punish the people responsible."

Sam knew that voice. Had heard it... Where?

A face drifted out of the mist that his thoughts were descending into. A round face, with a small mouth, a dinky nose in too much skin. Obsessed gimlet eyes, fixed on Shyla...

...The people responsible.

Sam floated deeper into the mist, thoughts beginning to scatter. Responsible. Re spon si ble. Four syllables. Nice word. Meaning... Meaning...

And then even that question drifted into a gray oblivion.

CHAPTER FOURTY-SEVEN

* * *

THE SIMILARITIES TO HERDING CATTLE WEREN'T LOST ON BREEZE TAPPAN. LIKE PUSHING beeves, the freed hostages balked, bawled, and just didn't have it in them to hurry as they lined out on the trail. Also, like cattle, some moved the herd better than others. Especially Shirley Mackeson, the gray-haired woman. Turns out she was a Park County commissioner who'd defied Edgewater's takeover of the county government.

Others just couldn't get it into their heads that they had to travel. Including Tom and Sally Visange, who'd owned one of the auto dealerships. Also slow and stunned were Harry Nelson and John Baker. Both bank presidents who'd had their vaults cleaned out by Edgewater's goons.

Unlike beeves, however, the freed prisoners understood a verbal threat.

"You're going to move," Breeze insisted as she leaned down from Joker and pointed a finger at the black-haired young woman with startling blue eyes. She claimed her name was Joelle. "If you don't, we'll leave you for the wolves."

"What do you people want with us?" Joelle cried, fists knotted.

"Is it so hard?" Danielle asked, striding up. "We're trying to save your lives."

"Here?" Joelle stared around at the slopes, trees, and sky. "In the wilderness?"

"Where are you from?" Breeze demanded.

"Marin County," Joelle declared. Then, seeing it made no impact, added, "That's in California. Across the bridge from San Francisco." She pointed at another woman, a busty brunette. "Michaela and I were trying to get home from Minneapolis when they...they..." Her expression began to cave.

"So, get it together," a strawberry blonde in her early twenties said as she came walking up.

Breeze recognized the woman—one of the few who'd taken immediately to the situation back in the stable and led the way up the canyon. The strawberry blonde—who she'd heard called Mary Lou—looked to be in her early twenties, pale pink in complexion with green eyes and a perfect body. But then the freed women were all physically attractive. Apparently, that was the single criterion that damned them, along with being from out of state.

"So, let's move it, huh?" Shirley Mackeson snapped as she strode up. "Or would you rather be back in that stable still being gang-fucked by whatever shit heels unlocked that door."

Joelle—who'd been the center of attention—nodded, and added, "Do you trust these people? I mean, they've got guns and they're marching us into the wilderness." She shot a suspicious glance at Brandon and Willy where they were leading the pack mules up the trail.

Mackeson snapped, "Get your ass moving, California." Then she raised her voice. "All of you! We've got to move. Get away from here. There will be a time for payback, but we've got to stay free in the meantime."

"Shirley?" Harry Nelson asked. "Where's Frank?"

"Who's Frank?" Breeze asked.

"From the Buffalo Bill museum," Harry told her. "You know. Older guy. He was with us. Why isn't he here?"

"Yeah. White shirt. They shot him when he couldn't go any farther."

"They shot a lot of people," Shirley said bitterly. "Now, let's go. From here on out, everyone does what Breeze orders. Got it?"

They nodded, glancing uneasily among themselves, and started along the trail again, letting Breeze bring up the rear with Danielle.

"Should have brought more horses," Danielle said, glancing at the sun easing past its noon high. "How fast can they walk? How far?"

"Maybe we can make five or six miles today," Breeze answered, looking back across the meadow to where their camp had been. Would there be pursuit? Would Edgewater try and take the prisoners back? Hell, was he even alive? Or had he been crushed when the house collapsed?

The strawberry blonde had dropped back, looked up from where she walked. "You're Breeze Tappan," she said. "I know you."

"From where?"

"Saw you ride. I did some rodeos. Wasn't nearly good enough." She paused. "I'm Mary Lou Finch. From Greybull. Finch Ranches."

"I know some of the Finches. How'd you end up back there?" Breeze nodded back toward the South Fork.

"Got accepted to the University of Washington. I'd driven out to check out the campus. Figure out which dorm and all. I was headed home when a couple of Frederick's guys stopped me at a roadblock north of Cody."

"Thought they didn't take local girls," Danielle said as she walked her horse behind Joker.

"Yeah, well, lucky me." Mary Lou spit the words. "Figured that if I was coming back from Washington, my folks would think I vanished somewhere along I-90. Edgewater told me that as long as I 'held his interest' he'd keep me alive. After that, I'd join the rest along the south fence."

"The south fence?" Breeze asked.

"Yeah," Shirley Mackeson called back. "That's where they buried the people they executed. Anyone they'd arrested who was no longer useful to them. Made us watch so we'd understand. They'd shoot the person, toss the body into the bucket and drive the backhoe up to the south fence. Dig a hole and drop them in."

"How many?" Breeze asked.

"Maybe twenty-some that I know of. Probably a lot more."

Mary Lou said, "Most of the girls don't make it past their first night with Edgewater. I kind of had special dispensation because the director knew that Frederick wanted me for his private property."

"Private property?" Breeze asked.

"His alone," Mary Lou said. "The alternative was communal property, which means anyone, anytime, in any number up to what they called group screw."

"Jesus," Danielle whispered. "How long were you there?"

"I stopped counting days," Mary Lou replied. "After the director was done with me, I did what I had to do to keep Frederick happy." A pause. "You never know what you'll agree to, how far you'll go to justify it to yourself. Wasn't any ambiguity left. Either I was one un-Godly fucking machine, or I was dead."

Mary Lou glanced back at Breeze. "Doesn't get much simpler than that, does it?"

"Nope." Breeze shook her head. "Shit. Wish I'd killed more of that trash back there."

"I can't believe this is real," Danielle cried. "It's America, for fuck's sake!"

"Yeah," Shirley Mackeson almost spat the words. "It's real."

"Then maybe what we paid is worth it," Danielle told her. "Amber and Sam? I mean, they were our strength. Kept us together. But for them, there's no telling where any of us would be now. If we'd even be alive."

Breeze narrowed her eyes. She'd had her doubts about Amber Sagan and Sam Delgado, but would she have been willing to sacrifice herself like they did?

Did these people—especially the ones like Joelle—understand?

"Mary Lou?" Breeze called, "Do you get it that people died to get you out of there?"

"Yeah. As much as I ever can."

"I'm relying on you. We've got to keep all of you alive. You understand that don't you? The fight's not over. We're going to bring Edgewater down."

"So, like, what's the plan?" Shirley Mackeson asked.

"It's a hard, three-day hike to the field camp. Then it's a couple of days to check out the situation. Get a hold of the right people. Get your statements."

"What are you thinking?" Danielle asked.

"People can stand giving up property when the country's against the ropes, but they won't stand for the executions or what Edgewater and his goons did to these women. Word gets out, it won't matter how many men he's got. As long as these witnesses are alive, he's vulnerable."

"So he's going to come after us?" Danielle asked.

Shirley Mackeson shot a look over her shoulder. "I've been thinking about what you did back there to Edgewater. Taking us. Ruining up his ranch. Killing his men. The guy thinks he's an emperor."

"No shit," Mary Lou told her. "Dressed in a sheet one night and made me call him Caesar while he raped me. You better bet he's going to send someone after you. And they'll be coming for blood."

Breeze nodded, seeing it unfold. "Change of plans," she said. "Today we make tracks. Tomorrow, we take to the timber and the rocks, figure out how to hide our trail."

Danielle asked, "What if they've got someone as good as Brandon?"

"Then we'd better figure out how to kill him before he can kill us."

CHAPTER FORTY-EIGHT

***

LIKE A MOUSE SURROUNDED BY FLAMES, SAM'S SOUL SHRANK BACK, TRIED TO CRINGE, and would have done anything to escape the pain. Nothing had ever hurt like this. He hadn't *known* he could hurt like this.

Words would not describe.

The truck bounced, and Sam gasped, wishing for silence, wishing any hint of movement would stop.

"How are you doing?" a woman's voice asked.

He pried his eyes open, surprised when even that hurt, as if a spear where thrust through his brain.

In the dim light he could barely see her, aware that he lay on a gurney, and was riding in the back of a van. Ahead of him, a driver and another man were illuminated in the dash lights.

"He's coming out of it," the woman said. "His pulse is elevating."

Sam caught the doctor's profile as he turned in the passenger seat. Yes, the same doctor from the hospital.

"Hang in there, Sam. It won't be long now."

"Long for what?" Sam whispered dryly.

"You're a very important person," the woman told him. In a flash from an overhead light, he caught a glimpse of her. She had clipped her hair behind her head. Looked to be late thirties and was wearing scrubs. A name tag hanging from a lanyard was too dark to read.

"Is every bone in my body broken?" Sam rasped.

"Not quite," the nurse said with a smile. "The ribs took most of it. The crack in your hip will heal just fine. You should be over the worst of the concussion. The rest is pulled muscles and some pretty awesome bruising.

"Go left!" the doctor called. "That driveway."

Sam felt the van lurch. The nurse grabbed for the strap holding his gurney as she was flung sideways. Sam whimpered as the vehicle was slammed to a stop.

"Did they see us?" the doctor asked, sounding half panicked.

"Guess we'll know in a second, Doc." Sam heard the driver shift in his seat, then a clunk. The bolt worked on a rifle. "If it gets hairy, Doc, I'll bail and shoot. You switch to the driver's seat, slam it in gear, and drive like hell."

"Dear God," the nurse was whispering. "Please, don't let them catch us."

Sam tried to muster some semblance of worry, but his thoughts had all the acuity of mush. He couldn't even remember how he'd come to be here, let alone where here was.

Lights grew brighter in the front of the cab, the doctor and driver crouching low and out of sight. Sam could see the shine passing through, the angle changing as a vehicle passed behind them. The sound slowly diminished and dwindled into complete darkness.

"Damn," the doctor hissed, righting himself in the passenger seat. "That was close."

"Good thing I thought to pull the bulbs out of the brake lights, huh?" the driver asked. "You owe me for this one, Doc."

"Wasn't curing you of cancer good enough?"

"Close, Doc. Close." The driver was chuckling. "But you know damned well what they'll do if they catch us with this guy."

"People are going to die either way," the doctor said. "As if we didn't have enough problems."

"Catch who?" Sam asked in his hoarse voice.

"You, Mr. Delgado." The doctor looked back as the van's engine started; the truck backed out into what was apparently a street.

"What did I do?"

The nurse was taking his pulse again.

The van shifted into drive, and Sam winced as it accelerated. Damn it, what he'd give for just a few minutes without the agony.

"If you're to be believed, you raided the director's compound. Freed political prisoners and mysterious women who were being raped and abused. Flattened his house and burned his garage, not to mention killed about fifteen men and left another ten in the hospital."

"Good," Sam said, trying not to breathe since it hurt his chest to do so. "Just wish...we'd gotten him, too."

He longed to take a deep breath but could only wince and try and suck shallowly as the pain built.

"That makes you the most wanted man in Wyoming," the nurse told him. "By both sides."

Sam's mind was clearing. "Where are we?"

"Headed someplace safe," the doctor told him. "Senator Briarson's."

"Who's he?" Sam worked his lips, trying to conjure enough saliva to swallow.

"Served three terms in the Senate back in the day. One of the most respected men in the state. Has a place on the outskirts of town." The doctor made a gesture. "As long as we don't run into another one of Edgewater's patrols, you'll live to meet the man."

The van hit a pothole. Sam heard himself cry out. And that hurt his lungs even worse. When he could even out his desperate breath, he said, "Hey, just make this pain go away, and I'm yours for whatever."

"Sorry, Sam," the doctor told him. "But you're going to need your wits here real soon." To the driver the doctor said, "There, that's the drive. Head back behind the house, and a garage door should open. Drive inside and we're home free."

The van bumped over something.

Sam thought his body was breaking up.

He would have gritted his teeth, but that made his head hurt too much.

"Just put a bullet in my brain, will you?" he whispered as the van bumped again, slowed, and came to a stop. The driver put it in park and killed the engine.

"Yeah, well," the doctor said, opening his door, "that's exactly what Edgewater would love to do. But only after he tortured you for a couple of centuries. The guy's actually talking about crucifixion, starting with you."

The rear doors opened, and a light was switched on that sent white pain through Sam's eyes and into his skull. He whimpered as the straps were loosened and the gurney was rolled out the cargo van's back.

"Easy with him, easy," the nurse warned as she climbed out beside Sam. Two men in casual clothes had his gurney, one at either end.

Sam was being wheeled through a large garage that housed a sleek and gleaming GMC Denali and a BMW 7 series sedan. Four-drawer file cabinets, a work bench, and assorted tools were the only furnishings.

At the door, he was carefully lifted, wheeled into a mud room with hanging coats and hats, and then through a door and into a hallway. Sam caught a glimpse of photos and paintings on the walls, passed a couple of dark bedrooms, and was wheeled into a very nice den.

Bookshelves covered two of the walls, another was packed with photos of men and women in suits, citations, framed parchment-like awards complete with ribbons, and shelves with glass, bronze, and silver statuary, the type of which awards were composed.

Sam's gurney was rotated so he could see the two men who stood by the desk. He recognized Sully Richardson of course. The officer gave him a slight nod. The highway patrolman might have been in a light cotton shirt and Dockers, but he still looked like a no-bullshit cop.

The tall and elderly bald man beside him wore a powder-blue button-down shirt open at the collar, belted chinos, and loafers. He'd been stately for so long it was part of his aquiline face and prominent nose. Age had taken its toll on the flesh, but nothing had slowed in those knowing eyes.

"So, this is the man of the hour?" the tall elder said, stepping forward and offering his hand. "I'm Sandy Briarson."

Sam managed to extend his hand and shake Briarson's. It left him panting, with spears in his chest, and sweat popping from his brow.

Sully Richardson said, "You know Doctor Simpson here, and Delgado's nurse is Dorothy Malone."

"Hey, Hal," Briarson shook the doctor's hand. "Ms. Malone, my pleasure."

"Pleasure's all mine, Senator," Malone told him.

Briarson turned to Sam, "Anything I can get you, Mr. Delgado?"

"New ribs?"

Briarson chuckled. "The good doctor, here, tells me your old ones will heal just fine. Now, Hal, what's the situation back at the hospital?"

Sam watched Dr. Simpson check his watch. "About now they're figuring out that Sam's guard is passed out in Sam's hospital bed. As soon as they do, the shit's gonna hit the fan. Expect Edgewater to turn this town upside down looking for Sam, me, and Dorothy. It was the middle of the night, and I don't think anyone saw us wheel him out. But they'll know it was Dorothy and me. We've relocated our families to safe houses."

"My watcher thinks I'm asleep at home," Sully Richardson added. "For the time being, no one has any clue about where Delgado would have been taken."

Briarson smiled again. "Well, well, so, Mr. Delgado, would you mind telling me who's behind sending you and your people to tear up Clark Ranch?"

"I'm Sam. Mr. Delgado was my father, and when it's all said and done, probably twice the man I'll ever be. But to get to your point, no one sent us. Me, I'm in it because Edgewater killed my wife. Breeze and Brandon, they're in it because Edgewater's men raided their home, shot their mother. Amber was in it because she couldn't stand the thought of all those women and girls being raped like she was."

"How many women and girls?" Briarson asked.

"I think seven made it up the canyon. I hope, anyway. I was sort of busy."

"Doing what?" Richardson asked.

Sam frowned, trying to pull the memory from his aching head. "The Jeep was coming. Two big guns. Breeze had to get the last of the hostages across the open spot to the safety of the big boulder." His dry throat made him cough.

Which sent a whole new level of agony through him. What seemed like an eternity later, he blinked tears from his eyes, and tried to breathe without moving his lungs. Call that the trick of the century.

Nurse Malone placed a straw to his lips and let him suck cool water into his jangled system.

"Go on," Briarson said when Sam was almost back to normal.

"I thought about shooting, but the only cover I had was under the Polaris. I needed them to get closer. So I couldn't miss. But they drove right up to the back of the Polaris and let loose with those big machine guns.

"I heard a guy order Breeze and the girls to stop, so I figured it was only warning shots. I crawled back under the Jeep, pulled the pin from the grenade, and stuffed it between the frame and gas tank.

I was already squirming my way back under the Polaris when the grenade went off."

Sam swallowed hard, trying to pull the truth from fractured images in his imagination. "It was sort of like the whole world went away. And then this giant fist smashed down..."

Richardson crossed his arms, leaning against the desk. "How many people attacked that place? Edgewater's men claim it was at least a full company."

"Me, Breeze, and Amber went in. Brandon and Shanteel provided cover from one ridge, Willy Star from the other. Then Amber blew herself up along with the guys behind the breastwork to get us in."

"What do you mean, blew herself up?" Briarson asked.

"She took one of Breeze's hand grenades, hid it in her pants, and surrendered herself to the goons. They were so intrigued they crowded close. She..."

He tried to still his pounding heart. Damn, why did it still hurt so much? "She unsnapped her pants, pulled the pin, and handed them the grenade."

"Like a suicide bomber?" Dr. Simpson.

"Amber Sagan died to free those people." Sam closed his eyes. "But for being armed, my Shyla would have ended up in that stable. Servicing those men." A beat. "What's her life, or mine, compared to getting those girls out? And those other people? In that fenced compound. It was something the Nazis would have done."

The room was silent, and for the first time Sam realized that a clock was ticking somewhere off to his left.

"Okay," Briarson said. "I'm convinced."

"Six of you did this?" Richardson asked. "How?"

"Three of us came down the canyon. Amber got Breeze and me in, I got Breeze and the freed hostages out. But not all. Most ran the wrong way."

"Fifteen men died up there," Dr. Simpson said. "Ten more wounded, some critically. Not to mention the house is destroyed and the garage burned."

"You didn't see what they were doing to those people," Sam tried to keep his voice calm. "I wish I could have killed them all. If Edgewater got out alive, that's my biggest regret."

"We need those people who escaped," Briarson said. He looked at Sully Richardson. "Any sign of them?"

"Nothing. But Edgewater's got every outfitter in the valley headed up onto Boulder Ridge and into the Carter Mountains. If the Tappan kids are thinking to hide those people up there, they'll be rounded up and back in chains within days."

"Someone's got to warn Brandon," Sam said. "If he knows he's being hunted, he'll keep them safe."

"Warn him how?" Richardson asked.

"Airplane," Sam replied. "You don't even have to find him. Just buzz around like you're searching."

He took a shallow breath. "My turn. How's Pam?"

"Alive," Sully told him. "There's hell to pay down in Hot Springs. The sheriff and deputies are dead along with some locals. My guess, the Willson-Smith faction's going to come out on top. Especially since Edgewater can't send his soldiers down to back up that FEMA guy down there."

"What about Tank and Barry Lehman?"

"Sheriff Madden arrested them the day they got back from Cheyenne. They're charged with sedition and conspiracy."

"I need you to get a message to Frank and Bill Tappan that Breeze and Brandon are alive, and that they got some of the girls and hostages out."

"I'll do that." Sully crossed his arms.

"What about the Basin? Anyone talked to the governor?"

Sully said, "Eastern side of the Basin is firmly behind Agar. It's just Cody now that's the problem."

"We need those young people," Briarson was fingering his chin. "They tell their story, and Edgewater's life won't be worth a pebble in the street."

"And we have to keep Sam, here, as far from Edgewater's hands as we can," Dr. Simpson said. "Edgewater was serious. If he can get Sam alive, he's planning on crucifying him in the middle of Sheridan Avenue, and to hell with the consequences."

"Yeah, well, Doc, you shoot me full of digitalis or something if it even seems like that's a possibility, huh?" Sam asked wearily.

"Let's just ensure that it doesn't go that far." Dr. Simpson reached out and laid gentle fingers on the back of Sam's hand.

At that moment, the phone rang. Briarson stepped behind the desk, lifted the handset from the cradle, saying, "Yeah?"

He listened. "How the hell would I know? I'm in bed."

Another pause.

"Sheriff, this is just my advice, but if I were you, I'd start acting like the Constitution was still the law of the land, and to hell with what Edgewater says." He tilted his head, lips grim as he listened, and then said, "You've got my last word on that. Now I'm going back to sleep. And if you had any sense, you would, too."

Briarson replaced the handset on the cradle and said, "They know Delgado's been taken. Sully, you'd better get home. Just in case they check."

Sam watched the Highway Patrol captain nod and thoughtfully remove himself from the room.

Briarson arched his bushy gray brows and rubbed his forehead. "I don't think they'd dare to search here, but let's put Sam back in my documents room. Just to be safe, you know."

"What happens next?" Sam asked, his body so exhausted he didn't care.

"Everything hinges on producing those young women and freed prisoners. Their testimony sinks Edgewater and avoids a civil war."

"But he's sent people up into the mountains looking for them," Dorothy Malone reminded, her expression pinched.

"Yeah." Briarson crossed his arms. "Let's hope they don't find them, hum?"

CHAPTER FORTY-NINE

***

THE AIRPLANE SHOULDN'T HAVE BEEN A SURPRISE BUT DID CAUSE A NEAR PANIC. BREEZE immediately worried about being strafed from above. Fortunately, so far as she knew, Edgewater's people wouldn't have drones capable of long-distance flight.

Brandon, however, quickly routed people, horses, and gear into the trees. For the captives, it was a relief to throw themselves on the ground. The pace was hard enough on the freed women, but they were young. Mackeson, the Visanges, Marley, Baker, and Nelson were on the verge of collapse.

Then, as the plane weaved its way back north, Shirley Mackeson held up a hand. "Wait. We can't do this."

"You've got to," Breeze told her.

"Kid, at this stage of the game, the only thing I have to do is die someday. I don't even have to pay taxes." She glanced at Brandon. "The drainages east of here, they drop into the headwaters of the Greybull River, right?"

"Yeah."

Shirley indicated the rest of her party. "We've been talking. We can't make it across the mountains. We're not as young and fit as the rest of you. And more to the point, we're not dressed for back-country travel. It makes more sense if we split up. All we have to do is follow the creeks down. They'll take us to the Greybull River, which will drop us at the Pitchfork Ranch. I've got friends there. People who will keep us safe."

Brandon turned to Breeze. "What do you think?"

"Hey," John Baker piped up. "I used to hunt elk up here with my Dad. I can get us down."

"Breeze, think it through," Shirley said reasonably. "Two parties doubles our chances that someone is going to live to expose Edgewater."

Brandon pointed east. "Commissioner Mackeson, follow that little valley. Keep to the trees. Take your time. You should make it in two days, three at the most. Wild onions are up. *Don't* mistake them for death camas. Shooting star and biscuit root are blooming, too. It won't be much, but it will keep you going."

One by one the freed hostages shook Breeze's hand. Each offering their thanks.

"What about us?" Joelle asked.

"You come with us," Breeze told her as she watched the Cody contingent walk away.

"Time to hide the trail," Willy told them. "Head north. Toward Cody. That's what they expect."

"And then?" Brandon asked.

"One by one, we leave the trail. Double back. Last to split off are the horses. They're shod. Have to split off the trail onto thick duff, in water, or on stone that won't scar. That way our trail just sort of vanishes."

"Where'd you learn this?" Shanteel asked. "Old Indian trick?"

Willy looked shocked. "You mean, you didn't read Louis L'Amour when you were a kid?"

"Who the hell is Louis L'Amour?" Shanteel asked.

And for two days, they did exactly as Willy said.

The most daunting problem was the slow pace. And it wasn't just the time it took to hide their trail. The freed women weren't dressed for back-country travel. Physically, they were soft, sexually abused, some had been beaten, and none were acclimated to the high altitude.

Brandon showed them how to keep from hypothermia at night, digging long trenches and filling them with stones; then they kindled fires and let them burn down. One thing they were not shy of was firewood. Shoveling dirt back over the trench left the ground warm through the night. And though the women huddled together for additional warmth, they were constantly turning the cold side down onto the warm ground.

The other challenge came from empty bellies. They consumed the packaged food the first day. Rations were lean on the second, consisting of a couple of rabbits that Willy had brought down with an ad-hoc throwing stick. Sego lily, wild onion bulbs, and balsam root were boiled into a thin stew that didn't go nearly far enough.

Brandon finally risked a rifle shot in a thickly timbered canyon to bring down a yearling bull elk. As the report echoed off into the distance, Breeze thought it sounded like the clap of doom.

"Think they'll hear that?" Joelle asked, nervous eyes flicking in the direction of possible pursuit.

"Maybe." Breeze placed a hand on her hip, wary eyes on the back trail. "Depends on how close they are. Empty bellies will doom us just as quickly as Edgewater's goons."

She indicated the women, resting now, looking bedraggled. "The rest of you, pitch in. We've got to drag that elk out and cut it up. Fast."

She turned to Willy. "Want to do us all a favor?"

"Sure, boss," Willy told her. The way he said it took her off guard.

"Scout our back trail. See if anyone's following."

Now seven abused, broken, and desperate women were all looking to Breeze for salvation. She hated it.

"I've got the horses," Danielle assured her as she took to picketing the lead ropes.

"Come on, all." Breeze led the women down into the steep-sided timber where Brandon and Shanteel were already gutting out the elk.

For city kids—with the exception of Mary Lou, who'd become Breeze's sergeant at arms—they actually exceeded Breeze's expectations when it came to the butchering. Maybe they were hungry enough, desperate enough, or just so battered as to be beyond shocking anymore.

A half-hour later, they were on the move again, heading higher along the peaks. Here the women labored, tripping and stumbling as they gasped for breath. On steep up-hills, it was Mary Lou who suggested that the weakest could hold onto the horse's tails, letting the animals help pull them up.

"Amber and Sam died for us. Can't let them down." Breeze heard the words as they passed back and forth between the freed women's lips. It had become a sort of mantra, the thing that kept them moving.

Bless you both, wherever you are.

Breeze kept hesitating on the high points, sitting on Joker, using her binoculars to stare back down the trail for as far as she could see.

Searching for any sign of movement.

No sign of Willy.

No sign of pursuit.

But she could feel them back there.

Then she scanned the sky, smoke-thick from distant fires, searching for any sign of an aircraft. If anything would be their undoing, it would be that damned airplane. Especially here, where the trail skirted timberline. The scanty trees, the glacially scoured cirques and hanging valleys left no place to hide eleven people and ten horses and mules.

As the women reached the end of their endurance, they started to stumble, fall, and it took longer each time for them to stagger to their feet. The weakest were rotated onto Amber and Sam's horses, and the previous riders took to foot. Watching them, Breeze realized with a sense of pride, that they weren't giving up.

So much for the human condition in the last days of the world.

Brandon was the first to ride back, dismount, and lift Michaela Jenson—the busty brunette from Marin County—into Midnight's saddle. There she slumped, tears of relief streaking down her face as Brandon took the reins, leading his big blood-bay gelding.

Danielle was next, offering her dapple gray to Rosa Bertolli who staggered on blistered feet that had gone bloody.

Brandon called a halt to the march a little before seven that night, leading them down onto a timbered ridge that stuck out like a defiant shoulder from the steep slope of basalt. Dark clouds were rolling in across the high country to the west.

Worn and fatigue-clumsy herself, Breeze recovered her entrenching tool from the boogie bag and set about scraping the duff back and excavating the trenches. Stumbling, staggering women went about the chore of dragging in wood, snapping off dead branches, and preparing the camp.

Brandon and Shanteel untied the diamond hitch and dropped the elk quarters from their respective mules before Danielle went about tying up the picket line.

Once the fires were built, and the women were shown how to roast meat on an open flame without burning it, Brandon squinted up at the darkening sky. Then he broke out the chainsaw.

"You think that's a good idea?" Breeze asked. "It was bad enough we risked a shot this morning."

He squinted from under the brim of his black Rand's hat. "It's gonna rain like hell tonight, Sis. You really think those women can take it if it turns to slush or snow?"

"Probably not."

Brandon went about burning up the last of his gas as he cut down lodgepole pines, then dropped a thickly branched fir tree, and began limbing it.

"We're building a shelter, guys," he called. "Give me a hand here."

Breeze, however, just had that prickly feeling.

Taking her M4, she pushed her weary legs back up to the trail. A chainsaw could be heard across long distances.

No doubt about it, as thick and black as the clouds were, the night—and maybe all of tomorrow—was going to be damned miserable. Even in midsummer, people died of hypothermia in the high country.

She climbed up on the ridge and scanned the backtrail with her binoculars. Carefully studied each of the stony gray outcrops of cracked basalt, checked each dip and ridge they'd crossed. Nothing moved but a small herd of mule deer does, yearlings, and a couple of fawns.

No sign of Willy.

Nothing.

"Where are you?"

The first rumbling of thunder rolled down around the peaks.

And then a real flash, followed by a deafening crack, as a bolt discharged into the peak above her.

As it rumbled away into the distance, the first drops of hard, cold rain splattered around her.

She was turning back when she heard it: the distant sound of a rifle shot.

Seconds later a faint crackling reached her ears. A fusillade of answering gunfire that was carried away by the wind.

Then the storm broke in earnest.

CHAPTER FIFTY

***

AS COLD RAIN FELL, LIGHTNING ILLUMINATED THE SURROUNDING TREES AND CAST WEIRD, actinic shadows across the smoking fire where it struggled to hold its own against the downpour.

Breeze—her hat soaked and streaming from the brim—walked over and tossed another section of deadfall onto the hissing and sizzling flames.

The wet surface steamed until it burned down to the dry wood beneath. Lightning flashed again to gleam in the water that ran down her slicker.

"One thing about it," she called. "Tracks will be washed out in the trail."

"Yeah," Brandon answered from the other side of the fire. "As if they didn't know which way we were headed. Only so many trails up here. Even if the steep parts are washed out, anyone with a half a sense can still find the shadow of a print in the flats. That's the thing about a shod horse ridden on damp ground."

"I'm worried about that shooting Breeze heard," Shanteel added. She stood beside Brandon, head bowed so the rain dribbled from the brim on her hat, shoulders slumped in her rain-coat.

"Me, too," Breeze added.

From the shelter of the lean to, Mary Lou called, "It had to be Willy, right?"

"Most likely," Breeze answered. "Hope he got one with that first shot. Hope even more that he got to cover before the bunch of them shot back." She gave them a grim smile, illuminated by the flames. "You get to feeling really small inside when a bunch of bullets go clapping past your head."

"So what do we do next?" Kylie Havel, the redheaded girl from Oakland, asked in a small voice. She had her sleeves pulled over her hands for warmth as she snuggled against the rest of the bedraggled females.

Brandon looked at Breeze and shrugged, then turned his attention to the women crowded shoulder-to-shoulder in the lean to. "That depends. The temperature's down in the forties. Up this high it can stay that way for days. Smart money would be stay right here, fix up the shelter better, haul in more firewood. Shoot another critter to keep our bellies full. But somebody's shooting at somebody else back down the trail."

"I don't want them to catch us," Joelle said, her breath clouding in the cold.

"So where are we?" Shanteel asked, glancing at Brandon.

"Just to the west of Frying Pan Canyon."

"Why do they call it that?" one of the girls asked. "For its shape?"

"Nope." Brandon smiled. "It's because it's so steep, and the downed timber's so thick, that if you ever kill an elk down there, you'd better have a frying pan, salt-shaker, and fork. You're going to have to cook that elk and eat it right where you shot it because you'll never pack it out."

Shanteel tilted her hat so that the rain ran off the other side. "Y'all aren't laughing. I didn't get it either. It's local humor."

Danielle appeared out of the dark, rain pattering on the hood of her slicker. "Horses are good. But I've got an idea. This is that really hard section of trail, right? The one that skirts the head of Frying Pan Canyon. Lots of slippery climbs and descents."

"Yeah," Breeze told her. "You spent most of the time slipping and sliding, and that was on two feet."

Danielle looked east into the night, toward the field camp. "The other side of Frying Pan Canyon, that flat we could see from the canyon edge, that's where Brandon and Shanteel holed up during the storm, right?"

"Yeah," Brandon told her.

Danielle turned back, staring thoughtfully into the fire. "Took us a hard day coming this way. Probably be two days getting back given how the girls are moving. And there's no place to camp in all those rocks and steep places."

"You got a point?" Breeze wondered.

"How long would it take us to climb down Frying Pan Canyon through all that deadfall, then climb up the other side?"

"Most of a day," Brandon told her. "Assuming you didn't have packs."

"And how long would it take you and Breeze, both excellent back-country riders, to bring the horses around on the trail to meet us on the other side?"

"Most of a day," Breeze answered.

Danielle raised her hands and gestured, as if to say, "Well?"

"Taking these poor women down into that mess?" Brandon asked. "Do you know what you're asking?"

"We're primates." Danielle stuffed her hands into her belt. "We can crawl up, over, around, and through. And we're a team. Michaela, and Kylie, and Rosa are in the worst shape. Shanteel, if you'd come, help Mary Lou and me, together, we could all make it. Help each other." She lifted her chin defiantly, "And it would leave us no more than a half day from the field camp. There's food there. And the morning after, we can scout the situation at the ranch."

Breeze eyed the huddled women who were watching from the lean to. "Do you understand just how tough this will be?"

Courtney Volusia, an auburn-haired beauty from Chicago, said, "Could Sam and Amber cross that canyon in a day?"

"Well, sure. But they were—"

"Then we can do it," Rosa Bertolli told her. "If my feet get so bad, I'll *crawl* up the other side."

"Fuck that," Mary Lou told her. "We'll pull you up."

"We won't like, run into a grizzly bear, will we?" Joelle asked.

"Might," Brandon offered. "Frying Pan Canyon? Just about perfect habitat."

"Screw 'em," Michaela muttered where she huddled cross-armed, damp hair in strands. "After what we've been through, and as many of us as there are, what's a grizzly bear?"

"I'll have a rifle," Shanteel told them. "And Danielle will have her pistol."

Shanteel turned to Brandon and Breeze. "Come morning, we feed these girls the rest of the elk, pack up before daylight, and you make tracks. Meet you at the wickiup."

Brandon nodded as he studied the huddled women. "You be damned careful down there. No risks. You fall? You break a leg? It could be days before we get you out of there."

Verla Tollman—a sixteen-year-old blonde from Seattle—brushed her hair back. "Brandon, we'll make it. If we've made it this far there's nothing we can't do."

Breeze exhaled a breath that fogged and rose into the rain. Just back there, maybe two or three miles, someone finished the day in a gun fight.

CHAPTER FIFTY-ONE

***

PATTERNS OF RAIN CAME AND WENT THROUGH THE NIGHT. BREEZE, BRANDON, AND DANIELLE spent most of the long, wet hours keeping the fires going, cooking the last of the elk.

Piled together as they were in the lean to, the women actually slept. Breeze suspected that not only were they exhausted, but they had full stomachs for the first time in weeks. And she suspected that they were coming into their own. They actually had hope. Part of it was tomorrow's challenge of Frying Pan Canyon, part of it had to be bonding among traumatized survivors, that sense of "we few".

Must be nice.

An hour before dawn, Shanteel awakened the women. Told them that they needed to eat.

Breeze shivered, having munched on elk loin for most of the night. As the camp was packed onto the mules, she stood in the drizzle in an attempt to get Joker to take the bit.

"Hey, old fellow," she greeted, slicking the water off his back. "We've got a tough day today. But it's make it or break it time."

Joker did his best to search her pockets in forlorn hope of a treat—and only got the cold bit in reward. Then she helped Shanteel, Danielle, and Brandon saddle up the pack animals; last she pitched her boogie bag onto the roan mule's crossbucks and lashed it tight.

"You be damned careful," Brandon told Shanteel for the umpteenth time. "Watch out for the deadfall, wet like this, the wood's gonna be slick as snot on a doorknob."

"Who you worrying about? We'll be fine."

"Just trying to remind you that these women aren't like us. They're city people."

Shanteel laughed. "Go on with you, Brandon. Now, you hear me. You don't hurry on that trail out there. On those steep sections, you give Midnight his head. Don't you go crowding him. Let him pick his way."

"Telling me how to ride my horse?"

"Only 'cause I think it will keep you alive." She pulled him close, hugging him to her. "See you on the other side, lover."

"You, too." Brandon stepped into the saddle. "You get in a mess down there, I'll be coming to look as soon as I can."

Breeze stepped into Joker's stirrup and threw a leg over the cantle, taking the reins. After checking the way her M4 hung under her slicker, she walked Joker around to grab up the lead rope for the rest of the string.

Then they were off, climbing up onto the trail as the first gray of dawn began to filter through the clouds and rain.

The horses' hooves clacked on wet rock as they made their way south along the canyon rim.

"Think they'll be all right?" Brandon asked over his shoulder.

"Hell, I don't know." She paused. "But then I don't know much anymore, little brother."

Another ten minutes passed before she asked, "Think you and Shanteel will have kids?"

"She'd help me raise 'em right, that's for sure."

"You really love her?"

He turned in the saddle. "Sis, you got a problem with Shanteel?"

"God, no. Now turn around so you don't fall off your horse and look any stupider than you usually do. No, I was just wondering what love was these days."

"It's kind of wonderful. Kind of scary. I just want to be with her. I mean, every minute. It's like it's all perfect. How she thinks, the things she says. The way she just takes what comes along. Thomas says she's got an old soul."

Breeze let Joker tackle a steep ascent, shifted to help him keep his balance when he slipped, and stuck with him as he buck-jumped his way up the rocky trail. Behind her, the pack animals followed with a clattering of hooves and loosened rock.

"Yeah, well, nothing's the same anymore." She tilted her hat so the water ran off. "Let alone human life. At night I think about what I've done, who I've become. I don't even think twice about killing a human being anymore." A beat. "What kind of monster does that make me?"

"About the same kind as me, I suppose." His shoulders slumped as he settled into Midnight's gait. "Shanteel and I have talked about it. How the only thing that matters now is keeping people you love alive."

He was silent for a time, then said, "I never would have thought I'd be killing people. Let alone that I'd be less bothered about it than I am about shooting an elk. What's that say about who we are?"

Locked in their thoughts they might have been alone, motes lost in a hazy gray mist, sole occupants in a universe of wet and gray. Breeze remembered the long climb the horses now tackled, the trail appearing out of the mist, rocks, scrubby subalpine fir and whitebark pine passing by, only to vanish into gray nothingness behind them.

"What about you?" Brandon asked as they crested the top of a knife-like rise; Midnight slipped and slid his way down the other side.

"What about me?" she asked, staying loose in the saddle as Joker felt his way down ahead of the pack string.

"You were going to conquer the world. Had your sights set on a place in Manhattan, didn't you? Big time stock-broker? Not that I doubt you'd have made it, but what now?"

"Haven't a clue."

"We get home, I want you to spend some time with Thomas."

"Whoa. That came right out of left field."

"I guess what it boils down to is I didn't think you were coming back. Not given the way you left. Not after you went off to school. And most particularly not after you, Sam, and Amber headed down to raid that ranch."

"Why'd you think that?"

"I know you, Sis. You had that 'I'm going to hell' look. The one you get when you hate yourself so much all you want to do is destroy yourself."

"Suicide ain't my thing."

"There's a difference between suicide and getting yourself killed. I figured it would be Sam who came back if anyone did. He's solid, even if he is from New York.

"Amber? Yeah, I can see her blowing herself up if she could take bad guys with her. She'd been too badly broken. But tough as nails when she needed to dally-up on a hard situation."

Breeze snapped, "So, when—while you were branding calves and fixing fence— did you become the world's psychiatrist?"

He ignored her. "You? I figured you'd be the last one out. That you'd make it an Alamo kind of last stand, with bodies piled all around. Given what I saw from up on that ridge, you gave it a fair shot, what with that D8 and all."

"Sorry to disappoint you."

"Nope. Made me a happy man when you showed up behind those poor people you rescued." He paused. "But you've still got that self-destructive thing burning inside you. Pissed at the world, and damn the consequences." He shot her a look. "What we are to each other? That mean anything to you?"

"Oh, hell, Brandon, of course it does. You're the only person in the family that never passed judgment on me."

"Then promise me that you'll spend some time with Thomas. That's all. After that, I won't say another word."

"So...I promise."

"Good."

They tackled another tough section of trail. Breeze considered herself an expert horsewoman, but several times she and Joker came within a whisker of disaster on the steep down hills where the trail descended over slithery-slick rocks. Rather than heart-stopping, she was wondering if her chest would burst from blood-pulsing cardiac exuberance.

Joker snuffled, as if he understood.

Not ten minutes later the echo of a shot carried through the clouds.

Brandon pulled up, asking softly, "You hear that?"

"Yeah, behind us. Definitely not Shanteel. Didn't come from the canyon."

Brandon let the horses blow and rest, his head cocked, listening for anything.

"Willy?" Breeze guessed.

"Yeah." Beneath the shadow of his hat brim, she could see Brandon's concern as he said, "Edgewater's hirelings couldn't have followed us this far without help. They're not backcountry people. I'd say they drafted an outfitter. A local. Someone like Bradley Cole, but from the Cody area. Maybe one of the Mathew bunch. Or the Ackermans."

"Hard hunting in this fog, little brother."

"My money's on Willy. He knows how to hunt men."

"Damn them. They've got us killing each other." She thought back to the day she and Sam had shot up the posse, how her first burst took Bradley Cole out of the saddle. Just a man hired to do a job.

"Horses are rested." Her brother clucked Midnight onward.

Brandon did know her better than she knew herself. She *had* been at war with the world ever since she was a little girl. What the hell was wrong with her that she always had to fight her way through, only to realize she felt disappointed that the world had somehow let her win?

But then, Brandon hadn't mowed down those men, women, and children on I-25. Guilty of no more than empty stomachs and an association with a desperate bunch of thugs in search of a way out.

A half-hour later they descended beneath the cloud layer to the point that she could see a couple hundred yards in every direction.

The mountain solidified on her left, rugged with cracked outcrops, talus slopes, rocky precipices, and peppered with whitebark pines and denser stands of firs and spruce. The trail led them out from the canyon head and dropped them just above the flat on the eastern side of Frying Pan Canyon. The gently sloping shoulder of the ridge lay before them—thickly timbered as it extended to the north. The trail here bent east, clinging to the base of the soaring basalt to finally top out on the ridge where it tied into the trail above the field camp.

For all intents and purposes, this was her back yard. Home.

The sound of a horse whinnying made her turn in the saddle. Back up in the clouds, a tumbling rock clattered and cracked as it bounced down a steep section. The faint strike of a shod hoof on stone could be heard.

"How the hell did they get so close?" Brandon asked, a note of disbelief in his voice.

Breeze chewed her lips, bringing Joker to a halt. Behind her, the pack string snuffled, one of the mules shaking its head hard enough to slap its ears back and forth.

What to do?

"Bro, here. Take the pack string." She walked Joker up beside Midnight and handed Brandon the lead rope.

"What are you going to do?" Brandon asked warily, his eyes

thin-lidded.

"I'm going to hold them here." She gestured at the trail. "It's a bottleneck. Slope on one side, drop off on the other. Slow 'em down at least."

"And then what?" he asked harshly. "I mean after they shoot you dead?"

"I won't let it get that far." She pointed east. "When it looks like they're coming through, Joker and I will make a run for it. I can stay just far enough ahead. Lead them over the pass and down the south side. Right into the headwaters of Horse Creek. Lose them in the timber above Dubois."

"Why you and not me?"

"Because the woman you love is waiting for you down in those trees. Because you've got a future with her." She grinned. "Me, I've got my war with the universe."

He reached across, taking her hand, squeezing it. "You promise me you're not going to get yourself killed just to say 'fuck you' to the world, all right?"

She gave him a bawdy wink. "Yeah, I promise. And I love you, too, little brother."

"I mean it," he called as he spurred Midnight off the trail, leading the pack string out onto a section of bedrock.

In a sweeping move, she doffed her hat, then wheeled Joker around. She slipped the M4 from beneath her slicker and checked the magazine. She had sixteen rounds left.

The hollow sound of a hoof on stone carried to her. Closer. They were coming fast.

Glancing over her shoulder, it was to see Brandon leading the pack string down into the timber. An instant later he was out of sight.

Looking at the ground, he'd barely left tracks. Good. As soon as she could see to shoot, she'd fire a couple of rounds to get their attention, do as much damage as she could. Once she had their blood up, she'd wheel Joker and run for the pass. The trick would be to stay just far enough ahead they could catch glimpses of her, but not be close enough that they could shoot her or Joker.

"You know what we're about," she told her buckskin horse, stepping down and showing Joker the rifle. He twitched his lips and pulled back on the reins, ears pricked.

Joker had never liked gun shots, but she'd trained him to tolerate them without pitching into a rodeo.

That had been a couple of years back. There was no telling what bad habits Dad might have instilled in her beloved gelding in the meantime. Just to be safe, she stepped off the trail, clipped the lead rope to Joke's halter, and tied it off on a sapling.

Perching on a boulder, she shouldered the M4, flipped the fire control to semi-auto, and took a deep breath. The sound of hooves could be heard clearly now. Close.

Back along the trail, she could see two horses emerging from the low-hanging clouds. One, a black, was awkwardly leading the way. Riderless. The saddle had slipped down under the horse's belly; the stirrups were flopping and bouncing off to either side. The second, a sorrel, limped along behind, ears pricked, what was left of the reins dangling. At least the sorrel's empty saddle was still on the animal's back.

Joker whickered, the black answered and galloped forward, in apparent relief. The sorrel hobbled along afterward, obviously hurt.

"Here you go," Breeze called, setting the M4 to one side. She stood boldly in the trail, reaching out and getting a hold on the black's bridle. The nervous gelding tried to toss his head, eyes rolling.

"Easy there. Easy now." Breeze patted the animal's sweaty neck, felt it tremble under her hand. "Looks like you've had a tough morning."

She led him to one side, used the single rein still dangling from the bit to tie him off, and walked over to where the trembling sorrel mare had stopped, head hanging, bloody foam lining her lips where the bit had cut into the mouth. Scrapes and cuts, a bloody gash the length of her left front cannon bone, and scuffs on the saddle showed where she'd taken a nasty tumble.

Breeze squinted back up the trail, picturing what the thick cloud now hid. Someone had pushed too fast, too hard. Or didn't have the skills to keep his seat. Or the horses weren't used to such difficult mountain terrain.

"Looks like you two dodged the bullet, doesn't it?" she asked as she stepped around to the black, loosened the cinch, and pulled the saddle and blanket back into position. As she tightened the cinch, she said, "People sure make a good horse's life difficult, don't they?"

She untied Joker, retrieved her M4, and stepped into the saddle. Riding over, she took the black's single rein, and stared thoughtfully back up the trail. If there was pursuit back there, they'd be busy cleaning up a nasty wreck.

She no more than started off on Brandon's tracks than another horse whinnied, this one off to the east. Between her and home. And from the sound of, it, not far either.

Before she could react, Joker answered back, his returning whinny loud in the still air.

"Shit!" *How many damn horses are up here, anyway?*

Breeze pulled Joker up. The slight breeze was at her back, blowing straight toward the trees that masked the unseen equine.

A couple hundred yards to the south, just down in the timber, Brandon would be picking up the rest of the women. She didn't dare try and head back up the trail. That would put her smack dab in the middle of her pursuers. That left her trapped betwixt and between.

She spurred Joker eastward, angling down the slope, wondering if she could get into the trees, cut lower on the mountain below the trail. With a little luck—and no more knot-headed horse interference—she might be able to just sneak around the side, get behind whoever this was.

Damn it! The only explanation was that Edgewater's people had somehow figured out which way Breeze and Brandon were headed. They'd trucked men and animals to the ranch, headed them up the trail to intercept the girls before they could make their escape.

Breeze ground her teeth, a sinking feeling dragging her guts down. So close. They'd been so damned close.

"And you had to promise Brandon you'd try and get out of this alive."

Well, shit. She'd meant it when she said it, but that was then.

Reaching back to her pack where it was tied behind the cantle, she fished the last hand grenade from the zippered pouch on the side.

Sure as shit they wouldn't be expecting a grenade. Dropping it into her coat pocket, she grasped the M4 by its pistol grip, reins in her left.

She was crossing a decades-old burn on the mountain's north slope; lodgepole and firs had come back over the years, growing up in a mosaic of timber patches. She wound her way around and through them at a walk, head cocked, listening for the slightest sound.

Assuming she heard them first, she could turn away at a right angle, seek to avoid contact. Once she was behind them, she could hit them from the rear. Shoot a couple, turn, and race for the pass, leaving the way clear for Brandon and the girls.

If she rounded a clump of trees and ran smack into the middle of them, she'd flip the fire control, fire a burst, and slap heels to Joker. If the gunfire over his ears didn't send him into a bucking fit, she'd charge right through them, firing all the way.

In the process, she'd drop the two riderless horses to add to the confusion. Then, as soon as she was past, she'd pull the pin, toss the grenade over her shoulder, and light out for the Dubois side.

Brandon and Shanteel—hearing the gunfire and explosion—would be well aware of the danger.

Meanwhile, if nobody shot her, and if Joker hadn't pitched her off, she'd lead the pursuers a merry chase down into the Horse Creek headwaters.

"Gotta love a plan." She patted Joker's neck and whispered, "It's going to be loud, old friend. Don't buck me off, all right? Get me out of this, and you'll roll in oats for the rest of your life."

Her heart began to hammer as she searched the screening trees, her ears cocked for the slightest sound.

"Where the hell are they? How many?"

Images flashed in her memory. She was living the I-25 checkpoint all over again. Her mouth had gone dry, every nerve on edge.

I'm tired of it. Let's just get it over with.

She reined Joker downhill, skirting another stand of young fir trees. On the damp ground, the light drizzle falling, the only sound of their passage came from the labored steps the wounded sorrel was taking.

Water dripped from the fir branches; a chickadee sang melodically to the morning. In reply a squirrel chirred down in the trees below.

She thought she heard a stick snap somewhere up slope. Was that them? One thing was sure, this wasn't any bunch of townies, clumping and clattering along. She heard no clink of metal, no nervous chatter, not even the strike of a hoof on stone.

The raven gave them away. The big black bird was flying from tree to tree, only to stop, peer down at something below, and then flap to the next tall conifer to repeat the process.

Breeze had seen it before. During hunting season when the ravens acted just like this. Following hunters. Knowing that after the gun went off, the humans would leave a hot, steaming pile of entrails. A perfect raven feast.

Here we go.

Breeze pulled Joker to a stop, raised the M4, and flipped the fire control with her thumb. Joker tensed, every muscle bunched. His ears were pricked, attention fixed in the same direction the raven was headed.

The faintest creak of saddle leather could be heard through the trees. Then a soft clumping sound as a hoof knocked a bit of dead wood.

Please. Just ride past.

Her breath went shallow, the tingle of fear and worry eating at her nerves. The wall of green between her and her nemesis seemed so fragile, as if at any second it would be torn by bullets.

She heard the soft thunk of a rifle butt on a saddle horn.

Okay, so it was the worst. She took a deep breath, fished out the hand grenade, and aimed the M4 at the break in the trees where the rider would appear in the next few seconds.

When the voice spoke right behind her, she flinched so hard she almost triggered the gun.

"Please don't shoot Meggan. That would really piss your grandfather off."

She whirled, heart in throat, to see her father, leaned forward on his saddle, a grin on his face as he walked Jackpot out from behind the screen of trees.

"Daddy?"

"Good to see you girl. Now, where's your brother and these mysterious women? We've got things to do, places to go, and people to see."

CHAPTER FIFTY-TWO

***

THE COURTROOM LOOKED PRETTY MUCH LIKE SAM FIGURED A COURTROOM WOULD LOOK: Judge's raised bench made out of fancy wood in the back, the jury box with cushioned chairs off to the left. Two tables, one for prosecution, the other for defense out front. Off to the right the bailiff and recorder's tables. A railing, and then bench-seating all the way to the back of the room.

Governor Agar—freshly arrived from Cheyenne, having flown up special despite the weather—sat in the judge's chair behind the raised desk. The man's close-cropped black hair actually shone in the light. His brown eyes had a thoughtful look, and he leaned slightly to the side, head cocked.

Evan Holly, along with Court and two of the governor's aides, sat in the jury box. Senator Briarson and Sully Richardson both hunched forward over the prosecutor's table, and four Highway Patrol officers—two women and two men—stood in the rear, guarding the door.

Sam sat uncomfortably in a wheelchair just inside the railing. His ribs were tightly bound; his bruised body felt distinctly uncomfortable as he shifted to ease the sore spots.

Old Bill Tappan, wearing a leather vest, his battered black cowboy hat on his silver head, sat with his arm extended on the first-row pew. The man's 1911 could be seen in the holster at his hip.

Every eye was on Director Kevin Edgewater where he hunched in the defendant's chair. His body appeared more bulbous than it had been last time Sam had seen him. The mousey brown hair had grown down over his ears and reached to his collar. If anything, Edgewater's cheeks were rounder, his nose smaller, but his blue eyes had gone from lazy to quick.

Sully Richardson's troopers and a collection of picked deputies and Cody city police had moved with precision the moment the word had been radioed north. In force, in the wee morning hours, they'd raided the top floor of the Irma Hotel where Edgewater had set up residence in the Phonograph Jones room.

They'd arrested him neatly, quietly, and efficiently, handcuffing his five-remaining bodyguards. The rest of his lackeys—it was no secret—were up in the Carter Mountains, looking for "the paramilitary commando force" that had destroyed Clark Ranch. Sources from within the Sheriff's Office also reported that any stray women that might be found up there were also to be rounded up and "interrogated".

"You really don't want to make this worse for yourselves than it already is," Edgewater insisted in his high-pitched voice. "I am the duly authorized federal authority. And you're playing with trouble like you've never seen."

Governor Agar mildly said, "Under the Wyoming criminal code you're charged with kidnapping, rape, sexual trafficking, extortion, theft, first-and-second-degree murder, assault, brandishing a deadly weapon, nonpayment for products and services rendered, destruction of cultural property, theft of antiquities, rustling, and, well, just about everything in the code when you get right down to it."

"Under 36 C.F.R—"

"Yes, yes, and all the Executive Orders, as well. We've heard it," Agar snapped. "Your stint at playing God is over, Mr. Edgewater."

"You try and jail me, and half the town is going to come after you," Edgewater promised. "I've got my backers, too. Powerful families in this town. People I've made promises to." He pointed with a thick finger. "People whose sons, husbands, and brothers have been *murdered* by your hired mercenaries. And you can bet, they're going to be wanting blood."

"You think they'll back you?"

"You bet. I'm the duly constituted authority in a time of—"

"If he spouts that shit again," Agar told Sully Richardson, "break his jaw."

Richardson squirmed uncomfortably in his chair.

Agar continued, "You kidnapped and executed innocent citizens, people whose loved ones are only now realizing their family members lie in unmarked graves. You kidnapped and trafficked in young women. Call it what it is: sexual slavery. When word gets out about what those young women and girls endured, you won't make it half a block."

"Any relations with females were consensual. You don't understand what some women will offer to a man with power."

Agar looked at Sam. "You were part of the raid, I understand?"

"Yes, sir." Sam wheeled himself forward, taking time to shoot a hard glare at the director; the man was glaring back, that slight smile on his small lips.

Agar tapped papers on the judge's desk. "Mr. Delgado, this is your sworn testimony. That there were only six of you. That Amber Sagan blew herself up in order to allow you and Breeze Tappan to get past the blockade. That you and Ms. Tappan freed the women and girls from the stable, that you used a bulldozer to knock down the concentration camp and free the people Edgewater had taken prisoner?"

"That is correct."

"Was there any way those young women in the stable could have been there consensually?"

"No, sir. Two were shot down by Edgewater's men as they ran for the trail. The others will testify as to the nature of their captivity."

"That's a lie," Edgewater said easily. "This deluded young man would have you believe it was seraglio? His band of raiders merely stumbled upon a barracks where I quartered some of my men." He smiled. "You'll just have to take the testimony from my men when they get back from the mountain."

"Won't need to," Agar told him. "We've got statements from the surviving young women. All the way down to young Kylie Havel. She's fifteen, you sick son of a bitch. And worse, she says your man Tubb shot her parents when they tried to keep you from abducting her."

"Never heard of her." Edgewater lifted a disdainful chin.

But Sam could see the piece of shit squirm for the first time. Apparently, the news that the girls were safe came as a real shock.

"Mary-Lou Finch?" Agar asked. "Joelle Masters? Michaela Jensen? Verla Tollman? Rosa Bertolli? Courtney Volusia?" and the list went on. When he'd finished, Agar asked, "Never heard of any of them?"

"No."

"Very well, the court calls Shirley Mackeson."

Edgewater stiffened as the side door opened, and the tall gray-haired woman from the fenced compound entered. Sam barely recognized her, washed, and elegantly dressed as she was.

She barely gave Edgewater a glance, stopping before the bench, greeting, "Governor."

"State your name and position, please."

"I'm Shirley Mackeson, I serve as County Commissioner for Park County."

"You know the defendant?"

"I do."

Agar lifted a thick sheaf of papers. "This is the sworn testimony of you, Bill Marley, John Baker, Sally and Tom Visange, Harry Nelson, Terry Tanksley, and Barry Lehman?"

"It is."

Agar fixed on Edgewater. "I'll cut to the chase. These are all prominent people from Cody that you ordered arrested and locked in a fenced enclosure at Clark Ranch. These witnesses claim you executed thirty-two people without due process, legal representation, trial, or right of appeal."

Edgewater's eyes had narrowed, his jaws working. "Here's the thing, Governor. It's a whole new world. Now, you're a man who understands what's what. My last communication informed me that two Chinese divisions had invaded Portland and Seattle. That an American carrier group had been attacked in the South China Sea, and that our banking system had been brought down to keep us from responding to—"

"Actually, it's three entire Chinese armies." Agar corrected.

"Which is why you need me to—"

"We don't *need* you for anything," Agar said, slapping his hand on the desk.

At that moment, Richardson plucked his radio from his belt. "This is Sully."

"*Captain? We just escorted the women into the Hot Springs High School gym. Most of the town's here to listen to what they have to say.*"

"Roger that." Sully slipped his radio back into its holster. "You get that?"

Agar nodded, stood, and descended to face Edgewater across the table. "Based on what Shirley, here, has told us, and what those re-markable young women have told us, we've sent a crew up to Clark Ranch with a backhoe to dig up the graves along the south fence line. Tank and Barry Lehman are driving up to supervise, along with some of your 'leading supporters' who we want to serve as witnesses."

"Look, we can come to an agreement." Edgewater gave Agar a knowing grin. "Sure, you might get a lot of things done, but think about how much quicker and easier you could do them with"—he hooked his fingers—"federal approval."

"You really think you're getting out of this, don't you?"

"Actually, Governor, yes. I do. Like I said, I can help grease the wheels, and I know the system. How things work."

Edgewater shrugged his round shoulders. "So maybe there were some accidents along the way. How about we sweep that under the rug for the time being? Sure, I have appetites, but I've controlled my appetites before, and I can do it again."

Agar turned to where Sully and Senator Briarson sat. "Verdict?"

"Story's out," Sully said. "We're done with him."

"I don't see any choice but to be rid of him," Briarson said. "Make it quick and tidy."

"Unmarked grave," Dr. Holly added from the jury box. "Just an-nounce that Edgewater was found guilty and justice was rendered."

"Sure," Edgewater said easily. "And once that announcement is made, I can work from behind the scenes. Do what you need done. Change my name. Perhaps act as a liaison with some of the other governors and DHS heads."

"You don't get it," Agar said, pulling a pistol from his pocket as he walked around behind Edgewater.

"You call *this* a trial?" Edgewater demanded, a faint sheen of sweat breaking out on his jaws. "I demand a real trial. With a judge and jury, and a defense attorney. I've got my rights, and—"

"And the Constitution's suspended," Agar reminded. "I'm told you bragged about that often enough you should remember. That's what you told the people you robbed, arrested, and stood before a firing squad. The same words you quipped to those young women and girls you stripped, raped, and locked in a fucking stall, you piece of shit."

"Kill me, and you're messing with the federal government!"

"Down in Cheyenne, I've got a passel full of federal officials from the Bureau of Land Management, Environmental Protection Agency, FEMA, the USDA, and host of other agencies that are standing in my way. By killing you, I send a really clear message that, yeah, you're a special piece of shit, but maybe they might want to work with me."

Agar extended the black pistol.

"Sir?" one of the aides interjected uneasily. "In this instance, I'm not sure you want to do this yourself."

"I take my own dogs to the woodshed," Agar replied, and Sam could see the man's facial muscles straining.

"Someone else," Dr. Holly agreed. "Edgewater isn't just some common criminal like the others."

"No," Agar cried, "he's worse. Listen to the man, not even a hint of remorse."

"Remorse, remorse," Edgewater said, bargaining for time. "That's why you need me, Governor. Like I said, I can be a most remarkable asset."

Sam winced at the man's self-assurance; the monster still couldn't understand just how far he'd transgressed.

The movement was fleeting, and when Sam looked, there he was: *Nynymbi* danced in the shadow of court recorder's chair. The haunting concentric eyes, the waving three fingers.

You do it.

Did he really hear the words?

Sam took a deep breath. Locked the wheels and stood, saying, "I'll do it, sir. My wife died rather than be raped by him. My friend Amber gave her life to bring him down. Mr. Tappan's daughter, Pam, was shot by his goons when they went to raid for women."

"You, Mr. Delgado?" Agar studied him thoughtfully. "Vendetta?"

"Justice, sir. The first step toward rebuilding."

Agar's eyes didn't waver as he handed Sam the slim black semi-automatic pistol. The design was the same as a 1911 like old Bill's, but slightly smaller. A Browning in .380. Sam did a chamber check, walked painfully around the table, and looked Kevin Edgewater right in his surprised blue eyes as he put three rounds through the man's heart.

Sleep in peace, Shyla.

CHAPTER FIFTY-THREE

* * *

SAM HAD LOST COUNT OF THE DAYS HE'D SPENT ATOP THE LITTLE KNOLL WHERE THOMAS and Willy had buried Shyla Adams. Morning, noon, evening, midnight. It all sort of ran together as he'd sat by the mounded soil and relived every single instant he'd shared with Shyla. With intricate detail, he'd carried in stones and arranged them in artistic patterns atop her grave.

In the lucid moments between bouts of tears and the times he shrieked in rage, Sam wondered if he'd gone completely insane. He reveled in the memory of how he'd shot Tubb, and as he did, he placed his forehead on the grave's surface, willing the image through the dirt and rocks to Shyla. Desperate in the hope that he could communicate the man's death. The same with the shocked disbelief in Edgewater's eyes as the first bullet tore through the man's heart.

For a time Meggan brought him food. Then Thomas told him he was on his own.

That morning he'd watched from the grave as they brought Pam home in the college van. And Sam had finally roused himself enough that he'd come down, taken a shower. Having eaten, he now sat despondently on the porch, where he studied the cold bottle in his hand.

Pam had been placed in a nest of pillows on the love seat Frank and Brandon had carried out for her. "What are you going to do about the bullet holes?" Sam asked as he swirled his beer.

This, he'd been told, was the first bottled stout from the Big Buffalo Brewing Company in Hot Springs. Word was that people who bought bottles of beer, couldn't buy more unless they brought the bottles back—and they would receive discounts on future purchases by providing clean, brown-glass bottles with their first purchase. Since crown caps were nonexistent, wooden stoppers were wired on.

Pam—looking sallow and thin, glanced up at the pock marks on the logs. "Most of them were nine-millimeter or .223 slugs. Didn't even get through the logs. I think that's what you'd call character. The bullet holes in the windows? Those we're going to seal with epoxy and hope they hold. It's not like I can order a new picture window anymore."

Sam nodded and sipped his stout. No windows, no tires, no cinnamon, the list went on. In the month since he'd executed Edgewater, the world continued on its downward spiral. Food shortages were being felt in town, but the first gardens were putting up shoots. The last two winters, it was said, had been mild, so the numbers of antelope, mule deer, and elk were up.

The local game warden—on orders from Governor Agar—now coordinated a carefully managed hunt. From this time forward, game populations were to be managed like livestock. At Evan Holly's insistence, local groups were now foraging for bitterroot, sego lily, desert parsley, bladderwort, and a host of other wild plants to supplement the shortages.

Ranchers were allotted fuel on a priority basis depending upon how many calves they were raising; and the same system on a per-acre basis was keeping tractors running on the farms. Expectations for the fall harvest were high. Because out-of-state wheat harvester crews from Texas and Oklahoma weren't coming, anyone with a gleaner now sat at the top of the heap.

News trickled in from the Northwest. The Chinese were largely stalemated in the cities they'd taken. Word was that China hadn't sent their promised reinforcements. That four EMPs had laid China prostrate.

Rumor also had it that Russia had invaded Europe, and both were locked in a titanic struggle.

And America had been completely broken.

"You don't look so good, Sam." Pam sipped her glass of mint tea. "Sleep last night?"

"Haunted. *Nynymbi* keeps creeping around the room."

"So you're going to tell me the cabin's haunted?"

"Oh yeah." He pinched his eyes closed. "Shyla slips through the shadows. I hear her sometimes when her voice mingles with the wind's. I feel her. Just that faintest touch on my cheek, or maybe my shoulder. When it gets to the point that I can't stand it anymore, she fingers strands of my hair. I see her smile of encouragement every morning when I make myself get out of bed and will myself to live another day."

"This, too, will pass, Sam." She fixed her gaze out in the field where Jon was walking through the alfalfa, a shovel over his shoulder. Ashley was carrying the plastic sheet tied to a two-by-four that they used to dam the irrigation ditch. The two, together with Frank and Brandon, had finished swathing, baling, and stacking hay but two days past. Now a big green haystack stood on the far eastern corner of the field.

Pam studied him from beneath a skeptical eyebrow. "Talked to Thomas the other day. He says he's saddling old Tobe for you to-morrow morning. He says the spirits told him it's time. That you're healed up enough. He said Breeze was going to meet him up there."

"Breeze?"

"Brandon made her promise." Pam studied him thoughtfully. "What about you, Sam? Thomas said you told him you'd go to the cave."

Sam closed his eyes, thoughts in chaos.

Like, what's the point?

CHAPTER FIFTY-FOUR

* * *

BREEZE COULD HAVE REFUSED TO PARTICIPATE. FOR A LOT OF REASONS. IT WAS CRAZY. Indian hocus pocus. A healing and cleansing of the soul? Seriously? She could have dismissed it as fantasy, shaken her head, and walked off. The way Thomas looked at her—that knowing twinkle in his dark eyes—he knew it, too.

She hadn't expected Sam Delgado to show up, hadn't really seen much of him since he'd come back from Cody. Instead she'd hung out in the high country with Willy, keeping an eye on the field camp.

Willy didn't talk much about what he'd done after riding off that day on the trail. He just got a faraway look in his eyes. His expression and slumped posture barely masked a bruised and tortured soul.

Then Thomas had shown up. The two Shoshonis had disappeared for a couple of days, and when they'd climbed back up to camp at dusk one night, Willy was like his old self again.

But when it came to herself? She probably should have said no.

But I promised Brandon.

And yes, damn it, she'd go through with it. Not that she had a hell of a lot of other things on her plate.

She'd heard about sweat lodges, but never been in one. When Thomas led her and Delgado down to the small dome next to the pond below the spring, she crossed her arms and studied it skeptically.

A fire was burning outside, hot stones shimmering in the heat.

"Take your clothes off," Thomas told them. "You can leave your underwear on, but it's better if you go naked."

Sam outright refused, looking horrified.

Something about the expression on his face goaded Breeze into taking off her shirt, playing an odd game of dare with him. She was sliding her pants over her hips, when he sort of started, blinked, and like a man in a trance, began unbuttoning his shirt.

Thomas held the flap for her, his eyes closed, face beatific as he chanted softly in Shoshoni. Sam ducked in next, and moments later Thomas used a shovel to drop three glowing cobbles on the dirt in the center of the lodge. The old man—wearing only a loin cloth—crawled in with a coffee can filled with water.

Draping the door hanging to seal the dome in darkness, he said, "You are both warriors. The spirits of the dead cling to you. They bother your thoughts, disrupt your dreams. Let us cleanse you, and then, when you are ready, ask the spirits to help you find the way forward."

When he sprinkled water onto the hot rocks, it exploded in steam.

Breeze had broken first, asking to be let out. She'd crawled from the lodge, loose-limbed and glistening sweat. Nor did she need to be asked twice when Thomas ordered her and Sam into the pool of cold spring water.

That had been the first time. And over, and over, they repeated the process, and for some inexplicable reason, she and Sam had endured.

It's as if we're punishing ourselves.

That night, at the fire, she sat next to Sam, poking the fire with a stick while venison backstrap roasted over the coals. Overhead, the night sky had a foggy look. Lot of smoke in the sky, and clear days were becoming few and far between. Periodically ash floated down from the haze, carried from who knew how far.

"Heard you calling out to Shyla last night," she told Sam.

"Might have." Sam sat on a bucked, round of wood, elbows on his knees. "She's stronger here, more clear. Like she's watching."

"Does she smile? Laugh?"

"Yeah."

"You don't."

"You either."

"Nothing to laugh about, is there?"

"Nope." His lips twitched. "If I could go back, there are so many things I'd change. I wouldn't have let Thomas talk me into going to Cheyenne, that's for sure."

"Maybe you had to."

"Why?"

"So that you'd go rescue those people. So that you'd get blown up. So that you'd be there to shoot Edgewater." She shrugged and chuckled. "Hell, maybe so that you'd be here, wondering what kind of idiocy we're enduring so that we could wish we'd made other choices way back when."

"What would you have done differently?"

She pursed her lips and finally admitted, "I wouldn't have won first place at the High School State Rodeo finals. I wouldn't have drank that pint of whiskey, and I wouldn't have ended up pregnant with Travis Labeaux's child."

Sam stared thoughtfully at the fire. "That's what went wrong between you and your folks?"

"History repeats itself. I mean, that's how Mom got pregnant. Which led to me and Brandon. But, hey, Travis Labeaux wasn't any Frank Tappan, you know what I mean? Even for a bulldogger he was dumber than a box of rocks."

She exhaled wearily. "So I had Trish Thompson take me to Billings. Had an abortion. And somehow the folks found out." A beat. "Hey, I had plans."

"Yeah, me, too." He slapped at a mosquito. "Mom and Dad scraped and saved all of their lives so I could go to college. Figured I was going to be a business major, maybe law or medicine. That I'd be there. In the neighborhood. Help them."

She glanced sidelong at him. "If you had an MBA you'd be just as dead as they are right now. The last of their line. Extinct. I'd be dead, too. Along with Joelle, Michaela, Kylie, and the rest of the girls. And those people from behind the fence. Shirley Mackeson, the ones who went with us. Some of the others—like Tank and Lehman—we freed from that compound, evaded, and weren't caught."

"Those men in that posse we shot up at slickside would be alive."

"And maybe Brandon, Shanteel, Meggan, and me would be dead or taken prisoner. I fit into that profile of Edgewater's, you know. Young, attractive, slim, with a good figure. Want to bet that Tubb would have let me walk away when he already had a beef with the Tappans?"

"Jesus," Sam whispered. "A person could go crazy thinking about this."

"Yeah. And we still have to survive whatever Thomas is cooking up for tomorrow." She reached out, punching him playfully on the shoulder. "You're a good man, Sam Delgado."

"No, I'm not," he told her, eyes on the distance.

CHAPTER FIFTY-FIVE

***

SITTING AT THE MOUTH OF THE SACRED CAVE—AT THIS PLACE OF *PUHA KAHNI*—THOMAS rhythmically beat his pot drum and sang the old songs. He called upon *Tam Apo,* and *Tam Segopia,* our father the sky and our mother the earth. He sang to Wolf who brought wisdom and order to Creation in the Beginning Times. He sang to Coyote, who had caused all manner of mayhem and chaos in those same early days.

Most of all, he sang to the Spirits of the Water World below and pleaded that they would come and help to heal his wounded friends. That they would convince the *navushieip*—the wandering dream souls of the dead—to leave Sam and Breeze in peace.

Yesterday evening, as dusk was descending, he had led them down here to Puha Canyon, carrying only blankets and a canteen full of *toyatawura* drink distilled from the ancient power plants.

He had made them drink, asked them to disrobe, and handed each a colorful Pendleton blanket. Then he led them into the cave as the last light dimmed. Illuminated only by a pitch torch, he'd guided them from carving to carving, watching their expressions as the holy drink had taken possession of their souls.

Sam was easy. Thomas had made him lay down before the image of *Nynymbi.* It helped that the young man already had a guide.

To his surprise, Breeze had chosen to sleep before the image of Water Ghost Woman. A decision which filled him with uncertainty and no little trepidation for what it might portend. He had no knowledge of what kind of women's *puha* Water Ghost Woman might share with a female of Breeze's strength and character.

Then he had taken his place outside the cave entrance, standing watch, singing, and praying the night through. Stars barely penetrated the thick haze overhead. Occasional bits of ash floated down like soft flakes. The air had that "burned city" smell.

Sunrise finally began to turn the cloudy sky from black to darkest indigo. And still Thomas sang, his words echoing in the narrow canyon.

To his surprise, Sam and Breeze emerged together, holding hands, as if to steady each other. He searched their faces, looking for some sign of the visions they must have shared with the spirits, and saw only weary acceptance.

"Hungry?" he asked.

"Totally empty," Breeze told him woodenly as she picked her way over to her clothes, shed the blanket from around her shoulders, and began dressing.

Sam's expression looked pinched, his eyes fixed on a distance, his still-bruised body shivering in the cold as he dressed. He paused only long enough to bend double and suffer through the dry heaves. A not uncommon result after dreaming with *toyatawura*.

Breeze steadied him, her own expression pained. "You with me, Delgado?"

"Yeah. Somebody's got to have your back and blow up the machine guns."

"You'll do, Sam." She patted him on the shoulder and straightened. Her expression had taken on a somber cast.

"You all right?" Thomas asked them both after the young man had wiped his mouth and straightened.

"Not sure," Sam told Thomas. Then he glanced at Breeze. "You saw, didn't you? You were there. In the vision."

She nodded, pupils like black dots in her brown-ringed hazel eyes. "Nothing to bounce around in glee about, is there?"

Sam gave her a weak smile, then led the way up the steep canyon trail to where the horses were tied in the aspens. Thomas was only halfway up, puffing for breath, when Breeze reached back, took his hand, and pulled him to the top.

A thousand questions ran through Thomas's head. As they rode back to the field camp, he glanced surreptitiously at the two of them. He had expected to see relief, perhaps a lightening of the burdens each seemed to carry. Instead, both appeared slightly depressed, introverted.

As much as he might wish to pry, a spirit journey was not the sort of thing to be meddled with. He would have to take a measured approach, ask only appropriate questions.

Thomas felt his years as he stepped down from his horse and tied him off at the picket line behind camp. He walked to the fire Willy had kept going and accepted a plate of pancakes with hot tallow for butter and chokecherry jam for sweetener.

He watched Breeze and Sam—each locked in their thoughts—take their plates and seat themselves warily by the fire.

"What you have just finished," Thomas said softly, "should not be approached lightly. What the Spirits have shown you, told you, is not granted frivolously."

"Call that an understatement," Breeze said as she nibbled hesitantly at her pancakes. "Was that real, or was that drink you gave us drugged?"

"It was an hallucinogen," Sam told her. "That's common for vision quests; medicine men and women use it to open their minds to the spirit journey." He snorted as if in self-derision. "Damn, does it work, or what?"

"The things I saw...seemed so...real." Breeze shook her head. "Impossible. Water Ghost Woman, the turtle, the dogs." She took a breath. "The dead, I talked to them."

"What did they tell you?" Thomas asked as casually as he could.

"That I've been tested. That I'm chosen."

Almost angrily, she jabbed her fork into her pancakes. "All I wanted was, like, to do my own thing. Now everyone thinks I'm so special." A beat. "'The hero of the Line.' 'The woman who got the girls out.' I didn't ask for this."

"Maybe you were chosen because you didn't want it," Thomas told her.

Sam was listening quietly, his own expression reflecting confusion and disquiet.

"So, do you think it's possible to see the future?" Breeze asked, shooting him a sharp look.

"Do you want me to answer as a puhagan or a physicist?"

"Either."

"If time doesn't exist as a thing, who is to know? Forces, inertia, observations that create reality, a cascading of events for which only one possible outcome must, of necessity, lead to another predetermined outcome. Yes, it is possible."

At that she turned her pensive eyes on Sam, jaws knotting. "How does it feel to be chosen?"

"Was it real? I mean, I've read the literature. I know what goes on in the brain, the physiological explanations." Sam forked pancake into his mouth and chewed listlessly. "But, wow, I mean I see *Nynymbi*. I'm supposed to be a scientist, an impartial observer."

"Sometimes you just have to believe," Thomas told him. Breeze was studying him with a curiously level look.

She smiled grimly. "Water Ghost Woman took me to visit with the dead. So, did I really get to tell them I was sorry, or was that just my mind allowing me to forgive myself?"

"What do you want it to be?" Thomas asked. "That's the power of spirit visions. They open a door."

She nodded, chuckled softly, as if amused at herself. "It's hard, that's all. We really had it good. People just took it for granted. Food, safety, a warm house. Now they ask me to let it all go the same way they have."

"Who?" Thomas asked.

Breeze picked at her food. "How do you say no to the people you've killed? Okay, so they forgave me, but these things they want me to attempt...?"

"And what did Water Ghost Woman say?"

"She grants me the power to take life, to measure myself against the future."

From beneath the brim of her hat, Breeze studied Thomas with those piercing eyes. "So, what's the real story on Water Ghost Woman?"

"She's dangerous. Very powerful. Seduces men, and when they're making love to her, she either drowns them or devours them. She can grant a man sexual prowess if he survives, and she has powers of fertility. She offers women different powers, but, being a male, I don't know the medicine. Nor do I know a *waip puhagan,* a woman shaman, who still knows the old ways who could guide you."

She took a deep breath, glanced around, and lowered her voice. "Wow. So, I've got a heavy-hitter when it comes to a spirit helper, huh?"

Thomas felt a chill run through him. "She is the most powerful of the female spirits. Bloody in her wrath, but capable of granting remarkable abilities to those she chooses."

Have I created a monster, or a hero?

Standing, she tossed her plate into the fire shook her head, adding, "Being what they want me to be? How can anyone live up to that?"

With a heavy sigh, she shook her head and walked away.

"Think she's going to be okay?" Willy asked from the cook tent.

Sam tossed his empty paper plate into the fire and rubbed his face with both hands. "What do you choose? Yourself? Your happiness? Or do you give that all up for a long-shot chance to save the world?"

"That was the question the spirits posed?"

Sam sucked his lips, nodded. Glanced at the forest where Breeze had disappeared.

"You and Breeze?"

"Tough times ahead, Thomas. I wanted to be a scholar, and now I'm a warrior for an impossible cause."

"What did *Nynymbi* show you?"

"We have a chance here, Thomas. A slim, fighting chance to hold the darkness and the barbarians back. It's already cost me Shyla...and part of my soul."

Thomas whispered. "I can't imagine the choices you and Breeze will have to make."

Sam cocked an eyebrow. "Breeze and me? Think again, elder. You are our lodestone, our moral compass from here on out."

Thomas smiled to himself, a sinking sensation in his heart. Yes, for a supposedly wise elder, he should have seen *puha* working through him.

"I could give up, Thomas. Find a way to join Shyla. But if I do? Well, I guess we lose it all."

"You saw this in your vision?"

A fleeting smile crossed Sam's lips.

"Sam...?"

"Shyla asked me to thank you. She's found her way."

"I wondered if I should have sung over her. Sometimes it's hard to know what is right and what only causes complications."

Thomas watched Sam rise, cast another glance in the direction Breeze had taken down into the trees. Sam picked his way up the slope, finally seating himself on the rocky outcrop he had once shared with Shyla.

WE LOST IT ALL

***

Who were we? What had we become? How did our world die? Who unleashed the maelstrom? Why did we turn on each other? What was it to be American? Why did we hate? Who was responsible? How could this happen to us? Didn't we care who we were? What kind of insane were we? Could we have been that selfish? Who fostered the hate? Why did we embrace it? Who did this to us?

If you could go back, what would you tell the Republicans? The Democrats? The religious right? The social progressives? The president? The social media tweeters? The TV pundits? Antifa? QAnon? The police? The socialists? The white nationalists? Black Lives Matter? The pro-life movement? The gun-control lobby? The secession movements? The social conservatives?

Who is to blame?

Who isn't?

And the questions never cease.

I was just a student, but I know we could have survived the cyber-attack. Freeze the banking system and credit. Find and expunge the malware, backdate the system a week, and restart.

It would have been difficult. Painful. The process imperfect and not without issue. Still, we could have endured, worked together. Like we did when we saw ourselves as neighbors, friends, as an imperfect but willing people. Back when we had a single identity. Before we separated ourselves, blamed each other.

Whoever perpetrated the cyberattack sought to weaken us, perhaps distract us. Instead the effect was like tapping an already fractured glass. Once the first shards fell, the cascade couldn't be stopped.

We didn't need an outside enemy.

We had ourselves.

ABOUT THE AUTHOR

***

W. Michael Gear is the New York Times and international bestselling author of over fifty-eight novels, many of them co-authored with Kathleen O'Neal Gear.

With seventeen million copies of his work in print he is best known for the "People" series of novels written about North American Archaeology. His work has been translated into at least 29 languages. Michael has a master's degree in Anthropology, specialized in physical anthropology and forensics, and has worked as an archaeologist for over forty years.

His published work ranges in genre from prehistory, science fiction, mystery, historical, genetic thriller, and western. For twenty-eight years he and Kathleen have raised North American bison at Red Canyon Ranch and won the coveted National Producer of the Year award from the National Bison Association in 2004 and 2009. They have published over 200 articles on bison genetics, management, and history, as well as articles on writing, anthropology, historic preservation, resource utilization, and a host of other topics.

The Gears live in Cody, Wyoming, where W. Michael Gear enjoys large-caliber rifles, long-distance motorcycle touring, and the richest, darkest stout he can find.